More praise for *TO ALL APPEARANCES A LADY*

"A powerful meditation on the past and present
of British Columbia."
The Toronto Star

"Bowering exhibits powerful control of poetic details in her
description.... A novel well worth reading."
Edmonton Journal

"Delights and instructs... An intelligent and enjoyable book, an
important book you will not regret reading."
Leona Gom, *Duthie Reader*

"Marilyn Bowering has brought to *To All Appearances a Lady* the gift
for compression and the spare sharpness of phrasing and imagery that
mark the style of poets when they write prose."
Books in Canada

TO ALL
APPEARANCES A LADY

MARILYN BOWERING

Harper*Perennial*Canada
HarperCollins*PublishersLtd*

http://www.harpercanada.com

HarperCollins books may be purchased for educational,
business, or sales promotional use. For information please write:
Special Markets Department, HarperCollins Canada,
55 Avenue Road, Suite 2900, Toronto,
Ontario, Canada M5R 3L2.

First published in hardcover by Random House of Canada Limited: 1989
First Fawcett Crest paperback edition published by
Random House of Canada Limited: 1990
First HarperPerennial paperback edition published by HarperCollins: 1997
First HarperPerennial Canada edition

Canadian Cataloguing in Publication Data

Bowering, Marilyn, 1949–
To all appearances a lady

1st HarperPerennial Canada.
ISBN 0-00-648537-5

I. Title.

PS8553.O9T6 1999   C813'.54   C99-932543-4
PR9199.3.B635T6 1999

00 01 02 03 04 RRD 6 5 4 3 2 1

Printed and bound in the United States

To Michael, and to Xan

ACKNOWLEDGEMENTS

To All Appearances A Lady is wholly fictional and is not intended to be a history, or a portrait of persons living or dead.

This book was written with the aid of a grant from the Canada Council. It also owes a great deal to the assistance of my family, friends, and colleagues. My gratitude first to Michael for his support during the inevitable moments of discouragement. Also to Capts. C.C. Wilson, Hill Wilson, and Rod Trail, all B.C. Coastal Pilots. Special thanks to Capt. Trail for his reading of the manuscript. Maywell Wickheim helped form my plan of the *Rose*, and Roxana Argast rocked the baby. Denise Bukowski was a friend and generous agent, and Ed Carson, my editor, thought like a poet when it mattered. I shall never forget his 'silent edit'. I also owe a debt of thanks to my parents; and to Giselle Coffey, Liz and Colin Gorrie, Richard Marks, P.K. Page and Arthur Irwin, Constance Rooke, and Robin Skelton. The Maritime Museum of British Columbia was an important source, as was (and foremostly) the British Columbia Provincial Archives. My heartfelt thanks for the patience of the Archives librarians.

The poems in Chapter Nine are adapted from "A 'Prison' for Chinese Immigrants," the *Asianadian*, Vol. 2, No. 4, Spring 1980 by David Chuenyan Lai. I found "Praise and Prayer," by R.L. Stevenson, in *Collected Poems*, edited by Janet Adam Smith (Rupert Hart-Davis: London 1950). I have also quoted from the "Constitution, By-Laws and Rules of the Order of the Workingmen's Protective Association," (McMillan & Son, Victoria 1898), and have drawn upon "The Lepers of D'Arcy Island," by Ernest Hall and John Nelson (*Dominion Medical Monthly*, Vol. XI, No. 6, 1898). Other sources which should be mentioned are two unpublished M.A. theses: "The Human Geography of Southeastern Vancouver Island, 1842–1891," by Patrick Donald Floyd, Dept. of Geography, University of Victoria, December 1969; and "The Context of Economic Change and Continuity In An Urban Overseas Chinese Community," by Charles P. Sedgwick, Dept. of Anthropology, University of Victoria, April 1973. I used an anecdote found in "A Victorian Tapestry," *Sound Heritage*, Vol. VII, No. 3, Provincial Archives, Victoria, 1978; and found *In A Sea of Sterile Mountains, The Chinese in British Columbia*, by James Morton (J.J. Douglas, Vancouver 1974), invaluable. *Clippers for the Record*, by Marny Matheson (Spectrum Publications: Melbourne 1984) added to my information on *Thermopylae*, as did *Thermopylae and The Age of Clippers* by John Crosse (Historian Publishers, Vancouver 1968). More information on sailing ships came from *Life On The Ocean*, by George Little (George Clark & Son: Aberdeen 1847); and *Pacific Yachting's Cruising Guide to the West Coast of Vancouver Island*, by Don Watmough (Maclean Hunter Ltd.: Vancouver 1984) provided important detail. *The Arrow War, An Anglo-Chinese Confusion 1856–1860*, by Douglas Hurd (Collins, London 1967) gave me a great deal of background on that period in China.

The epigraph from Yeh Ming-Chen can be found in the *Harvard Journal of Asiatic Studies*, Vol. 6, 1941, pg. 37; that from Boethius is reprinted with permission of Macmillan Publishing Company from *The Consolation of Philosophy* by Boethius, translated by Richard Green. Copyright © 1985 by Macmillan Publishing Company; copyright © 1962.

While my heart is disturbed by
Leaping tigers and the insistent bugles' blast,
I watch the white-throat blackbirds
Until they disappear with the sunset;
Only the spring returns as of old,
Everywhere are cotton flowers red against the wall.

Yeh Ming-chen,
Viceroy of Kwangsi and Kwangtung

Good fortune tends to enslave the one who enjoys it by
deceiving him with spurious happiness. Bad fortune frees
him from the bondage to mutable things by showing him
the fragile nature of earthly felicity.

Boethius
Translated by Richard Green

PROLOGUE

"In one of the dense fogs which sometimes hang over the entrance of the strait, a sailing vessel should not close the land; but should stand off sufficiently far to avoid the set of tidal streams and currents. If the fog is very dense, a stranger should proceed no further, but should anchor; it must be remarked, however, that not infrequently the weather is clear a few miles within the strait while the entrance is totally obscured."

British Columbia Pilot, Volume I

Spring 1957

I had stepped over to the closet hoping to get a look at the embroidered silk jackets that she knew I coveted when Lam Fan opened one eye and said, "Get away from there you silly boy," scratched at the bedspread with her long red nails, and died.

This scene, like so many others, took place in the small decaying farmhouse at the foot of Christmas Hill where Lam Fan lived. We had had our last argument over what I would do without her. "You must stay on in the house," she'd said, "it is your home."

"My home is the sea, Fan," I replied, "I've told you a hundred times that if it weren't for you I wouldn't be here at all."

Which wasn't quite true: although I'd run away at fifteen, just after Sing Yuen's death in an anonymous trench in France, I'd returned a number of times over the years and was by now nicely settled down into my job as a coastal pilot—a far cry from deep sea days when I sailed the world for months at a time. In fact I had my eye on the clock right then. The *Galafkos* had radioed in her ETA, and I was expecting a call from the dispatcher. As first man on the board, I had to be ready to go.

"What would Sing Yuen think!" said Fan. "He built the farm for you. You were his son!"

She was sitting in her chair with her long, elegant feet in my lap. I rubbed them vigorously to warm them.

"First of all," I said, "Sing Yuen's been dead for forty-two years, and I doubt that he'll much care, and secondly I'm not his son, nor yours, so even if I wanted to I couldn't carry on the family business. Besides, Fan, I'm fifty-seven years old, and I'll damn well do what I please."

My ancient stepmother withdrew her feet, snorted, and, gathering her long robe around her thin brittle body, stood up and made for the stairs.

"You think you know everything, Robert Lam," she called over her shoulder as she began her difficult ascent. "You think you can live your life all by yourself. You just wait and see!"

"I intend to try, Fan," I answered irritably. "So far I haven't had the opportunity. And what's more," I continued, "since it's what we're really talking about—I intend to keep the boat and fix her up with what I get for the house!"

I know I shouldn't have said it. Fan had hated the idea of my living on the *Rose* ever since I'd first mentioned it. She disliked small boats, although a forty-foot converted troller isn't what I think of as small, and would change the subject every time I talked about where I wanted to go: to some of the smaller islands, or all the way up the Inside Passage to the old whaling station at Rose Harbour. I was going to do it, too: my month's leave was a few weeks away, and all my plans were made. Although I'd sailed the seas since I was a boy, it would be my first long trip alone.

"You can sulk all you want, Fan," I cried out after her (she was taking the stairs particularly slowly), "but I won't change my mind."

"You'll be sorry, Robert Lam," she shouted down, "you are just as stupid now as when I took you in."

"And whose fault is that Fan," I answered. "I was an infant. You and Sing Yuen taught me everything I know!"

We weren't always so rude to each other, but I was tired of her bad temper. I wasn't used to looking after anybody but myself, and Fan was a poor patient.

I listened until she reached her room safely. I could hear her moving things around in her bedroom, scraping across the floor in her hard-soled slippers, opening and shutting drawers; and taking advantage of her absence began what I foresaw would be the long process of sorting through her effects after her death.

It was a warm, airless night. After a while I heard Fan snoring. She had a weakness, developed in the past few months (and forgivable in such an old woman) of falling asleep after the briefest exertion. When I had finished with the kitchen drawers, emptying out handfuls of tangled string, broken elastic bands, Christmas light bulbs, used stamps, and articles clipped from magazines ("Radioactive Clams on West Coast Seabottom"), I opened the front door. The frogs were singing from the ditch, and I could hear the munching of a cow that had strayed through a break in the fence into the orchard. A damp mist at ground level made the sky above seem heavy and thick, but as I watched, a sickle moon cut its way through. Then one by one the stars.

We lived in the house in which Fan had always lived. A gravel lane ran by it eastwards to the thumb-shaped peninsula of Vancouver Island. At one time, before the First World War, a railway passed nearby. It stopped at our sheds to load produce, and the farm workers, most of whom lived in Chinatown, travelled in and out on it every day. Where the roadbed skirted the hill, you could still find rusted spikes, rotted ties, and the occasional old bottle.

From our front yard, stretching across the lane and out of sight to the north, was the orchard. Long rows of grey trunks with the branches pruned to make wide bowls. In summer these filled with apples, and the labourers reached in with quick hands to twist the fruit free and drop it gently into their sacks. I helped to wash and pack it in boxes, and when I was older, carried the boxes on my back to the loading shed. I gathered the falls for Fan to put up, or fed them to the cows. Or threw them on the lane where they smashed into stars, staining the dry earth red. Now, of course, there were few trees and these—unpruned and neglected—were hung with strands of pale moss so that the little yard looked as if it had been swept by a tide. The bark was white and flaking, and I could count the number of blossoms on my fingers.

During the Depression, when I had been sailing the world for the SilverLine, Fan had cut down most of the trees and turned the farm over to potatoes and a half acre in vegetables. It was all that people could afford to buy. Those who had no money, like the army of starving men who straggled between the work camps on the peninsula, and the town, stopped at the farm anyway. There was always something to eat, since much of the food remained unsold and Fan needed little for herself. The men worked for what she gave them, cutting wood, feeding the cows, mending fences. All the jobs that should have been mine. I'd objected at first when I'd come home on leave. I didn't like the thought of Fan alone with them. They were hardened men, used to fighting to stay alive. Unwanted men, homeless and unemployed, with nothing to lose. Who were being made ready, so it came to seem to me afterwards, to be soldiers.

"You have never really been hungry, Robert Lam," said Fan to my objections, "or you would understand. It is the man you don't feed who is dangerous, not the one with a full stomach."

Fan and I on opposite sides of every question. Fan in the house while I wandered.

Lam Fan on the steps, banging a tin pan to call us for dinner. Lam Fan at night, twisting up her hair in front of the mirror, wearing gold and jade earrings, or sitting in her chair in the kitchen smoking, turning over the pages of magazines.

Lam Fan in the beginning, with my hand in hers as we walked the miles westwards to the city. Where there were tram cars and dentists and ladies wearing hats. Where telephone poles and steamers at the wharves made a network that linked horizons. Where, in Chinatown, I'd wait in a restaurant while Fan went about her business. Or going to the theatre, the Victoria, or the Pantages or the Chinese Theatre round the corner from where The Place of Ten Thousand Occasions had been. Or to the temple where the smell of joss was like the inside of Lam Fan's closet.

I sat on the broken steps and looked out into the darkened world I had known since childhood: the ghosting apple trees, the tilted greenhouses, and surmounting all, the dark face of Christmas Hill. In this International Geophysical Year, in which nations had joined harmoniously together to observe the marvels of the earth, atmosphere, and space, in which boys in their twenties handled millions of dollars' worth of rocketry, I, Robert Louis Lam, three years from retirement, had quarrelled with a one-hundred-year-old woman over my future.

I sighed and thought about the *Rose* and what it would be like to set sail in her and never come back. And as I did, an icy hand gripped my shoulder and a voice shrill with anger cried out, "Dirty Robert Lam! Dirty, dirty Robert!" I turned at that to see Fan standing there in her nightgown, holding a knot of papers in her shaking hand. Behind her in the hallway were the emptied drawers and the bags of rubbish that I had meant to throw away before she wakened. "Dirty Robert!" she cried again, summoning unexpected reserves of wrath.

I stood up and put my arms around her. Her head touched my chest, her arms felt like small dry sticks. She tried to say more, but her mouth was dry, and I could smell on her breath the sour fume of opium. So that was what the retreat to her room had been about—Fan taking refuge in her pipe. Well, I was used to that. But as for her outburst....

I suppose I deserved it. Certainly I was ashamed of myself, and it must have seemed to her as if I were hurrying her death. But the truth is that she'd picked an inconvenient time to fall ill. Cardboard boxes, old clothes, cupboards full of false hair, bleaching creams, and catalogues: it was a daunting prospect for a bachelor, and I had only a month each year to use for myself; if Fan was running out of time, well, then, so was I.

"I'll take you back to your room, Fan," I said, trying to steer her in the direction of the stairs. She stiffened under my touch, then she sagged against me, and tears of frustration or sadness, I don't know which, seeped out of the corners of her eyes. I had never seen her cry before, and I didn't know where to look.

"There, there," I said digging into my job bag among tide books and course books for a clean handkerchief, "there, there." I let her daub her own face. I put my hands into my pockets, afraid to touch her. I did not know what the tempest was about, but it deeply disturbed me. I was used to dealing with facts—they were the only terms on which a man could be a pilot. This was a different Lam Fan—one with uncertain depths—and I didn't know what to make of her.

*   *   *

We made our peace. I apologized for my lack of tact, and Fan offered to help me pack. There wasn't much to do, but I let her assist.

"Is this a long job or short job?" she asked, refolding the clean shirt and underwear I'd already put out.

"Just overnight, I think. As far as I know the ship's headed for Vancouver, but it could change course at the last minute. It depends on where the agent gets the best price for cargo—they call it 'subject to orders.' She could head up to Rupert or even Alberni for all I know, but that's unlikely. If we were going to the west coast I'd know by now and be on my way out to Cape Beale instead of Race Rocks."

I'd explained it to her maybe twenty times, but she'd never understood. She leaned against the kitchen windowsill and looked out. The apple trees bowed and straightened in the gently rising wind. The mist had blown clear, and a few moonlit clouds feathered the sky.

"I don't like it," said Fan. "Why do they send you out on such a bad night? There is a big storm on the way, the radio said it."

I turned away and put a book on top of my case. Since my interest in the whaling stations had been piqued, first by photos in a paper called *Seamen's Institute* taken by the Reverend Ratcliffe in the twenties (one showed a one-hundred-foot serpent in the cut-open belly of a sperm whale), and then by Captain Larson of the *B.C. Standard*, whose father had been captain on the *S.S. St. Laurence*, whaling in the Gulf of Georgia in the teens, I had been trying to find out more. The book, a history of whaling in the Arctic, was all I'd been able to find. If I were lucky, I would have a few hours to read it on my way back from taking in the *Galafkos*; if I were unlucky, like MacCrimmon two weeks ago, I'd have time to read half a dozen books: he'd been caught in a fog outside English Bay for eleven days. The sawmills were going at full blast, and it took a lot of wind and rain to disperse the smoke from their beehive burners. At last he'd spotted a little freighter with what he thought was a radar mast, and trailed her in, taking the chance only because they'd run out of fresh water.

"There's no storm coming, Fan. The forecast is good. I'll have no trouble at all with the *Galafkos*." Fan looked doubtful. I had made the mistake, some months before, of taking her out on the pilot launch. She had seen for herself, for the first time, what climbing the pilot's ladder meant, watching as I went up the side of a ship on the frail rope ladder, swinging out over the sea.

It had been a mistake in other ways, too. She hadn't known, and I hadn't thought to tell her, that I spelled my name at work as "Lamb." "It's for professional reasons, Fan," I'd told her when I'd seen her face as she read the board. I'd seen the faces of the others, too—the dispatcher and launch-men—when they met Fan. I suppose they'd never considered it—I took most of my looks from my European mother—but I was half Chinese.

I'd wanted to say that she was nothing to do with me. She was an absurd-looking old woman with a painted face, and her clothes were twenty years out of date. For the truth was I'd been ashamed of Fan. But in the end I hadn't denied her, at least I hadn't done that.

It was shortly after that that I bought the *Rose*. She was tied up—a lady in a junk heap—among the derelict boats at the foot of Fisgard Street. There, where time, rust, and rot had taken their toll, I also found the *Green*, last of the five identical whaling vessels, built in Christiania (now Oslo), Norway, that had made up the Victoria Whaling Company. The other ships—the *Black*, *Blue*, *Brown*, *White*, and *Grey* (the tender ship)—were auctioned off and scrapped ten years ago. The *Green* had made her last voyage out of Rose Harbour in 1944—which is what had given me the idea of taking the *Rose* north to that closed-down station. Call it a pilgrim-age, if you like, but I wanted my boat to test the same waters. It was too late to rescue the *Green* herself—she'd sunk at the end of her rope during a recent storm—but I could still resurrect her memory.

Not that there wasn't still whaling going on—on the northwest coast of the island at Coal Harbour, the air force station during the war—but the east coast had been fished out years before, and the great herds that had always schooled off the west coast were vastly reduced in numbers. I'd hear that Western Canada Whaling was in trouble and might not last out the season. It made no difference to me. I had no desire to see the actual killing, nor to voyage the west coast—the graveyard of the Pacific—in my untried *Rose*, even at this time of year.

When I returned from what had turned out to be a fairly typical twenty-four hours—the two-hundred-fifty-horsepower gas engine on the launch had broken down on the way to Race Rocks, the captain of the *Galafkos* hadn't seen the need to provide me with a lee to board his ship and had proven reluctant to take his vessel in to William Head to clear quarantine (he was afraid that one of the crew had polio), and there had been too many fishing boats in Active Pass—Fan was sitting in her chair in the kitchen. I could tell that she hadn't slept. She was wearing the same nightgown as when I'd left, and there were greyish circles on top of the deep yellow ones that had lately appeared beneath her eyes.

"I can see you have had a bad time, Robert Lam," she said. I threw my bag onto the kitchen table. Where I had left a clean cleared surface was now a mound of string, seed packets, and so on. Fan had retrieved all the articles I'd discarded, smoothed and folded them, and mixed them together in a jumble as close as she could approximate to the original. I took off my jacket, loosened my tie, and unbuttoned my vest.

"I had to wait outside in the rain while the other two pilots reported in," I said. It was an old complaint. The Pilot House was a little shack that had originally been a construction office during the building of the breakwater. It sat just off Dallas Road facing the water. It was cold in winter and hot in summer; and had room for no more than three people at a time, including the dispatcher. I was shivering. I had picked up a cold on the Greek ship, and the long wait outside hadn't helped.

"When I was a young woman," said Fan, "there was one famous pilot in the city. His name was Henry Glide. He used to climb to the lookout in back of his house to watch for ships."

"Do you mean you knew him, Fan?" I asked. Glide had had the first licence on the coast. His picture hung in the Vancouver office of the super-intendent. "I didn't know you knew him," I said, "why didn't you tell me?"

"Everybody knew Henry," she said dismissively. "He lived on Erie Street." Fan sat back in her chair and folded her hands together. She never talked about the past. She said it made her sad. She opened her hands, folded and opened them again, then said, "There were many many people here in those days. I wish I had told you about them."

I was stunned. For years I had tried to get Fan to talk to me about the old days. About her and Sing Yuen and Sing Yuen's restaurant, the Place of Ten Thousand Occasions, about her uncle, Lum Kee, and his herbal-ist shop—I remembered visiting there, long after Lum Kee had died, of course, when I was a child. About my mother, and about my father.

"It's not too late, Fan," I said, squatting down so that I could look into her face. She kept her eyes lowered, peering into the opening and closing bowl of her hands. "I'd like you to tell me about it, anything at all."

"There is not enough time, Robert Lam," she said. "I could not make you understand."

"About what, Fan? I don't even know what you mean."

She was silent after that and seemed to forget that I was there. Finally I stood up, put my things away, and busied myself preparing Fan's supper. I had eaten earlier, on the ferry boat back from Vancouver. It was a trip I always enjoyed, with time for a good meal, a visit to the barber, and a nap in the stateroom kept for pilots. I liked the lack of responsibility although I couldn't help but tick off the hazards as we steamed slowly into harbour: Brotchie Ledge, where the pilots were dropped off after taking ships out of Victoria, the breakwater at Ogden Point, Berens Island Light, Shoal Point, Laurel Point, Songhees. We tied up at the inner wharves, between Shoal Point and the Johnson Street Bridge, looking straight at the new cathedral and, below it, on the waterfront, the dome, with the gilded figure of Captain Vancouver, on the provincial Parliament building.

I scrambled some eggs and mixed them with a handful of dried field mushrooms that Fan had picked the previous autumn. I poured a glass of milk for myself and a dry sherry for Fan. And all the time I was think-ing: how can I get her to tell me what I want to know? I knew that Fan had emigrated with my mother, India Thackery, from Hong Kong colony in 1890. I knew that they were half-sisters—Fan had been adopted by India's English parents when she was a small child. The two women had been involved in business in Victoria after they had arrived, and eventually my mother had given birth to me and Lam Fan had married Sing Yuen. I knew nothing at all about my father.

I was still thinking when I felt Fan's cool touch on my hand. She was leaning forward in her chair. Her sherry glass was empty and the eggs untouched. "Help me take this off, Robert Lam," she said. I saw that she meant the chain that she wore beneath her garments. I undid the clasp and lifted out the chain and a key. It was shiny and thin, as if it had been worn next to her skin for many years.

"There is a metal box in my room," said Fan. "You may open it when-ever you like. My will is inside, and some other papers. As for the rest, I promise you that I will find some way to help you. I am tired now. I do not want to talk. Please help me into bed."

I put the key and chain in my pocket and carried Fan upstairs. I might have been carrying my job bag up the pilot's ladder, for Fan was no heavier. I tucked her in, looked around surreptitiously for her pipe, saw it peeping out from a rolled-up stocking beneath her pillow, and sat down to keep her company.

"You may go now, if you like, Robert Lam," she said. "You have many things to do. You do not have to stay with your stepmother. I am old now. I am not interesting. You go and visit your friends." Although she spoke sweetly, she could not stop her eyes from shifting in the direction of her opium. I was not being cruel, I was afraid of fire in that wooden house, and had no intention of leaving her alone to strike matches. There were scorch marks on her blankets, and a melted look to the nylon curtain that hung from the window above her bed. The normally fastidious Fan would not have put the house in danger with her habit. But these were not normal times, and her physical powers had failed to the point that I could not trust her. As for where she got the opium—she seemed to have an endless supply packed in one-and-a-half-pound tins marked "Tai June" and stamped with a rooster emblem. I only saw them when they were empty and had never tracked them to their source. It was one of Fan's many secrets. I did not mind her having them. I wanted her to keep them. I did not really mind her opium smoking—it had never harmed anyone—or that she dyed her hair and used cosmetics and pretended not to. I liked Fan as she was. She was the only family I'd known, and on the whole, she had always been kind. I could not forget about our earlier argument, however: it had left a sour taste in my mouth; it had bothered me more than I can say that she'd called me "Dirty Robert."

We spent the evening talking, and I asked her questions, some of which she would not answer. Such as why Sing Yuen, at age sixty, had volunteered to dig trenches for the army, disappearing into the ranks of unremarked Chinese who had died in France at that thankless task. But there were one or two questions to which she did respond.

"Why did you let me leave home when Sing Yuen died?" I asked her. "I was only a boy. Why didn't you try to stop me?"

"Many boys leave home at that age," she said. "You did not want to stay with me. You were afraid you would have to live here forever because I was on my own. Besides," she said, looking slyly over the bed covers, "I knew where you were all the time. I have friends who watched out for you."

"I had an accident on the very first job I took. I was in hospital for three months," I said with an anger that took me by surprise. I had not known that I had kept that old bitterness. "You never came to see me even once."

"How could I have helped?" she asked, surprised. "Would you have come home? Would you have let me take care of you? Would you have gone back to school?"

I looked away from her—at the closet that housed the silks I had always loved to touch, at the neat row of photographs of herself and Sing Yuen that were ranked across the dressing table. For now *I* had no answers. She was right: it was I who had turned my back on her, not the other way round.

"You know what happened, don't you?" I asked her. "We'd been towing hoggers—sawdust barges—across to Port Angeles in December, and I slipped on ice and fell into the hold. They thought I had broken my back. I had no working papers, and they were going to put me in the immigration prison until the Old Man intervened. He said it was my own damn fault, though, he'd told me to stay out of the way. The cook said it was because I'd opened a can of milk upside down when I made the tea. Everyone knew that was bad luck. But instead of throwing it overboard as I should have, I'd torn the label off so that no one else would see.

"After the hospital I stayed at the Sailor's Club until I was back on my feet."

"With Mother Beans, Robert Lam. Yes, I know."

That stopped me cold. How did Fan know that? Had I mentioned Mother Beans before, or had Fan actually had me under surveillance as she claimed? But I was not to be held up for long in my saga of self-pity.

"I was fifteen, Fan, fifteen years old! In the bed next to me there was a boy with rheumatic fever. I had to listen to him die."

"Poor Robert Lam," said Fan.

"I had no one to look out for me. I might have been shanghaied and sold—it used to happen, Fan. The crimps ran the boardinghouses and controlled the supply of labour. They used to drug the loggers and seamen on the waterfront and sell them to the ships for up to ninety dollars. Then the captains deducted the fees from the seamen's wages. You could work for months and not make it up, come home broke and out of pocket."

"Did that happen to you, Robert Lam?" she asked.

"Well, no, not exactly."

Fan smiled a gentle smile. "You were a nice young boy," she said, "that is why Mother Beans took such good care of you. You used to help her in the garden, I think."

I blushed. I had recovered from my childish anger and was remembering the facts. The club had been comfortable and friendly. There was a piano, a billiard room, a library, and I'd had a room to myself. Mother Beans had let me help her in the kitchen. We'd put up hundreds of quarts of preserves that autumn: pickles, jams, marmalade, green peas and string beans, asparagus and tomatoes, endless jars of salmon, venison and pheasant, and all kinds of jellies. I had been her small helper, safe and cozy, while all the real sailors were at war. The night the boys from the *Lancaster* had come in (they'd been torpedoed in the North Sea and had travelled across Canada by rail) it was pouring with rain. I had gone with her to meet them off the trams—six carloads of them—with hot coffee. "Mother, don't you remember me?" one youth had called. "Of course I do," she'd said. "I thought you were drowned." "They can't kill me, Mother," the sailor had answered, "I've been torpedoed three times since I saw you last." I'd never forgotten that. Nor the sailors' talk of the red dinghy that meant a sinking. They were a superstitious lot, and I'd thought less of them for that at the time. You made your own life, you took your chances. I still wanted to go to sea, though, and I got the captain of a fisheries boat to take me on as mess boy.

Fan closed her eyes and drifted off to sleep. I sat with her a while longer, holding her hand and listening to her fragile breathing.

After the funeral, which was a modest affair at graveside, I drove back to the house with Lam Fan's lawyer. There'd been no problem about the service. I'd found an accommodating minister just down the road who hadn't cared that Fan was not a church-goer, nor that I hadn't had the faintest idea of what her wishes had been in this regard. I knew only that she'd wanted to be buried next to Sing Yuen, and since whatever remained of him was still somewhere in France, it had been a simple matter of moving the stone marker with his name on it from the old Chinese cemetery on the water-front to the Royal Lawns nearer our house. The Chinese cemetery was an unkempt place, often flooded during storms, and, with its large altar with capacious furnace, to my eye far from restful. The flooding happened in other cemeteries as well. The island was known for its high water table, and there were tales told of coffins held down with shovels while earth was piled on. I did my duty by Fan, however, and her plot was high and dry.

The lawyer was an old man, not as old as Fan had been, but old enough to get away with saying, "What! No chickens, wine, and cakes, Lam? My father always said that if a Chinese ghost wasn't fed it'd come back to haunt you." He guffawed in that unpleasant way that lawyers have. The father, whom I remembered slightly, had been a friend of Fan's in the old days.

"There are one or two things in the vault I must look up for you," the lawyer said as we trudged up the stairs to Fan's room.

"When your stepmother first came in to make her will some years ago, she left some papers with us. They were to go to you after her death. Once we get this will business straightened out, I'll bring them to you."

"I'm leaving in a week and I'll be gone for a month," I told him as I knelt down and pulled Fan's tin box from under the bed. I took the key out of my pocket, where I had kept it since Fan had given it to me, and unlocked and lifted the lid. The scents of joss and opium came first, and with them other scents in memory that made the tears well in my eyes: rice cooking on a hot day in the greenhouses, the cooks handing me hot fried cakes; the strong strawy odour of the labourers' clothes as they came in from the fields to wash at lunchtime. I blinked the blur away, blew dust from the top papers, and quickly found what I wanted.

"I don't want to read it now," I told the lawyer, whose eyes were evaluating the contents of Fan's open cupboard. The silks were antiques and would fetch some money at auction. I handed him the will.

"You can let me know what I need to know when you bring the other papers."

"Aren't you going to look at the rest?" he asked, curious.

"I'll be away on my boat," I said, resenting his interest. "I'll have time enough then for reading." I locked the box and led the lawyer downstairs where I put the box with my kit bag before making him tea.

If I hadn't had to be on duty right to the end, if the *Rose* hadn't needed work on her engine the day before I was to leave so that I had no spare time, and if the lawyer had brought me the other papers earlier, I might never have gone to sea. As it was, he turned up at the last moment at the Upper Harbour Wharves where I'd moored the *Rose*, with a briefcase stuffed with paper. He heaved it aboard, shouted "Bon Voyage," and waved as I steered the *Rose* away. It was a calm, clear morning, and I wanted to take advantage of it. As anyone who sails the coast knows, the wind rises by noon.

"Goodbye, goodbye," shouted the lawyer, his shoes taking on water on the half-submerged dock. On his face was the smile that landlubbers reserve for sailors.

I lifted my hand in farewell, chugged the *Rose* beneath the Johnson Street Bridge, and aimed for the harbour entrance.

I was headed north, through the Inside Passage between Vancouver Island and the mainland. It was just possible, if nothing went wrong, to make it past the tip of the island, up through Queen Charlotte Sound to Rose Harbour, on the most southerly of the Queen Charlotte Islands, and back again in one month.

Trial Island, Seabird Point, and on into Haro Strait. I was already thinking ahead to the riptides at Turn Point, at the end of the strait, which I had to round in order to enter Boundary Pass, when I glanced up from the chart. My head had been down for ten or fifteen seconds, no more, and yet the vista ahead of me had changed utterly. The wind, which had been moderate since we'd passed Trial Island, had dropped. The *Rose* was gliding forward over a flat silvery sea, although moments before she had creaked and rocked her way across the steady chop. I looked behind me. A bank of fog had rolled up from the south obscuring all the nearby land. Vancouver Island had vanished. Her forested hills, the little communities on the shore that I'd watched sending out fishing boats and sailing vessels as I'd idly steered the *Rose*, might have existed only in my imagination. The fog was real enough, though, and I sounded the whistle at once and looked out for the Kelp Reefs light.

It flashed through the thick air, much closer than I'd expected, and I sounded the whistle again. I looked at the second hand of my watch, listening, but no echo returned, and when I checked the instruments, the depth sounder and direction finder, they were beaded inside with condensation, and useless. I slowed the engine. The *Rose* continued her slide across the mirror-like water, and I began to think about the freighter I'd seen coming up behind me, and the steamers that plied this channel, the border between the United States and Canada, with scheduled frequency. Where were they, and why didn't I hear their whistles in answer to mine? I slowed the engine another notch, and the engine began to miss. We were just off D'Arcy Island, where there was a line of rocks scattered outside the eastern shoreline, making my position dangerous, yet I hesitated to move out further into the channel with no information about the other traffic and not enough experience with the *Rose* to trust her spluttering engine.

A family of killer whales sported off the starboard bow, their calling muted and eerie in that muffled world. Then they disappeared, following the channel that I hesitated to risk, and I steered the failing *Rose* slowly westwards into the D'Arcy Island shallows.

The *Rose* had settled nicely at anchor in the cove I had found almost by instinct, and although the fog still filmed the landscape, I was in good spirits, my stomach lined with beef, bread, and coffee, and my hands warming round a mug of hot rum. I knew little of the island near which I sheltered other than that it had no inhabitants now but at one time had served as an isolation station for lepers. In all my time on the coast I had known no one who had set foot on it. Like most sailors I had seen enough leprosy in my travels to want to stay as far away from it as possible. There were still lepers nearby, however, on Bentinck Island, not far from where the pilots boarded inbound ships off Race Rocks. I had never passed by that desolate spot without a shudder of horror. The station was due to be closed once the last inhabitant died, and from what I had heard, that would not be much longer.

I raised my mug in the direction of the darker air that was the shore of D'Arcy Island, and saluted its ghosts, and drank.

I have heard men say that a spirit enters a ship like a rat. It travels along the bowline into the forecastle, and up the mast; or if there is no mast, it finds a perch on any high point. For there is not a ghost that is happy at sea: they long to return to land but have first to complete their undertakings, since it is living men who compel them by the strength of their memories. Not that I had seen any myself, but I knew men who had, and I had walked the deck of the *Silverbell* all one night to calm a seaman's fears. A woman had appeared three times on deck, calling for the captain, and it was true that he and many others on board that ship did not survive the voyage, and I had had to write the sad letters home.

I thought of the rising sun, the singing of birds, and the pale stretch of blue that made up the morning heavens, for I did not like the turn my thoughts had taken, and had learned long ago not to give free rein to them. But as I looked at the shoreline, which was only a shoreline, and raised my mug of rum to my lips, I heard a cracked voice singing, "I'll be with you in apple blossom time," and then a laugh.

I turned my head slowly in the direction of the scent of joss and opium. She was seated on top of the wheelhouse wearing the heavy black cashmere shawl that I had brought back for her from one of my voyages. And she was tapping her pipe out on my teak.

"Stop it, Fan," I said angrily, before I had time to think. "I only just had that repaired."

She smiled a slow smile and took her time at her work until the pipe was clean. By then I was shaking.

"Do not be afraid, Robert Lam," she said. "I am your old friend."

"I know who you are," I said, "but you're not welcome here. I'll have no stowaways aboard my boat."

She looked around the *Rose* disdainfully. "Is this your new home?" she asked.

"You know it is. We did nothing but argue about it at the end."

"Then what choice do I have, Robert Lam? I made you a promise, and now I am going to keep it. I have to go where you go."

My cup tipped off the rail, fell to the water, and sank as I raised my hands and pressed them against my temples. I closed my eyes, but when I opened them she was still there.

"I don't know what you're talking about," I said.

She looked at me with pity. "How is it that you remember everything except that which is important? You are a very foolish man."

That was it. When I looked again, she was gone. I heard the lapping of the water against the *Rose*'s sides, but no voices, no more of Lam Fan.

I awoke with a headache. My sleeping bag had drooped over the end of the bunk, and where it touched the floor it was soaking wet. A half inch of water sloshed from side to side as the *Rose* rocked at anchor. I sat up and looked out the porthole. The fog was still glued to the sky, and, if anything, had thickened since the night before. I put on my wet boots and got up to light the stove. A shimmer of fish scales, risen from the cracks in the flooring, floated on the surface of water in my flooded cabin, and as I splashed my way through the stores, I bumped into the briefcase the lawyer had thrown on board, which I had stowed beneath my bed. I lifted it up to a shelf to dry, went up to start the bilge pump, came down and made the coffee and reflected on the hours I would have to stay put and on Fan's "visit" the night before and what it could have meant. If it was grief that had summoned her, it ran deeper than I knew. And it was not grief but curiosity and the sure knowledge that I was afraid that made me summon my courage, take the key that Fan had given me the night she died, and open the tin box I had carried on board in my kit bag.

Still, for a moment, I hesitated as I lifted the lid; for I had remembered a bad night with Fan, and the trouble that had filled my mind at her angry words.

I had been through the Depression. I had been through the war. I had learned not to probe beneath the surface. Yet, when I saw the diary and flipped open the cover to read on the flyleaf my mother's name, "India Thackery," I could not resist looking further. But the diary, after the first half page, proved to be disappointingly blank. I looked back at the flyleaf. On it, in the same handwriting as my mother's name, was the date "January 1900." I glanced at the page of writing, but it meant nothing to me.

There were several yellowed folded papers clipped together inside the diary, and these I unfolded with care. Their edges were powdery, and in the creases the paper fibres were parting. But what was printed there was perfectly clear. My coffee cooled in my cup, my wet feet grew numb as I sat in the *Rose* and read:

An Act For the Relief of India Thackery Haack

[Assented to first day of January 1900]
Whereas India Thackery Haack, of the city of Victoria, in the province of British Columbia, wife of Robert Louis Haack, formerly of the said city of Victoria, mining engineer, but now residing in the city of San Francisco, in the state of California, one of the United States of America, has by her petition set forth that on the twenty-ninth day of November one thousand eight hundred and ninety-eight, she was lawfully married to the said Robert Louis Haack, of the said city of Victoria; that they lived together as husband and wife until November thirtieth of the year one thousand eight hundred and ninety-eight,

when without lawful reason or excuse he deserted her, and has since continued to live apart from her, and has committed acts of adultery; and whereas she has humbly prayed that the said marriage may be dissolved and that she be authorized to marry again and that such further relief may be afforded her as is deemed meet; and whereas she has proved the said allegations of her petition, and it is expedient that the prayer thereof should be granted:

Therefore Her Majesty, by and with the advice and consent of the Senate and House of Commons of Canada, enacts as follows:—

1. The said marriage between the said India Thackery Haack and Robert Louis Haack, her husband, is hereby dissolved and shall be henceforth null and void to all intents and purposes whatsoever.

2. The said India Thackery Haack may at any time hereafter marry any man whom she might lawfully marry in case the said marriage with the said Robert Louis Haack had not been solemnized.

I sat there, with cold hands, feet, and heart, for several minutes before I could take in what the document said. Growing up as an orphan, not knowing anything of my father, but believing my mother to have been a respectable and ordinary woman, was one thing. Finding out, at this late date, that my mother had married a man who deserted her after one day of marriage, and understanding (since Fan had told me my birth date) that I had been conceived and born out of wedlock, was another. Moreover, Robert Louis Haack was not a Chinese name, nor was mining engineer a Chinese occupation on the west coast of Canada in the late 1800s. Yet I was half-Chinese, and I was named Robert Louis. If Haack wasn't my father, why had India given me his name? And who was my father, and what kind of woman was my mother?

"I wish I hadn't asked, Fan," I said aloud. "Maybe your way, not telling me, was better." I resented, far more than I had ever thought possible, being a bastard.

I poured my coffee back into the pot and put it on to heat. I opened the hatch to let in air. I bailed the remaining water out of the cabin and turned off the pump. Then I sat down again at the table and read the next paper. It was a newspaper clipping, fragile as dust, from the *British Colonist*, Victoria, January 16, 1900.

Robert Haack Dead
A Former Resident of the City
Comes to a Bad
End

About 14 months ago, Robert Haack, former member of the Workingmen's Protective Association, once accused of crookedness in certain fiduciary matters, and connected in this city with instances of rowdiness and ill-fame, was deported to the United States from which he had come.

The town has recently been astonished to learn that Haack left a wife and some $4,000 of indebtedness behind him. In a short time the ill-omened Haack was heard of at San Francisco, where with his ill-gotten gains he purchased a fifth-rate boardinghouse on the waterfront called the New Swanston House.

Under Haack's management the New Swanston soon became a notorious place of resort for the bad of both sexes and all classes. Occasionally a well-to-do guest was induced to take up his abode there, and on three or four different occasions complaints were heard that guests had been robbed overnight of valuables, though Haack always professed innocence. Indeed he had conceived the strange impression that he had been a friend of the late Scottish poet, Robert Louis Stevenson, with whom he shared Christian names, and would tell anyone who could be compelled to pay attention, that he had once possessed a poem in the poet's handwriting. One night a stranger put up at the New Swanston, and after depositing with Robert a well-filled purse, got into an argument of a literary nature with his host. The next day the strange guest died suddenly. There were rumours that the man had been poisoned so that Robert might possess himself of the wealth that had been deposited in his unsafe safe. But nothing came of the rumours, except this—the money was never found. Shortly afterwards a man was murdered near the hotel. In a day or two another of the guests showed symptoms of poisoning, but did not die; and the police, becoming satisfied that the proprietor of the New Swanston was a dangerous citizen; gave him forty-eight hours in which to leave town. Robert went to Monterey, but did not stay there long as he was out of money. He then went to Los Angeles where he "put up a job" to slay a man, but the intended victim learned of the plot, which it is not clear that Haack intended to carry out, and the man shot him dead.

Robert Louis Lam, named after Robert Louis Haack. What's in a name but history, and this name, my name, meant (among other things) desertion, robbery, and murder. As well (I checked through the clipping to be sure) as a peculiar connection to a dead Scottish poet who also, coincidentally, possessed the same Christian names. I wondered about this husband of my mother's who had had so few virtues. Could my own father, whoever he was, have been in worse circumstances than the consistently crooked proprietor of the New Swanston?

I put the clipping down. I checked the weather, which had remained unaltered. I changed my socks and boots and hung the wet socks up to dry. I listened to the creaking of the *Rose* at anchor, thinking for a moment that I heard light footsteps.

Without Fan how would I ever learn the answers, for without her I could not even frame the questions. I knew so little. I had almost nothing with which to start. I'd lived my life to this point without knowing about my family, and it had made no difference. For whatever I had become, I had made myself. I owed nothing to anyone. And I could not help my name nor who had used it, or misused it, or so long ago.

When you find yourself telling yourself lies, and you are a middle-aged pilot on the road to retirement, sitting out bad weather in a stripped-down troller, with no one to talk to but yourself, and with your conscience uneasy as it unravels neat scenery; and the view through the porthole is a blank, and you wish and don't wish for your stepmother's ghost, then if you are to remain the man you've made yourself, you change direction. For there is no one saner than a mariner at work, and few less so when he is idle. And if you cannot navigate ahead, you turn around. Or plot a new course, or change destination. You adapt.

For what matters (I concluded) is not what the past contains, for it is only a threat if you imagine it. Nothing on paper could harm Robert Lam if it was only the facts.

I spent three hours working on the engine, cleaning the lines, adjusting the spark plugs, checking item by item all the repair work that had been done. When my back ached from bending, and I was covered in more grease than I'd seen since I was an apprentice, I stripped off my clothes and dove off the deck of the *Rose* into the milky waters of the cove. The cold took my fatigue at once, and I surfaced and dove again to the bottom, where the faint glitter of abalone shell promised bait for fishing.

But it was not just abalone that I brought up with me. When I cut the shells loose with my knife, I uncovered a spoon. It was nothing valuable, not even silver, and it had an odd looped handle, like on a child's spoon, but it was big enough to take an adult's fist through it. I toweled and dressed, put the kettle on to boil, and, with the spoon on the table beside me, sat down to read the last of the papers in Fan's tin box.

My mother's name, India Thackery, was written at the top of another newspaper clipping in Lam Fan's handwriting, and printed above the headline was the date, January 30, 1900.

Drowned Woman

The body of a Caucasian woman has been recovered from the waters off Clover Point. An informant reports that the woman, while out walking, two days ago, seemed to slip on the rocks, whence she fell into the frigid waters of the ocean. Our passerby ran for help. When he returned with a rope and another good Samaritan, the two were able, with some difficulty, to cast the rope out to the woman who had been buoyed up on account of her voluminous skirts. She seemed, our witness said, to understand what was required of her, although they heard her speak no words nor utter any cry for help. It was a calm day, and our rescuers were confident of a happy outcome to the incident. Alas, the woman, in the extremity of her situation, slipped the rope around her shoulders, instead of beneath her arms. When her new friends drew her in and lifted her onto the rocks, they found that the rope had encircled the woman's neck and that the poor female was quite dead.

To all appearances, she was a lady.

Friday is an unlucky day to set to sea. It was the day we'd sailed from Freetown in the *Silverbell* with thirteen merchant ships in the convoy, and not one of us made it safely past the Canaries. Sparks was playing the piano—"I'll be seeing you in apple blossom time"—when we went down. And Robert Louis Lam, called "China" behind his back, was a forty-one-year-old second mate.

I had just left the saloon to visit a sick apprentice when the torpedo struck us in number-five hatch; and the next thing I knew I was in the water. The sea, where oil had spilled, was on fire. The *Silverbell* was listing but afloat, and men were falling or leaping over the side of the ship into the water. I saw the periscope of the submarine as it came up to take a look at the damage, and I watched the Free French escort vessel, coming to our rescue, steaming straight for it.

I cried out loud, and I cried not for Lam Fan, nor for Sing Yuen who had been the only father I'd known, but for my mother. And when the sub dove and nothing happened, and the *Commandant de Boques* picked us safely up out of the water, I believed that my long-dead mother had heard me and answered.

I wanted to call for her again now. I wanted her to save me from unhappiness, from self-doubt, from the empty destiny that seemed to be my fate. I sat at the table with my head in my hands, and the full weight of loneliness, which I had not allowed myself to feel before, descended on my shoulders. I was a fifty-seven-year-old orphan. And with the only family I might have had on paper before me.

And so I turned back to that ending, which should have been a beginning, the only entry in my mother's diary for 1900, when I, her son was but a few months old. And I vowed to find out, however I could, what had happened. For if life was unfair, still it had its rules, and a mother did not easily abandon her child. Yet before taking her walk, before venturing out into the January cold, before her accident, my mother had written: "I cannot think that the world will continue to be so cruel. I washed and dressed the baby, kissed him goodbye, and gave him to Lam Fan."

CHAPTER ONE

"When navigating the inner waters of British Columbia, it should be constantly borne in mind that many of the minor passages have only been roughly examined; detached boulders from the broken shores and pinnacles of rock are still frequently found. Whenever, therefore, a broad and clear channel which has been surveyed is known to exist, there is no justification in using, without necessity, one of more doubtful character, even if there be some saving in distance."

British Columbia Pilot, Volume I

Although the usual route for smaller vessels going into the Strait of Georgia from southern Vancouver Island is by following inshore channels, avoiding the strong tidal streams of Haro Strait, I was taking the main sea lanes: up Haro Strait and thence into Boundary Pass westward of Patos Island. There were several reasons for this. I was still interested, despite my recent discoveries, in the project I had set out in the *Rose* to do, and I had more chance of sighting whales on my way in the deeper waters. Moreover I knew the coast and was not afraid of the heavy tide rips and eddies that kept some sailors in the less turbulent approaches;

and it was safer, in any case, in fog or thick weather to take the wider passages. Although I would miss out some of the former whaling ports (at Deep Bay and Hornby Island), which I had marked on my map as possible anchorages, I could make up lost time, using the strong tides to assist me, on my journey as a whole. The unscheduled stop at D'Arcy Island had taken a day from my calendar. There was no leeway: I had to be back on the job at the end of the month.

The day had dawned clear, but with a shirring of mare's tails in the east. A light sea breeze supported the gulls in my wake as I left my refuge at D'Arcy Island. I ran the *Rose* up to six knots and steered a course to take me a mile westward of Kellett Bluff and thence north-northwest to pass safely round Turn Point. I was humming to myself, watching for deadheads and possible whale spouts and keeping a weather eye on the solitary figure that had been my company since I'd put down the papers I'd been reading all night. The lawyer's briefcase had dried out enough to let me examine some of its contents: the rest were airing below, pinned flat on my table with lead fishing weights.

Fan was standing at the stern, holding on to the forestay, balanced neatly to take the rise and fall of the bow, with her knot of black hair half undone and flying. She seemed to be enjoying herself, from what I could tell. The sea glittered silver in the sunlight, and a fine salt spray stippled the air. I could feel its sting through the open window of the wheelhouse. Mostly Fan gazed ahead (with what intention I could not tell), but she'd throw the occasional glance my way, as if to check that I was following where she would lead. Not that I had much choice. We were in it together (whatever *it* was) for the duration, so she'd said when I'd questioned her last night; for she'd appeared in the cabin shortly after midnight.

There were puzzles in the archive that I was reading my way through: names, places, dates, events. And I could not give it shape; I lacked the context. I was moving in regions I had never mapped, and I needed help.

I was sitting there, stiff with fatigue, my eyes smarting from the smoke of the kerosene light, reading the pages of diaries, letters, and crumbling newspapers over and over, when, all at once, I knew she was back. The lamp dimmed and brightened as if a porthole had been opened, and I could smell her smell, the spoor of joss and opium.

"Do not be discouraged, Robert Lam," she said, touching the back of my neck with her cold fingers. "You start the work, and I will fill in the gaps."

I shivered, but I did not draw away. I made my decision in that moment: there was little to lose by accepting her offer, and likely some loss in shutting her out. And I could do what I liked so long as I was alone; I need give explanations to no one. Although what justification I could have found for believing in my figment I do not know, for I had no rationale to offer.

"I'm ready to listen, Fan," I said calmly, although my heart was beating loudly. My assent pleased her, and she assumed a more cheerful aspect, settling herself comfortably on the bunk above me. And so we began the story of my mother and father, which was Fan's story also, step by step filling in the blanks. And if I did not yet have it all, at least I had the outlines of my map. And was drawing in the first continent.

India's father, "Major" Thackery, my grandfather, died at their home in the Wanchai district of Hong Kong in January 1890. He was a man in advance of his time, and, as such, keeping true to form even at the end, he succumbed to the plague, although the epidemic itself didn't arrive in the city for four more years. When it did come, it fulfilled the "irresistible logic" that the major had prophesied. That is, that an epidemic of this nature was inevitable unless there were strong and complete reforms of sanitation. Although by the time it was evident he was right, it was too late, and irresistible logic had to follow its course. No one recalled the major's warnings, of course, except for his family, and he was not hailed posthumously as a hero, and in any case by that time there were other matters obscuring his record. Moreover, there were too many dead, and in a panic of whitewashing and disinfecting and mass burial, no one wanted a messenger, especially a ghost, pointing the finger and saying, "I told you so."

The year in which he had arrived in the colony, 1845, was a year of optimism, just the right climate for the reforming Thackery. In the settlement, which was damp and swampy and overcrowded, Thackery launched his schemes for better housing, more drainage, and cleanliness. Not that this was his job, but he would turn his hand to anything, and change—for the better—was his passion. In 1846 Wong Nei Chong Valley was drained and a road constructed around it; Jardine Matheson and Co., the major's employers, for whom he worked as a manager, subscribed a hospital overlooking Happy Valley; and the major penned a milestone report on cow sheds, pigsties, and stagnant pools. But as the years went by, and as fever and typhoid and cholera continued to overwhelm the colonists in recurring storms of pestilence, little more was done. Except for the construction of a few dustbins.

So it was that when a rat ran off a ship that had touched in at a plague spot on the coast, and, following a system of ineffable navigation, negotiated its way from the harbour past the Jardine Matheson warehouse, through the boat house, across the cricket ground, through the barrack kitchen, and up the Queen's Road straight to the major's doorstep, where its fleas, as if under instruction, bit the man who had written letters, drawn countless diagrams, and made speeches on this very subject... so it was that, as the unmistakable plague symptoms showed in the swollen glands of his armpits, the major found the justification for his life. "They should have listened to me," he cried as he lay dying. "I was right. Tell them, children. They must be told!"

Not that anyone *would* have listened at this point. For it wasn't just drainage, but agricultural machinery, education for girls, and the reconciliation of the Chinese religions and Christianity that made up the major's reforming program. And the fact was that they had long since stopped paying attention to him.

Year after year the major's schemes had accumulated in the files of the governor, and his drawings and writings poured before the public. Plan after plan, at first welcomed and discussed, for reasons inexplicable and political, fell away. So that, over time, even the enthusiasts abandoned him. For who could believe that so many ideas had anything in them, since they were never taken up.

And since, as we know, respect is the second vital element (after money) in keeping a man alive and sane, after some time in which the major's opinion, once sought, was largely ignored, the critics' and scoffers' whispers may have acquired substance. They said that he had lost his sharp edge, that pipelines and water-supply systems and curricula for women were but the manifestations of a softened brain. That in the damp heat, of which the major himself had warned of the effects, he had become no more than a local irritant.

It wouldn't be the first time that a good man had gone downhill in a difficult climate. I've seen it happen myself. In Indonesia, in the Caribbean, in Africa. Disappointed men, or those crossed in love.

"What do *you* know about love?" asks Lam Fan loudly in my ear. I nearly drop the cup I've been holding, as, lost in my thoughts, I was letting the *Rose* steer herself while I poured tea from a flask. Fan had slipped up behind me in the wheelhouse, although I swear I'd had her in sight all the time. "Look out, Robert Lam!" she cries suddenly in alarm, and I grab the wheel and spin it to avoid a deadhead that has appeared from nowhere in our path. The deadhead submerges as we pass it.

"Don't frighten me like that, Fan!" I say. My heart is thudding and I am shivering with cold sweat. If I am to believe my eyes, we have nearly struck a humpback whale, a species that has not been seen in numbers in the gulf region for some years. This must have been a baby, for it was no more than thirty feet long.

"Once there were plenty of those whales," says Fan, who appears to take credit for the sighting. "It did not have so much oil as the sperm whale, and was therefore often left alone. Some whalers didn't like to hunt it, since once one was killed, its mate would stay around until it, too, was taken. It was too easy to kill."

"Doesn't sound smart to me, Fan," I say, trying to concentrate on my steering. For a pilot I am doing a poor job. Somehow I've misread the tide tables, and we are in slack water, which means that within a few minutes we will be fighting the current—just as we meet the tide rips at Boundary Pass.

"They mate for life, Robert Lam," says Fan, as if I hadn't taken the point. "That is what you, a bachelor, cannot understand about your grandfather. When his wife left him he was a changed man. He couldn't go on as he had been going. He was lost without her. She had steadied him. You men, especially you bachelors, underestimate women."

"His wife left him?" I say, ignoring her jibes.

"It was partly my fault," she says, not without pride, as she stares unseeingly into the distance, and the *Rose* steers east between the islands.

The year 1857 was a pivotal one. Well-established by then, still well-connected, the major fought against the legalization of opium in China, although his employers, Jardine Matheson, had more than twenty ships in the opium trade and were pushing to expand their market. Opium, went the argument, was the means by which the Europeans could open China up, for so far the Chinese had shown surprisingly little interest in

European furniture or other goods. And the East India Company, which grew the drug on its plantations, had reorganized the whole of Indian agriculture and labour to supply the—so far—lagging demand. Not unexpectedly, despite his faithful service to the company and his unshakable belief in the inevitability of progress, the major, in his professional career, ceased to advance.

Of course he was right. History shows that the opium trade was wrong and led to nothing but sorrow. But the present offered no such comfort to a man on the way down, who could not ask the future to support him.

In this same year there was another occurrence of considerable import, at least to me. For this was the year in which my mother, India, was born, and named, to the distress of her parents' acquaintances, after the Indian Mutiny, which Britain had barely survived and suppressed. The earth, once so solid, was trembling beneath the colonists' feet. It was not a friendly act, they judged as they congratulated the major's wife on the baby's birth, to remind them of their danger. It was not the gesture of a patriot.

And if this weren't enough to affix the seal of disapproval to the major's house, his next act was. He acquired a second live-in child, another girl, a Chinese.

And shortly after this event the major's wife left him.

This child, this cause of so much trouble who appeared out of nowhere in a landscape shifting, floundering in the internettings of politics, this object of charity....

"No, no, Robert Lam. You've got it wrong," says Fan. "It wasn't at all like that. There was much more to it."

"All right, Fan," I say testily, trying to catch a glimpse of East Point light. There is a darkening on the horizon which could mean a squall. "Have it your way, it's up to you to make me understand. You said so yourself. You told me that what happened was your fault."

"Only partly, Robert Lam. The major did the rest by himself."

At issue (I pause for a moment in case Fan plans to interrupt; but she has gone back to the bow to play lookout), at issue, I repeat, was the vast market of China to which the Europeans were trying to force an entrance. As this matter was pursued by the diplomats, it took on a humiliating shape. For gradually it became apparent to the European officials that the Chinese considered the Europeans to be inferiors. The Chinese had no intention of letting the Europeans come and go freely in their country, or of establishing equal relations. Europeans could not meet the Emperor; they could not go to Peking; they could go only to the five treaty ports to which they (through military intervention) had coerced limited access.

Here was the problem. Each side believed in itself. Each thought it was superior to the other. There was no reconciling these perceptions. Imagine the effect of this on the European mind at the height of Imperialism.

So when, in 1856, a British-registered lorcha, the *Arrow*, was boarded outside Canton by Chinese authorities searching for pirates, and these same authorities arrested the crew and lowered the British flag, it was natural for the British to expect apologies and reparations. Almost as natural to use the incident to compel the Chinese to let the British traders inside the Canton city walls—for up to now they and other European merchants had been confined in factories or warehouses outside.

It was an invitation to escalation. And here is where Yeh Mingchen, viceroy of Kwangsi and Kwangtung, the province of which Canton is the capital, comes in. For Yeh would not back down. He said it was the right of the people of China to say no to the Westerners if they wanted. "The chief consideration is the people," wrote Yeh, a good Confucian. "It is said in the Book of History, 'Heaven sees as my people see; Heaven hears as my people hear.' Is this not an additional reason why I should be unable to constrain the people?"

Far from constraining them, Yeh encouraged their opposition, and, after some shelling of Canton city walls by the British navy, the foreign factories between the walls and the river were burned by the citizens of Canton to the ground.

For there is no law in Heaven that places one people above another (although my experiences at sea should have taught me differently: since there is no lower form of marine life than a boy apprentice, unless it is the *colonial* apprentice just starting out); and there are times indeed when an act of aggression is an act of self-defence; as when I sailed the North Atlantic for the first time and got in a fight with the captain.

"What's this, Robert Lam?" says Fan, who has come in off the deck as raindrops begin to fall. "You never told me this before."

"Never mind, Fan," I say. "I was lucky to get out of it with my job. The captain said, 'You, boy; you've got a black eye. The best thing we can do is to forget how you got it. You go and turn in.'"

"You always were lucky," says Fan, losing interest as we both watch the squall miss us by a hundred yards. We are passing Monarch Head, and I take a fix on the Alden Point light.

Action and reaction. It's not often that luck gets you out of a jam. For once a pattern starts it takes a miracle to put an end to it. And there was no such event to stop the chain that had begun at Canton. The pattern spread. In Hong Kong colony servants abandoned their masters. There were, in fact, about eighty thousand Chinese on the island, and Yeh Mingchen was in touch with the fishing villages on the Kowloon Peninsula. The colonists were outnumbered and surrounded. At night, near the harbour at Victoria or on the Queen's Road (the Queen's Road!), Europeans feared to tread. Even though it was the Chinese who were forbidden to appear after curfew.

It was during this turbulent time that my mother was conceived, for the major, like everyone else, stayed close to home. And with the servants gone he had to go to the morning markets himself. Where he saw, much to his disappointment, that the refuse buckets he had paid for out of his pocket, and caused to be placed in the streets near his house, were being used as lavatories.

"Heaven sees as my people see," as the Viceroy said.

In January of 1857, that critical year, the Chinese government attempted a blockade of Hong Kong in hopes of starving the Europeans out. It didn't work. It was far too late to close those doors that had been pried open between East and West—whatever Yeh thought. There were, of course, many sides to the issues, but they showed only two faces— European and Chinese. To a man with reforming principles this was unacceptable. The matter was too complex; there was good and bad on both sides. The Europeans had sanitation and voting on their side, but the Chinese were against the opium trade. The major stepped carefully down the middle. In an ideal of reconciliation, which appeared nowhere else but in his letters to the editor of the *Friend of China and Hong Kong Gazette*, the major set forth his opinions. But reconciliation brought him no friends, and he found that along with the hatred of the colonists, he had this as well in common with Yeh Mingchen: a belief in imminent disaster. For it was obvious that no good would come of this confrontation, and that the Chinese would suffer the results of cause and effect.

What happened was this as recorded little more than a year later in a soldier's diary:

"A heavy pall of smoke rose from the Summer Palace obscuring the light of the sun; it drifted over Peking and deposited an ominous layer of ashes in the streets of the city. The world around looked dark with shadow. When we entered the gardens they reminded one of those magic grounds described in fairy tales; we marched from them upon the nineteenth of October, leaving a drear waste of ruined nothings."

Fan and I sit quietly, watching the empty ocean rise and fall. It is patterned, to the northwest, by rain, but the sky and sea make a blanket of otherwise unrelieved grey, which shuts us in. We can see the islands, Saturna and Patos, but they are no more than neutral frames for the flatness.

"How do you stand it, day after day?" asks Fan.

What can I answer? That I'm used to it? That I like it this way? That it isn't as bad for me as for an ordinary seaman? "I wait for it to change, Fan," I say. And she smiles.

In Hong Kong on the morning of January 15, 1857, the Europeans sat down to breakfast. They had endured one more of a hundred sleepless nights spent in fear of the assassin's knife. As they drank tea and buttered their toast and covered it with jam, they basked in the security of broad daylight. For what could be safer than breakfast with the family on a rainy morning?

They ate the bread that was delivered each day from the E. Sing bakery on Pottinger Street, and, to a man, woman, and child, they vomited.

For while patrols had been watching for arsonists and for Chinese out late coming home from parties, the bakers of Pottinger Street, with the compliance, if not the direction, of the owner, Cheong Ah Lum, were stirring in an extra ingredient. But at this moment, when the fate of the entire British colony at Hong Kong was in their hands, they overdid it. There was so much arsenic in the bread that the poison had no chance to take effect. It was rejected, with vigour, by the European stomachs at once.

"I am shaken by the effects of poison," wrote the governor of the colony bitterly, expressing no thanks to heaven for his escape from death.

"Every member of my family being at this moment suffering from this new attempt upon our lives." So ungrateful was he for the heavy hand of the bakers that fifty-two of the workmen and underbakers of E. Sing were arrested and kept in a room fifteen feet square. Which allowed (just let me do the mathematics, Fan)—just over four square feet per person.

So that they couldn't sit down or lie down or move their limbs freely. So that they had ample opportunity to reflect together on their errors. So that some of them, later, died.

Oh yes. There is one more thing, Fan reminds me (as if this is something I could possibly leave out). The owner of the bakery, Ah Lum, plus his wife and all of his children but one, fled to Macau. The child left behind, a little girl, forgotten or abandoned we do not know, was that very same child that the major, for reasons best known to himself, took into his home and called Lam Fan.

"I don't understand, Fan," I say. (We are in mid-channel between Alden Point and East Point. Boiling Reef is behind us and we are about to alter course northwestward, into the Strait of Georgia.) "If your father's name was Lum, why did the major call you Lam?"

Fan looks at me oddly. "But you yourself do the very same thing."

"What on earth do you mean, Fan?" I say, then I understand and am embarrassed. I busy myself with the charts. We are skirting the boundary between the United States and Canada, and I take my time determining where on the border we are.

"At the Pilot House," she reminds me, since I haven't said anything. "Remember what I saw in there? They spelled your name on the board as Lamb not Lam."

I put the charts down.

"Well, the major thought Lam sounded better in English," she continues, "just like you thought Lamb was even better. He said it would make life easier for me in Hong Kong, it would help the English forget about my father who had frightened them. Lum is too hard for them, too Chinese."

I digest this information uncomfortably.

"Of course what counts," I say, "is not the name but the person who bears it. Changing a name doesn't change who you are."

"No," Fan agrees, "but it changes what you can do."

A light slowly begins to dawn in my brain. "Is that what my mother did, Fan, give me her husband's name, Robert Louis, to make my life easier? So that people wouldn't know I had no father? Of course, she had something to hide as well. Like the fact that she wasn't married when I was born. Like the fact that her lover was Chinese.

"Maybe," I add, after a self-sobering pause, "she didn't know who my father was."

"Oh, my," says Fan, giving me a withering look. "I didn't know you sailors were so nice. Or are these the thoughts of a disappointed man, one crossed in love?" She is mocking me by repeating my earlier words, and I find I am not amused.

"At least I've never been left," I say, taking the offensive. My cruel words hit home. I think for a moment that she will cry.

"My husband, Sing Yuen, believed it was his duty to go to war," she says quietly. "He felt that if the Chinese did well for Canada, they would be recognized as soldiers, as heroes."

"Well that didn't happen, did it."

"No, Robert Lam, it didn't. But it isn't because he didn't try." Fan regards me thoughtfully.

I count to ten and look at the birds in the water, and identify them. There is a Brandt's cormorant, a western gull, and a pigeon guillemot. We keep score, at the Pilot House, of how many species we see on each trip. It is something to take our minds off the boredom of making the same journeys, day after day, harbour to harbour, going nowhere but where we have often been before.

She was cooed over and stared at, then neglected and mistreated. In the overheated atmosphere of the pivotal year of 1857, she became a symbol. She stood for any number of contraries: Christian forgiveness, for example, or Chinese barbarianism. You could take your pick, according to your lights. Soon, however, for such is the nature of political events, as the news came in of the Indian Mutiny, and the possibility of a general uprising against the British in the East, and the great winds of change began to blow, the little leftover baker's daughter faded into insignificance. Even the *Friend of China and Hong Kong Gazette*, which had printed editorials on what should be done with her, forgot she existed. She was still left behind, though, and friendless. For who in his right mind would want to be responsible for a reminder of rebellion and ingratitude and near death?

Except the major. That champion of progress, of the underdog, of reform.

For the reforming mind likes challenges. It conducts tests, it is experimental. And in this case, at least, the reforming mind was also compassionate, and had noticed what others had missed. That as well as a symbol, the child *was* a child. Who needed parents and guidance and love. Who needed a home. Perhaps it was the birth of his own daughter that had set the major thinking. Whereas his child would receive food, clothing, and an education as a matter of course, the baker's daughter would be lucky to survive; and most likely would be sold and worked as a prostitute before she was twelve.

The child's life had come to a dividing point, and at this fork in the road stood the major.

Lam Fan nods her head. So far so good. But what about the mother? What about the major's wife?

Since there is no mention in the papers of her, I have to ask. And although Fan looks grim and stays silent, it isn't too difficult for me to guess the rest. For the major's wife had a baby in her arms whom her husband had christened after a seditious country. She had a husband on her hands whom her countrymen thought was a traitor to established British principle: a man who had lost the respect of his contemporaries. And now he had brought, into her home, and expected her to care for as her own, a baker's daughter, the child of a would-be murderer. For murder had been the intent if not the outcome: and between the two, in her mind, there was little distinction.

Everyone, even in the nineteenth century, even a woman bound to a husband, has a breaking point. And for India's mother, my grandmother, this was it. Out of the house on the Queen's Road she went, away from the reformer and his inflexible reforming principles, out of British colonial life and into an Italian Catholic convent. Which was a giant step for her to take but a momentous one also for her babies. For who was to be their mother now? And how could they grow up without one? One orphan and one half an orphan: that was Lam Fan and my mother. For three-quarters of their parents had disappeared. And what about me? Was it like mother like daughter that made my mother leave me?

"Poor, poor baby," says Fan. And I'm not sure I couldn't weep on her shoulder.

*   *   *

Night time. We are running up the Strait of Georgia, virtually mid-channel, with course set for Upwood Point on the south end of Texada Island. And rest stop planned for Blubber Bay on the north end. There is a dock there and little else: the ramshackle wooden houses common to the coast, and a few diehards remembering boom times while the forest takes back the land.

We are climbing a chain of islands in whaling country. Mayne, Galiano, Valdes, Gabriola. And Ballenas Island, called "Islas de las Ballinas" by the Spanish—Island of Whales. And Hornby and Denman islands where whale bones litter the shores.

Lam Fan stares with distaste into the cup of steaming tea that, without thinking, I have poured for her. Does a ghost eat and drink? I watch to see if she takes a sip. Do I cook for one or for two? I have put off getting my supper because I am uncertain. On a long trip like this, it is not an unimportant question. She puts the cup down without drinking, but I'm still uncertain of the answer.

"I was told," she says, "that a whale once towed a sailing whaler all around Texada Island. I also heard of two sisters who rowed a boat from the mainland to Van Anda followed by nine whales. There is another story, you know," she says, "I was told this by a Klootchman, that whales like human women. Do you know about that, Robert Lam?" Fan gives me a sly look to see how I react. I know the story she means. I've heard it, too, from one of the Indian guides up the coast. It is a story about jealousy. In the end, a woman eats her lover's privates. Of course this is an accident, but she does it just the same.

The thump of the bow waves fills the next moments while I resist the impulse to respond. For who knows where this might lead? And I have other questions to ask my stepmother, more important than those about a whale's loyalties.

The major's papers, for example. Essays on education, on water closets, on language. I have examined these leaden skies without hope. I need her to make them make sense.

Two female children, of different races, alone in a house with a middle-aged man. A runaway wife, housed in a convent. A predilection for impossible schemes. The colony had made its assessment. And the believer in education found the school doors shut against him. He tried every one of them, and at last he put the children in Miss Jane Baxter's Diocesan Native Female School, which was meant for Chinese only. They stayed a few months, India helping the others with English, until the major realized that the Chinese girls, who were not allowed to speak their native tongue, and for whom there were few Christianized English-speaking Chinese men to marry, were ending up as mistresses for Europeans.

The major brought Fan and India home.

There was a succession of teachers and governesses in the Queen's Road home, now belonging, in fact, to the major's employers, Jardine Matheson. For the major had run up certain debts. For the fact is, he had lost heart for his former way of life, and was slipping.

His wife, now a Catholic, wouldn't see him. His employers kept him on out of indifference, and he was scorned by all society, forced back on his own and the children's company. And the girls, those experiments in progress, were growing up half-wild, out at all hours in the streets, speaking both Chinese and English. For a believer in progress, it was one thing; for a Victorian father, it was another. In brief, the major, too, found his breaking point, and the man who was not soft-brained to begin with took steps to alter that fact. In the Bombay Tavern and the Old House at Home for the most part.

While the two young women learned their lessons. What Lam Fan learned was not what India learned. India yearned for rescue, and Fan for oblivion. So India kept a diary, and Lam Fan began to smoke opium.

In amongst Lam Fan's papers I have found two photographs. I have tacked them up in the wheelhouse on the bottom of the chart table, so that when the table is latched, I can see them. In the soft tipping light of the lantern, which hangs to my left illuminating the compass shelf, the faces age, then recover their youth.

The photograph of the major was taken not long before his death. He is wearing a tennis costume—white flannel trousers, white shirt with a high collar around which is tied a scarf. All the buttons of his single-breasted blazer are done up. It looks too tight for him, and his hands protrude out of the sleeves grotesquely. He holds a walking stick between his legs as he sits in a brocaded chair. It is clear that he has not seen a tennis court in years. He is a large man, but his flesh hangs loosely on his bones. His face is ugly, good-natured, and weak, with a large chin, spreading nose, and high forehead. He squints, and seems to blink, behind wire-rimmed spectacles.

It is a face, I think (throttling the engine down another notch to meet the wake of a tanker, probably the *Standard Service* on its way south), for all its drinker's traits (the veined nose and cheeks, the dull puffy eyes), that retains its innocence. As the lantern swings again I see my own face, smaller, flatter, less thoughtful and more cunning, peer out from behind his features. My grandfather.

The day he died, India found an unfinished letter, addressed to the governor of the Hong Kong colony, on his bed table. It began, "The authorities, once again, have bungled the question of the water supply." As if nothing had changed. As if he'd forgotten his failures. As if he, after the plague spots had patterned his body, after the buboes, in abscess, had burst in his groin and his armpits, after the pain that had blackened his face... as if, still, he had remained true to the call of the future, as the future left him behind. She had put a scented handkerchief to her face to disguise the smell of the sad poisoned flesh, leaned over him where he lay, and tucked the letter into his shirt next to his heart.

In the other photograph, India and Fan are together. India stands behind a seated Lam Fan, resting her hand on Fan's shoulder. Behind them is a pillar. Next to it is a summer bottle, the large stoppered glass encased in wicker in which the most perishable of household goods were kept against the humidity: the biscuits, writing papers, and cigars. Fan looks as I knew her. Hers was the type of face that develops its look in infancy. It is a knowing face, never innocent, with exquisitely arched brows, finely drawn nose and lips, black hair groomed straight back and looped at the neck.

And India, wearing the family expression of hope. Tall, slim, dressed in wool with a closely fitting bodice, high collar, tight sleeves. She is the image of practical womanhood. A spinster ready to brave the darkest of continents armed with nothing but her belief in herself. She is no beauty, not because she is not pretty. All the right parts are there: the full mouth, expressive eyes, abundant loosely arranged brown hair. But because beauty plays no part in her reality.

At least not then. Not for the girl inside her. Who wants to get away. Who wants to be on her own.

One last detail: on a stool visible in the portrait is a paper knife. It is the knife that Lam Fan used to open the letters that came for her, now and then, from an uncle who had emigrated to Canada. He alone of all the family had not forgotten the baker's daughter. Who was not, after all, completely abandoned; for someone somewhere was thinking of her.

And he, in his loneliness in a strange land, perhaps not knowing that his invitation would mean so much, suggested that if need should arise, Lam Fan could go and live with him in Victoria, in British Columbia, where he worked as an herbalist.

In the 1850s it was to California, and then to the Cariboo gold fields; in the 1880s it was to build the railways that the Chinese went. There were, after all, a dozen reasons for leaving China, among which were poverty, unemployment, a destitute family to support, not to mention the ambition for a better life. But the main reason, the one that caused every potential immigrant to sit up late at night blinking in thought or tears or mere sleeplessness, was that there was no other choice.

CHAPTER TWO

"The approach from southward to Desolation Sound may be made through Malaspina Strait, and thence by skirting the coast of the mainland northward of it; by way of Algerine Passage or Shearwater Passage, thence following the coast northward or through Baker Passage; all these routes are wide and deep."

British Columbia Pilot, Volume I

The procession started out. It halted, started again, then, finding its flow, jolted into the Queen's Road, following the blinkered horse (owned by Jardine Matheson) pulling the bier (on loan from Jardine Matheson) on which the major's casket rested. Into that solemn silence in which a funeral party moves. A silence packed thickly not with peace and resignation, but with questions.

Questions, furies, ghosts. Running back and forth between the past and the present. Not just the electrical discharges of minds under stress, faced with the order of death, but something other: and it showed in the horse's nervousness.

The Baptist contingent went first, holding their Bibles in front of their chests like shields, the Bibles, coated with anti-cockroach varnish, reflecting the sun; then the merchants and their ladies, the civil servants and business colleagues and all the other Europeans who formed the community. So that it might have been the gleam of an army that was seen that day, winding its way from the house on the Queen's Road to the Happy Valley cemetery. An exemplum of solidarity. For though not one of them in life, the major was given his place among them at his death.

Yet, despite the bravery of appearances, many maintained later, in the privacy of their homes, that they had walked that day with spirits. Not the common ones, often wakened by such occasions—the mothers, fathers, and other long dead relatives—but images of themselves. Dressed like them, like-mannered, walking quietly alongside. As if the damp, as the sun drew it forth from the cold earth in a mist, or disturbed nights and unexamined consciences, had resulted in mirage; or as if the future had come to visit.

But like the planets and stars, luminous gases, drifting cold hydrogen, these ghosts stayed with them; walking and faltering, only to pull themselves to their feet and fall again, as if by repetition they might drive their lesson home.

Even the bandsmen, blowing out march tunes, heard the phantom clank of musical instruments dropping from dead hands, and felt the sizzle of quicklime on their skins. And so the mourners met other mourners, procession after procession, mirroring their own, on the way to Happy Valley. And no voice interrupted that uneasy dark into which each individual felt himself plunged until after the coffin was placed in the ground.

So it was that the funeral anticipated the deaths of hundreds. If one rat could find its way to the major's doorstep in Wanchai, so could a million more. Climb the Peak, ride in sedan chairs, nest between the boards of the tramway cars. They could and did. It is a fact that few of the major's countrymen long survived him.

"Lucky that nothing like that happened at my funeral," says Lam Fan.

I have only just got on board the *Rose* after casting off from the dock. Fan's comment shocks me. "You were there?" I ask stupidly. And she laughs.

We are leaving Blubber Bay: where there are wharves belonging to the saw mill and some lime works, plus the government wharf where we were tied up. Where there is a post office, telegraph, and telephone. Where the harbour is a sand-and-mud bottom and is subject to north-westerly winds. Where, on the beach, there are a few of the big black rendering kettles left from the whaling.

I had walked down an arbutus-shaded lane. I had talked to the skipper of the *Cinnamon II* as he stood on his porch. I had climbed aboard the mail steamer and played whist with the mate. In brief, I had resumed my human contacts. But bow line, stern line, and spring let go, and Lam Fan was back in my life.

"No, no, Robert Lam," she says to the unspoken question in my eyes. "I will always stay with you. How could I desert my child and not share with him the burden of sorrow he carries, a burden caused by me?"

She starts to hum as we chug out from under the shadow of a heavily wooded hill. Three seals surface to starboard. She slides open the door of the wheelhouse, taps her foot on the caps, and sings to them.

I sigh and watch out for rocks. My wet clothes, draped around the exhaust shroud, are steaming. The rain clouds, which had brought a shower as I walked from the store with supplies, have blown to the east. The side windows are open.

"There's something I don't understand, Fan," I shout above the noise. "What made you and India leave Hong Kong when you did? How did you have the sense?"

"It was luck!" she calls, waving farewell to the diminishing buildings of Blubber Bay, and to the seals, which have ducked under. "We had good luck!"

There is a saving spirit, deep in the universe where galaxies collide and send out signals, like the magic twist of the wheel that saves a ship from icebergs, like patches of sky that emit radio waves, yet do not correspond to any visible object: we do not need to understand it; we know it by its presence.

This luck or gift or intuition, which cannot be purchased, which you must be born with, it was this which saved Fan and India from the epidemic.

On the one hand they had lost their father, their property, and all expectations; on the other the future stood open before them.

Of the unexpected, of the contrariness of life that can lift those who have tumbled down the furthest, no one would think until later.

But at the time, when they returned to the Queen's Road house, after brows were wiped with handkerchiefs, after tea was made and served by the major's daughters, and the sense of keeping an enemy at bay had faded, those who had followed the coffin regained their sense of purpose and remembered why they had come. Which was to give advice.

"We were two young women on our own," says Fan. "We had no husbands, we had no money." And to be precise, they were both more than thirty, and one of them, although adopted into a European household, was a Chinese baker's daughter worth less than forty-five dollars on the servants' market. The other, erratically educated, would quickly have to find some means to support herself.

"They suggested that India be a governess. They said, 'Try the Blind Females of China Foundation and the Foundling Home. These charities always need good help.' They did not even look at me." So says my guide, at the same time pulling from her pocket a rock she has found on the island. It looks like a flower: black porphyry with bursts of white crystal blossoms. She sets it down next to the compass, which immediately starts to fluctuate.

On and on the advice-giving went until India, calling a halt, said, "That's fine for me, but what about Lam Fan? What's my sister to do?" In the silence that followed, a little too long extended to be polite, an elderly gentleman, hard of hearing, shouted, "Anything at all, anything we can do to help. Don't hesitate, just ask!"

But the truth is, and it shows if not in their manners then in their eyes, that what they want, if they are given the choice, is for all this to disappear: the emptied Queen's Road rooms, the grief-stricken faces of the major's daughters, the unmatched sisters. For such women, brought up in such conditions, might do anything.

As women sometimes did. Even Englishwomen. Who had marched alone throughout the interior of China taking photographs, scrambling over fields, preaching in markets, making themselves (and, by implication, all other English) ridiculous. *Curiosities*, as they were called, who were heralds of a precarious future in which women had no rules and no masters. A future difficult for the women as well: for without masters, without rules, they had no one to protect them. (Fan nods ruefully.)

And so, despite, "Terribly sorry about the major," and "We're always here if you need us," when the mourners had gone, when the door had shut behind the last one, India and Fan were alone.

They reread the letters from Lam Fan's uncle, Lum Kee. They darkened them with fingerprints and soaked them with tears. They considered the alternatives.

And then they went to call on the Jardine Matheson solicitor.

"We've seen lawyers before, Fan," I mutter, thinking of the one who had thrown his briefcase on board at the last moment, and of whether he'd foreseen the consequences; and at the same time wishing I'd kept the *Rose*'s stabilizers. There was a strong northwest wind and a heavy following sea as we emerged from Algerine Passage and eased north through a tedium of reefs and shoals: Grant Reef, Mystery Reef, Sentry Shoal. I would have to decide soon whether to stop at Whaletown, on Cortes Island, as originally planned, or to hurry on north to make up lost time. Cortes Island, where one of the first whaling stations on the coast was established in 1869, using a schooner named *Kate*, had been mentioned in my conversations with Captain Larson, whose father had been a whaler. Following seas, such as we were experiencing, "made the killing extremely difficult," he'd said. He'd told me a number of stories about the area—as when a whale came up under the bow of the *Kate* and spilled the crew, drowning several of them—stories his father had told him. A lifetime of experience passed on that shaped who he was, how he thought. I, of course, had had no one to do likewise for me.

I wiped the dome of the compass clear of condensation. There was Lam Fan, of course. She had tried her best to bring me up, and even if she'd made a mess of it, leaving me ignorant of my own parentage, at least she was trying to rectify it now. Lam Fan, my lookout, standing in the cockpit well at the stern, facing the wrong direction.

A solicitor then. Who is, as well, a man. A husband and father, with abundant natural sympathies. He understands the plight of the major's orphaned daughters. He is even moved by it, but his closest horizon is his employer's interest, especially where it concerns money and property. For he knows that a stroke of the pen can put others in his place. And yet he also knows, as we know, that there is more to life than money: there is respect from one's colleagues. And there is self-respect, less vivid, perhaps, in some people than in others, but still present.

He thinks. He imagines consequences. He strikes a balance.

"It may be that I can do something to help," he says thoughtfully, considering the women's request for assistance to leave the country. "A ship to take you to the New World? That's what you want?"

The women nod agreement. The lawyer shuffles his papers, for the fact is that he's relieved: for if someone were to tell the story of these two, made homeless by a company, sent away penniless by Hong Kong's wealthiest merchants, there is a perspective from which the company (and thereby himself) may not be seen as—well, merciful. Although it isn't his fault that the women have no prospects, and he is certainly acting within the legal limits.

That is, in fact, he is aware that Jardine Matheson's title to the house could be queried. And there was provision that the daughters be left to live in it. Items, hinted at in the major's papers and confirmed years after by Sing Yuen, acting in Lam Fan's interest, that might with time and patience have been revealed.

But let us not blame a man who is doing his job. It is not his sole responsibility. He does what he's asked to do; he finds them a ship, even if he is on his own lookout, for he has a family to consider. But happily for the human spirit, with the appearance of generosity, in dispensing a favour, there is balm for the conscience.

A ship. Not such a ship as might have been hoped for, perhaps. Not a steamship, for example. Not even a passenger ship, exactly, but one with a glorious history. A clipper ship, sold out of the tea trade into rice and flour cargoing between the Orient and Canada. A famous ship in her day, although her era of fame is growing distant. But she is sailing where the women want to go, and they will not be obliged to purchase tickets. Since no one knows better than the Jardine Matheson solicitor that the major has left no money.

There is one difficulty, however. Not insurmountable, not enough to hold the women back if they're determined to go ahead. For these are resourceful females, used to conquering obstacles. But the former tea clipper, called *Thermopylae*, isn't leaving from Hong Kong harbour, but from Saigon harbour, some one thousand miles away.

Thermopylae! I look back at Lam Fan, still standing in the cockpit well, with new respect. This isn't a ship we are talking about, it is a myth! Why, a painting of her hangs in the Pilot House to the left of the dispatcher. There are clubs named after her, and every sailor knows her sailing record. She was one of the most beautiful and quick of three-masted sailing ships ever built. I'd sailed on a five-masted schooner myself, for Canadian Transport, carrying lumber from Vancouver meant for the South African railway. But we never got there. All the sails blew out at Cape Horn, and we couldn't get round. We spent six months in Valparaiso, Chile, then auctioned the cargo off. Sailing on the *Alberni* was one thing, but to have sailed on the *Thermopylae*!

"Calm down, Robert Lam, calm down," says Fan as she comes through the door to the wheelhouse. She takes my socks, which have scorched, from the shroud. She looks from the charts to the waters ahead of us with an appearance of authority.

"So," I say, thinking I've found her out, "you have sailed before!"

"How did you think your mother and I got here, Robert Lam?" she says. "It was long before the aeroplane." She touches my arm to soften the blow to my pride, for I confess I'd never thought about it. "Never mind, Robert Lam," she adds, "you were not to know. Nobody told you."

The compass cap receives another wipe.

"We did not know what to do at first," she says, going on with the story. "We were very worried. We thought we should start for Saigon right away, since we did not know how long it would take us to get there."

Moreover, they knew, with an inner sense honed on experience, having watched the major wear out public patience, that they were on their own. The solicitor had done what he could, as had Jardine Matheson, as had everyone. That is, they had all lost interest.

All the same, something had to be done. And when the circle of your world is the parlour lamplight ("Don't be silly, Robert Lam, we were much more experienced!"), yet you must leave its safety and venture out: when you fly like a moth against the flame of the present, it is not so easy to take the first step.

Still, it was an unlikely opportunity that presented itself. Call it Fate. Call it what you will.

Only a few days after the solicitor brought the news that *Thermopylae* was sailing from Saigon on April twenty-sixth, India and Fan saw an advertisement in the *Friend of China and Hong Kong Gazette*. An extensive gambling community had grown up in Kowloon, across from Hong Kong island, on the mainland peninsula. Businessmen, combining the attractions of a day trip, something for nothing, and the pleasure of taking a risk, were offering free launches to take customers across the harbour to the gambling houses. This was the opening the women decided to take, since if they were going on the journey, they had to start somewhere, and particularly since, with no money and little time, there seemed no other choice. Moreover, Kowloon was a different community, they were not known there, and they hoped to find opportunities in anonymity that were denied them at home.

It was a first step. A beginning. And like the major's refuse bins in the streets, a gesture of hope.

Down the steps, through the gate, and into the morning street they went, as the sun topped the horizon, and well-dressed men with clean faces stepped from sedan chairs, gripping the day's papers; and the club doorman was telling the maid about last night's dinner, and the maid was watching an older woman, with a baby tied to her back, as she rounded the corner. A policeman stood in front of a bank where all the shutters opened at once on a signal, and customers sprang forth—from shops and offices and from the strip of gutter along which the men of the stock exchange were already conducting business, clamouring their interests and waving documents as if the whole of life depended on it.

Eastwards from this point at which Fan and India began their journey were the other institutions of the Europeans. The barracks and polo course, the parade ground, cricket pitch, the racecourse and cemetery at Happy Valley. On these Fan and India turned their backs, shouldering their bundles and proceeding westwards. Into narrow dusty streets where the crowds were forced against the walls by passing rickshas and chairs, and where hawkers appeared, informed themselves as to the prospects for business, and vanished in a blink.

"Did no one know that you were going, Fan?" I ask, curious, as I decide to miss out Whaletown and take a bearing for Cape Mudge. A flashing white light on a red buoy marks the southern edge of the foul ground southeastward of the cape, but the Cape Mudge lighthouse can't be seen when the bearing is less than three hundred and seven degrees.

"No," Fan answers, peering over my shoulder at the chart. "We told no one. We were on our own."

"But anything could have happened to you, anything at all!"

So (as Fan gives me one of her looks), they inched onward through a swirl of hanging baskets, brooms, and feather dusters. They stepped over mats set out with earthenwares, struggled past piles of firewood, ducked whirring ginger grinders. And were transfixed, for a moment, in this cacophony of movement, by a glimpse, high above the melee of dirt and noise, of the cool green courtyards and gardens of the Europeans on the slopes.

Ferns, vines and flowers, out of which, down the steep steps and ladder streets, flowed a river of white-faced men.

The streets rose with their tide of humanity, sweeping the women along towards the Praya. Here the food vendors had set up shop and children sat beneath bamboo mats strung on poles, eating barley congee and drinking lemon water. The sun changed from soft gold to white, bleaching behind a fog that obscured the Peak and the oases of green, and all else but the milling, half-slipping images of moving people.

The mist dampened their clothes. Rose apples and plums, set out on a cloth, were beaded with moisture, and fowls, sleeping in baskets, woke up and protested at the falling droplets.

("Look!" says Fan, as a killer-whale fin cleaves the water ahead of us. "We are on the right track!")

Lam Fan and India, stumbling in the wake of vegetable carriers (watercress, spinach, and celery), shifted their burdens but did not falter, for they were the major's daughters and believed in progress; for the name of the ship to which they were journeying, *Thermopylae*, with its evocation of bravery—King Leonidas and his Greeks and Spartans against the Persians, outnumbered, but smarter—had aroused their courage. Moreover...

"Moreover," says Lam Fan, "as I've told you many times, there was nothing else we could do."

And so they arrived safely at the dock where the sampans waited to take customers of the gambling houses to the Kowloon launch.

Ribbons of white cloud, in strands across the sky. Thin bands of light on the waves. The motion of the *Rose* a steady lift and fall as the waves catch the stern and roll under us. Straining eyes for the cream-coloured cliff face of the cape, with its smudge of forest atop. The killer whale, alone as far as we can tell (although that would be unusual), continues ahead of us on the same bearing. Fan is fiddling with the stove-top cover. The tiny bones of her fingers straining as she pries the pan ring loose and lets it drop. Clank. Pause. Clank. It is the mindless repetitive act of a child, of a nervous old woman; of an addict.

Lam Fan. Trying to look like a gambler, in the company of my mother, that day in Hong Kong; a woman interested in nothing but pleasure. But her face belying the attempt with its complexion the colour of flour. A baker's daughter indeed. Who is becoming sicker by the minute.

But it is not the ferryman's responsibility, nor the launch driver's, to make a judgement. The women sit quietly, ignoring the looks of curiosity directed their way; all too aware that sex, age, and dress, plus the baggage they carry, as well as Lam Fan's pallor, argue against the roles that they play.

Yet, uncomfortable as they were, and worried as to how long Lam Fan could last between opium pipes, since there had been no occasion to put this to the test, since neither had guessed it would be so bad, they could not help but turn to watch the city they knew fall away behind them. Piled up the steep sides of the island as it was, with all its faults of overcrowding and lack of sanitation evident; and hopeful as they were against all odds, raised on a diet of reform—still, they were leaving with regret.

For so it is we sadly turn away from childhood ("Robert Lam, we were grown-up women!"), and so we find ourselves adrift in a world without reference, no home to return to, no refuge. Facing the unknown without map or compass....

("There it is," shouts Fan, "there's the white cliff!")

In any case ("I see it, Fan, of course I do"); in any case ("If you'll let me continue") the launch plowed its way through the harbour. Around junks and ocean steamers, tramps and men-of-war, carrying passengers and merchants and ordinary workmen, sailors and soldiers, even a pilot or two; with every flag of every country of the world, or so it appeared, being raised or lowered as the ships left or entered. So that the surface of the harbour was continually disturbed, traversed, circled, and roughened, and the launch hauled away or fell off, or hesitated like a horse at a jump. Moving through the confusion of traffic nonetheless, until at the appointed time, for no schedule is kept like the schedule of business, they landed at the dock at the base of the Lion Rock. With the Nine Dragons, the Kau Lang, red on the horizon.

But by this time Lam Fan had begun to shiver. Her forehead dripped sweat. Her hands jumped in her lap as she unloosened her fingers to gather up her bundles. Her feet, which she had kept hidden beneath her long skirts as she sat, began to twitch and dance.

It was unfortunate all around. For of course Fan's condition was noticed. And recognized. So that as the passengers disembarked it was with some annoyance—grumbling, losing their natural reticence and politeness—for these were gamblers on the brink, about to try their luck, and Lam Fan's state of nerves struck them as a bad omen. The women were jostled, elbowed, shoved aside as the gamblers moved off, led by a houseman, up the hill towards the gambling establishment. So that it would have been impossible, even if Fan and India had so wished, for them to go, too. So that the others, hurrying within a thunderstorm of dark emotion, cast angry looks at the two women. So that where the others turned left, the women turned right and found themselves at the market.

Where waiting for them—that is, it appeared as if she were expecting them—was an old woman. Who came to stand there every day, at the intersection, scanning the faces of all who passed for signs of sickness. Not just any sickness. But that unique illness to be seen in Lam Fan's face. With its ghastly hue, and expression of tremendous need.

The afternoon light was only just fading. The blank sun rolled along the horizon as if it would never set. Even the flies grew tired of waiting and stood still on the mats of debris that blocked the drains in the passageways. All the little houses, perched on the rock, tilted unevenly in the slowly dimming light as India and Lam Fan followed the old woman into the cool darkness of the Abode of Ten Thousand Happinesses. It was a place of business where, if not ten thousand happinesses, there was at least one: opium. Its odour permeated the cracked stone walls of this building that had been divided into a dozen rooms, all of them small, dark and clean. A safe harbour for the women on this afternoon, where every action had been performed through a haze of tension.

That is, what had just passed—the major's death, the loss of the house—and what was to come—a journey thousands of miles in length to the edge of the ocean. Farewells to the past. Greetings to the present. Normal for a sailor, of course, but for two untravelled women...

The old woman drew the curtains then went out. She returned with a tray containing pipe, opium, and lamp. India helped Lam Fan lie down on a platform, although it was difficult for Fan to keep still. She rocked a little, talking soundlessly to herself and licking her dry lips.

Now India (for there was no time to be anything but practical) set to work. She wasn't thinking, really, of what she did (although Fan was thinking of nothing else), but was doing it because it was required. Not out of habit, but because long ago she had made herself familiar with the ritual.

"She did not like to do it," says Fan quietly in my ear, letting her hand drop from the steering, "but she was my friend. She knew it was what I had to have."

"Poor Fan," I almost say, but don't. It isn't the time, and I do have some tact.

Now the wire on which India had lifted a small amount of the opium was heating over the lamp. She continued to warm it, and to dip the end into the jar; then she pressed the opium on the flat bowl of the pipe, turning it and working it on the end of the wire until it was a porous, swollen mass.

India shaped this into a ring around the wire, then inserted it into the round hole of the pipe, and by twirling the wire around while withdrawing it, deposited the opium in the pipe. I know how to do it myself. I have watched often enough.

She helped Fan to sit. Keeping the bowl of the pipe over the lamp, Lam Fan inhaled until there was only the dross. The *yin shee*.

Complicity? Is that what it was? Or compassion? It is a hard question. Perhaps there is a moment when it is both, as the hands that give touch the hands that receive. I don't know. But if such an instant exists, it is quickly over, swallowed up in this night that is not quite a night. Since one woman sleeps but does not rest, and the other is wide awake between the wall that faces the rock and the wall above the sea. India leans against the window, and smells the cooking fires, and hears the chattering of men sitting in small groups outside. Where, beside the straw-choked henhouses and the open water barrels, they watch the sky change from grey to red and to a deeper grey.

She walks up and down. From time to time she glances at the bundle of silk that is Lam Fan, who lies still now, knees drawn up to her chin. India wonders, I imagine, just what it was she had taken on.

Besides Lam Fan, there is the unknown. An empty land to which they are committed. With no plan, no diagrams, no working papers. No map to follow, no notes left them by the reformer. And no rule of thumb to trust, but solitude.

The door handle turns and the old woman comes in. It is comforting to drink tea with her, to erase one ritual with another, to watch the tea steam in the cups, and drink, sip by sip, the whole story of curing, drying, patting, throwing, heaping, roasting, drying, and rolling. A labour of weariness for which children are paid six cents a day. A labour that is their life. From the white end of birth to the black end of death. A circle. ("Cheer up, Robert Lam," says Fan, looking worried.)

India drinks and waits, watching tea leaves curl in the bottom of her cup while the old woman, who has something on her mind, gives a lesson in patience. Time stretches out. As if this woman, who stands at a dividing line from which one shore of her life is growing far distant, has all of eternity in which to think.

At last she speaks. It is about a son who is never there when he's needed. It is about the problem this creates in an old person's life. It is, in fact, about renewing the divan licence.

The Abode of Ten Thousand Happinesses was not large as divans went, but it made up for its size with the numbers of its clients. For the privilege of offering its service, the divan keeper paid a fee to Her Majesty's Government. But far away from the Lion Rock, in the British Parliament, it had been decided that too many licences were being given out and that the numbers had to be cut back. Each divan owner was to be given the opportunity to present an argument as to why his or her licence should be exempt.

But the old woman spoke no English. And the authority in charge spoke poor Chinese. The son, who should have attended to this matter, was away on his junk, on a trip through the China Sea; and although he would soon return, it would be days after the deadline. Who better, the old woman delicately suggested, to speak for the divan than an Englishwoman. It was a chance sent from Heaven. In return, perhaps, the grateful owners could do something for the strangers. For from the appearance of their luggage, and what they had told her, she had guessed they needed help on the next stage of their journey. Could her son not take them? He would have to voyage south soon anyway. What did India say?

And so it was agreed, and India took the opportunity that had fortunately appeared. In return for a word with the Civil Service of Kowloon, they would sail on the junk to Saigon. There was no time to lose. And any route was better than none when your ship was leaving in less than a month from a thousand miles away.

*   *   *

A clap of thunder. Lightning, from an almost clear sky, touches the red roof of the lighthouse as we round the southwest tip of Cape Mudge. The flat line of the cape; the serrated edge of forest tipped pale green with new growth. A kingfisher spins down from a branch and dives into the sea not far from us. We are entering Discovery Passage, with Quadra Island to starboard. If the wind rises easterly or southeasterly, we are in trouble. But so far so good. Touch wood.

CHAPTER THREE

"The navigation of Discovery Passage is very simple except in Seymour Narrows. Here, the tidal streams, which at some stages of the tide, attain a velocity of 14 knots, make careful navigation essential. Elsewhere in Discovery Passage, it is only necessary to steer mid-channel.

"Unless in possession of intimate local knowledge, the passage of Seymour Narrows should only be attempted at or near slack water.

"At night, the greatest caution must be observed at all states of the tidal stream, even if in possession of most intimate local knowledge."

British Columbia Pilot, Volume I

The killer whale has left us. We follow the low wooded western shore of Discovery Passage to the mouth of Campbell River, where, against Fan's advice, I decide not to stop. She looks tired, sitting on deck with her back braced against the hatch combing, although she doesn't seem to feel the cold that, as the afternoon light fades, makes me shiver and light the oil stove.

Orange Point, with its red cliffs redder as the sun slides away to the west; Gowlland Island; Steep Island; May Island. We pass the last safe anchorage at Duncan Bay. Then the passage trends northwestwards on its eastern shore, with steep, copper-stained cliffs, followed by a rough rocky coastline fringed with boulders. As we near Race Point, I check the tide tables. The south-going tidal stream rushing past the point can reach up to ten knots, causing heavy overfalls and eddies, which extend for some distance eastwards.

But still no easterly or southeasterly winds to get us in trouble.

And I am a pilot, in possession of local knowledge. It should be a piece of cake. Although I haven't tested the *Rose* like this before. Although a capability of seventeen knots would make me feel easier. Although the south-going tidal stream has increased since Canoe Pass was closed. If I even had thirteen knots...

"Sperm whales, humpbacks, blue whales, finbacks, sei, and right." Fan sets up a chant. Her toes stretch over the sill of the open wheelhouse door. "There she blows! There she blows!" she cries. When I look at her, hoping to make her stop, for I need to concentrate, she winks.

"Many ships have been wrecked up here," she says. "The U.S.S. *Saranac*, U.S.S. *Wachusett*, the whaling brig *Byzantium*."

"Not the *Byzantium*, Fan," I say, biting the pencil I have in my mouth—I could do with one of Fan's cigarettes—we should be about four cables out as we round, and I am still too close to the point. "The *Byzantium* wasn't sunk, it was stolen."

"Salvaged," says Fan.

"It was piracy. The Indians found her at anchor and hid her behind Malcolm Island."

"She was abandoned," Fan corrects me. "The crew left her after she hit a rock in Weymton Passage."

"For Pete's sake, Fan!" I burst out at last. "Please don't argue. I need your help!" For suddenly—I had forgotten how suddenly it can come at the entry to Seymour Narrows, where the shores are high and rugged, and mist cascades through the blue-black forest—it is dark.

We take the wheel together, the ghost and I, feeling our way around the heavy swirls, steering the *Rose* by instinct, as once I steered a merchant ship through ice in the North Atlantic, making that ship dance, when one slip would have sliced us through. I don't know how I did it then, I don't know how we do it now; but we round the point safely, the *Rose*, Fan, and I, with straining hearts and engine. For the *Rose* is alive, too. That is, while we're in harmony.

I sound the whistle, and listen for echoes, then steer the bearing for Stephenson Point.

"It was a mistake," says Fan.

"I know, I know. Don't rub it in. We should have anchored until daylight."

"I told you but you didn't listen," says Fan, not very helpfully.

So it was that a red-sailed junk, owned by the divan keeper's son, called in at Kowloon and with the old woman waving goodbye from a seaside window, set off with India and Lam Fan on board.

Their course lay south, with a short stop at Macau, then down through the South China Sea, keeping far enough offshore to avoid pirates or *Ladrones*. "There are many islands, " said their captain, encouragingly. "It will be very pleasant. We will have no trouble." He smiled at his passengers, Lam Fan and India, and two others, Dutch merchants, whom the captain intended to land at Java. It was an ambitious program for a small boat, but no prospect seemed to daunt the optimistic skipper.

"He must know what he's doing," India assured Fan, who, well supplied with opium, was evidencing some scepticism. "Why would he take us unless he was sure?"

Why indeed? It was a question that neither really wanted answered. At 11 A.M. they made sail with a fresh easterly wind. At 4 P.M. the coast lay like a thick cloud, east and west, and the Ladrone Islands were disappearing in the distance. At sunset the islands were out of sight, and the junk was on the ocean, where north, south, east, and west there was nothing but water and sky. The passengers retired to their bunks in the fo'c'sle while the crew kept watch. In the morning the cook set out breakfast—rice and tea—on deck, and Fan and India were each given a basin of water in which to wash. Lines were trailed in the hope of catching fish, and the passengers occupied themselves with their private thoughts.

The wind continued fresh and fair, and with her light cargo of sugarcane and rice, the junk sped over the sea like a tiger, the crew raising all sails, until no more could be spread. That night Fan took out her opium pipe and lay in her bunk, and India sat on deck, next to the rudder man. She watched the stars and hummed the songs of her childhood; she saw a crewman shake a black snake from a fishing pole, and watched a water-spout run alongside them, keeping pace until the junk altered course. The next morning they weathered an island, passing between two small rocks about a quarter of a mile distant and abreast of the island, the current obliging them to pass through this channel, while a crewman was sent aloft to watch for rocks and breakers.

The wind moderated, and the weather became cloudy, remaining thus until the morning of the fifth day, when the wind veered round to the north-west with dark, threatening weather. Heavy black clouds rolled in from the west, and the captain took steps to secure the sails. At sunset a heavy cross sea rolled in from the northwest with severe squalls of wind and rain, accompanied by heavy thunder and flashes of lightning. One of these flashes lit up a rock, until then unremarked, that was alive with pelicans. The captain sent all who could be spared below, where most of them prayed.

Not that prayer would have done much good if they were caught in the change of the monsoon—we nearly turned turtle once on the way down to Java in similar conditions after leaving the graving dock in Singapore; and that was on the *Silverbell*, which had power a junk could only envy. For prayer may make you feel a little better, but it won't change the weather.

"No, Robert Lam?" asks Fan, as we alter course in the narrows gradually to starboard, heading up mid-channel between Maud Island and Ripple Rock. "In any case I am praying now," she says. For she has noticed, seconds before me, that the southeast wind we fear has made its appearance. And with a wind to oppose the tidal stream, the races and eddies in this vicinity become very dangerous: with treacherous whirlpools that seize small craft and pull them under. Moreover, it is dark. And the moon the wind has chased from behind the clouds gives only enough light to frighten me, and not enough to help. I open the throttle and the *Rose* labours against the flood, inching onward. If we can hold on until the Maud Island light beacon is abaft the beam, and edge towards the eastern shore...

Fan clutches my hand while I pray, yes, I do, for the shuddering *Rose* to hold together.

The storm in the South China Sea continued all night, but on the morning of the sixth day, it cleared, and the wind shifted to eastward. The passengers poked their heads above the deck, and were set to clearing up the mess below. Everything unsecured—luggage, dishes, tables, and chairs—was upended, and all the passengers and most of the crew had been sick. But they had been lucky, all in all—since some of the cargo had shifted—that the junk itself had not overturned.

The wind continued light but fair for the rest of the journey, and at last they began to see numerous seabirds, meaning they were approaching land. There were other ships in sight, as well, and soon they were in company with several junks. Sails in tatters, nerves frayed, but having endured, having travelled the first thousand miles of their journey.

We are through the narrows, past Ripple Rock and Maud Island. I am shaking with sweat and cold. Lam Fan, my spiritual pilot, has fallen quiet. I had put us in danger, and I should have known better. I only wanted to prove the *Rose*, I only wanted to show that I could do it.

Which I have. But not without cost.

I can feel the strain in the boat. Some of her planks have spread, and water is pouring into the bilge. I have set the bilge pump working. When we anchor, which we will do at Granite Bay, I will have to take a hand to the deck pump. The engine, a Chrysler Crown six-cylinder, is functioning at low power. We've blown, I think, two of the cylinders; and I am not looking forward to the work this means, cramped in a crawl space too small for a child, a ridiculous space for a grown man to manoeuvre in. I had thought I was out of the dirty jobs. I had thought that part of my life was behind me.

"Yes, I know," I say out loud, not giving Fan the chance to say it first, "it was my choice to buy the *Rose*. But why is there always trouble? Why do things never go well?"

There is no one to feel sorry for me but myself. Fan isn't interested: she shrugs as if it doesn't matter.

Well, let it go. It doesn't help to dwell on one's mistakes or on questions that can't be answered. It is best to forget them all and get on with it.

"No," says Fan, unexpectedly. "You must not forget, you must remember. Else what you've done wrong you will do again, over and over."

And so, with a difference of opinion, not for the first time, we putter into Kanish Bay, where, at the southeastern end, there is an anchorage, plus the logging and farming community of Granite Bay, with its government dock, post office, telegraph and telephone, and gasoline scow. Nothing we haven't seen before, of course, or that we won't see again.

Saigon Harbour spread out in inlets like the fingers of a hand. Along these lines ran barges, black and rusty, which carried loads of rice, coal, matting, and timber to the great ships that lay anchored, crowded together, in the deep water. If there was a plan to the movement, the loading and unloading, it was not evident, crisscrossed as it was by dozens of fishing boats and the little junks, with beet-coloured sails, that seemed to flourish within the network of commerce. The Kowloon junk joined this assortment, searching in and out among the steamers and clippers, with flags of every description—black eagle, white ensign, yellow crown, and dragon pennant—for the three-masted *Thermopylae*.

At last that noble ship appeared, in the slanting light of evening, and with the whole scene overlaid with the fragrance of spice and rotting vegetation. The junk drew alongside. Fan and India, with their letters of accreditation from Jardine Matheson, were taken on board, ready to sail for the New World. Along with a cargo of grass mats and 1,350 tons of rice.

> The old *Thermopylae*, my boys,
> The old *Thermopylae*.
> We wish her luck and give three cheers,
> For the old *Thermopylae*!

As the men of the *Thermopylae* Club in my city sing to this day. For she was the only full-rigged ship ever to call Victoria, British Columbia, her home port.

They say that ship was alive. Indeed, she was christened with the death of a sailor, Peter Johnson, on her maiden voyage. He fell from the jib boom on the fifth day out, to the west of Portugal, and some say he sailed with her ever after. But she made record time on that first voyage, sixty-one days and eleven hours, pilot to pilot, from London to Melbourne.

A ship built in Aberdeen in 1868, painted green above her copper plates, topped by teak bulwarks, and with a topgallant brass rail running her entire length; lower masts and yards painted white; upper masts and spars varnished; with gold leafing on her name and decorating the carving under her counter and on her bow.

Her figurehead was King Leonidas, all white and facing forwards, with his helmet on his head, a shield on his left arm, and on his right a downward-pointing sword, which it was the apprentice's job to sheath at sea. She was a ship that was said to "walk the waters," sailing ninety-one days, pilot to pilot, in the tea trade, from Foochow to London, where she flew a gilded cock at the masthead, and the crew were fed on champagne for a week.

A wonderful ship, a lucky ship with consistent speedy voyages and few accidents.

But time is what matters in business, and with the opening of the Suez Canal in 1869, which sailing ships could not efficiently use, the steamers began to take over. Still the clippers carried on, for the "steam kettles" required coal and frequent maintenance, but eventually the inevitable happened: the steamers monopolized the tea trade and *Thermopylae* began carrying wool.

Yet the legends persisted: that a man could walk round her decks with a lighted candle while she sailed at seven knots, because she required so little wind to move her; that while sailing at thirteen knots, with her helm amidships and all sail set in steady quartering breezes, a small boy could steer her. "She went to windward like a witch," they said, "and she rode out the worst sea like a duck."

But in 1890, Aberdeen White Star, having purchased a fleet of steamers, sold her for five thousand pounds to Redfords of Montreal for use in the Pacific rice trade.

If a ship can feel shame, then she felt it. For after bringing her with a load of coal to Singapore, her captain auctioned every piece of movable gear on her. She was stripped, this beauty, this ship with the bas-relief crowing cock, stamped "Dum Viram Canam," carved into her forward deckhouse.

The captain was fired, and the mate, Wilson, given the job in his place, took the ship on to Saigon. Despite the fact that Wilson was a notorious drunkard. Regardless of the fact that my mother and Lam Fan had entrusted themselves to a long ocean voyage in his care.

Granite Bay. Where I pull the steps leading down from the wheelhouse aside, and worm my way into the cavity that houses the engine. Where my mate, Lam Fan, takes a powder, although strictly speaking all ship's maintenance should be her—the mate's—responsibility. Where a woodsman, or as close to one as a man can be in sight of a government float, wanders down to supervise. He insists on telling me what's wrong: not just with the *Rose*, but with the world. Moreover he stands, butt saluting the head, bracing his arms against the locker, repeating that I'm wasting my time. The engine can't be fixed. I should give up on it and civilization. He also wants to read my palm.

"It's been read before," I tell him. "It didn't do me any good." But I don't say when that was, or where, or what happened after. I say nothing of the price a young girl paid, before we sailed from Freetown on the *Silverbell* in 1941, for my fear of going blind. Of the kind of man I was, with the world at war and believing we were losing; a man who didn't like what the doctors told him about his tropical eye infection, not knowing the Old Man had taken steps to help, procuring a wonder drug called sulpha from the navy hospital, on my behalf; thinking that whatever I did it would never be found out. There was so little time left for the world. That is, thinking only of myself. For who was there to speak for her?

The woodsman, called Joe Alexander, who is from Russia, he tells me, having walked overland from Siberia—a story I pretend to accept, out of indifference—stares at me as if he would read my thoughts. I am glad that my ghost, Lam Fan, who lets nothing go by unremarked, is absent. For here is a man who, surely, she would question; and how would I deal with a complication like that? He thinks he is better than everyone else because he has so little; yet he wants what I've got. He covets the blankets on the bunks, the supplies in the locker, the charts in the wheelhouse, the clothing, equipment, gear of the *Rose*. He knows that I know it.

"I would know what to do with her," he says with a lift of his jaw, indicating the *Rose* and meaning that I don't. That I have no right to what I've worked for all my life.

I give him a beer and ask him why he's come out of the bush, away from the homestead he's talked of, if he dislikes the world and the rest of us in it so much.

"I'd go crazy if I didn't," he answers. "I get bushed. I come down and watch the steamer land two, three times, then go back home. That's enough." He looks around for cigarettes. I shake my head no. Then he reaches into his pocket and brings out a coin, a Chinese coin made of bronze with a hole in the middle of it.

"Some woman gave it to me once," he says. "You take it. For luck. It ain't brought me none that I can think of."

And with that he's gone, lifted himself up into the wheelhouse *sans* steps, and out the sliding door. He pads around on the deck for ten minutes, though; but I resist going up to see what he's taken in exchange for his coin.

It makes me think of Captain Jenkins of the *Thermopylae*. Who auctioned that ship down to the bare bones so that no one else could have her. For only *Thermopylae* at her best was *Thermopylae*. Anything less was a different ship. Almost as if he knew what would happen: her masts shortened, cut down to a barque; then loading lumber; finally used as a coal hulk near Lisbon, in Portugal. As if the future was in the air for all to see—if you had the courage to look. As if the *Thermopylae's* life, her real life, her dignity, was for him alone to dispose of.

Ah, well. A ship has her own kind of being, with or without men, and *Thermopylae* did go on, into a new frame of reference, a lesser one, perhaps, like the *Rose* here, who has seen better times; and like some others of us.

Thermopylae left Saigon on April twenty-sixth, sailing north through the South China Sea, past Hong Kong and out through the Luzon Strait into the Pacific Ocean. The irony of that return, past the point at which they had started out, was not lost on the women. But the earth is a circle. It brings us back to where we began, at some time or other. Even so...

"Even so," says Fan, who has appeared on deck, checking the manifest of the *Rose's* movable gear—as she should, it is her job—"we were not happy about it."

No, certainly not. But conditions on board the clipper ship were better than on the junk.

The captain had a well-appointed suite aft, to which the ladies were invited to dine, with a steward waiting at table. The captain's bathroom and water closet, off his saloon and chart room, were also made available to the women. They slept in a cabin vacated by the third mate and were mothers to the apprentice boys in the midship house. The men were housed in the fo'c'sle—if there was grumbling as to the women's presence, it was kept quiet. And for the first few days, at least, neither captain nor crew was drunk.

Sixty-one days to cross the North Pacific. It shouldn't have taken much more than forty—but they met nothing but fierce gales, varied with dead calms, from the start. A trip like most others: they started out, then they arrived.

Lam Fan squints at me over the manifest. She puts it down on the fir planking of the deck. The stranger has left footprints from the wheelhouse door to the well at the stern. Everything has been touched, but nothing, as far as I can tell, has been taken. I finger the Chinese coin in my pocket, unconvinced that somehow I won't be made to pay for it.

Fan looks at the pieces of the *Rose's* engine that lie strewn over the wharf. She seems to be puzzled.

"It's all right," I say, "I know how it goes back together."

"No, Robert Lam," says Fan. "That is not what bothers me, it is what you said."

I have to think for a moment before I remember. "About the *Themopylae* and your voyage on her?"

She nods. "All journeys are different, Robert Lam. Surely you know that. How else could you be a pilot?"

"I disagree," I say, holding a pocked bearing up to the sunlight. "The sea is the sea, a boat is a boat, and there are only so many things that can happen."

Fan shakes her head sorrowfully. "Poor, Robert Lam," she says, "to have travelled so much and seen so little."

Which annoys me, of course. "What do you know about it? Who are you to judge?"

"I only know what you tell me," she says, and goes back to looking puzzled.

And so, a voyage that was not like any other. Beating up the South China Sea in the teeth of a gale, making slow headway at the tail of the northeast monsoon. But once through the straits, the wind died away. India stood by the hour on the poop deck watching the crew turning braces and halyards end for end, drawing and knotting yarns, making and trimming sail. She listened to the talk in the saloon where the mate or second joined the two women, when not on watch, for their meals. Lam Fan, who was taken to be India's servant, sat quietly, not at all displeased to be left alone, for she had decided to give up opium, and tins, pipe, lamp, and spoon had been consigned to the deep off Hong Kong.

Their route lay north towards Yokohama, picking up the Kuro Shio, then east, at about forty-two degrees north to catch the North Pacific current, crossing the meridian of one hundred fifty degrees west in about forty-four degrees north. It was a journey of some seven thousand miles, although ships had been known to cover seventeen thousand on a particularly bad crossing.

At midnight the larboard watch was called and the starboard watch ordered below. The wind began to increase until it blew a strong gale, obliging them to close-reef the topsails. No one slept that night, nor for the next three, what with the noise of the wind and breaking water and their fear of foundering.

Lam Fan snorts. "I was not afraid," she says from her perch on the rail from which she is watching me.

"You were a better man than me, then, Fan," I tell her. I have given up on the engine and hired a local man to fix it. There was nothing else to do, since I could not buy the parts I wanted. This man, however, has four or five similar engines in his basement. I am letting my feet dangle over the dockside, keeping watch on some children further down the wharf, fishing for minnows.

"No," I reiterate. "Not once did I go to sea without fear."

"Why go then?" asks Fan with straightforward logic.

I pause to consider my answer. "I never knew what I wanted to do, so I kept on searching. Going to sea is one way of looking."

Fan blows through her lips dismissively. "You did what you wanted to, and that's that."

"Like you did?"

"Like anybody."

"You know what they say about sailing in ships, Fan. It's just like being in prison, but with the added chance of being drowned."

"Who said that?"

"I read it in a book one day, waiting for the tide to turn."

"You read too much, Robert Lam. You should be a man of action, like your...." Her voice trails off.

"Like who, Fan? Like my father? Well, who was he, then?"

I think she is going to turn away from the question as she has before, but this time is different. I am given an answer of a sort.

"I was going to say your mother," she says. "Your father was a

Chinese man. His name will mean nothing to you now. And anyway, I am telling you."

"Telling me?"

"I am telling you about him every day."

A journey like no other, with variations of wind and calm, fear and peacefulness. A sailor comes down with smallpox, the telltale blisters appearing on the bottoms of his feet, and India, in the absence of a ship's doctor, is asked to lance his soles. She does so with Fan swabbing the pus as she cuts. It is a job that has to be done. And besides half the officers and crew are drunk.

"A.B. was this day beastly drunk, and incapable of doing any work.... All hands were this day called aft, and in the presence of the steward, each man took lime juice.... A.B. has fits, and I am feeding him the medicine prescribed."

So ran my mother's diary.

On May thirteenth a typhoon was encountered. The glass began to drop alarmingly, and the captain readied the ship for a storm. In the late afternoon, dense black clouds appeared in the southeast quarter, driving furiously to the northwest. All the light sails were furled, and the yards braced so as to take the wind on the starboard tack. Spray clouded up from the surface of the ocean, and the wind and rain struck with such violence that the gunwhale lay in the water. Quickly the mizzen topsail was furled, and the lee-main-topsail braces were slackened; the helm was put to starboard, and the ship ran before the wind.

For several days neither sun, moon, nor stars were seen, and the ship stayed under close-reefed sails, with a heavy sea running.

Just as they thought the worst had passed, another black wind arrived, driving from eastward. Once more all but the fore topsail was furled, and it was close-reefed. The ship ran before the wind again, and all that had not been properly secured on deck washed overboard.

With night the scene worsened. There were thunder and lightning, seas breaking on either beam, the stern lifted by the sea, then the head plunging into the vortex below, tossed like a twig upon that ocean. Even the most experienced seamen feared for their lives when the sea stove in the stern boat and also took both swinging booms. But towards daylight the gale moderated, and within twenty-four hours the wind fell away to almost nothing.

"It plays with you, Fan," I say. (The local mechanic has pronounced on the engine. The *Rose* will be herself again, he says, by morning.) "Just when you know you're going down, when you've made your peace with yourself and all creation and are ready to die, the storm abates. And so the whole thing starts over. Once more you are full of hope, looking ahead. But the storm that's going to finish you off is only biding its time. It is still out there somewhere. And so you have a false sense of comfort."

"False, Robert Lam? Why false? Is it comfort or isn't it?" She opens her mouth, and I'm sure she's about to lecture me.

"It's all false, Fan," I say before she can start. "War and peace, storm and calm. Even the atom bomb. It's no more than another shift of weather."

They had been at sea for more than a month, and now lay drifting. To cheer the crew the cook made lobscouse—salt beef with potatoes cut up with broken biscuit and some fat, mixed together with fresh water and boiled, and considered a treat in the circumstances. The crew were set to duties such as making new sails, laying rope, and stripping and overhauling the ship's rigging; that is, every yard and mast, except the lower masts, were sent down. The yards were stripped, all the rigging was taken off the mast heads, then put on a stretch. The service and parcelling were stripped, the rigging tarred, service and parcelling were heaved on afresh, then the rigging clapped on again. Captain Wilson, wanting to make a good impression when they arrived in port, relied on calm. Otherwise, nothing transpired of importance to interrupt the monotony for days, and Fan says she would have forgotten all about this part of the voyage if it hadn't been for a singular event—a battle between a thresher shark, a whale, and a swordfish.

They heard a noise like a cannon going off, then about two hundred yards from the ship they saw the combatants. The shark, raising his whole length nearly out of the water, fell with crushing force on the back of the whale. Again and again the shark leapt and fell as the whale, throwing its flukes high in the air, dove, only to reappear at the surface to be again attacked. For while the shark was striking the whale on the surface, a swordfish was harrying it from below. The battle lasted only a short time, then the whale went down and was seen no more.

And since Nature is full of correspondences, even as the sailors had predicted, with the end of the battle, the wind rose.

The night was terrifying. The gale had increased almost to hurricane, with a short, high cross sea breaking in almost every direction. But the ship, a gallant ship, a wet ship, behaved beautifully.

Although all on board, including Lam Fan, who had succeeded in her struggle with opium, were looking forward to the journey's end.

"At which point, do you think," I muse aloud, as the *Rose* enters Johnstone Strait on the morning of the fourth day after our arrival at Granite Harbour, "does the outward journey end and the inward one begin? I mean to say—" I am addressing Lam Fan, who is gazing awestruck at the mountains that rise from the southern shore "—there is always a moment when you cease to be interested in what will happen next and just want to get it over. You want to arrive."

Fan answers without turning her head as an icy wind drops down through the snowy passes. "There is no such point, Robert Lam. At least not for me. Whatever journey I am on, I am always at the start of it."

"Then you've never had a bitter or a boring moment, Fan. Because the way to get through it is to look ahead, hope that what comes next will be better. Want to start over."

She shakes her head. Mist lies over the calm surface of the water, despite the wind, which blows steadily. An unnatural wind, which I can feel in my bones and see in Fan's swirling black hair, but not otherwise sense. Fan sighs. "Have it your way, Robert Lam," she says quietly. "Then the journey is over."

We pass the light at Rock Point. We see the square summit of Mount Eldon. Ripple Point goes by, with its west-going tidal stream of about three knots: from Camp Point westwards the shore is steep and cliffy, and in Race Passage we encounter a faster current and strong eddies and swirls, but the *Rose* takes them on like a dream.

We pass the mouth of the Salmon River and the settlement of Kelsey Bay, the terminus of the highway that connects to home. From now on there is no safety net. There is no way back but in the *Rose*.

"What's next?" asks Fan. She is jiggling the flower rock, which she has picked up from the compass table, in her hand.

"Whirlpool Rapids and a dozen other hazards. And safe anchorages," I answer.

"So you assume," she says.

*   *   *

Thermopylae approached the coast of Vancouver Island, holding south-west of Tatoosh Island before opening up the entrance of Juan de Fuca Strait. She had been sighted by the *West Indian* on the Wednesday after-noon and sailed into Royal Roads about midnight. On the morning of the following day, June twenty-fifth, she was towed by the tug *Pilot* to the Outer Wharf.

We dream, we imagine, in ignorance. And so the greatest dreams are born, unhindered by reality. There had been time to dream on that voyage, time to hope. At sea there were no familiar landscapes, no houses, no businesses, no daily routines (at least for the passengers), no undermining neighbours to whisper of failure. All seemed possible: free-dom, for example, uncluttered by prejudice or conflicting philosophies. A dream world indeed, in which the reformer could work unhindered.

Expectations, in short, which could not be lived up to.

The *Pilot* pulled them from one grey-green shoreline to another. Along the coast the vague, bent shapes of oak trees, topping the rock, stood out in the mist. Lam Fan and India looked down on calm grey waters and up at seabirds calling and wheeling above them. When the mists lifted, they saw forest, and a meadow where animals grazed: they saw shadow change to substance, and were disappointed.

The sea, the land, those birds, that cow—how were these any differ-ent from what they had left behind? But as day filled in the outline of the wharves and other boats; as officials came on board to clear them of quarantine; as the stale, dirty ship rode at anchor, and, with the loosen-ing discipline of the crew, as the routine delays of landing were met, that disappointment muted. For what mattered, of course, was not the land, but the people in it.

Mr. Redford, son and namesake of *Thermopylae*'s new owner, came on board to inspect the cargo. Once he had done so, he asked to meet the passengers. He carried in his hand an explanatory letter that had been sent ahead by Jardine Matheson. What was in it he didn't indicate, but it was clear from his face, when he saw the two women, that it hadn't explained enough.

Mr. Redford, with a kindly nod at Lam Fan, offered India his arm, and they took a stroll around the deck. It was not that he was unkind—far from it, he was the most liberal-minded of men—but there was a question of the laws of the land. He knew about the major and that he had left no money; he had been glad to let the major's daughters have free passage. It was just that no one had thought to tell him that one of the daughters was an Oriental. And the fact was that the laws of the new land were rooted in the old, and the fact was that all Chinese entering the province had to pay a fee. A head tax. No doubt there were reasons practical, economical, and social for the arrangement, although it was not the type of regulation he would have thought of, but as far as he knew there was no way around it.

India looked at the meadow a little ways distant; she watched the dockworkers and the horde of male onlookers.

"Did you not know about the tax, Miss Thackery?" Redford took out a handkerchief and patted his brow. It was, by all accounts, a humid morning.

India's eyes adjusted, until they no longer absorbed the scene before them, but examined circumstances: fear, prejudice, habits, the baggage that the New World settlers had carried along with them. She sighed.

"If you'll forgive me for saying so," said Mr. Redford as his companion remained quiet, "I think that you don't have the money to cover it. Please don't take it amiss. I am going by the letter that was sent to me. If I am wrong, please correct me."

"How much is it?" she asked. Not that the amount made any difference. Whatever it was they hadn't got it.

"It's fifty dollars," he said. "Everyone has to pay it. All the Chinese, that is."

They both examined the scenery: the trees bent landward, the tug that was approaching to tow them to the rice-mill wharves in the inner harbour, for the quarantine officers had cleared them at last.

Now it was Redford's turn to sigh. "Look," he said, speaking softly. "Give me a little time, let me see what I can do. You'll be all right on board the ship for another day or two?"

India nodded. What else could she do? She glanced at King Leonidas, the figurehead, with his unsheathed sword. He stared straight ahead, weapons at the ready, fully prepared.

Small broken-down boats scuttled across the waters in front of them as they moved into the confines of the inner harbour. The city itself clustered close to the skyline dead ahead. There were six church spires, the pagoda-shaped bird cages of the legislative buildings to starboard, and coming up to port, Deadman's Island, the Indian burial ground. Sculls put out from a rowing club at the water's edge below the government buildings, and parties of walkers and riders could be seen along the roadways fronting the sea.

As the ship slipped onwards on the first leg of the inverted "L" that formed the harbour, they saw buildings—hotels, clubs, offices, and theatres—all built of stone.

But as the ship eased northwards, up the inlet towards the rice-mill docks, the scene changed. Westwards were the white canvas tents of the Indian encampment on an open muddy flat, and along the eastern shore, stone changed to brick and brick to grey wooden shacks stacked next to each other, on top of pilings, on top of nothing—so it appeared—but thin air.

There was a crowded, tumble-down, dirty huddle of buildings from which white clouds of smoke issued. In and out between them, and up and down around the pilings, hurried Chinese laundrymen carrying baskets slung on poles, or with firewood gathered in their arms. It was, to Fan and India, a familiar picture, much like the Hong Kong settlement, also called Victoria, that they had recently left behind.

A divided city.

From Churchway to Pandora Street, land cost from $225 to $450 a square foot, but from Pandora Street north to Chatham Street, from $90.00 down to nothing. And what marked this boundary, this change of value?

"The colour of skin, Robert Lam. You know that, why ask?" says Fan, crossly. We are passing the last of Hardwicke Island, making our way towards Blenkinsop Bay where I shall look for an anchorage. Fatigue has caught up with me, perhaps the aftermath of Lam Fan's death and all the business of clearing up; not to mention her reappearance, and whatever I am to make of that. I am coming down with a cold, caught, no doubt, from my Granite Bay visitor, Joe Alexander. Perhaps that was the price of his coin—a day or two of sickness.

I button my flannel shirt and put on my jacket.

"Too late for that," says Lam Fan unsympathetically while I sniffle.

"I'm not asking for much, Fan," I say between sneezes. "I want to be well, I want to get on with my journey."

Waterfalls dropping from great heights, splashing onto the dark rocks of the beach; thick coniferous forest; indented coastline; Indian summer villages built on middens of shell; rock paintings; petroglyphs—of many-legged insects, angle-legged men, women, and children; direction posts, signs and signals pointing heavenwards, whose meaning is lost in history. A coastal world with no inference, for there is no one to interpret it. It slides by, atmospheric blue slipping to grey to paler hues: each deadhead a possible canoe or drowning sailor; each small island a ship going down. My eyes shift back and forth along the shoreline, over the waves, up to the sky and down to the deck of the *Rose*. Scanning, trying to understand shape, identify. No whales for days. But dark blue kingfishers, young eagles, schools of herring. Attempting to make sense of the world I have known since childhood and passed by.

"It takes no print," I say out loud to Fan. "It looks like no one's touched it."

While she, in her own world now, says, "Little Foochow faced Little England in the new place we had come to. We had seen it all before, but there was nothing to be done about it."

By the time the crew had been in port for two days, Mr. Redford was forced to advertise that "Hall, Ross & Co. will not be responsible for carrying debts contracted on account of ship or crew." For the crew, let loose in town, were making up for lost time: spending wages they had earned plus money they didn't have. But Redford had been active in other spheres as well, as he'd promised, and with the rice and matting safely on shore in storehouses, his emissary, a tall and well-built man, but a little pale in appearance, and rundown, was making his way from Chatham Street, along Government Street, down Fisgard Street, in the direction of the rice-mill docks.

He was a man, let me suggest, who was full of promise, but whose talents remained largely in the abstract; that is, neither he nor the world had found a use for them yet. He was a man who scanned the horizon, a sailor at heart though he lived on land; a man who was capable of almost anything, except discipline.

A charmer, a legend in his time.

("Don't overdo it," says Fan. "I am warning you. Please listen to what I tell you.")

This man, as I was saying, who was a little down on his luck, living in a hovel on the wrong side of town, near the Chinese market gardens, because he was recovering from an accident.

Although even then, in the split second between the time he'd seen the descending coal bucket and the moment he was struck while working on one of Mr. Redford's barges, he'd known it would turn out all right. So that what passed before his eyes in that instant of insight was not an ending but a new beginning; so that when he awoke in hospital with a cracked skull and with bandages thick as newspapers round his head, he was not especially surprised to see Mr. Redford bending over him. Nor to see the expression on Mr. Redford's face change to one of relief as he saw that Robert Louis Haack—for that's who it was, the originator of my name, my mother's future husband—had regained consciousness.

Yes, this man who could not now return to his former heavy labours, who had become Mr. Redford's right-hand man and jack-of-all-trades, was on his way into my mother's life.

For Mr. Redford dared not take the necessary steps himself. But if a third party were to intervene, and if, under his influence, justice, fairness, chivalry, and compassion were to be served, that is, if they could find a way to evade the Chinese head tax, Mr. Redford would not object.

And so Robert Louis Haack, alert to the workings of destiny, adjusting his thinking for the task ahead, stepped off the boardwalk on Fisgard Street, waited for a tram to pass, then ambled across Store Street and down the ramp behind the rice and flour mill. Here, in the finger of commerce that crooked round the west end of Chinatown, was also an ironworks, a shoe factory, and matchworks. The smell of wheat, of dust, mouse droppings, and rust combined with sulphur and leather; so that the stevedores wheeling sacks of grain to the tied-up *Thermopylae* breathed in air from which the sea, lapping at the dock pilings, had been excluded.

The ship itself was relatively quiet, as the crew, like children set free from school, had gone rushing up the ramp towards the town some hours earlier. Left on board, attending to the loading, were acting Captain Wilson and his mate, as well as Lam Fan and India.

Haack's plan was simplicity itself, and like many simple programs had evolved from a lack of alternatives. The facts were as follows: when a ship arrived in port it was inspected by quarantine officers, who then turned it over to customs. At every stage goods and passengers were checked against the manifest, and the passengers interviewed to be sure that their answers corresponded to what was on paper. Thus, it was not possible to hide Lam Fan's existence: customs was already waiting for payment of the head tax. All that could be done was to try to change the customs officer's mind about what it all meant.

And hope of accomplishing this difficult task lay in Robert Haack's pocket, in a whiskey bottle from which only the smallest amount was missing.

Robert Haack approached the customs shed. The officer, sleepy on this warm summer's day, sat inside, paring his nails, waiting for the signatures and money that would release him at day's end to his family. It was a lonely job for a sociable man, and having finished his manicure, the officer was more than ready to answer Robert Haack's greeting; which was to the effect of, "Sure is a nice day. Sure is a fine place for a man to keep himself company."

And it was pleasant, pleasanter then, I think, than now, when the air is thickened with smog from the mill up-water, and rusted automobiles stud the stagnant waters that once flowed freely round the ships at the docks. But then as now, water, especially in sunlight, is like a poem, imbuing us with feeling; and the sunlight on the trees on the far shore, and on the distant blue-green hills further west, produced a tranquillity of mind, internal music, that made men under its spell seek a common bond.

Few words are needed. Only a smile and a nod to establish the beginnings of friendship. Moreover, in a city where hundreds of men are out of work, foraging through the waste produced by other men's employment, the customs officer felt that generosity of spirit that comes from being on salary.

He offered Robert Haack a bite of his apple, and Haack took out the whiskey bottle. Thus, in a few minutes, during which the scenery and the boats were examined and a little local gossip was exchanged, mostly about that aldermanic worthy, that notable speechifier, Noah Shakespeare, one thing led to another. They toasted the prime minister, John A. Macdonald, a well-known friend of the bottle; they drank to history, to their parents and grandparents who had brought them to this country; to the children yet to be born; to business ventures. Even a possible partnership in import-export was envisaged: for so it is that we try out possibilities, speculate in land, dig mines with strangers. Sharing a vision of self-improvement unsullied by commitment.

Drink by drink, Haack's hopes of success improved.

Until at last, made inevitable by the falling level of the liquid in the bottle, Haack brought up the critical subject—the customs law, the Chinese head tax, and certain exemptions from it.

"See here," he began, throwing his arm round the shoulder of his new friend, "isn't it a fine thing, when local business is in sore distress, when, for crying out loud, we are desperate for jobs and overseas investment, that right in front of us, on board that ship there [Haack pointed to *Thermopylae*], we should be throwing away an opportunity." Haack shook his head in disgust while the customs officer looked on, bewildered.

"Right in front of us," Haack repeated, "are two fine ladies who want to start up a factory here in our city." He shook his head again, sadly, while the customs officer blinked and tried to keep up.

"See," he explained, "these Hong Kong people have got money. You've heard of Jardine Matheson, haven't you?" The customs man nodded. "Well, they say that company is setting these ladies up. Thirty jobs to start with and more after that.

"The strange thing is," Haack went on with an air of puzzlement, "somebody's told them, even before they can get off the ship, that because one of them is Chinese they have to pay the head tax. Why, it's an insult! If I was them two I'd turn right around and go back. They're here to give us jobs, and what do we do? We stand in front of them with our hands out. I think it's a shame!

"No!" cried Haack, amending himself, "I think it's a crime, and, by God, you and I won't stand for it!"

The customs man, a kindly man, it is true, was upset. His troubled eyes wavered over the beautiful lines of the ship before him, and he struggled to his feet to stand before his newly risen companion.

As to what would have happened, if he would have broken or bent the regulations or done nothing, we cannot tell. For as the moral battle was being waged, the first shouts were heard of the sailors returning from their spree, having worn out their welcome, having run ahead of the law and a number of outraged citizens.

They flung themselves aboard *Thermopylae* like a wave. They fell into the fo'c'sle, sprawled in companionways, tripped, fell over, were trapped below. At which the master and mate got out the belaying pins and set about with vigour, raining down a frightening storm of blows on the miscreants.

It was the last of a number of such episodes, and *Thermopylae*'s officers and crew were soon fired by Redford and shipped back to England as distressed British seamen.

But in the midst of the melee, as Haack and the customs man looked on with amazement, two female heads appeared above the teak railings, like swimmers in danger of drowning. At this sight, without a moment of doubt or hesitation, Haack and his officer friend sprang into action. They leapt on board *Thermopylae*, fought their way through the confusion to the women, and rescued them.

It was an act of chivalry, a test each man passed to his personal satisfaction.

Not another syllable was spoken, not another thought given to the head tax.

Fate had intervened at the critical moment. What an instance to inspire confidence! What a springboard to achievement!

Anchored in Blenkinsop Bay, thinking of time rushing by, of less and less chance to make it north to Rose Harbour, lying in my bunk, sneezing, too weak and stuffed up to make tea or squeeze a lemon. And Lam Fan, unaffected by virus, sitting at my table, looking over all my papers, says, "What did you want to be when you grew up, Robert Lam?"

"Be?" I say, incredulous. "What I am, a man. Nothing else."

"Ah," she says, impenetrably, "a man."

"Yes."

"Indeed."

"So what's wrong with that?"

We listen to the sea below us. The hiss and murmur of the tides around the *Rose*. The bump of creatures small as dimes against her sides. Or maybe it's nothing more than inflamed ears and running sinuses.

"What's wrong with that?" I ask again, beginning to think I need an answer.

Fan fiddles with the wick on the oil lamp, turning it up and down.

"Don't, Fan. You'll ruin it."

"When I was a girl," she says, ignoring my protest, "I wanted to do something, anything that no one had ever done before. I didn't know what it was, I just wanted to be the first at something new."

"And so instead you started smoking opium."

She does not get angry, as I expect. She cocks her head as if listening again to what I've just said. "I suppose so," she says. "I did it at first because the major didn't like it.

"Then, too," she continues, "I missed my family. When I lit my pipe I could think of them happily, without sadness, forgetting that they had left me behind. I even dreamed I would find them. Or that one day my mother and father would come to the door. Every time there was a visitor to the Queen's Road house, I was sure it was them or a message from them."

"I'm sorry, Fan," I say between sneezes. "I hadn't thought about it. I didn't know you felt so..."

"Abandoned," she finishes for me.

Something knocks against the side of the *Rose*. A drifting log?

"I went to sea at first to get away, to make some money. I wanted adventure, too," I say.

"You wanted your mother," Fan tells me with a smile. "When you were a little boy you used to tell me when you'd go outside that you were watching for her. I don't know where the idea came from. We wanted to be your family, Sing Yuen and I. I guess we failed."

"Like the major did, Fan. Like my mother failed as your sister."

"Yes," she says, pulling out from a pile of papers a picture of India, "you are right in a way, but failure isn't so important. Some of us start with a loss and never make it up."

We cannot forecast consequences. We do not know how any act will turn out. They could not know, in the good old days along the coast, when they used to anchor at dark, particularly in winter, wherever the darkness overtook the ship, that one day all would change. We have seven grades of lights now, gas and electric, totalling three hundred; there are thirty-six diaphones, many lighted spar buoys, floats, and dolphins, together with buoys rigged with bell and whistle devices, some of which are operated with wave action. In addition, there are approximately four hundred fifty unlighted buoys, dolphins, spindles, and beacons. There are two lightships, too, one located on the Sandheads at the entrance to the Fraser River, and the other at Swiftsure Bank; plus radio beacons, which send out a signal once an hour in clear weather and continuously in foggy weather, some synchronized with the foghorn signals. And every channel leading to an important harbour is well defined. Aids to navigation. Yet still we make mistakes, still there are shipwrecks.

When I was small, sometimes I'd go with Fan into town, and we'd visit the temple in Chinatown to have our fortunes told. There was an altar—a gift from Canton—and a bell, banners, and fans donated by various families. On the offering table were three sets of semilunar fortune-telling blocks, two bamboo cylinders of fortune-telling sticks, one of them for medical advice. Fan would light incense, and I would take a stick from a cylinder and give it to the caretaker. He consulted the number on it and matched it to a piece of paper in a pigeonhole. There would be my answer. Though I can't say I always understood it.

Generations of experience behind that ceremony. Yet were we enlightened by it? I don't know. We always left cheered up, more confident.

Then, long ago, before I was born, when my stepmother was a young woman newly arrived in town, it was Robert Haack who, leaning against the wall in that same building built by a gold miner out of gratitude for his good fortune, watched as my mother and Lam Fan selected their sticks.

Whatever the answers, they are dust and ashes now. Dust and ashes and ghosts. Which mean less than nothing. Except here and now to me, anchored on the *Rose*.

CHAPTER FOUR

"Johnstone Strait—The tidal streams turn everywhere from 1 1/2 to 2 hours after high and low water by the shore. In the wider parts, the rates are from one to 4 knots; but in the narrower parts, they may attain a rate of 6 knots at times, and in places tide rips are formed."

British Columbia Pilot, Volume I

Anchored in Blenkinsop Bay, westward of Blink Rock and Elf Shoal, with the light from the escape hatch, which I have raised for ventilation, dancing its watery way up and down the wall of my cabin. My fever has gone, and for the first time in three days I am strong enough to stand. But I am sitting, wrapped in a blanket, feet up on the lounge, leaning my back against a storage cupboard. My hands, gripping a cup of hot soup, are pale and nearly transparent. Soft hands, clean hands, but with the dirty, blunted nails of a working man. It is reassuring to see that the *Rose* has left her mark, that I am still myself.

Thank God we didn't drag anchor. Thank God the wind stayed calm.

"I have been wondering," says Lam Fan, my shadow, a little thinner after the illness, like myself, "why you never married. You never brought home a girlfriend. Wouldn't you like to have had children?"

I close my eyes. Through the lids, the dancing light still moves. I wish she would go away. At least until I'm better.

"Everyone likes children, Fan, even you. You never had them, either." Silence, while we both examine our pain.

"But no woman, Robert Lam? Nobody to give you comfort? I had Sing Yuen. I don't know what I would have done without him."

"You didn't have him for long."

"More than twenty years, Robert Lam, from the time we married until he died. And I had known him before that. He was my uncle's friend."

"How did you meet him?" I ask, interested, certainly, but anxious to turn the subject away from myself.

"My uncle, Lum Kee, introduced us, and he gave India a job in his restaurant, keeping the books. She also kept the accounts for his factory, Tai June, where they manufactured opium. She was good at it. She had done the major's accounts, too, keeping him out of trouble for longer than he deserved."

"Opium! He made it legally?" I ask.

"Oh, yes," she answers. "It was not like it is now. There were eleven factories in the city at that time. Sing Yuen was very proud of his management. He knew where every tin they made was sent. He was not in league with smugglers like some of the others."

"Pretty convenient for you, Fan," I say. "I always wondered where you got your supply."

She blushes, but she is also angry. "I had quit at that time," she says, "Sing Yuen never liked my smoking opium. He said it was a habit for old men. But he also let me do what I liked."

We sit in silence. I blow my nose and wonder if I can find the lemons. I could do with a toddy. I would have to heat water, find the whiskey bottle, scrounge in the bilge amongst all the vegetables. I decide not to bother.

Fan is fidgeting with papers, uncurling edges, smoothing out with her palm, rearranging.

"What are you doing?" I ask, slightly annoyed. "I thought that was my job. You've had your chance."

"You should take better care of them," she says, "not leave them lying about like this, they could get damaged.

"Besides," she says, having made her point, willing to be friendly again, "there is something I want to show you. Ah, here it is!" she exclaims, pulling out a sheet of paper with a frame drawn around it. "This hung in Lum Kee's shop. He was an herbalist, you know. I worked for him until he died, and later I ran the shop myself."

"You, Fan? People trusted you to give them medicine?"

She smiles like the Cheshire cat. "I did many things long before you were born, Robert Lam."

I take the sheet she hands me and read.

Us Chinese men greeting Thee Excellency in first degree, Thee in first Rank Country Name Vancouver with hangers to it.

All us here be dwellers at Victoria this island and Columbia British, much wish to shew mind of dutiful loyalty to this Kingdom Mother Victoria Queen, for much square and equal Kingdom rules of us.

Just now most humbly offer much joined minds of compliments to Thee Excellency Governor, on stepping to this land of Vancouver, that thee be no longer in danger of Typhoon, us much delighted. Us be here from 1858 and count over two thousand Chinese.

Chinese countrymen much like that so few of us have been chastised for breaking Kingdom rule.

This Kingdom rule very different from China. Chinese mind feel much devoted to Victoria Queen for protection and distributive rule of him Excellency old Governor Sir James Douglas, so reverse California when applied to us Chinese countrymen. Us believing success will come in obeying rulers, not breaking links, holding on to what is right and true.

Us like this no charge place, see it grow higher to highest; can see a Canton will be in Victoria of this Pacific.

The maritime enterprises will add up wonderfully and come quick. China has silks, tea, rice, sugar, &c. Here is lumber, coal, and minerals, in return, and fish in exhaustless supply, which no other land can surpass.

In ending, us confident in gracious hope in Thee, first degree and first rank, and first link and trust our Californian neighbours may not exercise prejudice to our grief.

I put the paper aside. "What's this supposed to mean to me?" I ask.

"It is part of your past, Robert Lam," Fan says indignantly. "Lum Kee helped to draw it up. It was presented to the governor by all the Chinese merchants. It is a link to the very beginning of the city. And to me."

Then she starts to sing the words of a numbering poem that catalogues the medicines, and that also tells the story of the creation of the earth.

"Let's get going, Fan," I say, throwing off my lethargy, for Fan's singing is always off key. "I'm tired of hanging around. If we want to make Rose Harbour we had better get rolling."

I drop my blanket, and, dressed in long johns, go up on deck to start the anchor winch. The chain rumbles through the roller. We will take a mid-channel course, which should lead us clear of all dangers to the western end of Johnstone Strait. After that, who knows, for there is Blackney Passage with its tidal streams and races. It will depend on the weather, it will depend on the tides, and there isn't a thing I can do about those.

Boardwalks and dusty streets. Peddlers loading up with goods. Notice boards, advertisements, businessmen sweeping their premises. And a grid of Chinatown streets in the early morning light. The whiskey sellers in the ravine at Johnson Street rolled barrels of tangleleg into carts, and Indians set out in canoes from the canvas settlement across the harbour to meet the shipments.

Mussel gatherers filled their baskets, cutting the shells from the rocks by the bridge with sharp knives, and fishmongers met the fish boats, paying twenty-five cents for two baskets of fish, which they would sell that day at a two-hundred-percent profit.

The sun rose over Pandora, Cormorant, and Fisgard streets: streets banded north-south by Douglas, Government, and Store; streets fronted

by poulterers, shippers, provisioners, and inter-penetrated by the multitudinous alleys that ran, like so many cracks in stone, through the heart
of this network of commerce. A maze where tenement piled on tenement
like so much waste.

While Lam Fan, at her job with her uncle, the herbalist, Lum Kee, an
elderly man who wore spectacles, rinsed herbs in the sink, taking care
not to bruise the leaves, and placed them in the bamboo drying trays,
and India got on with her work at Sing Yuen's restaurant.

India was seated, wearing a green eyeshade, in her office at the back,
copying out a list of the restaurant's debtors that Sing Yuen had given
her. Sing Yuen—who affected Western dress and who had already cut his
queue; who approved of Lam Fan's different ways, her education and
experience; who would make speeches and support Doctor Sun Yet-sen
(then finishing his education in Hong Kong—"It was the British who
made me what I am," he would later explain) in his program of reform,
and who would invite that great man to Victoria for a visit... Sing Yuen,
a man with connections and plans and morality but not prejudices, with
whom India, the major's daughter, felt at home.

But the list, slowly copied out in ink, presented difficulties. How was
she to know who these people were? How on earth could she collect
from them? These had been Sing Yuen's first questions, but India had
already solved the problem. Since she couldn't do the collecting herself—
she didn't know the town well enough, she didn't know whom to trust—
she had asked, the night before, during their walk, her new friend Robert
Haack if he would help.

And he, a man-about-town with his ears to the ground, in need of
work, unable to return to his former job with Mr. Redford, now running
errands for that gentleman (which wasn't enough to keep him, even in the
manner to which he had become accustomed), had said that he would.

And so India noted names and figures and added up the total of
unpaid bills, which came to a little more than five hundred dollars, an
important sum to Sing Yuen's business.

Butcher $18.00
Captain of Schooner $50.00
Cook in Ship's Galley $8.00
Red Shirt Man $27.00

Man Come Late $10.00
Cap Man $8.50
Lean Man White Man $20.00
Fat Frenchman $30.62
Captain Tall Man $8.00
Whiskey Man $18.37
Blacksmith $39.00
Barkeeper $5.00
Workman $10.00
Workman Friend $6.50
Little Shirt Man $10.00
Double Blanket Man First $15.00
Lame Leg Man $40.00
Fat Man $9.25
Old Workman $7.50
Red Whiskers $18.50
Indian Joe $10.00
Lick Make Coal Shovel $25.00
Ya Yip Earring $25.00
Flour Pantaloon Man $16.00
Shoemaker, Gone to California $15.00
A Man Butcher's Friend $39.00
Stable Man $15.00
Get Tight Man $7.50

When she had finished, she gave the list to the cook's helper and sent him off in the direction of the Chatham Street shack where Robert Haack—that man in whom so many pathways converged, engineer and future husband, who once, Fan tells me, had met the poet Robert Louis Stevenson, and who carried as talisman a poem in the poet's handwriting; that complex, simple man who, by stumbling beneath a falling coal bucket, had joined himself to my mother's destiny and thus to mine—where Robert Haack lived and was waking up, shivering, with a headache.

Headaches: some caused by colds (like that I've got myself), others caused by weather as the blood vessels respond to the change in barometric pressure; some due to tension, difficult circumstances, unusual work. And some due to drink.

Intending to stop but not. Trying to forget, or hoping to become someone else. In sorrow, in loneliness, in company, and in order to celebrate—emptying the bottle. Which was exactly what had happened to Robert Haack.

Who had met his friends at the Colonial after leaving India, and who had happened to say that it was his birthday coming up, and that he had had a letter from his mother in California, who had asked him how it felt to be twenty-eight.

Which question had worried him. *Did* he feel any different? Was life passing him by as his mother meant to suggest? For he was past the full flower of his youth. What, after all, had he made of himself? It is a question to make a man think—not just at twenty-eight, but in later years, at fifty-seven, say, a few years from retirement, with no attachments, no children, dogs, or a garden to keep ("I mean it, Fan," I say, as we pass the kelp-covered entrance to Port Neville Inlet, "I am still selling the house.") And so, as if to prove, after a few more drinks, that he was still a youth, Haack, accepting a dare, went round the back of the hotel where the proprietor kept a chained bear and let it loose. A mistake that compounded itself, for as the bear shambled into the street it attracted the attention of the police. Who arrested the celebrants and charged them with mischief. Which meant a court date coming up. More bad news for Robert Haack, for there were details concerning his past that he desired to suppress. There was more, but for the moment Robert Haack stopped himself thinking about it.

For something else had claimed his attention as he lay on his back, eyes closed, on a soaking wet mattress: there was the damp itself, there was the movement of air over his body, and the play of bright light across his closed eyelids. Slowly he dared to look, squinting against the sunlight. In the distance were the floating tops of the hills, Mount Tolmie and Mount Douglas, a trembling deep green above the meringue of fog that filled the valley; there were the bent backs of the labourers working in the market-garden fields across the road; there were peddlers filling their baskets at the sheds. None of this, of course, was visible normally from inside his house, the four flimsy walls made from packing cases, the curtained doorway and window. But the fact was that, while he slept, after he had been carried home by his friends after more to drink and after an extended visit to

Yong Sam's gambling house, his house had been dismembered. And there its remains lay, neatly stacked nearby as if to add injury to insult: a most deliberate and cruel practical joke.

Haack closed his eyes. There was nothing more he wanted to see. Moreover, he had remembered the worst of the worst (or was it?). At Yong Sam's gambling house, to which they had gone once released by the police, he had spent all his money. No, even worse. He had signed for his losses, placed pen to paper, written his name with his usual flourish after a sum of money owing. A large sum. An unbelievable amount.

How would he ever pay it back, he wondered in panic. He hadn't seen that much money in all his life! And there were Yong Sam's men to reckon with. Enforcers. Large men, belonging to a Tong. Determined men who would remember that debt the rest of his days.

He would have cried aloud if it hadn't been for the passersby staring at him, wrapped in his blankets in the open air, curious.

And finally, and this *must* be the worst of the worst, there was what he had promised India: that he would help her out by collecting the money owing to Sing Yuen's restaurant.

They had gone for a walk. He had told her the story about the Klootchmen, the Indian women, that he had heard at a Workingmen's Protective Association meeting. (Not that he had told her where it had come from.) About how the two Indians had been sitting on the walk, selling clams and potatoes, and how a society member—a working-man—with some talent for magic had come along.

"Can I buy some clams?" he had asked.

"Certainly," one had replied, and had given him a clam to try. He had taken out his knife, opened the bivalve, and produced from inside it a fifty-cent piece.

"Oh!" cried the woman, "I can't sell you that one!" Then she had given him another clam to try, and the same thing had happened. The magician said, "I'll take all of them." And she had said, "Oh, no, I can't sell these, no!"

He had left her there with her friend opening every one of the whole bag of clams. He had gone away laughing.

As Robert Haack had laughed. As India hadn't. "I hope he went back and paid her for what she'd lost," said India.

"But he'd already given her a dollar!" said Haack defensively.

India had let the subject drop, and they had continued on to the foot of Johnson Street, where the ex-miners lived and where there were buildings with trap doors set right over the water so the whiskey sellers could unload their goods into the canoes.

The bells had started tolling then, one after the other, from each of the six steeples. They had stopped to listen; everyone on the street had stopped—the unemployed men and the drunks, the women in their evening dresses looking for business. The sky had glowed pink over Deadman's Island. Just then, when he was still smarting from her criticism of his humour, she had put her hand gently on his arm and had said, "Robert, could you help me out? Would you like a job?"

And of course he said yes.

And perhaps that was why he had gone out drinking, for it was only later, after he had said goodbye to India, that he had let himself think about what working for Sing Yuen's restaurant really meant. Blacklisting. No hope of future employment. Loss of friendship. Ruin now and forever.

How, how, how could he have done it?

For in Robert Haack's world, in the world of all the workingmen who had joined with Noah Shakespeare, that aldermanic worthy, that political hair curler, it was conflict of interest. Worse than that, it was betrayal, suicide, breaking of an oath. For the one thing that Robert Louis Haack, charter member and informer for Alderman Shakespeare's Workingmen's Protective Association must not do was to help out a Chinese business. Even when asked by a woman. A young woman he liked and respected.

Haack struck his head with his fists, oblivious now to how he must appear to others. And even as he did, tracing in his mind those fatal steps, his lips moved silently, repeating the solemn oath he had sworn, which was recited at the beginning of every Association meeting.

I solemnly pledge my word as a man to neither aid or abet or patronize Chinamen in any way whatever or patronize those employing them, and I will pursue all legitimate means for their expulsion from the country; and this society shall be for the mutual protection of the working classes of British Columbia against the great influx of Chinese, and to devise means for the amelioration of the condition of the working classes of this Province in general.

Which was clear enough, wasn't it?

"But why, Fan," I ask, "why did he do it?"

"He didn't like to be alone," she says. "When he saw that all his mates were joining, he went along with them."

While I ponder that, she takes the wheel. "Stay in midchannel," I urge her. "We're not that far from a reef."

"I know what I'm doing," she says, "there is a place I mean to take you. A special place."

"I don't have time, Fan. We've had too much delay already. I'll never get where I want to if you keep on interfering."

"So what, Robert Louis," she says. "So what."

And I am left with my question. How could my mother's future husband be so foolish?

Well, I say to myself, keeping an eye on Fan as she steers away from Cracroft Island, crossing the strait to follow the southern shore, it was an age of innocence. There was no radio or television or cinema. No space journeys. People had to do something for companionship and adventure. And what was there for a single man, who had no money, to do, except drink? For then, as now, it was an age of couples. Of families. Of tight social circles.

There was the theatre—the Savoy with its dancing girls, the Negro theatre beneath Goodacre butchers, the Theatre Royal—but there reserved tickets cost three dollars, far too much for a man like Haack. And who cared what would happen to him anyway? He was just another poor man in a country full of them.

In the year 1890, in that city of double aspect where the races faced each other across a boundary and men were lost, directionless, milling hopelessly in unemployment; where overtures of friendship, messages of goodwill, such as the statement Fan had shown me, drawn up by the Chinese merchants, Lum Kee among them, where such messages meant nothing because there was no one to interpret the gesture; and where small boys reversed the reins of the Chinese carter's horse so that left meant right and vice versa....

Where disease wore a foreign appearance, as ships arrived from the east flying the yellow quarantine flag, and a dress sent out from one of these to be mended led to an epidemic, and the doctors inoculated arm to arm as fast as they could but couldn't catch up with the deaths; where, when a storm destroyed the earthworks of the Chinese cemetery on the waterfront, there were bones from hundreds of casualties....

A man like Noah Shakespeare made sense. Bringing order to confusion, bringing purpose. It was, he explained, the immigrants' fault; the Chinese were taking jobs from the whites; they had to be stopped.

For sometimes it does not matter what a man believes so long as it takes him to brotherhood, to escape from despair and loneliness, and gives him a family of sorts. Which was exactly the case with the Workingmen's Protective Association for poor Robert Haack.

"I can't believe this," says Fan disgustedly. "Maybe we should turn back. I cannot believe you are defending him. You are half Chinese yourself!"

"But Haack was my mother's husband, Fan," I remind her. "My mother named me after him. Surely my mother knew what she was doing."

"Of course she did," Fan responds, "but it wasn't *that* she wanted carried on, not Robert Haack's prejudice."

"But you have told me yourself he did not believe in it, he did not actually act."

"Yes," she admits despairingly. "But he belonged to a group that persecuted men, women, and children. He reported on what he heard in Chinatown. He spied on the people who befriended him!"

"Aha!" I cry. "So it's something personal you have against him."

"No more than you have," she says quietly. Which shakes me up.

Still, I feel compelled to go on. "You have no proof. You are making it up. You never liked him. You never wanted my mother to have friends other than you."

"Am I so jealous, Robert Lam?" she asks gently. "Can you honestly say that?"

And so I stop for a moment and think. And am ashamed of myself. I was the one who wouldn't bring friends home. I was the one who had no confidence in myself, who thought that if folk knew who I really was, they would turn away.

But did I know yet? Had anything changed? Had I acquired more trust?

Coolly, Fan, who has indicated that we are almost there, wherever she is taking us, puts down the glass through which she has been examining the shoreline and gives me the benefit of her most critical stare. Not that I want it.

"In fact, you are just like him," she says icily. "You think you can do anything you want and it won't cause harm because it is you who do it.

You think that any price is worth your comfort, as long as someone else is paying it.

"You think you need friendship," she says, "when what you need is to be a friend to yourself. Not that you have much to offer. But you should not be afraid to do what you know is right."

"But Robert Haack...."

"I know, I know," she says, putting up her hand to stop me saying anything further. "You want to admire him. You bear his name. There is nothing wrong with that. Just don't close your eyes to the truth. He was wrong to sign such a document; he shouldn't have taken that oath. He should have had more courage. Let me assure you, he would have been much better off."

So ends the argument. Although I still see his side of it. I know what it means to be on a ship with men and officers, to be part of a team, to belong. And I know what it's like without.

Robert Haack: who had crossed a border, unwittingly at first; who had walked out with my mother one night when the air was as soft and potent as laudanum; who had listened to her troubles, who had told her his, along with a tasteless joke; who had wanted her to like him, and who had felt the electrical current that ran from her hand on his elbow, and that flowed out, in turn, from his fingertips. A current that promised— what? A future, perhaps. And so he had said yes.

Keeping his secret. Hoping it could be kept and everything would turn out all right.

And here on the *Rose*, a boat full of secrets, too, there are atoms of paper spinning, colliding, coalescing like splitting and joining tides; long lines of memory scored and crosshatched with streets and buildings: Lum Kee's herbalist shop, Sing Yuen's restaurant, the Fisgard Street house where my mother and Lam Fan lived. Cigar factories, breweries, butchers, opium houses, the electric arc light at Johnson and Douglas, the red-light district at Herald and Chatham; streets where the balconies joined in endless procession up and down at the second and third levels; streets full of women, of men and children, dogs, rats, mice and other vermin.

Streets where I walked with my stepmother, and where, a young child, I watched Sing Yuen, my stepmother's husband, stand on a platform outside the Chinese Nationalist office, and where there were the sounds of breaking glass and the screams of women, and the thick, muffled sound of wood striking bone as the police waded in. It was the day of the arrival of the news of the revolution in China. It was the day that the men cut the queue, the symbol of the Manchu rulers, from their heads.

And it was the day that I, a boy, neither yellow nor white, cut myself off from my Chinese self, turned my back on it.

Cut away the past, freed myself from it and the mysterious burden I bore in my blood. That could not be talked of. That set me apart from those I knew and loved.

"We're here!" Fan shouts suddenly. "This is what I was hoping to see!"

So I look out from the *Rose*, out from the midst of my memories. And there, along the smooth rock shoreline called Robson Bight, named after a seaman who died in a fall from his horse, the whales have gathered. Hundreds of them, it looks like. Roiling and boiling, sounding and diving. Grey, blue, black, and white: wart-backed and smooth, blowing, splashing, feeding, playing, and rubbing the barnacles from their skins on the rocks. Families of them. Families and friends and relations. Tears spring to my eyes, and I feel like I've come home.

"Thank you, Fan," I say, not sure what my gratitude is for.

And she smiles. "We'll anchor here for now," she says.

CHAPTER FIVE

"What strange fatality envelops nearly every enterprise set on foot in this colony and paralyzes the efforts of our most public-spirited men? Look at the Roys' Whaling Expedition. The party start for the West Coast and kill a few whales— the oil from any one of which would have defrayed two months' expenses of the expedition—but no sooner do they make fast to the monsters than fierce storms arise and the animals, cut adrift, float ashore and are taken in hand and claimed by the savages. Next, despairing of a lull, the party repair to Deep Bay, a sheltered locality and famed for visits from the oleaginous tribes; but not a whale enters the bay during the stay of the party. Next, they strike off to Knight's Canal, where shoals of whale are reported to be; but not a fish appears after their arrival. Then they return to Nanaimo, coal and come on to Victoria abandoning the expedition—when, the very day succeeding the one on which they leave the locality of black diamonds, into the harbour dart a dozen great whales, spouting, sporting, and fighting like mad all day long; and, to make the case all the more provoking, if possible, one of the big fish impudently runs aground at low water and actually lies upon the beach over

one tide—as much as to say, come and catch me, if you can!—before he floats off. Too bad. Too bad!

The British Colonist

"The sperm whale is the only one with teeth," I say, to my stepmother. "It's the one that produces ambergris. The humpback is similar to the sperm. Its spout is short and thick, and it can stay down for fifteen to thirty minutes. The sulphur bottom or blue whale is larger. It has no teeth, but in their place are gill bones from eight to twelve feet long. Then there is the finback...."

"Don't tell me things I already know," says Fan. The surface of the bight is quiet now. The whales, possibly tiring of our presence, have moved off, but the air seems to hold their radiance: there are rainbows everywhere. Even the lapping of the water against the sides of the *Rose* has a charged quality, as if still resonating with the whales' calls.

Leviathan. Monarch of the oceans that ships tread with caution. Sailors' saviour or nightmare: for while some whales have ferried seamen to land, others have swallowed them. There is Jonah, of course, both swallowed and vomited up, unlucky man, whom his shipmates threw into the sea to calm a storm. Because it was all his fault: he had dared to disobey his orders from Fate, had tried to outrun it. Jonah, who gave his name to all bad luck at sea.

On our ship, the *Silverbell*, that night we were struck by torpedoes, there had been things said among the men: "Thirteen ships in a convoy that sails on a Friday, and carrying *him*." They had fixed their looks on the bo's'n, an innocent man if ever there was one, but who had survived without harm three earlier sinkings. And whose crewmen had sustained several injuries while working with him, repairing the gun deck. A Jonah, they called him, and tried not to be near him.

Whereas they should have picked on me. I don't know why they couldn't see it, I wore my guilt like a colour, and I could not stop myself from thinking about it. I never stopped working, and when I didn't work, I had to hide my shaking, although now I see they would have thought it because of my illness: they knew I had nearly gone blind.

"The sei whale stays down three to seven minutes," says my stepmother, taking up my lecture, "and the right whale is the only whale with a double spout. Oh, yes, Robert Lam, I know all about it. They do not hunt the bottle nose and grey whales any more, although the killing of the right is the only one prevented by law." She smiles at me, having given proof of intelligence.

"Do you know how they kill them, Fan?" I ask (but don't wait for an answer). "They shoot a harpoon with barbs in it, and with a bomb attached. When the bomb goes off, the barbs spread open."

"We are very different people," Lam Fan says bitterly, looking away from me. "I would never have thought about killing after what we've seen." A slight wind has come up. The waves, under this freshening, wear the stiff, brushed look of a mat.

Because there's no way to explain what I was thinking, I say, "It's how men have made their living for hundreds of years. Even the Indians hunted the whales. In fact, those who did so were thought to be heroes."

"But they didn't use a gun and a bomb!" she says.

"No," I agree.

"No."

We stand quietly together, Fan a dark presence in her black and grey silks on this grey, damp day, and I think about moments like this. How they pass. The good and the bad. How life goes on and on, without respite, until it ends.

"Sometimes they had to leap onto the back of a whale to deal the death blow," Fan says.

"Pardon, Fan, I'm afraid I've lost track...."

"The Indians," she says. "Like Jonah in the Bible."

"Fan, I don't think that's quite right," I say, trying to correct her gently. "That's not the way they told it at the Chinese Christian School for Boys."

"I know what I'm talking about, Robert Lam," she says. "I knew some of the whalers long before you were born. Chief Atlin practised holding his breath under water so that he could stay with the whale when it dived."

"Really, Fan?"

"It's true," she insists. "Just because it's new to you doesn't make it a lie." Which is a point.

"There was also Chief John Moses," she goes on. "He used to get ready for the hunt by fasting and praying, bathing in the sea, and rubbing himself with twigs. He also wore a headdress made of cedar bark and decorated with eagle feathers and wooden figures of whales. In the center of it there was the harpoon head used in the hunt. He danced in imitation of the whale. He sang and prayed for power over the whale. And you know what?" she finishes, "he did it, he was able to kill it."

I look at her until she blushes. "I didn't mean..." she says. "It's not the same thing."

"That's what it's all about, Fan. That's what I said in the first place."

She looks at me sadly. "You've still got it wrong, Robert Lam. You'll always get it wrong. I was talking about a single person. I was telling you something important."

Well, and so we are at odds again. To try to make it up a little, I change course, as she'd suggested. Instead of Blackney Passage, the logical route into Queen Charlotte Strait on our way to Rose Harbour, I head for Broughton Strait, fiddling along the inside lane, passing Beaver Cove, Yellow Bluff, Haddington Island (avoiding the reefs), steering mid-channel with Yellow Bluff astern, and passing northward of Neill Rock. And coming out of the western end of Broughton Strait (where I didn't want to be in the first place) southward of Kelp Patch with Pulteney Point lighthouse behind, bearing about one hundred twenty-four degrees.

Tricky navigation, and time-consuming. When I have no time to spare, when the fact is I'm worried by the calendar. It may already be too late. We could get caught up north in bad weather. But why come this far if not to go on?

Time. Time passing too quickly.

Time that can't be saved, that seems lost before you start.

Summer had gone, and Indian summer had come. Then that, too, had ended, and the rains had started. Court dates had arrived and been put back while Robert Haack lived on tenterhooks, stretched to the limit of patience, fearful of what was to happen.

Watching (as it were) the weather.

It rained and rained. Late October ran into early November. Storms altered the shoreline of the harbour and swamped the laundrymen's shacks and left a high-tide wrack on the posts of the whiskey sellers' houses where, above the pilings, the trap doors opened. Scavenging weather. Flu weather. In which the muddy streets were picked clean of refuse by coughing men, and every wood chip and stray length of grass was put on a fire and burned. In coal-oil tins or on cast-iron grates scarcely big enough to balance a cup.

Pooled water overran rooftop gutters, and the horses struggled to lift their hooves from the sludge; and from the tin chimneys and half-open windows and doors of Chinatown came slipstreams of smoke, spiralling upwards into the smoke-coloured air.

Then, as if having worn itself out, the rain stopped. The emptied clouds rose and fled high across the icy surface of the hard blue sky. Not the lazy leaden blue gaze of summer, in which Haack and India had walked, discussing business, but the arctic blue stare of approaching winter, which awakens horses at dawn and sends early risers to the window first thing to look out and question, as if something is wrong.

The vegetables in the market gardens lay shrunken and stiff—bush potatoes, yellow lettuce, scraggled, collapsed vines, left in the ground too long. They were late plantings, the labour of farmers who wished the seasons would change to suit them. Farmers who used every bit of ground, including the space where Haack's shack had been. For long since, before the rains had come, Haack had found a new home.

And it was here, in his rented room in the Metropolitan Hotel and Roominghouse, presided over by the landlady, Mrs. Lush, that he laboured over a letter.

With his jaw clenched, fist tight on the quill and nerves on edge after a day of avoiding Yong Sam's debt collectors as he went about his errands for Sing Yuen's restaurant, Robert Haack rubbed his eyes and started over. It was a small job for the "brotherhood," keeping his hand in by composing an anonymous letter to send to the *British Colonist*. He had been given instructions personally by Alderman Shakespeare.

To the editor [Haack had written]: Passing down Cadboro Bay Road this morning I was attracted by the sound of hammering from the other side of the road. Looking across I saw a Chinese carpenter engaged in putting up a fence. I made inquiries and ascertained that the land that was being enclosed is the property of Mr. Grant, town councillor, and a large shareholder in the *Times* newspaper. I should like to be informed whether there are not among Mr. Grant's constituents and subscribers several carpenters

who would have been glad of the job, which has been
given by him to a heathen.

Yours very truly,
A Citizen

Haack wiped his forehead with a handkerchief and leaned back in his chair. Not a bad letter if he did say so himself. Surely it would help if (God forbid) worse came to worst and his treachery were found out. Surely they would remember useful acts like this. And, thank God, he said to himself, as he often did, that his mother, an ex-schoolteacher, had taught him to read and write. Not that in the everyday sense he made much use of it, but still it came in handy.

He stood and went to the window of his room. It looked out at a red brick wall and down onto an alleyway. There, in the shadows on the ground, catching sight of him and wagging his tail, stood Charlie, a scabby, long-haired dog that had adopted Haack when he lived in the shack on Chatham Street. The dog had moved with him, too, trotting along beside the wheelbarrow that Haack had borrowed to transport his goods, and refusing to be discouraged although Mrs. Lush would not allow the dog inside her premises. And Charlie had remained loyal, waiting all day and all night, if necessary, for Haack to make an appearance. Haack did his part, when he could, by dropping Charlie scraps from the inedible breakfasts Mrs. Lush cooked. He liked the dog. They had a straightforward and comforting relationship, better than most people did, and it was all the more consoling in its simplicity considering the mesh of other complexities in which Robert Haack lived.

Such as this. In the midst of composing this letter (a task that had taken him several weeks to complete, for he had wanted to get it right), Haack had gone with India to lay a complaint with the police against the white employer of the small son of Kung Fong, a vegetable peddler. Robert pulled down his hat, hoping not to be recognized, hoping against hope that the long-put-off court date would not suddenly be announced in front of India by the constable on duty, yet feeling good about what he was doing. How could he have turned away when he had found the boy himself, by the roadside where his employer had left him, with black bruises striped across his legs as if they'd been painted there with the cane, a deep cut on one thigh, and a knee swollen large as a bowl? It was all right for a man to suffer, but a child!

And there was more to it. With India beside him, taking time out from her work for Sing Yuen at the restaurant and the opium factory, which indeed kept her busy, and with the child in his arms as they hurried along, Haack had felt quite peculiar. As if the pieces of his life were coming together. As if the walk to the police station, just the three of them, meant something special. Although it was hard to put a finger on it exactly, it meant something... different.

Haack knocked his fingers against the window in greeting to Charlie. "Two minutes, boy," he mouthed, "I'll be right down."

That feeling, that sense of floating free but being firmly held to earth as well, had stayed with him, and he had found that it tended to reoccur in India's company. Although what he could do about it, considering his financial and other circumstances, he had no idea.

Moreover he had more immediate difficulties with Miss Thackery to concern himself with, important ones, for the court appearance had come and gone—at last—with surprising swiftness, and, to his dismay, although he was the one who had given her name, they had summoned India as a character witness. It wouldn't have been so bad if he had prepared her for it, but he hadn't said anything at all. He really hadn't thought it would go so far. Although her testimony had helped, certainly, in reducing the sentence to a fine from a jail term. He had to be grateful for that. But she hadn't spoken to him afterwards, and he was fearful of what she thought. A woman like that.

Haack picked up his hat and jacket from the bed. He was managing, barely, to get by on the generosity of some of his workingmen friends. That plus the small amount he earned as Sing Yuen's debt collector and running Redford's errands. He needed new clothes. He needed shoes, a warmer jacket. He'd have no trouble making a list. These were hard times, there was no getting around it.

Before he left his room Haack glanced in the mirror, pulled his hat to an angle of jauntiness over his dark brown hair, tested the length of his beard as to need for a barber, brushed off his trousers, and spat on his boots for polish. He was ready, he thought, for whatever came next.

At the southeast corner of Pandora and Government streets, where Pandora joined Cormorant Street in a vee, and across from where the government liquor store is now, the only place in the length and breadth of the city where you can buy a bottle of rum or a case of beer, not noted for its decor but for the brutes wearing armbands who patrol its counter.... ("Enough, Robert Lam," says Fan, as we make our way past Masterman Island and into Goletas Channel, where we must keep in mid-channel until nearing Nahwitti Bar, which itself protects the channel from heavy swells during westerly gales, a fact for which I'm grateful as the *Rose*, for some reason, is labouring.) At this corner, in the layering of time natural to cities, stood Sing Yuen's Tai June opium factory, India's other place of employment.

It was a modest two-story building, made of red brick like its neighbours, but with a white-painted balcony and carved white wooden posts supporting the veranda. With smoking chimneys, and a flag flying bearing the Tai June emblem, a crowing rooster. Down the street were Van Volkenburgh's butcher shop, Fullerton's shoes and the St. Nicholas baths, the latter often of service in the toilet of Robert Haack—buildings which, by the way, would endure along with Delmonicos Hotel and Restaurant, long after the Tai June and other opium factories were no more.

For before the rafts of overhead wires strung on telegraph poles, marking the streets as channels, had ceased to be remarked, when theatregoers still flocked after performances to the oyster bars on Government Street, while vendors cried their competing virtues—"Fries, roast, stews, everything you chews in the way of eating, Peter'll be repeating, oysters (halo clams), tidbits broiled in hams, everything just right, both by day and night, one and all, give me a call—Peter—at Charley's, on the corner"—that is, before the Great War, which put so much of the world I had known out of existence, including my childhood; even before then, the opium factories had been demolished.

Although I could just remember them; and they might have gone on for decades, importing, processing, exporting, paying their annual licence fee, making the Dominion government about $150,000 annually, all quite legally, if it hadn't been for a pudgy, straitlaced bachelor sent out by the federal government in 1907 to investigate the anti-Oriental riots on the coast. (Yes, Fan, even I admit that bachelors have their blind spots.)

This emissary, from far across the mountains and plains, from the other side of the continent, this man named Mackenzie King, who would one day be prime minister, who loved his mother and his country as no one had before him, had not known that opium was legally manufactured, sold, and smoked in his native land. No one else—no one who counted in politics, that is—appeared to have known, either. Despite the large sums paid and collected. And didn't know (they claimed) about the smuggling of the drug from Canada to the United States, although it was obvious to anyone who cared to think about it that, one way or another, there was a great deal of money to be made on the sixty to sixty-five tons of opium produced in Victoria annually. It was a great deal of opium for a small town to absorb by itself.

And so Mackenzie King, alerted by the damage compensation lists submitted after the riots, with claims for six hundred dollars each by two Vancouver opium manufacturers for the loss of six days of their business (while the rioters smashed windows and threw rocks and held rabble-rousing street meetings), was nonetheless startled to find on the front page of the Victoria *British Colonist* an advertisement that ran, "For Sale: Olives, onions and opium. Choice grades of opium direct from British plantations in India and processed at our own island warehouse." He was more than dismayed, he was hopping mad. "This is not only a source of human degradation but a destructive factor in our national life," King reported to Ottawa, and as quick as could be, drew up the new "Opium and Drug Act," which prohibited the "importation, manufacture, and sale of opium for other than medicinal purposes."

His report was presented to Parliament on June twenty-sixth, 1908. And the law erasing the opium industry from Canada was passed in Parliament less than three weeks later.

A black day for my stepmother, Lam Fan. Although I can't recall it affecting her much. But then she had connections and contacts, a life of which I was ignorant.

"Keep trying, Robert Lam," says Fan, eyes glued to the binoculars, "but don't imagine I will respond to your baiting. You're no good at it. You never were." I watch what she's watching—Miles Cone on Doyle Island now behind us, an oddly regular drinking-cup shape set against the high, wild shorelines north and south of the channel. We have passed the Noble Islets light, riding a tidal stream of about three knots. And now Fan swivels the glasses to focus on Mount Lemon, on Nigei Island, with its steepto and cliffy shore. "Why mountains, Fan? Why always the land?"

She turns and looks at me blankly, and for an instant I see through those eyes to the sea. Nothing but weather. Nothing but foreordained pattern and movement. I blink, and Fan is solid again.

"Why?" she answers. "You are in charge of the ocean. I am only a passenger. You are in charge, Robert Lam," she says, smiling, but with emphasis. "It is your story."

The earth, the earth all around us, encircling. The high mountains, the broken shoreline, the litter of woods on the islets; the life of the ocean surging beneath the bow of the *Rose*. As permanent as anything I can envisage, and as yet untouched. Snow on the mountain peaks, the plunging waterfalls and stony beaches. It unrolls before us, as if Fan and I both are ghosts on this voyage; as if space has come down to earth, and we are its witnesses.

And so Robert Haack arrived at the Tai June offices on the corner of Pandora and Government streets, where Cormorant made its vee, looking for India.

He carried flowers, borrowed from Mrs. Lush's lobby; he carried his hopes, waiting outside for India to be finished with business, wandering into the yard where men worked, unloading the raw materials and readying the processed tins of opium for shipment. Men at work. Men with regular jobs. Men who had money.

Overseers and labourers, with sweat-stained handkerchiefs tied around their heads, who had been down to the docks and met a ship; who had lifted the crates of unrefined opium gum (from Malwa and Benares) into the carts; who had whipped the horses up the hill; who had unloaded in the yard and filled up the warehouse while, from the other side of the lot, men were carrying the crates of processed opium to other carts to tally up the Tai June orders; and other men moved tins to the factory itself; and still others answered calls for more and more of the unprocessed drug from a factory window. Perpetual motion. What came in going out, only at so many times the original cost. For each tin of one and a half pounds sold for $3.50, and was about a month's supply for a user. And there were thousands and thousands of tins.

Robert Haack returned to the front of the factory and cooled his heels on the porch. Inside, he knew, for she had told him, India was conducting an audit. Sixteen hundred pounds of crude opium shipped to make one thousand pounds of refined drug. Tins at wholesale, tins at retail. Minus the annual licence fee of five hundred dollars, and the duty of one hundred sixty dollars per case. Counting up costs, reckoning profits. Haack drummed his feet on the porch, then edged round the side to the windows.

Besides the receiving room and warehouse at the rear, there were, as well as the office, two large processing rooms. In these, as he saw, having wiped away the dirt and steam from the glass, there were about thirty employees. The room in full view (the other he could see part of through an archway) was much like a kitchen. A long table stood against one wall. Here the workers scraped the crude opium from the coconut shells in which they had been shipped. At intervals, the material was checked by an overseer for quality. India had told Robert how it was done: the inspector checked for colour (blackish), odour (strong and fetid), and texture (hard and viscous, heavy). Robert watched as the final test was done—a rubbing between the fingers to feel for the roughness or grittiness that meant the opium had been adulterated—which it occasionally had, sometimes with cow dung or the stalks and dry leaves of the poppy. As Robert watched, the overseer nodded his satisfaction: the material, at this stage at least, was pure.

It was because of the danger of adulteration that Tai June did its own grinding. India had told Haack what had happened when they had tried sending the material out to be ground on contract: it had come back the same weight as it had left, an impossibility, of course, because of the moisture inevitably lost in the grinding process. When they had checked, they had found, among other added substances, stones and gravel, wheat and flour, and the residue left from preparing tincture of opium.

Along another wall there was a set of stoves, one great stove, actually, which one man was employed to keep fed with fuel, and on which other workers, with their hair tied up in white cloths, fried great balls of opium in huge pans. The balls, Haack estimated, were twice the size of his hat. Even standing where he was, Haack could feel the odour of the cooking opium seeping into his pores. It made his eyes water, and he rubbed his hand under his nose.

In the far room there were more stoves on which the opium was boiled into jelly form in giant copper vats. The walls ran with condensed vapour, and it was a labourer's job to wash the walls down after each day's work, and in the daytime to sweep the running rivulets from the floor down a drain. It was a busy scene, with workers hurrying to keep up with demands from the yard.

Powdering, canning, and packing: all this went on in the second room, behind a screen, out of Haack's view, but he felt as if he knew it by heart anyway, having listened to India discussing her work on their daily walks, and having talked over with her a number of Tai June's problems. Such as whether to fill orders for local brewers, although everyone knew that the opium went into the beer, which was against the law, but if Tai June didn't supply the drug, another manufacturer would; or how to handle the retail trade—to do more than they did, selling powdered opium in dried-out lemons mostly to seamen leaving on voyages, would require expansion of the premises. And it was a business of fashion to some extent: now thought by some to remedy tetanus, always popular for strengthening children, and used as a remedy for impotence. And Tai June's greatest problem of all, to which Haack had given some thought, which was security.

For it was easy to carry away some of the drug—in shoes or hatbands, knotted up in queues (although India said it was unheard of for a Chinese to smuggle)—at any stage of the manufacture; and even though preparation at home was tedious, it could be done by a person who knew how to shred and simmer, knead and skim.

One of the security guards whom India had hired, at Haack's recommendation, caught Robert's eye at the window.

Haack jumped down from the box on which he stood and dusted his hands.

It was, all in all, nothing out of the ordinary. His friend, India, treated it much like any other business, like Sing Yuen's restaurant, for instance, and tried to make sure that no one was hurt by it. For she had grown up, in Hong Kong, with opium a part of her world and had seen its potential for harm and for good. For good in medicines to heal the body and mind; for ill in those who relied on it overmuch. Those like her sister, Lam Fan.

Employees who were opium addicts did not keep their jobs at Tai June, and so there were few who took up the habit, since they were good jobs to have, reasonably well paid and with other benefits, including money for families during sickness and time off for festivals.

Opium. An industry as old as mankind. A drug that began life in a flower, *Papaver somniferum*, and that seeped out of the incised poppy capsules, was collected with much labour, and ended up in laudanum, paregoric, Battley's Sedative and Dover's Powder, not to mention

Cholorodyne and Godfrey's Cordial and Street's Infants Quietness. Not to mention in pigeon's egg opium pipes. The kind of pipes my step-mother liked.

Robert sighed. He had had more than a passing acquaintance with the drug, although that was long ago, in an unfortunate incident of transferring opium from bond at the San Francisco docks, raw opium meant to be shipped to Victoria but passed over the side to the Sacramento boats. Unfortunate because he had been caught. Although because he had been so young and scarcely to blame—he had hardly known what was happening; he had needed the money—the judge had been kind. Six months in jail was all, although it had cost him more than his pride; it had cost, he believed, a certain friendship. But now he was most of all grateful that it had not been read into his recent court record. That would have been all he'd needed, to have that brought up.

Let bygones be bygones, he said to himself, still waiting for India. There was nothing in any of it for a man like himself, a man with talents. A man with potential, however unrealized.

For it was hardly worth the trouble to cross the border, not after the supplier was paid, and the transporter, not to mention the local distributor.

Still, customs took it seriously enough. With ten dollars duty paid or lost on each tin, it was nothing they could afford to sneeze at.

But a business for dopes. A business for men at the end of their ropes.

Haack picked up the flowers, which he'd rested on the steps. He checked his shoes' appearance, and armed himself with patience.

"I meant to tell you," said Robert, following India across Government Street, where she had looked both ways for traffic, but not at him.

"Somehow it just never came up." As she waited for a dray to pass, he produced the flowers from behind his back.

"I'm sorry," he said. "It was the wrong thing to do to you. But I didn't want you to think badly of me."

She turned to face him reluctantly.

"Think badly of you?" she said. "But what did you believe would happen when the police came to get me? I didn't know anything about it! I didn't even know you were in trouble! If you had told me, asked me, of course I would have helped. You've done plenty of favours for me."

At some point during this speech, she wasn't sure when or how, she had accepted the flowers. She looked at them with bewilderment.

He took her arm, and they crossed the street together. "I didn't think they'd make you testify," he said. "I thought that giving your name was enough. I don't know what I thought. I was upset."

Clouds, grey and snow-filled, lowered over the sea, and down the street ahead of them ran a file of quail, late migrants from some backyard brush.

"I thought they'd get you to write something, maybe," he went on. "I just didn't want to get you involved."

"Then you shouldn't have given my name," she responded logically. "You could have asked somebody else."

"Somebody else?" he echoed. But who was there to help him but her? Mr. Redford, possibly. But Haack didn't want to jeopardize his chances there. And it certainly wasn't a matter for the Association. They were committed to lawfulness, at least publicly. Although one of the attractions of the monthly meetings was the quantity of beer served.

"I wanted it to be you," he said stupidly.

India, stopping in front of a fish peddler, preparing to buy, looked up quickly. "Robert," she began, "I don't want you to get the wrong idea."

Perhaps she had more to say: that he wasn't her type, that she was a few years older than he, or that the kind of work she was committed to, reforming work, not the work that paid her bills but the work that was close to her heart, wouldn't interest him, and that it was the most important thing in the world to her. Whatever, it had no chance to come out, for as she looked, and Robert Haack read the rest of the thought unsaid, in her eyes, his hand clutched at the piece of paper he carried in his pocket and had kept there since, as a boy of fifteen, he had met a poet.

He brought the paper out and unfolded it. "Here," he said to her, his action stopping her words, "this will tell you what I can't."

Puzzled, India took the paper and read.

Praise and Prayer

I have been well, I have been ill,
I have been rich and poor;
I have set my back against the wall
And fought it by the hour;

I have been false, I have been true;
And thoro' grief and mirth,
I have done all that man can do
To be a man of worth;

And now, when from an unknown shore,
I dare an unknown wave,
God, who has helped me heretofore,
O help me wi' the lave!

It was signed, "Robert Louis Stevenson."

"Where did you get this?" she asked, puzzled. The name of the writer was known to her. Indeed, he was known to many English readers since the publication of *Treasure Island*, *Dr. Jekyll and Mr. Hyde*, *Kidnapped*, and other stories and poems.

"He gave it to me," said Robert, "I met him a long time ago."

"You know him?" she asked, quite taken aback. "You've met him?" she repeated, as if unable to believe it.

Haack nodded twice. "I met him at home in California," he said, as if that should explain everything.

It would be hard to express just how surprised India was. She had known of the writer since the appearance of *Travels With a Donkey in the Cevennes*—her father, the major, had kept in touch with developments in literature through Old Country friends, and she had tended to think of Stevenson as her own discovery. And yet Robert Haack, a man she knew and liked yet whom she now suspected she had underestimated, had not only met him but had a holograph copy of one of his early poems. "Do you like poetry?" she asked. "Do you read it?"

"My mother was a schoolteacher," Robert answered. "She kept all her books on a shelf in the house. She used to read from them at night."

Which wasn't perhaps what India meant, exactly, but it was enough for the moment. She paid for three crabs from the fish peddler, forgetting to haggle, and put them in her basket. One of them twisted itself around the handle and Robert, trying to free its claw, had his hand nipped. He sucked at his fingers, then took his poem back.

"Why couldn't you trust me?" said India, resuming their former conversation. "How do you expect me to be your friend if you won't tell me the truth?"

Robert, sensing a victory, although not quite sure how it had come about, said, "I appreciated what you said in court. It was good of you."

"I know."

"You didn't have to."

"I know!"

They continued walking to the bottom of the street. A butcher's van and a baker's cart raced by in dangerous competition. Robert put his arm protectively in front of India as she was about to start across Store Street.

She turned to him. "Would you tell me about it sometime?" she asked hesitantly, almost shyly.

"About what?" he said.

"How you met him, the poet Stevenson."

Robert took a deep breath. "Of course I will. But you have to remember I was very young. There isn't much to tell."

Although there was, of course, more than he wanted to think of.

"Promise?"

He smiled at her as they drew near to the conglomeration of dwellings that had grown up and around the abandoned wharves where India was due to meet Sing Yuen.

"I promise," he said. "We'll find the right moment."

Perhaps the truth was that my mother was not without her own literary ambitions. Consider the diaries she kept. It could be that she, as a girl in Hong Kong, had once hoped to live a literary life, or at least move in those circles, but that circumstance (her father's deterioration and death) had prevented it. If so, then Robert Haack, who had brushed shoulders, at least, with a poet, might be seen as a window, a glimpse into a world she had thought she had lost forever. And how unexpected it was: that a man like Haack, with his frontier talents, should be a person whose mother had been a teacher, a man who carried a poem in his pocket for reference. Well, didn't people often hide who they were for fear of rejection? And what else could a sensitive man be expected to do in a town and a time like this?

So India reasoned. And had a lot to think about.

"It is the small things that interest a woman in a man," says Lam Fan sagely. "How he puts his hands in his pockets, how he wears his hat or uses his fork. These tell her more than his words do. Everything else she learns of him is seen through that perspective. Much is excused, much is forgiven if in these small things he is truly, originally himself."

"And Sing Yuen, Fan, what was it that he did that you liked?" I ask.

She stops to think as we come abreast of Hope Island, heading straight for the swell of Nahwitti Bar. The bar extends right across the western entrance of Goletas Channel, and on its southern part are the Tatnell Reefs. The waves aren't breaking there yet, and I think it will be safe to cross. We are keeping Hope Island at a distance of half a mile.

"There were many things," she says at last with a smile. "He dressed beautifully, he would do his shirts himself if the laundry didn't get them right, but his arms were short: he wore armbands to keep the sleeves up, and he always carried a toothbrush. He had the nicest teeth of any man I've known. He was proud of his strength, and he could run very fast. He liked to run barefoot, and he used to race me home when we had the farm."

She thinks for a moment. "Yes," she says, "the first time I saw him, saw him to notice him, I mean, he was running towards me barefoot in snow."

Sing Yuen: my stepmother's husband, who too soon went out of my life, who had come this late afternoon to meet my mother on the water side of Store Street, where men in permanent hibernation lived in shacks made of packing cases, closed off, with the humiliation of their lives, from the rest of the world by a few strips of old blankets. The wind fluttered the blankets like tattered flags, and let out pale fibres of dust.

India and Sing Yuen, trailed by Robert Haack, who had attached himself to them, entered one of these makeshift lodgings and found a group of men sitting on an ice-covered floor around a small pile of leaves, which one man was attempting to blow alight. Another man was being shaved by a companion, and another lay on straw, smoking a pipe. They nodded politely to Sing Yuen, but had eyes for the food in his hands. In a corner, a man wrapped in rags and newspapers tried to hide the rat he'd been skinning with his fingers. His limbs were swollen with dropsy.

India had been here before, but it was Robert Haack's first time, and he could not control his revulsion. How close he had come, he thought, living in the Chatham Street shack, to this. How little there was now, in fact, to keep up the difference. It was a fine line. And the question was— as he looked around remembering his troubles: the overwhelming debt, the thin string of income he counted on, plus Yong Sam's collectors, and the potential of the Association to do him harm—how long would he have, if disaster struck, before he crossed it?

Since the basis of starvation is no money, and even worse than no money is overwhelming debt. He saw for the hundredth time in memory the paper he had signed in the gambling house. He heard the judge in the courtroom pronounce his fine. He had no idea how he'd pay it. Not that any of this was news, but he was seeing the probable future in front of his eyes.

It was a tableau he bitterly feared, and excusing himself with a lie— some matter to do with Mr. Redford—he eased himself out of the room. And once outdoors stood immobilized with his head in his hands.

But since, in this world at least, it is up to every man to help himself, and since Robert Haack was desperate, casting about for any way out of the straits he foresaw for himself, in the shock of seeing men his own age bent double and toothless, a door of possibilities that he had firmly kept shut, now opened a crack.

It wasn't much. It was the tiniest shift of emphasis, but suddenly every experience he'd had that day began to add up.

The anonymous letter he'd had to write for Noah Shakespeare; his excuses to India; even the flowers he'd stolen from Mrs. Lush. Humiliations forced upon him one after the other. And what was the answer? How could he be free of this prison of poverty that was hindering his movements?

He wasn't positive, but he believed he might have glimpsed it through the window of the Tai June opium factory a few hours earlier.

Opium, Fan. And we should know about that.

We have crossed Nahwitti Bar without incident, emerging from the shelter of the east coast of Vancouver Island to feel the full thrust of the open Pacific Ocean on our bows. I am steering northwest, into Queen Charlotte Sound, for the long crossing to the Queen Charlotte Islands and our destination, Rose Harbour. Although I am wary of this stretch of sea, for in a storm the big ocean swells roll in through the gap between northern Vancouver Island and the Charlottes, strike the ocean shelf, and rise up in tremendous steep seas, fifty feet high. But I am glad to be free of coastal navigation, out in the clear, watching the weather, which is blowing in from the northwest, and riding the edge of the tidal stream, which flows north-northeastward into the sound.

"What next, Robert Lam?" asks Fan, with her hand on the red dinghy, which is tied to the boom. Several Leach's storm petrels are gliding and swooping, following our pointed stern.

Hearing her question but not bothering to reply, since she knows the answer, my eyes tracking the petrels, I say, "Brings back old times, Fan. We used to see these same birds in the South Pacific, but they were darker there, I think. See the forked tail?"

As I speak, the darkness of the birds that I remember becomes real and fills my eyes. There are pricks of light in this darkness, but they are not pleasant. Each is like a tiny electric shock. For minutes I am not sure of where I am, although I think I am still on my feet near the door of the wheelhouse. But my sense of balance is gone, and my stomach feels sick. Both these sensations feel strangely distant. And then the wings of the petrels brush my face. But how could that be?

"Fan? Fan? Help me!" It is no dream I am dreaming, for I can feel the thrum of the *Rose's* engine hum through my body, and I have the sense that, pilotless, we are turning in circles. The wings brush my cheeks again, and, blind and helpless, I am afraid the birds will go for my eyes.

"Fan? Fan?" As my vision slowly clears I see the solid fir planking of the *Rose* below my nose. I don't know where on the boat I am, for I cannot turn my head. "Fan?" I call again, but I am aware of how useless this is. I am alone on the ocean. No ghost can help me. And I am suddenly not a man in his prime but elderly, full of physical frailties and dreadfully afraid. What if I don't recover, or what if I don't recover in time? There are rocks and reefs, there is the ocean itself which forgives neither innocence nor accident, and we are not far enough from land to escape the risk of running aground. We could be minutes from help, or weeks.

The deck of the *Rose* is comforting, smooth as skin and warm from the cloud-filtered sunlight, and so, because I have no choice, I rest, feeling my body on the warm planking turn as cold as though I had fallen overboard. Stinging cold; an abrasive cold that only the cold sea brings. And then there is a voice, quiet at first, but soon loud enough to stir my blood and thaw the icicles in my veins. My ghost hasn't left me at all; she is doing what she can. She sings to me.

A tree top blown by heavy winds will bow its head,
but when the weight is gone the tree looks back to heaven.

The sun sets at night beneath the cavernous waves,
but by a secret path returns to its beginning.

Feeling returns to the tips of my fingers, pin pricks, which work their way up my arms until I can push my chest up. Then my legs come back, and I struggle to my feet. And so, dragging my heavy head along with me, numb on one side of my face, and badly bruised, I reach the wheelhouse and cut back the throttle. I look at the compass, but the needle is jumping unhelpfully. I tap it, I move everything away from it, but still it won't settle.

Time. How much time has this taken? How much time have we lost? I check the chronometer, but it appears to have stopped. I look at my watch, strapped to my wrist as always, but its face has been smashed in my fall. I glance out at the sky, but the sun's position is hidden by cloud.

"Fan?" I call softly. I hold my breath, listening. Somehow, in some way, I think irrelevantly, I have got to get back to the surface. Like those men my stepmother spoke of, the whalers who rode on the whales.

I open my mouth to breathe, and, as if the air has turned into poison, my world blacks out again.

Some years ago, when I first joined the pilotage, I went out with one of the senior pilots in answer to an emergency. A gill-netter had been seen circling furiously in the straits off Brotchie Ledge. The cause of this peculiar behaviour was not apparent, but it was clear that, if left to itself, the gill-netter would sink.

We had trouble catching her: the skipper had left the throttle wide open, and we went round and round after her, blowing whistles and ringing bells. Finally we were able to cut into the middle of the circle, and from this vantage point we could see the owner of the gill-netter slumped over in the wheelhouse. In ever-closing circles the gill-netter was approaching the breakwater where we feared it was bound to capsize. Before this could happen, however, the boat began to ship water, and, with her decks awash, we were able to jump aboard and rescue the mariner. He was not ill or dead, as we had feared. He had had, he told us, the deepest, sweetest sleep he had ever known.

Just so, when I awaken this time, with my back against the cold wheelhouse stove, I feel curiously refreshed. I remember everything, from the moment of Fan's question to now, with the spaces in between filled in with a series of pictures, like stills taken from a film. I remember being asleep or unconscious, although I have had no dreams. I remember the infinitely slow passing of time, a series of grey slides without horizon, through which I was travelling.

We are among islands. Strikingly high islands inhabited by seabirds. I see tufted puffins, Cassius and rhinoceros auklets, and pelagic cormorants in my first quick look. The *Rose* is piloting herself, caught in a heavy tide rip, which seems to be carrying us safely enough for the moment, but I can see the need for caution. There are reefs here, and a wind, which, though gentle now, can quickly blow up. And I know where I am, somewhere in the western Scott Islands, heading south, back the way I have come but off the outermost northwestern coast of Vancouver Island.

I do not need a calendar to tell me what I know. That there is no way I can continue north. My accident, or small stroke, as I suspect it was, is cause enough to turn back.

But there is more to it than that. It is time to be thinking of home.

My mother, India Thackery, and her employer, my stepmother's future husband, Sing Yuen, had a program. It included the solicitation and distribution of food and clothing in the slums of Chinatown. It contained concern for the fate of women held captive in the upper stories of Chinatown buildings and the establishment of a refuge for them. It was measured in meetings with other like-minded citizens. It was called "reform."

Putting aside the mistakes of the past, changing the order of things.

They moved through the underside of the commercial section of the city, the network of tenements, where real estate was leased and subleased until there was only the slightest connection to a landlord; where rooms, licensed to hold four people, contained fifteen to twenty, and where eight men might wait to eat the seven two-inch fish that Sing Yuen had been able to send to them.

In this land of Gold Mountain, to which so many had come, there were lessons to be learned. And Robert Haack, following in the tracks of his friends, fingering his poem, worrying, absorbed them.

But there is more than one kind of lesson.

Just as there were days when the winter wind blasted through the tunnel streets, and men brushed ice from their eyelids and the tatters of their clothing, so there were days when the sun struck haloes from the buildings, and India and Haack sat outside on chairs from the restaurant, reading. When Yong Sam's men took a holiday, and the Association meeting was three weeks away, and anything seemed possible. When the world was expanding, and the circling planets spoke not of repetition, but of endless mystery. When the boy from Carmel Valley in California, who had listened to poems and novels at his mother's knee, who had lived, except for those times, a life of utmost misery since his father, the goat farmer, had banished the boy and mother to a hut on his property and had only fed the child for what he would gain from his labour... when Robert Haack knew, beyond a shadow of a doubt, that the story of his life would end happily.

"It makes me think," interrupts my ghost, who has returned now that I'm heading south (as I believe she has always intended), "of Jim Post at the Savoy."

"Pardon, Fan?" I say, trying to pay attention, although I have a splitting headache and am plotting our course for Quatsino Sound and Coal Harbour, the old air-force base, where I hope to get medical attention. And from where the whales are still hunted. "I'm sorry but I don't understand."

"It was before your time, Robert Lam," she says. "He was a vaudeville comedian at the Savoy, like I said. He put his thumb to his nose like this—" and she demonstrates a rude hand gesture "—and blew very loudly through his lips."

"What?" I say, for it takes me a moment to get her drift. "Oh.... It's called a raspberry, Fan."

"Yes." She nods. "He was famous for it." And she keeps on nodding, as if what she's said is important.

One night, while Robert Haack lay sleeping in his room at the Metropolitan, and while a thin layer of snow shrouded the streets outside and blew in through the open window, there came a knock at his door. He awoke to that knocking with a pounding heart, for all his fears had awakened with him. It was just such a summons that he had long feared, whether it be from the men of the Association, who were at that time engaged in a boycott of Chinese businesses, and on whose charity he relied for the payment of his rent, or from Yong Sam, who had grown tired of waiting for payment of his debt. Haack cursed himself for a fool for neglecting to prepare for danger and rolled silently out of bed and onto the floor. He lay there listening to his own quick breathing until a voice from the hallway called out quietly, "Robert Haack, please wake up! It is important!"

The men he knew didn't announce themselves. Whether workingmen or Tong, he doubted there'd be any warning or any awakening either, except, perhaps, to take his last breath. Moreover, against all probability, the dog, Charlie, who kept a lookout beneath Haack's window and who had always proved faithful, had given no alarm. Haack thought for a moment, then stood up, pulled on his pants, and spoke through the door.

"Who is it? What do you want?"

"It is I," the voice said helpfully, "the herbalist, Lum Kee."

Robert eased open the door and smelled the aroma of herbs and grasses that clung like a signature to Lam Fan's uncle. Lum Kee stepped forward, smiling his apology and polishing the snow from his spectacles. "I am sorry to awaken you," he said, "but I need your help. My niece, Lam Fan, has disappeared. Her friend, Miss Thackery, and I are going to look for her, and we both hoped that you might come with us. We are very worried," he added unnecessarily, for Robert Haack, who knew the old man's reputation for steadiness and common sense, could read the concern on Lum Kee's face. There was no need to explain. With the shortage of Chinese women, women sometimes did vanish in Chinatown, although most of the trade was in children or in women who were already known as prostitutes.

"But everyone knows that she's your relative," said Haack, puzzled, as he put on the rest of his clothing. "I can't believe that anyone would dare to harm her."

Lum Kee simply shook his head, as if the world he had trusted had come to an end.

They went into the corridor together. "There is one more thing," the herbalist said reluctantly. "India tells me my niece was once addicted to opium. It could be that she has slipped into her former ways."

Opium. The abandoned baker's daughter's original friend. A disease of grief and loss, of rootlessness, in my opinion, which offers, as does all addiction, a return to the mother's breast.

But hadn't she given it up? thought Haack. Hadn't her life, according to India, changed for the better?

He was puzzled. Could India's sister have been so unhappy and no one have known it? Why had nothing been said? Weren't they all family? Wouldn't she have asked for help, if not from her sister, then from her uncle, Lum Kee, whom she deeply admired?

As Mrs. Lush, the landlady, opened her door to hiss at them to be quiet, Robert Haack added it up. It was like hunger and thirst; they didn't exist until there was emptiness, or until they were brought to one's notice. Say someone laid out a banquet in front of you, even if you had eaten two hours earlier, might you not be tempted to eat anyway? Especially if you were often alone, and your best friend, your sister, had other concerns? Especially if that sister worked at the Tai June opium factory and took home on her clothing, every night, its odours? Especially if you were reminded of opium by day and by night?

Robert Haack sighed. He found it difficult to listen to Mrs. Lush's words. "Don't worry, Lucy," he said automatically to her rumble, "we'll be real quiet."

"You know the rules, Mr. Haack. It's after ten o'clock." She turned her lace nightcap, mounted above a face that was pale and contoured like a rough field in uncertain light, towards Haack's companion.

"Ah, Mr. Lum!" she remarked. "I take it there is an emergency."

"Yes," said the herbalist, politely. "I am sorry to disturb you."

"Mr. Lum needs help with a patient, Lucy," said Robert in his best conciliatory manner. "He wouldn't have fetched me if it were not necessary."

"Well, all right, then," said the landlady, withdrawing from the hallway, "but don't think you can make a habit of it."

"No, ma'am."

"No!"

One look at India's face as she waited outside with the lantern told Robert that she had reached the same conclusions as himself. She would not meet his eyes and kept glancing into the gloomy distance. "We have to find her," she said. "We have to bring her back before anything happens!"

There was no answer to that, and so the three of them, each occupied with troubling thoughts, followed the chain of brick and wood that lined the street, their footsteps printing the snow, and crossed Cormorant Street and stepped into the labyrinth of tenements that housed the opium dens of the city.

Shed roofs and gables overlapped each other. The white-bread texture of snow lay softly against cold chimneys. In a doorway, his head resting on his chest, stood a poorly dressed old man. His eyes glazed in the lantern light, oblivious.

"Here is such an example," said Lum Kee as if thinking aloud. "So many are like this man. He is half awake, at most. He feels nothing." The three would-be rescuers gazed pityingly at the old man's sunken chest and the dried, almost mummified texture of his skin.

"But suppose," Fan's uncle continued, still as if to himself, "he goes without his opium, what then? He has half a fish to eat at most, and he quarrels over it with his friends. He has no wood to light a fire to cook it."

"You don't mean you think it's all right," said India, "you don't mean you don't see its harm?"

Lum Kee looked at her as if at last taking her in. "Suppose," he said, "a man like this takes too much opium. What happens then? He sleeps and sleeps and dreams and dreams. But suppose a man gets drunk with liquor? He shouts, he sings, he beats his wife and gets put in jail."

India looked at Haack and Haack at India. Haack cleared his throat.

"But that's not what we're talking about."

"It is white people, too," said Lum Kee, "not just Chinese. Sometimes they give their clothes away if they have no money. It is always the poor who suffer."

India touched Lum Kee's arm. "It's my fault, isn't it, Kee," she said. "It is because of me and the factory. Fan wouldn't have thought of it otherwise."

The herbalist shrugged and took off his spectacles to clear them of snow. "Nothing is certain," he said. "We have not yet found her. Anyway," he went on as India was about to interrupt with further protestations of guilt, "nothing like this is because of one person. It comes from many things. No, it is not your fault."

"Why now, when she seems so happy?"

He shrugged again. "I think she is lonely sometimes. Opium is something to count on."

We are setting a course to clear Kains Island, then into Quatsino Sound for Coal Harbour. My stepmother's ghost stands close beside me at the wheel, her silks whipping in the wind. I have left the window open, letting in the chill, for I am fearful of the aftereffects of my stroke, concerned that I might fall asleep.

"Why did you start to smoke opium again, Fan?" I ask. "It couldn't just have been because of where my mother worked. If it had begun to bother you, you could have told her. I'm sure together you could have solved the problem.

"No," I go on, interested in a theory I am building, "I am sure it was because of your childhood. It left its mark upon you, and you never recovered. Everyone knows that opium is used as relief from pain. You were suffering, perhaps not physically, but mentally, and that's why you smoked."

She looks at me wryly. "Is that what happened to you, Robert Lam? Somebody was mean to you as a child, and you never grew up?"

"Fan!" I am hurt beyond all reason. "There's no need for that. I am trying to understand what happened."

She looks at me, clear-eyed. "I liked to smoke my pipe. It was calm. It was peaceful. I could forget about my troubles. I only stopped to please my sister, not to please myself."

"Ah," I say, nodding wisely. "So the moment you felt she was less interested, less committed to you, that she was getting involved with a man—Robert Haack—you strayed."

"Not strayed, Robert Lam," she says stubbornly, "I told you, I liked to smoke. It was my habit, and it never hurt me. Besides," she says, before I can marshal an argument, "nothing happened that time. That was not when I started up again, that came later. This was the time I met Sing Yuen."

"Sing Yuen?"

"Yes," she says proudly, "he was the one who came to rescue me. He was the one who ran through snow with no shoes on."

What makes a man look up from his work in his restaurant as he supervises preparations for the Festival of the Dead, as tables are loaded with dressed pigs and goats, pastries, fish, and sweetmeats, and as the remains of one hundred and sixty Chinese, in clay jars, are made ready for shipment to Hong Kong? Perhaps he expected to see the arrival of flowers, or the instrument cart with its drums, bells, and bows, its roof of carved figures, human and animal. What Sing Yuen did see when he glanced up, however, alerted by a prickling of the hairs of his neck, was a solitary female figure making its way from Fisgard Street into an alleyway which led as he knew well, nowhere but to the brothels and opium dens of the inner labyrinth of Chinatown.

Sing Yuen: a man who could make decisions, who felt his heart turn over with dread as he recognized Lam Fan; who ran after her, barefoot as he was, and, taking stock of her symptoms, not trying to change her mind, walked with her, walking, walking, walking for hours until the hunger for opium was pushed out of Lam Fan by exhaustion.

But what happened to the others, who had no way of knowing of these events?

For Lum Kee had led the others to a particular door, and had knocked on it and walked in. Inside, one Chinese and three white men shared a pipe while sitting around a table. A fourth white man was rolling a cigarette, and two other Chinese were dreaming on couches. The room was clean and well-kept.

"What do you want?" asked the Chinese who was overseeing the pipe. He looked old beyond counting, his body a mere scaffolding of bones.

"We are looking for someone," replied India, glancing about her.

"There is no one here," the man said, and he turned his back to them. Lum Kee dropped his eyes at this rudeness, and Robert Haack coughed into his handkerchief nervously.

The white man who had been rolling a cigarette picked up his hat from a chair beside him, put it on, and pulled the brim low to hide his face. He edged to the door, trying to squeeze past India, who was blocking his way.

"I am so sorry you should have found me here," he said to her politely. His companions, ministered to by the divan keeper, continued to smoke.

"I am sorry, too," said India, making room for him to go and turning to leave herself. There was no point in staying where they were not wanted, and where clearly Lam Fan wasn't present. The air was heavy, the room gloomy, and she wanted to go outside. Lum Kee had preceded her.

But the man who wanted to leave was prevented by Robert Haack.

"Wait a minute," said Robert, looking him over, "don't I know you?" He reached out and tipped the hat up. A look of horror crossed his face, and he blurted out the man's name— "Henry McMullen! What are you doing here?"

"I could ask you that," McMullen replied sullenly, repositioning his hat and losing his air of apology. "I could ask you what you're doing here."

They glared at each other, each wishing he was somewhere else. For they both had similar thoughts to contend with.

Such as Noah Shakespeare reading out the names of firms and individuals who had had dealings with Chinese; Noah, who had, at the last workingmen's meeting, produced a queue, which, he had said, he had gone to great pains to obtain, and which he intended (he said, drawing laughter) to keep as an heirloom.

"No yellow slave shall eat our children's bread," and "Cut out the Chinese cancer," they had shouted. Not to mention, "Boycott the Chinese employers," and, "They that are not with us are against us."

"You were on that committee!" cried McMullen, breaking the silence. For he had recalled a recent report in favour of the Association starting its own laundries to break the Chinese monopoly on that business. "You're Robert Haack!" Both men had turned pale.

"I guess we both know what we're talking about," said Robert.

For, of course, they both were workingmen.

It was then, know it or not, outside in the cold and damp night air in which all the smells of poverty had combined—cooking, smoke, fatigued bodies—that Haack's future crystallized. Yet Henry McMullen had slunk away, and it appeared that Haack had been lucky, since McMullen had his own good reasons for keeping quiet about the encounter. He was the one who had been found smoking opium, he was the one with most to lose if the news got out. And there was no hope of explaining it away.

And, on the other hand, what could McMullen say about Robert Haack? That Haack had arrived there after him in the company of a white woman and a Chinaman? That he had stood at the doorway and listened? No, it wouldn't do. And besides, there were other white witnesses to support Haack.

But, despite this. something had changed in the balance of Haack's life. Two paths, his and McMullen's, had met to make one wide road, and there was no going back.

The divan keeper skidded up through the snow behind the would-be rescuers as they left. He hoped, he said to Lum Kee, whom he knew, that they would forgive his poor manners. They could see that his difficulty had been with his other guests, he hadn't wanted to speak in front of them. He thought he knew for whom they searched: he thought it was Lum Kee's niece, who had, indeed, entered the divan some hours earlier, but had left almost at once in the company of Lum Kee's friend, the restaurateur, Sing Yuen. No doubt if they went to the restaurant they would find her safely with him.

Smiles and bows all around, even some shaking of hands: for all felt they had come out rather well from the outing with whatever it was that most concerned them. India, that her failure to consider her sister's weakness when she had agreed to work at the Tai June factory had not resulted in disaster; Lum Kee, that his niece was safe with his friend; and Robert Haack, that he had passed through a nightmare unscathed.

There were twenty brothels in the city as a whole. Seven of them were at the east end of Fisgard Street at Blanchard Street, where city boundaries lost meaning in the general dissolution of town to country, and where muddy fields and rickety dwellings dispensed with the pretension to civilization.

But at the other end of Fisgard Street, it was a different matter. Here, deep in the underpinnings of Chinatown, out of sight of the merchant and upper classes, the trade in girls was part of the fabric. Over one hundred girls, young children, most of them, and none older than twenty, who had been sold in China and brought to the land of Gold Mountain as property, spent their lives in the star houses or in slatted crates in the alleyways, none larger than twelve by fourteen feet, with five or six other children. There was a pallet, a wash basin, a mirror, and a couple of chairs for furnishings. Here the girls lived beneath the clean bright sky of the New World as the men took their turns and shivered and coughed and starved as they had in China. And when, after seven or eight years of service, they were worn out and were turned out into the streets, most died, within six months. Or committed suicide by swallowing matches or acid or opium.

Yet, despite the commonplaceness of it, there were men in the midst of their own desperation, the numbing effect of suffering, thousands of miles from their families in China, who, in the crowded rooms of the tenements, listened to the cries of these children with pity and sent word to the reformer, Sing Yuen, telling of some particular girl's situation. Although there was no law to protect those who interfered, and more than once the children were returned by the law to their owners.

In this work, which required a delicate touch, Sing Yuen was glad to have India's help: together they turned several of the rooms in the Fisgard

Street house in which Lam Fan and India lived into a shelter for young runaway women. And with this work, as well, Robert Haack gave his assistance. For where Robert Haack went, obstacles disappeared: customers melted like snow in spring from out of the brothels, and arguments against removing the children were stilled. For the question was (and the problem occupied many Chinatown tongues for some time), whose side was he on, and who would one offend by offending him? It was this uncertainty that helped India's work go well, and that kept (though he'd never have guessed it) Yong Sam's men from pressing Haack's debt: there were motives, contacts, forces at work beyond understanding, and in this complex net it was wise (it was thought) to tread with much caution.

Robert Haack: a man who liked to share himself, waiting for my mother at the Tai June factory or having a coffee in Sing Yuen's restaurant, acting as escort, friend, companion, supporting the reformer's daughter in her vocation, talking about books, or not so much talking as listening, and offering with his obvious flaws (his vanity, his occasional drinking) material for shaping. For so it must have been that India saw in Haack a man to her liking.

And of course there was chemistry, and of course there was the fact that he needed her, for what would become of him on his own?

"How much chemistry, Fan?" I ask my stepmother.

She looks up from the stove where I've put the kettle on to boil, askance.

"What kind of a question is that, Robert Lam?"

It won't be long now until we pass Kains Island and proceed up Quatsino Sound. "It is my question, Fan, I'm India's son, I have a right to know."

"To know things that should be private?"

"Well, was he my father or wasn't he? They did get married eventually."

"You know he wasn't," she snaps. "You are only asking to be difficult."

"I bear his name, Fan, that must mean something."

She scrapes her nails absently down the window glass, for she has turned away from the stove to look where we're going.

"Please don't, Fan!"

"I was wiping away the steam!"

"You were not!"

"I was!"

119

There is a moment's silence while we both try to recover our dignity.

I take a deep breath. "It is a question I think is important, Fan. I'm not asking out of curiosity, believe me. The whole thing puzzles me. There's something missing from what you've been telling me. The part of the equation that would put them together, make them fit properly."

"They enjoyed each other's company."

"Fan," I say warningly.

"They were near in age; they were not like others in the city. Who else lived in two worlds, white and Chinese, like they did?"

"How much, Fan?" I ask again.

She sighs deeply, steaming up the glass, then wipes a circle clear with her finger. "Enough," she says.

"Enough?"

"For me to worry about her."

He talked to her. He told her things about himself he hadn't thought of since he was a boy. Colours, for example: the dead grey-green of the river in the Carmel Valley in winter, or the liquid blue of the lupins in spring; the first snow he had seen, which he had mistaken for salt on the grass; the rattlesnake that had killed his pony, and how he was beaten for it by the man his mother told him was his father, although he had never believed it, it was so unthinkable; the stars at night as he sat out with the goats, guarding them from coyotes; that is, who he believed he was, what he thought he'd become.

Chemistry: which removes the brakes of logic and ignores the warning signs. Which does not ask, But what about after, what did you make of what you had to start with?

Chemistry: which puts strontium 90 in cow's milk, which makes the atom bomb. For I know what its power is, I know what it's like when it goes off.

Robert Haack: continuing, despite the warnings he had given himself, to follow my mother around, advancing deeper and deeper for longer sojourns into dangerous territory, who knew that Yong Sam's men would never give up, and that the Association, once crossed, could ruin his life. Yet all might still have been well for him, going about on this charitable business, if it hadn't been for coincidence, which could put a man not once but twice where he wasn't wanted. And that man turned out to be Henry McMullen, workingman.

Haack stood behind India as she opened the door to star house number sixty-one at the top of a flight of stairs. It was as cold inside as out, and Robert blew on his hands and peered down the corridor, which was lit at its end by a droppings-encrusted skylight. This mottled radiance revealed a length of closed doors.

"Did he say which one?" asked India. Robert, who had begun rattling doorknobs, shook his head.

India touched his arm. "Be quiet a minute, listen." A tuneless voice rose and fell somewhere nearby. It was halfway between crying and singing. In mid-hallway a door opened a crack, and there appeared the face of an elderly man. He wore a black silk cap, and they could see his rag-wrapped shoes.

"Are you Ah Luie?" asked India. "Did you send Sing Yuen a note?" The old man bowed but said nothing. A shower of sleet struck the roof, making Robert Haack jump. The outside door slammed shut, pushing in cold air up to their knees.

"It's all right," said India. "We come from Sing Yuen. This is my friend, Mr. Haack. He is here to help."

"I have seen him before," said Ah Luie. Robert blushed and twisted a few more doorknobs.

"Could you show us where she is?" India asked. "Then we wouldn't have to disturb you further."

"It does not bother me," he said. "I do not like to see the child in here, that is why I sent the letter. My children are in China. I have a boy and girl." His face twitched, and he rubbed at the circles beneath his eyes. "I will go home soon, in five years maybe."

Answering India's unspoken question he elaborated, "I make dresses for ladies." He gestured at the series of closed doors. "Nobody responds to knock before lunchtime. They must sleep sometime. But the child's owner goes out in the mornings. Her name is Tai Ho. She is a very wicked woman."

He led them a few doors down and stood and waited while India rapped. There was a scurrying sound, back and forth, then it stopped. India opened the door. Inside the room, below a window, a child sat on the floor. She was tied to a table leg. An empty rice bowl was set a few feet from her. She looked to be about twelve years of age. Robert went over and began untying the rope that held her.

"You like me?" the girl asked him, and tried to stroke his hand.

"Tai Ho beats her," Ah Luie said from the doorway. "I hear her at night. Tai Ho beats her three or four times a day." On the girl's wrist, a mass of bone showed a badly healed break.

"What is your name?" asked India, who had led the child to sit on a cot, which, besides a stove and a chair, composed the room's furniture.

"My name is Gook Lang," she said. "Ah Luie is correct. Tai Ho beats me with that." She indicated a broken broomstick, which stood in a corner. She smiled almost proudly.

"You don't have to stay here," said India. "Would you like to come and live with me?"

"Do you have much money?" Gook Lang asked. "Tai Ho paid three hundred dollars for me."

"I'm not going to buy you, Lang."

The child pouted. "I am worth much money."

They heard the sound of Ah Luie's door softly closing and turned to find that he had gone. "I think that means we'd better get out of here, India," said Robert. He went into the hallway and tapped at Ah Luie's door. The old man whispered through it. "Tai Ho is a very bad woman. She will come back soon."

As if summoned, there was a clatter on the steps, and a woman, angered at once by the sight of the open door of her room, ran in spilling water from the bucket she carried.

"What are you doing in my house!" she screamed. India drew the child close.

"I am taking this girl with me."

"She is mine. She belongs to me." Suddenly, Tai Ho, as if struck by a thought, changed tack. She arranged her mouth into a smile and began to inch towards India and the child on the cot. "I am a good woman," she said. "I look after her for nothing." She picked a blanket up from the floor and held it out towards the girl. "She is a sick girl. She is always cold. I take good care of her."

"How did she break her wrist? How did she get those bruises?"

"She is a clumsy girl. She all the time falls down." Suddenly Tai Ho darted forward and thrust her hand beneath the cot's mattress. And fumbled there fruitlessly.

"My friend, Mr. Haack, has your knife," said India coldly, rising and manoeuvring the child ahead of her.

There was another noise in the hallway as one of the locked doors Haack had tried opened. Robert went out to investigate.

"Excuse me, but you'll have to let me by," said the man who had emerged, stopped short at the sight of them, then pulled his hat over his eyes. Black stubble broke up the planes of his face so that he was at first difficult, in the grey and spotty light, to recognize.

Robert Haack put up his hands to stop the man. "You're not in too much of a hurry to give us your name, are you?" he asked imperiously. As they looked at each other at close quarters, there was a dual intake of breath.

"You!" said both.

"What are you doing?" asked Henry McMullen in genuine astonishment. "Are you having me followed?"

"Mr. Haack is doing his job," intervened India, to whom the appearance of Henry McMullen was a reminder of a night she would rather forget. "He has every right to be here, as I'm sure you have not."

"Is that so?" said McMullen, who looked from India, holding Gook Lang's hand, to Tai Ho and back to Robert Haack.

"There's no need," said Robert to India. "I'll take care of it."

But India was not to be stopped.

"This is the second time, Mr. McMullen, that you've been caught out in circumstances that hardly do you credit. The second time you've been found, I say; not the second time you've been where you shouldn't."

"India, please," said Robert desperately, but to no avail, for she was swept away by that unfortunate zealousness to which the reforming mind is prey.

"And by what right are you here, if I may ask," said Henry McMullen.

"It's my job to be here," said India. "I was asked to be here. I work for Mr. Sing."

"Ah," said Henry McMullen with a lift of his eyebrows. He caught Ah Luie's eye peering through an inch of open door. "Then it's Chinese business that brings you."

"Yes," said India, ignoring Robert Haack's signals to be quiet, "both Mr. Haack and I are here at Mr. Sing's request."

"Mr. Haack, too?" asked McMullen. "You don't mean to tell me that he works for Mr. Sing as well?"

"Of course," said the reformer's daughter. "We are here by rights; we are in his employ."

What made it worse, as Robert Haack knew, was that India was trying to protect him, lift him out of the context that men like Henry McMullen represented. It was more than enough, however, to demolish the fragile edifice that supported Robert Haack's life.

"Well," said Henry McMullen, looking very self-satisfied, "I guess you're right, ma'am. People like me should stay away and leave it all to people like you and Mr. Haack here, who know the Chinese mind so well. No, I couldn't say I was as close to them as all that."

Too late sensing that she had made a mistake, India took heed of Haack, who had gone stiff and quiet.

"Robert?" she asked.

"Get out of the way, India," he told her, gently moving her aside. "McMullen here is annoyed at losing money. He can see we're going to stop this child from earning his keep."

McMullen's skin, beneath the stumpage of whiskers, paled.

"You get going with the girl. I'll be right behind you," said Robert.

India obeyed. And although she couldn't grasp what it was about—how could she have known?—she felt that she had stepped through a door and found, instead of dry land, a vast expanse of waters, for which she had no experience, no compass. And in that expanse, measureless between horizons, stood the stranger she had known as Robert Haack.

Gook Lang blinked in the deluge of light outdoors. There were two thuds, one after the other, inside, then Robert Haack came running down the steps behind them. His masquerade was at an end, and on his face was a mixture of relief and panic.

He waved at them. "I've got to be going," was all he said as he left them.

"But Robert!" cried India, in need of an explanation. But there was none forthcoming. Haack had vanished from sight.

Although in two days' time the whole town knew what had happened. For Robert Haack's name, printed in red and posted on every notice board in existence, was put on the Association's blacklist.

CHAPTER SIX

"As I listened to the why and the wherefore of procedure, the line slackened, there was another flurry of flashing foam on the surface as the winch wound up the slack, and the engines of the boat turned free again. Down the whale went, and when it showed it was accompanied by another which seemed to snuggle against it for an instant or two as they sped on ahead together.

Only slightly smaller, it was the mate which had been feeding with the harpooned "fish" earlier in the morning. The sight thrilled me no end as the line was rapidly running out again, with the two sulphurs, side by side, headed for the wide expanses of the Pacific.

It really looked for the moment as if the female had created an impelling desire in its harpooned mate to break away."

The Victoria British Colonist

"What did he say?" asks Fan.

"I told you," I answer.

"What did he say, Robert Lam? I want to know."

I am taking the *Rose* through Quatsino Narrows. It is like being at the bottom of a long narrow well. The sides are sheer, and the rushing waters, the product of the tide waters of Holberg Inlet and Rupert Inlet, run black and fast. There is no sound other than the gush of ocean through this bottleneck and the *Rose*'s engine, of course. I am gazing straight ahead, concentrating.

"Come on, Robert Lam," she implores me, putting her hand on my arm.

"Careful, Fan," I say. "If you jerk the wheel we could be in trouble. I'm taking a chance as it is going through here on the tide. It's a fast stream, maybe as much as seven knots."

She takes her hand away and says nothing, but her face keeps asking the question.

"I couldn't wait to get out of there, Fan, to tell you the truth," I say to her. "Not even another hour. If you'd seen what I'd seen...." I make a face to illustrate my disgust. "The smell of it! Boiling blubber and digesting bones!" The memory—or more than a memory, for if I sniff, I can still catch the odour of cooking whale in the air—almost makes me retch.

"And the doctor?" she persists.

"If you must know," I answer as we leave the narrows and prepare to negotiate the islands in Quatsino Sound, "he said there was nothing wrong with me."

"Oh!" she says. "Then what does he think happened to you back there? It was very dangerous, and you were seriously ill, whatever it was."

"I agree. I don't know what he thought, Fan. He didn't want to speculate. He did his tests and said it wasn't a stroke and asked me if I was under any strain.

"I told him no, not more than I was used to in my work, and that I was on holiday. He shrugged and gave me some pills, which neither of us expected would do any good."

I fish for these now in my pocket, tear open the small envelope in which they are sealed, and hurl them out the open window of the pilot-house. "He was dead drunk, Fan, as a matter of fact. I don't think he liked being what he was, a company doctor in a whaling town. I gathered he had seen a better life. He spent last night sitting on the dock. He didn't move for hours, and when I walked down from the hotel where I'd gone for dinner to ask him if he was all right, he pointed west with his thumb. 'Japan,' he said. 'It's our nearest neighbour, and look what we've done to it. They deserved to lose the war, all right, but not like that. Who wants to bring children into a world that's capable of infinite murder?'"

"I suppose he meant the atom bomb," Fan says.

"I suppose," I agree.

We have met up with a tender called the *Western Express*. She has a whale, which has been pumped full of air, in tow, and has been waiting for us to clear the narrows. She is on her way to the processing plant at Coal Harbour.

We wave at each other as we pass. It seems to take hours to run clear of the carcass, a finback, I think, from its length and smooth black top. Its belly, which I catch a glimpse of as the whale rolls with our wake, is pleated and white.

Fan and I are silent for a considerable length of time. Although I am not feeling any better, I am not feeling any worse. From time to time my hands and arms tingle with pin pricks, but I feel in no great danger of blacking out. Perhaps the doctor was right, perhaps strain is at fault. I admit there is some wear in travelling with a ghost.

We pass Hecate Cove, then the low wooded shores of Drake Island. At East Point, Fan comes out of her reverie to say, "There was an Indian village here once. Can't you feel it?"

"No," I say, "I don't feel anything." But I peer around, as she wishes me to. There is forest dark as a cave and a few moss-encrusted totems. Shafts of sunlight filter through and light up the softened angles of the wooden emblems: ravens, thunderbirds, bears, eagles. It is hard to make them out at this distance.

I know, from having visited similar sites on other parts of the island, that the hollowed-out backs of some of these poles will be filled with bones.

"What's so special about a graveyard, Fan?" I ask. And shiver as, at my words, a gust of wind makes the *Rose* heel over. I push the throttle forward a notch to speed us by.

But not before I remember what I've been trying to forget: the whale I had seen on the slipway at Coal Harbour, the men wearing spiked boots and carrying knives shaped like hockey sticks swarming all over her. They were flensers, cutting the fat from the body and peeling it off.

It was a cow, I was assured by the doctor, who had taken me there to look. This particular whale, a humpback, had grown a leg on one side instead of a fin.

"You see them like that sometimes," the doctor had said. "They are more like us than we care to think."

I didn't want to think. I wanted to head on down the coast and resume my story. I wanted to live. And let live.

"Too bad about that doctor," Fan says.

"Yes," I say, "but it's none of our business."

"I meant that he couldn't help you."

"I know what you meant, Fan," I say closing the subject.

"I meant," she tells me anyway, "that we don't seem to do too well on land."

Land. Mother Earth. Terra firma. Mother.

My mother in shock on learning Robert Haack's true position in the city. That is, as traitor, informer, carrier of tales for the Association, and now blacklisted by them. An announcement to that effect had been published in the *British Colonist* as well as posted throughout the town. No one could have missed it. It was enough to cast doubt on all relationships. It was enough to crucify love.

My mother, going about her business, but with head down, thinking. How could he have done it? How had he taken her in? And weighing it up: on this side treachery, on the other all the help he had given, what he had said, how he had *been.*

Could they have helped him, she wondered. Had they ignored the symptoms? Had it been her fault?

Back and forth the questions went, repeating themselves, until she was sick of them. If only she could talk to him, find out the truth; for she was in no doubt that there was more to it than she knew.

But where was Haack to be found? He was not in the Metropolitan, for Mrs. Lush, when she'd learned he could not pay his rent (the Association's subscription having suddenly been cut off), had thrown him out. He was not in the bars, for Sing Yuen, on India's behalf, had looked through all of them, although it was unlikely, she'd had to admit, that Haack would show his face in public: for who would drink with him, let alone speak to him? Not the workingmen nor any of their friends, not the Chinese who now knew he'd been a workingman, nor any but a few gentle souls who wondered why a man couldn't do what he liked, especially here, in the New World, but who had families to think of, businesses to run. In short, who wouldn't have cut him dead, but who would certainly avoid him.

"And did it take money to set up shop?" he asked ruminatively. "Why, no! A man's word was his bond. You could trust a man back then."

"Sure you could," Robert agreed as Jimmy caught his eye. He was holding out his coffee cup for a refill. Charlie, supine on the floorboards, lifted his head to sniff at Jimmy's trousers.

"What's put an end to it," Jimmy Carroll said, hooking his thumbs into braces that tracked the contours of his stomach, "is the law. It interferes with a man's rights. What's it matter how a man gets his money, so long as he gets it, doesn't harm anybody, and looks after himself?"

"All the law has done," Jimmy concluded, not without bitterness, "is to hang some damn fine men."

At this Robert wiped his mouth reflectively with his napkin. "I believe you have had some experience of the wrong side of the law yourself, Mr. Carroll," he said.

"Why, yes, sir," said Smiling Jimmy unabashedly. "It's nothing I'm ashamed of, except that it's made me grow old. You miss out on life, locked up in jail. It's not good for a man's health, or his soul. I'd die before I'd allow myself to be locked up again, Mr. Haack. But you'd be knowing what that's like yourself, or so I've been told." He winked.

Robert, about to resume his breakfast, paused and held up his knife for emphasis. "Whoever told you that's a two-faced liar," he said strongly. "I'm not saying I've never been in trouble," he continued for the sake of honesty, "but I was no more than a boy back then and I had nothing to do with the wrongdoing. Even the judge said so."

"Is that a fact, Mr. Haack?" said Jimmy Carroll, as though he could, if he would, say more.

"That's so," said Robert firmly, closing the topic.

Both men examined the tablecloth in front of them.

"Well," said Jimmy, "I'd better get to the point. You're a good man, Robert—if I may call you that. I respect a man who stands up for himself. You're a hard worker, I'm told, and smart, but I know you've had bad luck. Let's call it an accident. From the sound of things it wasn't your fault, but that's your business and I won't go into it. In any case it seems to me you could do with some work, am I right?"

Despite his resolve (so far kept) to keep his distance, Robert looked up with dawning hope.

"A job?"

Where was Robert Haack? And why would he hide from his friends who wanted to help him? Who only wanted him to explain? Friends like India and Sing Yuen, kind men like Lum Kee, sceptical but good-hearted acquaintances like my stepmother, Lam Fan, who were prepared to be reasonable but who had hurt feelings?

A man who thinks that he is alone is alone. It does not matter who his friends are if he cannot believe in them. He is shunned by his former companions, hunted in earnest by those he owes money to. The world turns within its shroud of cloud. The sun, the moon, and stars have lost their meaning. The futility of his life takes hold of him, and even his dog grows worried and licks at his face to enliven him.

Robert Haack, who had made a nest for himself in the rubble of the Johnson Street ravine, huddled around a slipstream of smoke, ignorant of the manner in which he was discussed, of those who longed to see him, feeling only his failure, regretting what he had done, having no way to make amends. Suffering.

He did not move except to gather fuel or make tea or scrounge a few scraps from the rear of restaurant kitchens for his dog. He grew thin. Chilblains blistered his hands and feet; rain, snow, sleet, and hail fell on his hat brim and rolled down his face. He sneezed. He coughed. His boots reposed in mud. In short, just as he had foreseen, he had crossed the line of chance into the packing-case-house life. Although he did not even have a packing case with which to house himself, for it was too much effort to look.

Poor Robert Haack. Who had come to the end of his rope; and who wound it around his neck himself. Who could not stop himself from thinking about what he should have done. Who did not know that even the worst of woundings is temporary, that the world forgets us long before we acquit ourselves; that nothing lasts, not even disgrace: it is only injured pride.

But hurt pride is self-increasing. It infects the core of being. We worry at it like a dog with a flea, until in self-absorption we consume ourselves, and what is left is only what we cannot stomach: it is the cannibalism of self-pity.

("Ho, ho, ho!" says Fan as we clear Kains Island and turn south to pass Restless Bight and so leave the southern boundary of Quatsino

Sound. "What is this? Has something touched a nerve? Does Robert Lam feel sorry for himself?"

"Shut up, Fan," I say to her rudely.)

Robert Louis Haack, down on his luck, although one day he would be my mother's husband and give his name to me, with no one to help him; with Yong Sam wanting his money back; with only the dog for company. Who did what his mother warned him not to, which was to talk to a stranger when he should have resisted. For the man who bought him breakfast was Jimmy Carroll. Smiling Jimmy Carroll, as he was called, a well-known smuggler.

"I think we should talk about dogs," says my stepmother unexpectedly. I have set my sights on Cape Cook, the cape of storms on the tip of the Brooks Peninsula, whose mountains rise like a black wall before us. I am watching the sky for the cap on the cape, a thickening cloud belt that could herald treacherous weather. For when the cap is present, strong winds are on their way from the west-northwest. And there is no place to shelter.

"For Pete's sake, Fan," I say, "get on with it. Robert Haack is at a turning point, and you want to talk about dogs."

"It is not any dog," she says. "It is a particular dog."

"What dog, Fan?" I ask patiently, but with a sigh.

"The dog Charlie," she answers. "Robert Haack's dog. The one who has stayed with him all along. The loyal dog who does his best to keep Robert Haack from trouble."

"Oh, *that* dog, Fan," I say sarcastically. "Dog in the manger, in the blanket, hair of the dog, dog's body, dog's collar. That dog!"

"You never had a dog, did you, Robert Lam?" she asks accusingly.

"You wouldn't let me have one when I was a boy! You wouldn't have one on the farm! You said it would chase the cows! And how could I have taken a dog to sea?" I don't know why I'm so defensive about it; it seems that she has rattled me.

"Some are good dogs," she says noncommittally, "and others are bad dogs. It all depends."

"Go to the dogs, Fan, let the dog have his day, love me, love my dog!"

We look at each other, both of us on the verge of anger. But suddenly it all seems ridiculous and we turn away from each other to compose ourselves. We are passing the oddly manicured field called Lawn Point.

"Robert Haack had a dog," Fan says persistently, trying to sum up without starting another argument. "He was called Charlie. He was a good dog sometimes, and sometimes bad, like Robert Haack himself."

And so Robert Haack, accompanied by his dog, Charlie, sat down to a meal of pancakes and pork hash and eggs with Smiling Jimmy Carroll. Who had worked on the Pacific boats as long as anyone could remember and who had captained the *Idaho*, which had been seized with a cargo of opium some five years previously. Forty-four thousand dollars' worth of the drug, on its way from Victoria to Portland, Oregon, detoured via the captain's cannery on Prince of Wales Island, labelled as furs; and Jimmy would have gotten away with it, too, if it hadn't been for a disgruntled seaman named Hansen who had lost his job and who betrayed him. All this was common knowledge, as was the episode in which Jimmy had been found, but not charged with, for nothing could be proven, shipping opium by rail to Chicago where, as compared to the ten dollars it fetched per pound in Victoria, it could be sold for twenty-five dollars. Five hundred pounds of opium in two packages. All this Haack thought over as he chewed his food, drank his coffee, and warmed his feet on Charlie's back— Charlie who lay recovering his strength beneath the restaurant table.

"It used to be," said Jimmy warmly, leaning back in his chair and lighting a cigar, "that a man could make his way in this world by his wits." He shook his head sadly. "Not so any more, my friend. They want you to follow the rules. They want you to conform." Jimmy gazed at the lighted end of his cigar as if seeking explanation. Not finding it, he raised his eyes to Robert Haack's face. But Haack was examining the pile of pancakes still to be tackled.

"Yes," Jimmy went on reflectively, "once upon a time a man who was willing to take a chance could make money in this country."

He paused for Haack's response, and Haack, sensing that to be quiet, although his mouth was full of food, would not be diplomatic, said as thoughtfully as he could manage in the circumstances, "I know what you mean."

"Take the Cariboo, or California before that," said Jimmy, stabbing out compass points with a hand on which a diamond ring glittered. "Why, if a man didn't find gold there, what did it matter? He could still make a living with his muscles, digging in a mine or packing supplies. He could get into business for himself.

"Now, don't get excited," said Jimmy, holding up his hand, "it's not so much a worker as information I want, and I can't pay much."

Haack's smile faded. "Yes?" he said guardedly, for we know what happened during his last career as informant.

"They say you have a friend, a lady named India Thackery," began Jimmy. Robert flushed, and Charlie growled.

"Don't say another word, Mr. Carroll, whatever it's about. I won't have the name of a lady spoken in public."

"Now, now, don't get me wrong," said Jimmy calmingly as Robert stood. "Please sit down a minute and hear me out." Robert sat.

"It's nothing to do with your friend," he said softly. "It's just that she works at the Tai June factory. I suppose she's talked about it with you."

"What if she has," said Robert. "I wouldn't betray a confidence."

"Of course you wouldn't," said Jimmy. "I wouldn't ask you to. I'd only want you to use your eyes. Like I said, it's information I need, and you're the man on the spot. Next time you're down there to pick her up, just make a few notes about what comes in by way of shipments, and what goes out. There's no harm in that, is there?"

Robert considered. "Maybe not," he said after some thought. "But I'm afraid you're too late. I don't see the lady any more, and I wouldn't want to be found hanging around that factory by anyone who'd tell her I'd been there."

Jimmy looked disappointed. "You don't say," he said sadly. He touched Haack consolingly on the arm. "Don't worry about that blacklist, young man. It won't last long. People forget." Haack looked down bleakly.

There was a pause during which Jimmy examined the disconsolate figure before him. "Let's change the subject, Mr. Haack," he said, kindly, "let's speak of my interests and not yours. Now how much do you think a pound of opium is worth in this city right now?"

"About ten dollars," said Robert.

Jimmy nodded. "The duty on the American side is also ten dollars. Thus if all were as it should be, it should cost about twenty dollars a pound across the border in Port Townsend."

Haack nodded agreement.

"The trouble is," said Jimmy, "you can get all the opium you want at the Port Townsend auction for fifteen dollars a pound, duty paid. It's not worth the trouble to smuggle it. And they put you in jail, you know, if you get caught." Jimmy grimaced, and Haack looked sympathetic.

"I'm saying, if you've been listening," said Jimmy very quietly, "that it's not worth it if you have to pay for it in the first place." He looked meaningfully at Robert.

Haack rubbed his foot across Charlie's back for reassurance. "I don't know that I catch your drift," he said.

"Look," said Jimmy, "we know that most of the opium made in this town crosses the border one way or another. I have a friend, a half-breed, who's tried running it from here to San Juan Island. It is received there and stored until an opportune time, when it is placed on vessels engaged in carrying lumber. It's not much of a trick to get away with it if a little common sense is used."

"Customs are on to that," said Robert, lowering his voice conspiratorially. "The Americans check every vessel that goes in or out of San Juan Island."

"Where there's a will there's a way," said Jimmy. "That's my philosophy. You think about it, Mr. Haack. To be blunt, you'd have to get the opium for nothing and have a foolproof place to keep it until you could get rid of it.

"My time is gone now. I'm getting on in life, and I've had my run at it. But I'd be glad to help a younger man get started." He sat for a moment in thought. "If you had some place where the goods could sit, maybe for months, you could slip them over the border little by little. Customs would lose interest: there's too much going over for them to keep track of where it's all come from. It would work. I know it."

He smiled and snapped his braces. "Where there's a will, my friend Robert! Don't you forget it."

There was a feeling of companionship between the two men as they sat, stomachs full and appetites satisfied, while Jimmy paid the bill. They smiled at each other.

But Charlie, operating within his own parameters, seemed to hold his breath. Flea-bitten, mangy, suspicious, a rubbish heap of a dog, but a friend to Haack when everyone else had left, the hackles slowly rose on Charlie's neck.

"The great trouble," said Jimmy placidly while cleaning his teeth with a toothpick, "is that men who smuggle will get to quarrelling among themselves. That's why you've got to know who you're working with. Two weeks ago, for instance, a large shipment on the way to Portland had to be divided up before it got there amongst those employed to carry it. None of them would let the others out of sight so long as they had the cargo with them.

"No," he said, "my day is done. It's up to you younger ones." He slapped Haack on the shoulder as he stood up. "I'd like to think of you as a son," he said. "I'd like to do what I could to help."

At which point Charlie, who had barked and snapped at Jimmy the moment Jimmy had entered the Johnson Street ravine to ask for Robert's whereabouts, scrambled to his feet as well, and bit Jimmy's ankle.

Jimmy shrieked, then kicked Charlie in the belly with all his strength. Charlie fell, rolled onto his back and lay still while a little brown liquid dribbled out of the corners of his mouth.

Which brought Haack to his senses. For he hated viciousness. And he loved his dog. For there are few loyalties as profound as that between dog and master. It is more than a contract, it is a vocation, each taking upon himself the well-being of the other. As Charlie had fended for Haack throughout the winter, keeping him warm with his body, protecting him, sharing his bones, now it was Robert's turn to stand up for Charlie.

He said, "I'll say thank you for the breakfast, Mr. Carroll, but don't you ever touch my dog again or I'll kill you."

Jimmy, clutching his wounded leg, bent double in pain, his eyes red with rage, said, "We'll see, Mr. Haack. We'll see, or I'll be hanged. I won't forget this." He hobbled from the table.

Robert stroked Charlie's belly until Charlie wheezed, coughed up more liquid and struggled to his feet.

It was a near escape. For both of them.

"It reminds me," says Fan, as we prepare to go round the outside of Solander Island a mile southwest of Cape Cook, for it is too dangerous to pass between the island and the Brooks Peninsula, "of when I went fishing."

"*You* went fishing, Fan!" I say, surprised, looking at her long, slim hands and trying to imagine them baiting a hook. Fan and worms? Or Fan gaffing a grilse, then clubbing it to death? It simply did not fit.

"The trouble with you, Robert Lam," she complains, "is that you have no imagination. You think everyone is like you, always the same. No wonder I never liked to tell you things."

"I'm sorry, Fan," I apologize. "It's just that you're so—" I search for an acceptable word "—feminine."

She checks my expression to see how I mean it. Satisfied that I'm not pulling her leg, she goes on. "It is not your fault you have little experience

135

with women, Robert Lam," she says kindly. "I know that things have not always worked out for you. Women are different from men. They do not stay at one job like a man, they do many things. They learn about life in all its aspects. Sing Yuen knew that. But then he was my husband, and you are a bachelor."

"Tell me about the fishing, Fan," I say, refraining from comment.

"It was very long ago," she says, "right after Sing Yuen had died and you had gone away. I didn't know what to do with myself, so I went out with a friend on his boat."

"Just like that," I say.

"Yes," she replies. "He was a commercial fisherman. He knew I needed to get away, so he took me with him. He had known Sing Yuen and me for many years. It was only for a few days. We were fishing for halibut."

"Halibut!" I say, although I can't think why this should surprise me particularly.

"Yes," she continues. "It is not a fish I eat myself—at least not since then. You may have noticed."

I think about it. It's true. In fact I can't remember Fan eating anything much but vegetables for years.

"When you catch these fish," she says, "you must be careful what you do. You have to calm them, stroke them on their bellies to soothe them. Otherwise they can be dangerous—even lying on the deck of a boat they can hurt you. They have strong muscles, and you cannot kill them outright. They take many hours to die."

I nod. I think I have heard this before from one of my colleagues. He is the only other pilot I know who has his own boat.

"There is something else you must do," she says. "You must place them on the deck so that their bellies are uppermost. This is not just so that you can stroke them, as I said, but so they cannot watch what else you do. Their eyes are on the dark side of their bodies. If you place them so they can see you as you are cleaning other fish, they will try to escape. They push themselves up from the deck. They cry out to each other. It is not a pleasant sight or a pleasant sound, Robert Lam, I assure you. They know what is being done to them, and they do not like it. They don't want to die like that."

"And so, Fan?" I say.

"So, Robert Lam? What do you mean?"

"Why do you tell me this now? What is the point of it?"

She looks at me as if I am an idiot. "One thing leads to another, Robert Lam, in this as in all else. If you do not know that a fish has feelings, you can eat him. But once you see his anguish, it is different. You cannot forget what you know, except at your peril. Your spirit will not stand for it."

"Fishermen manage, Fan," I say.

"Oh!" she says in anger, "you are truly hopeless. I don't know why I bother. You do not see anything at all, you are so stupid!"

And she stomps out of the pilothouse.

But what have I done, I ask myself, except be what I am? If I don't ask questions how will I know? How will I remedy my ignorance?

Solander Island: rocky, treeless, desolate, storm-swept. As bleak as, and not unlike, Cape Horn; and home to hundreds of seabirds, including the tufted puffin; and sea lions; and with a light on top of its three-hundred-foot height. We are just over halfway home.

Something had happened to the weather. Overnight, almost, it had changed to spring. The trees were in bud, birds sang from the gutters, shoots pushed up through the mud. Doors were opened, front steps swept, windows washed. Even in the depths of the Johnson Street ravine the effects could be felt. Charlie lifted his head and sniffed, then set to grooming his coat. Robert Haack unbundled himself from the piles of rags in which he slept. He took off his hat, scratched his head, blinked.

"Let's go, Charlie," he said. "Let's get out of here. I don't know why I didn't think of it before. What are we doing here, anyway?"

He packed up their few belongings. They went into the street and sampled the air. Then putting one foot in front of the other, or two and two, in the instance of Charlie, they walked away from the town that had brought them nothing but trouble.

They travelled east then northeast past the market gardens and the peddlers, past the brothels on the frontiers of Blanchard Street, across rain-flooded fields in which ducks paddled, past milk cows and swine and knots of baaing sheep on the brink of lambing, all the way to the farms at Cedar Hill, then further. Charlie ran in circles, nose to the ground, then he dug up turnips and buried them, then abandoned these to chase some horses.

They were running away and enjoying it. Waving at children who espied them from windows, shouting at wagoners: oh, the urge to keep moving once it takes hold! It won't let you go, it pushes you forward, it pumps up the blood, loosens the muscles, rejuvenates the bones.

("For heaven's sake, Robert Lam," says Fan, who has entered the pilot-house, "keep an eye on your chart. There are reefs around here."

"I know, Fan. I am watching out. It's just that I feel good. I want to get going."

"You are going," she says scornfully. "You've been going all along but hadn't the sense to know it. Don't feel too good," she warns crushingly, "I don't think you're built for it.")

Robert Haack and Charlie walked, ran, skipped, and ambled down paths and through meadows. Where bees were beginning to move and ants to venture afield; where lilies and trillium bloomed, and beneath the soil roots took hold. Travellers who arrived at the foot of Mount Douglas, one of the hills Haack had viewed from his Chatham Street house, and began to ascend it. A feature, a summit, rock-ribbed and ancient.

("Robert Louis," says Fan impatiently. "Get on with the story.")

Robert threw stones and sticks of wood as they climbed, and Charlie fetched them; and the higher they ascended, the more distance they put between themselves and the town, the happier they felt. Since the whole complex of trouble—the gambling debt, the Association and Smiling Jimmy, even Haack's thwarted affections for India—needed buildings of brick, wood, and stone to support it. As did his humiliation. And so shame was left behind, and with it poverty and disgrace. For these, as we know, are endemic to place.

Up and up they went. A deer trail wound through the red cedars and hemlock. The upper slopes were covered in Douglas fir. The trail dipped through swamps clotted with skunk cabbage and fringed with spindly alders; it edged along cliffs and scrawled across boulders. It carried them out of the world of their worries, and at last, at the very height of the little mountain, it brought them to a cluster of oak trees. Where ravens croaked their laughter as Charlie, nearly crazed with the infinity of scents kaleidoscoping through his brain, rushed back and forth wildly.

At the edge of a granite platform they looked eastwards to the ocean and the islands between Vancouver Island and the mainland. James Island, Sidney Island, D'Arcy Island near the border, and San Juan Island just over the border with the Americans, had emerged from a cloud bank and were treading water in the distance. Seeing San Juan Island brought the first unpleasant memory, since they had arrived, of Smiling Jimmy and his assault (for so Haack now saw it) on his conscience—for it was from there, Smiling Jimmy had said, that his friend had smuggled opium; but it wasn't enough to spoil things. That world was behind them.

Victoria, to the southwest, could stay lost within its muddy swath of smoke. It was none of their concern. There seemed no reason, none at all, that they should ever have to return to that olive-grey horizon.

Falling and cutting logs. Collecting moss and mud with which to chink holes, cutting poles to weave a roof, laying and tying down sod. Smoothing the floor, making chairs, a bench and table. Lighting fires, hauling water, snaring rabbits and pheasant for food, stalking deer, digging for edible roots, noting the berry patches. Carpentering, cooking, planning, constructing. While the weather continued to improve and Haack's clothes, rusty with wear, acquired the dignity of camouflage.

They were a team, Haack and his dog. Charlie found a cache of flour left down the mountain by a squatter. Haack picked burrs and ticks from Charlie's coat. They were free, self-sufficient. They could do what they wanted. And all their troubles were over.

Except that what we are is also what we've been before, and a change in surroundings doesn't alter that fact (though it helps). We cannot revise our biology, for instance, and we cannot order up the dreams we want. And perhaps that is God overseeing the line that we travel. It is God keeping us honest.

Or so I was taught at the Chinese Christian School for Boys. And so, for a time, I believed.

Whale sound. Calling one to another as they swim away from the hunters. Travelling in families. Not lonely, like the boatmen are. Not part of a process in which magnificence is killed and dragged to shore: then stripped and cut and boiled. Not killers. And it is a funny thing, when I think of it, that the whale hunt ground to a halt during the war and was only started up thereafter. As if, as the doctor at Coal Harbour implied, we had come to the end of our instincts as we stood at the edge of the world, facing outwards, west, to where the last of the whales were. Facing what we had done in Japan with the atom bomb. Facing a mirror in which we had to look or perish.

Ah, me. It's not as if we waste them, Fan. We use up every scrap. For margarine, and perfume, and dog meat. It's not as if there's nothing to learn: the skeleton the doctor showed me had four-foot-long limbs. It was going somewhere, or coming from somewhere. It had a story to tell.

And it's not as if the men weren't heroes, just like we were in the war: one killed three humpbacks, basking together, with one harpoon. And one of the skippers piloted his boat into Cachalot Station—where we are going—without looking where he was headed, by listening to his whistle and looking at his watch. He didn't have to see; he could navigate by timing. That was something, Fan, there was achievement for you.

I wait but Fan makes no comment. She stands nearby, feet planted wide to take the rise and fall of the swell. We are going shoreward, through Checkleset Bay and the Barrier Islands, through Gay Passage between the two Bunsbys: where there are rocks visible and submerged, so many dangers that I dare not think of them singly; then hugging the shore of Vancouver Island near Malkscope Point, running a course towards St. Paul's dome, then into Nicolaye Channel and Kyuquot Channel, and thus to our anchorage.

"Not so fast, Robert Lam," says my stepmother. We are facing a rocky, broken landscape marked by high mountains. Colonies of sea lions plunge from the reefy islands we pass as the engine of the *Rose* disturbs them.

Mist rising as the afternoon fails. Midway between Rugged and Chatchannel points just entering Kyuquot Channel, in fact. The beacon on Rugged Point flashing its warning.

"Not so fast, Robert Lam!" Fan repeats, crossly. "Why are you hurrying? You are like a tourist who spends all his money travelling, then when he gets to his destination is too tired to look around him and stays inside his hotel. You have seen nothing of this place, its wildlife, its beauties."

"I have to watch the charts, Fan. I can't afford to get too interested."

She sniffs. "There are plenty of places we could have tied up earlier. Now we have to go to an anchorage that's known for its winds. What kind of planning is that? What kind of a pilot are you?"

"A tired one, Fan. I can't seem to keep my eyes open, yet we've got to keep going." It's a feeling I've had before. Not just when I blacked out at the top of the island, but on the job. As if I didn't know where the ship I was piloting was supposed to go, but had to guide her in anyway. As if all I'd learned in my life, in my profession, was, after all, guesswork. As if no one was in control. I didn't think such thoughts for long, of course.

I couldn't have and stayed with the work. But it bothered me more than I cared to admit that I was that vulnerable. And what if something had gone wrong? For the waters were full of hazards. What if, in my care, a ship went down?

"Wake up, Robert Lam!" Fan is shouting in my ear. "Wake up. You must not fall asleep."

"I'm sorry, Fan, I just can't seem to stay awake." I start to nod off, to dream the dream that I want to dream. But she pinches my arm.

"Silly old fool," she shouts. "It is not a time to be weak. You are a grown man. You can do better than that."

"Really, Fan," I protest, "I can't. I've known all along I wasn't up to it."

She pinches and pinches and pinches.

Empty landscape, I think, looking at the rocks and the trees, and between these shores the undulating pavement of water. How strange the cities have become. The tongues of whales, which the Indians eat raw, the tongues of spirits.

Where have I come from, where am I going? Robert Haack asked himself staring from his mountain aerie at dawn. He could see the farms on the Cedar Hill plain with their neatly sculpted fields. He could see the beach at Cadboro Bay, near the foot of the mountain, strewn with fishing boats. And the islands in the strait, set out like finger bones and fingernails all separated. Links and chains; pieces broken off. He went through his naming: James Island, San Juan Island, D'Arcy Island, Sidney Island. He had been to almost all of them at one time or another. They made gunpowder on James Island—he had tried to get a job there. There was abalone off Sidney Island—he had dived for it and sold some to a restaurant when he needed the money. And San Juan, of course, where the Americans had their settlement and which had been disputed territory until after mid-century when a German emperor had settled the problem to the satisfaction of his countrymen, and to no one else. Haack scratched his head. Borders never had made much sense to him. Which was one of the reasons he had never considered smuggling across them to be much of a crime. Although the penalties were stiff enough. As Smiling Jimmy had pointed out.

He pondered a minute longer, thinking about the island he had never set foot on. D'Arcy Island. The island of lepers. Nobody went there, except the lepers, of course. They were supplied by the City of Victoria, which was responsible for imprisoning them. It was not a subject much talked of: it tended to be bad for morale. And the lepers were all Chinese, so far as he knew. Once sent to the island they ceased to exist for the rest of the world. Even passing ships avoided their shores, arcing away from the coastline where the lepers had their colony. People were superstitious about it, as well as frightened. The Indians said the island was cursed. It was too small and too unsheltered to be much good for anything. It might as well not have been there at all for all the use it was.

He was a man on a hilltop, surveying the landscape he knew best, where ships crisscrossed and farmers worked and there was the pull of a city in the distance.

Cities. And islands. All of which could be blotted from his sight by his uplifted hand. It was that simple. He could do anything, he thought, if he could only decide what the anything was. He was on the verge of mysteries, of visions, of answers.

And so he slept that morning after breakfast with his dog by his side. And, as was bound to happen eventually, for the present had come to a halt and he had finished his building and made himself comfortable and there was nothing more he could do to stave off the past, which, with its knife, cuts through the shelter of our habits and lets in the night, which is the future... he dreamed and remembered.

Dust obscured the vision at first. Hot, dry, Carmel, California dust. The dust of his childhood. He blinked his eyes at it, and wanted to sneeze. He suppressed a cough. For there was someone in the vision, just emerging from the cloud in which she moved, whom he didn't care to disturb. It was his mother, but dressed as he had never known her, in a travelling suit and delicate shoes. Her pretty auburn hair, from which his had taken its glint of red, was gathered up beneath a hat. She wore a travelling cloak, and the dust she brushed from her shoulders had been made by a rapidly departing horse and cart.

His mother sat on her luggage at the side of the road looking down at her idle hands. When the dust had settled, Haack noted that the hills above the valley were tinged with green. The murmur of a nearby stream competed with the chirrup of birds. It was spring. Eventually, perhaps when she had rested enough, Robert's mother stood, then bent to the task of moving her luggage ahead of her down the track. Eastwards, into the interior of the valley. Away from what, he did not know, unless it was the job she'd had teaching school, and towards, amongst other matters, his own birth.

More dust. This time approaching from the west. And now the goat farmer made his appearance. He was long-bodied and short-legged, this much was clear even as he sat his horse. What was not clear was why Robert's mother climbed up on the horse behind him. Unless, as it suddenly occurred to Haack, she had determined to surrender to chance.

Time passed, as it does in dreams and as it does for unhappy children. That is, it scarcely passed at all, although there were some consolations: tree frogs, golden as fire, to be watched; the tinkle of the goats' bells as the flocks wandered the hills; the white puffs of angora wool caught on branches and lifting like feathers as the boy ran by.

There was his mother, with whom he lived in a shack a quarter mile from the farmhouse; there was the goat farmer, who ignored him, except to make him work or to teach him what it meant to be a man—that is, suffering—and to drink. And to play a game of cards. All this by the time he was twelve.

And so time passed as if for all his life he would be locked in this valley with no way out, until the day, at seventeen, when, pretending a courage he did not feel and abandoning the mother he had promised to rescue, he walked out of the valley and away from his childhood without looking back.

Not at the hills or at the restless dry trees or at his mother, who stood at the door of the shack with a book in her hand, shading her eyes to follow him.

Not at himself, until this very moment.

Robert Haack, on top of his mountain, slept in daylight. Not a quiet sleep as one sleeps in a room, but a wakeful sleep as one sleeps at sea, aware of the wind, the creaking of ropes, of the strain in an engine or sail. Of others' voices, and orders and duties neglected. Of possible hazards, of sea life and shoals, shipwrecks on islands. Submarines. Cannibals. Submarines.

The little Spanish town of Monterey was spread neatly over the foot of a hillside topped by pines. The boy, Robert Haack, crossed the railway line, then gazed down at the sea and the white sailing ships and whalers that encrusted it. The blue water was roughened into grey by a wind cooled with fog. The boats tacked and tossed, drew near to each other then shied away like horses. What he had been told by his mother and what he had read had not prepared him for this. It was so much less magnificent yet more vital than he had thought. The sea. It was like opening his veins to the wind. He felt painfully, unbearably, all he'd already missed in his life, what he had to make up for: the passing of time.

He ran down to the little town, scarcely watching where he was going, stumbling and tripping in his eagerness to begin. There were red roofs on top of whitewashed adobe dwellings. A few wooden buildings with painted signs: the Bohemia Saloon, at the intersection with Alvarado Street, outside of which a man with a shovel was aimlessly digging; restaurants and general stores and ships' chandlers. And Indians holding up doorways, and Portuguese sailors and Chinese and Mexicans and Americans. What seemed to the boy like crowds of people; although there were, in the little town, but three hundred and fifty people in all.

Suddenly he stopped. He had passed into a residential district. Here windows were shuttered and the houses were decorated with iron balconies and flowering vines. There were walls embroidered with flowers, and gates from behind which came the sound of women's laughter.

Directly ahead of him was a small, two-storied rose-covered adobe cottage. And although most of the sidewalks were made of wooden planking, just here, where he had halted, they were shining whalebone. A pony was tied to an upright Spanish cannon. Somebody was singing in the garden in a tuneful baritone. There was the sound of coughing. More laughing.

How to describe what happened then? Dreaming about it, so many years afterwards, made Robert Haack shiver, although it was daylight on top of his mountain, and Charlie lay snugly next to him.

At the entrance to the garden of the rose-covered cottage, there was an arch made of the curving jawbones of a whale. The door on the far side of the archway opened, and through it came a woman.

She was small and pretty and tawny-skinned. She had thick, short, dark-brown hair, which shone in the sun. A cross hung around her neck, and a fringed shawl was draped over her dress. She was laughing and calling out to the man who followed through the gate behind her. "Lully, Lully," she called. "Hurry up or we'll be late to dinner."

The man was cadaverously thin. He had long, lank, brown hair, and wore a threadbare velvet coat. His expression was mischievous. He did not answer her at once, but began to whistle. The lady, puckering her lips, whistled also, waited for him, and took his arm. And so the two of them swept down the street, whistling and laughing, until they turned the corner and were lost to sight.

Robert, as if suddenly jerked to life by a string they had tied to him as they passed, ran after them. He did not know why he did so, unless it was due to their happiness: there had been little enough of that in his life. Or perhaps it was the woman herself, her liveliness and prettiness. He could count the number of women he'd met on one hand, and none of them had looked like that. They were farm women, neglected like his mother or worn out from work in their houses and fields.

Robert ran through a grove of cypress trees: he could hear the ocean at his back, urging him on. He saw a calf, caught in a fence, bawling for help, and although the plight of the beast tugged at his conscience, he did not stop. The whistling led him on, then dropped him off in time to see the woman's disappearing back as she slipped through the door of a fishermen's restaurant. What to do next? That question was solved for him as a rough hand grabbed the back of his neck and spun him around.

"Why!" the man said in surprise, "you're only a lad!" It was the tall thin man who, with the lady, Haack had been following. "What on earth do you want with us?"

Robert blushed and looked down at his feet. He wore no shoes. The bundle of his few belongings hung from his fingers.

"What is it?" the man questioned him, more kindly. "Are you hungry? Have you travelled far?"

Weakly, Haack nodded his head. His blush would not subside. He was embarrassed, so early on in his independent life, to have been found in the wrong.

"Come on, then," the thin man said with a smile, "I'll take you inside." And he guided Robert Haack up the steps in front of him.

It was a simple enough place in appearance. Six or eight tables covered with red-and-white checkered tablecloths. Men—there were no women other than the lady who had so recently entered—sat eating in their shirtsleeves. There was a large stove in a rear corner, and beyond that the entrance to the kitchen. Steam rose from a brimming kettle.

"That's Donna Martina's famous fish soup," said Haack's new acquaintance, taking in the aroma. "You must have some with us."

There was something different in the way the man spoke. As if the words were formed, then half rubbed out. This contributed to Robert Haack's shyness.

The boy blushed more deeply as he was seated next to the dark-haired lady.

"This is Mrs. Osbourne," said Robert's host. "My name is Robert Stevenson."

"Call him Louis," said Mrs. Osbourne, making room at the table.

"You called him Lully," blurted the boy. "I heard you."

"Why, so she did," said Robert Louis Stevenson quickly, to cover Fanny Osbourne's look of astonishment. "And you shall call me Lully, too, if you wish."

At which point the proprietor, a bearded, white-haired old man called Jules Simoneau, came to their table. The meal was discussed and ordered in terms Haack could not hope to follow, but soon the fish soup arrived, as promised. Robert stared at his cutlery, wondering which spoon to pick up as Stevenson poured out wine.

"You haven't told us your name, yet, you know," said Stevenson. "Would you like us to guess?"

"Oh, no, sir," said the boy, who was beginning to feel more comfortable as he drank the wine and ate the bread provided.

"It's the same as yours."

"Not Lully!" Stevenson exclaimed. He turned to Fanny Osbourne with a smile. "Is there room for two of us in this town, do you think?"

"Please," begged the boy, fearful of being misunderstood. "That's not what I meant. My names are Robert Louis, like yours are. That's all I meant."

"A coincidence!" cried Stevenson. "Jules, Donna!" he called out to the kitchen, "did you hear that? Now you've two poor vagabonds to feed, both called Robert Louis. I call that luck!"

Fortune smiled upon the company. The couple warmed to the lonely boy, and Robert Haack poured out to them his dreams. It was the first time ever he had spoken so freely. Of the goat farm he had come from, of his schoolteacher mother, of his father's cruelty. Of his wish to make his way in the world by his own honest labour (although he wasn't sure how, just yet).

Of the books he had read or hoped to read. For by now he had learned that Fanny and Louis were artists, Stevenson a poet and Fanny a woman of many unusual interests.

"I'll find a way to pay you back," said Robert Haack to Robert Stevenson as they left the restaurant and walked through the streets in darkness. The couple had found a room for the boy by asking at the restaurant. They were showing him the way.

"There is no need," the couple demurred.

"It's a promise I made," the young boy said. "I swore to my mother I would never owe money."

Weeks went by. Robert Louis Haack and Robert Louis Stevenson walked together on the beach, often accompanied by one of Fanny's children. Stevenson tried out ideas for his writing for the *Monterey Californian*, or made up stories, always talking, always entertaining. Robert Haack listened.

They followed the sandy edge of Monterey Bay, or visited the lighthouse, or walked up the slopes away from the sound of the sea and into the sheltered soughing of wind among trees. They stayed until sunset, watching the fog roll in over the ocean. And, when the air grew chill and deadly, they went home.

All this time the boy was looking for work. And he found it where he could, going out on boats with the fishermen, helping with nets and unloading. He took fish to Simoneau's restaurant to be cooked for his dinner. He traded fish for his rent. He made friends with some of the other lads he met. And he started to try his luck at cards. For he had almost nothing to live on, and he couldn't buy clothes with fish, he couldn't buy boots. And he had promised to pay his debts.

How could he know that Stevenson had a horror of gambling? That he had once left his hotel in Monte Carlo after a suicide in the casino? How could he know what else had happened in the young Scotsman's life: that he'd been waiting for Fanny's divorce (no small matter in the late 1870s), and that at last it had come; that he was short of money himself, and in desperate health; or that Fanny's daughter, Belle, had eloped with a painter and provoked a family crisis?

How could he know that all these matters played their part in the poet's gentle disengagement from his, Robert Haack's, life? For the last he heard from the writer was in a note, left for him at Simoneau's restaurant, and accompanied by the gift of a poem—the one Robert Haack had shown to India. The note said that perhaps they'd meet again sometime, elsewhere.

For Stevenson and entourage had left for San Francisco.

A big city. Hilly, windy, colder. Crowded with people making their way in the world. Far lonelier than Monterey for this boy who had followed his hero, hoping to start things over. He kept the poem close in his pocket, believing it would help, that at any second the long, striding figure would round the corner ahead of him calling out, "It's Lully, Robert Louis. What are you doing? Let's go for a walk." And that at once they'd be engaged in talk.

Of the sun and the moon and the stars and the planets. Of life and death. ("No," interrupts Fan. "Not this poet. He never talked about death. He was too sick.")

Of his childhood, then, his beloved Edinburgh with its cliffy streets and precipices, and its darkly moral habits; of murderers and smugglers, and the Cow Gate and Grassmarket; of the view from Calton Hill and the folly of the castle; of foreign sailors arriving in port; of the windy Pentland Hills where the Covenanters met. Of politics and religious passions, and royal intrigue and armed rebellion. In short, of such a world as Robert Haack, son of a goat farmer from Carmel, California, could only dream.

But no such thing happened. Instead he wandered the docks with other young drifters, hopeless, penniless, until he was given the job of driving a wagon by opium smugglers.

And this was the story: thirty thousand dollars worth of bonded raw opium had been withdrawn from the bonded warehouses for shipment to Victoria on board a steamer, the California Navigation Company's *Brother Jonathan*. The opium was escorted down to the ship and stowed on board. Now while the steamers used one side of the pier, on the other were the Sacramento River boats, owned by the same company. While all was bustle and activity, the docks crowded with people, Robert Haack, following instructions, drove a cartload of empty trunks to the docks and unloaded them. Soon a number of trunks were passed down from the *Brother Jonathan*, and Robert Haack, with his empty wagon in the line of wagons loading baggage from the Sacramento River boats, drew alongside of them. When his loaded wagon was stopped (for customs had watched the whole procedure), it was found to contain about thirty thousand dollars worth of opium. In tins, in the trunks.

Bad luck, said the judge, who thought him quite innocent. But who put him in jail for six months.

A downfall, a very long fall, when he had scarcely begun to climb and was not even twenty.

The sadness of it woke Robert Haack on his mountaintop. Charlie licked the tears from his face. For a few more minutes Haack was a boy wondering how to repair the damage, how to recover himself. But as he blinked, he remembered he was a man, and these were not boys' tears at all but a bad spring cold. He watched the birds patrol the waters below him.

An Indian camp on the shoreline near the abandoned whale fishery. A bonfire on the beach. We are safely at anchor, or at least safe so long as the winds stay calm. "The southeasterly and westerly winds blow through with great violence," says the *British Columbia Pilot*.

But the pins and needles are back. The numbness. And I am lying on my back on the deck watching the stars. And listening to their singing in chorus. Learning from the emptiness.

I do not know how we arrived here, how I navigated or dropped anchor. It must have been intuitive. I smile with satisfaction. At least that's something I can do right. I am a pilot, if nothing else.

Familiar figures—the Great and Little Bears, Orion, Cassiopeia, Perseus—overhead. On the shore, the flap, flap of the native camp laundry. I can see the outlines of the huddle of shacks, fish-drying racks, canoes pulled up on the shingle. Despite the laundry, the camp is deserted. Not even a dog barks.

"How do you feel?" asks Fan. She is sitting on the hatch-combing near me.

"Fine," I answer. I try to lift my hand, but it doesn't move. "A little stiff, maybe," I say. "It must be the damp."

Fan nods. "You want to stay here awhile and rest?" she says.

"There's nothing here, Fan. This place has been closed down for years."

"Do you want to go on?"

I do not answer. "It's not a good anchorage, as you know. Let's see what it looks like tomorrow. I want to sleep."

She shuts up, as I intend her to. But sleep is beyond me. Not only the stars are singing. There are whales, great, strong companies of them calling and filling the depths below our little ship. The *Orion*, the *St.*

Lawrence, and the *Green* were whalers here in Kyuquot Sound at the Cachalot Station. Perhaps we are being checked out.

Blubber, meat, intestines, ambergris. Or a fetus eighteen feet in length. The whales go on singing all night long.

Charlie scattered swallows that tried to nest in the cracks in the cabin. Robert Haack improved the structure: he wanted it to stand. He had some dim feeling that he might stay here the rest of his life, living as a hermit or retreating to this spot when the demands of his busy life (for surely he had much ahead of him yet?) became too much.

It was a time of pleasant confusion, when he made no plans but felt that plans were being made for him beyond his knowing. The mountain was the hub of the world, and he, Robert Haack, turned at its centre. He watched the green growth at the tips of the fir trees expand. He saw the wildflowers take their turns: after the lilies came wild pea and blue-eyed mary, and there were many others, which he couldn't name. Bees jostled among petals, rabbits emerged from their burrows, and the sun steamed the damp out of the moss, which sent up yellow tendrils to wave in the air. His days were spent cheerfully attending to tasks to be done: kindling to gather, small branches to cut with his knife, food to prepare and to cook. He liked keeping a fire going and boiling up rabbit bones and nettles; he liked digging a trench to lead water from a nearby spring to a pool he used as a wash basin. He enjoyed cutting grass and drying it for a change of bed linen.

And he liked himself: the great shock of reddish-brown hair that stood out from his head, the beard that covered his face, his calloused, nicked hands.

And yet, as time went on, and especially at twilight, as the birds settled down for the night and the farms in the plains lit their lights and the dim glow of the city on the horizon rose to a certain height then spread flatly like a miasmic exhalation, he grew restless. Both he and his dog sighed.

Robert turned the poem in his pocket. He imagined conversations with India. He examined what-might-have-beens. For it is only human to be lonely sometimes, and to people an empty world with lies to oneself. And to have regrets, and self-doubts, and to balance them with fantasies in which what went wrong goes right.

And as for Charlie.... Well, if Robert Haack had been less engrossed in himself, more observant, he might have seen that his dog was troubled, might have understood why Charlie stood half the night with his nose up, sniffing, or scratched his backside on the cedars and pines, or groomed himself with close attention. Charlie responding to the change of planetary position as the earth tilted towards the sun. Charlie, not bored, but full of longing. For a dog has feelings, too, plus biology and a keen sense of obligation. For Charlie, despite the name Haack had given him, was a bitch in season.

One night Robert Haack lay down on his bed of pine boughs and grasses under the stars on top of the mountain. He was too restless to sleep inside the cabin, where he felt confined. The stars turned above him, and down below the islands floated on their bed of trembling oceans. He felt dizzy with spring, as if a seed planted inside his brain had sent out its roots and was growing.

He slept well and warmly, however, and yet when he awoke before dawn, he was colder than he had been all winter. For Charlie, who had always been with him, whom he counted on, who had snuggled next to him through all kinds of weather, had gone.

There was the usual calling: at first casual, then more concerned. There were forays to the edges of the mountain, glances over cliffs, scrambles into caves. But Charlie could not be found. And in a little while Robert Haack knew he would have to go after him.

It was a fast but painful climb down the mountain this time, anxiety making Haack clumsy and his heavy heart rendering him insensible to the beauty of his surroundings. In the fields there were mares plump with foals, and stick-legged calves trembling against their mothers' flanks. Lambs flicked their tails and gambolled. But Robert Haack trudged through it all with his mind on his problems. "Charlie!" he cried at intervals. "Here boy, come on, boy, here, Charlie!"

At length, a thin farmer with red hands, controlling the skinny beige horse that was pulling his wagon, pulled up beside our pilgrim. In this country, in this season, where every man had his own good reasons for going where he was going, there was no need to explain. Robert Haack climbed aboard silently, nodded at the farmer, asked the one necessary question, took in the farmer's no, and said no more.

Although in his mind the loss was like a bell tolling, a wolf howling. For Charlie's desertion had hurt Haack bitterly.

For when you think you count on nothing, then find that you are wrong, that the one thing you depended on without even knowing it is gone, then truly you are on the edge of oblivion. For a man can live so long as he knows he knows himself, but without that certainty he is lost.

("It's almost morning, Robert Lam," says Fan. "Why don't you get some rest?"

"Not yet, Fan. I want to know what happened."

"What does it matter, Robert Lam? It is only a story about a dog. Can't it wait a little?"

"Not any dog, Fan. As you said to me, this was a particular dog, Robert Haack's dog. I feel I am getting to know her."

"As you wish, Robert Lam." She pauses two beats. "I am worried about you. You do not look well. You are very pale."

"If I want your advice I'll ask for it, Fan," I say resentfully. "I've always looked after myself, and I'm perfectly fit, thank you. I got us here, didn't I?"

She looks at me reproachfully, and I search my memory for details of the last stages of our journey, but still they elude me.

I touch the Chinese coin in my pocket for luck.

"I want to get it over with, Fan. I just want to see it to the end.")

Buildings appeared singly, then they clustered in groups like raisins in a fist. The track grew rutted, and the wagon rattled back and forth from crest to crest, creaking and rocking until Robert Haack felt ill to his stomach. They passed a schoolhouse where children stood uncertainly as Robert Haack shouted out to them, "Have you seen my dog?" But one of the little girls nodded and pointed cityward.

The roads branched and forked, and the nearer to the town they travelled the less the streets were like accidents and the more they wove the tight mesh of a net.

Until, when the farmer dropped him off at the corner of Johnson and Government streets, Robert Haack felt caught. He turned in a circle. The same streets followed the same old gridwork, the same signs swung on hinges, the same smells pooled in doorways and poured from windows.

He felt like a fool. While he had been up on his mountain watching the world spin, here time had stood still. "Here, Charlie, here!" he began to cry, needing a sense of purpose.

He shambled down the street, a strange, unkempt figure with a wild beard and threadbare clothes. His loose boot soles slapped the boardwalk.

"Here, Charlie, here!"

There were peddlers and gamblers, ex-miners and prostitutes. There were restaurants and general stores and cigar manufacturers. But Robert Haack kept his eyes lowered.

"Here, Charlie!" he cried over and over. He examined niches and alleyways, open stairways, deserted buildings, slop pails at the rear of restaurants. Strange dogs curled their lips and snarled.

"Here, Charlie, here," rang out his chorus. It was an exercise in futility, an exercise in love.

And then finally, just off Cormorant Street, in the utter darkness of the juncture of two brick buildings at the rear of a right-angled alley, Robert Haack spied two familiar gleaming eyes. It was Charlie!

But what was this? There was no leap forward, no joyful reunion of dog and master, no emotional release as they discovered each other. Instead, Charlie stood her ground. And now that Haack's eyes had adjusted to the dimness, he saw that there was a second dog with its paws up on Charlie's back. And Charlie's tail was flagged aside. There were a few rapid thrusts, which Charlie received with equanimity, and then the dog dismounted and turned its back, still tied to Charlie.

The dogs stood calmly, Charlie regarding Haack and the other dog facing the wall.

Naturally Robert Haack understood at once the mistake he'd made. He even smiled about it, although it was a painful moment for this man who had considered his dog his confidant.

"Okay, old girl," he murmured, "but I wish you'd told me. What's a dog like you going to do with puppies?"

Robert gave the matter some thought, then eased the two dogs, still attached to each other, hand in glove, into better light. He had heard from somewhere, perhaps from his father, that if you can break the tie of two animals, that is, before they are ready to part, then the mating won't take. He had been told how to do it, although there had never been an occasion for him to use the technique.

It was a moment of trust. Of Robert Haack in himself, and of Charlie in Robert.

"Easy, boys," he said, edging closer while drawing the dogs into the open. "This is the way the Indians do it."

Concentrating fully, thinking only of Charlie, who could barely survive as it was and who would never, he was sure, be able to care for a half dozen offspring, he knelt down between the two animals. Who both turned their heads to watch him. He thrust his hand up the male dog's anus to search for the nub of the gland that, he'd been told, would release the hold. He twisted his hand and probed. The male dog whimpered in outrage. Charlie trembled.

Nothing happened.

Robert Haack bent his head to his sleeve to wipe away the sweat that ran into his eyes. He was aware as he crouched there that people had gathered to watch. He did not care. Charlie was his dog and she was his responsibility. He had to help her. He had to keep on trying.

"Come on, you buggers," he said. But still the dogs stayed tied.

At last Haack withdrew his hand to rethink the whole matter. As he puzzled, a pair of feet on the periphery of the onlookers crept closer. There were other feet also, and some laughter and murmuring. But there was something about this particular pair of feet that finally drew his attention.

Still contemplating the problem, plus the relationship of dog to man, Robert Haack looked up.

And saw India. "Robert?" she whispered. He could tell that until that moment she had not been certain that it was him.

"Robert?" she said again with an unfathomable expression.

Slowly, as if in a dream, he rose to his feet. The set piece of dogs broke apart, and Charlie took off at a run with the male dog following. Robert tried to speak, but he couldn't. Where were the words to explain what had happened?

Stumbling, blinded by shame and in a rage at the injustices that starred his life, Robert turned away from her and, moving with dignity, but walking faster and faster and ignoring India's calls to him to wait for her, he found an opening, and, pushing through chickens and past heaps of rubbish, lost himself deep in the underpinnings of Chinatown.

CHAPTER SEVEN

"Cachalot Inlet.—The southeasterly and westerly winds blow through with great violence."

British Columbia Pilot, Volume I

"You have cut yourself shaving," says Fan, pointing.

I put my hand to my cheek. My fingers come away sticky and covered with blood. "That's funny," I say, "I don't feel any pain."

She shrugs.

It is early morning. A calm day at anchorage at Cachalot Station in Kyuquot Sound. Blue jays screech at us from the shore. Swallows flutter and dive above the ruins of the oil house. Although thirty years have passed since the station was operating, its outlines remain. Besides the oil house, there is the wharf, and the slip for hauling out whales; the fertilizer dryer and cutting-up platform; the trying-out tanks; and bunkhouses, cook shacks, and staff bungalows. It was all left as it was so that as soon as the market improved, the whaling could be resumed.

The station grounds are overgrown with brush. The beach is a shambles of broken timbers and rocks. Behind the station clearing there are heavily forested hills. The screaming jays are joined by kingfishers, which dispute the territory.

"Not much here," says Fan as we row away from the *Rose* in the little red dinghy.

"What did you expect, Fan? Eighty men slicing up blubber? They were Japanese and Chinese crews, mostly. When the station was closed they all went home. There was no reason for them to stay."

"It seems a strange place to have built the station at all," she says. "Why here? Why not somewhere more sheltered?"

"The men who built the station were businessmen, Fan, not sailors. It looked like a good anchorage to them, and that was enough. Besides, the whaling boats weren't meant to remain tied up. They were working boats, out for ten days at a time, then taking on stores and coal and going out again. They say that when a storm hit, the whalers ran north to a bay on the other side of Kyuquot. The manager didn't like to see them tied up alongside the factory."

We bump up against a rotted piling. I roll up my pant legs and step out of the dinghy into a foot of water. "You could earn good money then, Fan," I tell my stepmother as I haul the dinghy up the shingle, wincing as I step on barnacles. "As much as ten thousand dollars a season as a skipper, or three thousand as a hand. There were tennis courts here then, and they hunted game for pleasure. The mail steamer, *Princess Maquinna*, called in regularly. It was not an uncivilized existence."

We are standing on the edge of nowhere. The birds have fallen silent. The mountains press us near to the rim of water. When we walk, clambering over the fragile, decrepit tangle of boards, ocean debris, and rusted metal, I have to shake my head to clear it of a noise like running water. I shake it, it clears, then the noise begins again. I stop still to listen.

"What's the matter, Robert Lam?" asks Lam Fan.

"Hush, Fan," I tell her, "I'm trying to hear something."

We both stand listening. "I don't hear anything," she says. "There is nobody here, you said so yourself."

I start to walk again, and immediately stumble. When I look down to see what my feet have caught on, I stumble once more.

"I can't feel anything, Fan!" I say. "My feet have gone numb!"

"Five minutes ago you complained about cold water! I don't know what you're talking about, you are not yourself."

"But I am, Fan, this is me, Robert Lam!"

She regards me coldly. "Sit down then and get hold of your thoughts. I have told you before, you read too many books. They are not good for you. You should get out more, take up sports."

"Play tennis, Fan?"

"You know what I mean. Now look around you and pay attention."

I do what she says. I see the outlines of some buildings overrun with grass. I see the green of the forest, the mottled blue sky, the blue-green water. I hear a stream running, outside, not in my mind, and when I look for it, find it tumbling down some rocks a few yards behind me.

A hummingbird flies up for a look at the beached red dinghy. The sun shines hotly through a haze of cloud. I wipe the sweat from my brow.

"Oh!" gasps Fan. I look up at her quickly.

"What is it, Fan?"

She averts her eyes. She toes a hole in the beach. "Nothing, Robert Lam, it is nothing important."

"Fan," I say warningly. "Don't do that to me. Whatever it is I am better off knowing. Don't keep me guessing."

She takes a breath. I watch a butterfly settle on her wrist then skitter away, plant to plant, along the beach. She lets the breath out. "It is your face, Robert Lam. When you wiped your hand across it your eyebrow came off."

She still won't look at me. "I don't think that's funny, Fan," I say. "I thought you were in real distress, that you were worried about me. God knows I'm worried enough about myself. I told you, I can't feel anything in my feet."

"Please yourself, Robert Lam," she says. "You asked me to tell you what I saw that disturbed me."

"I'm still waiting," I say crossly.

The hummingbird returns to the dinghy, then it whirrs along for a look at Fan's red fingernails. "Ha, ha!" I cry. "That proves it, Fan. I knew you were real."

It is her turn to be cross. "You are such an idiot, Robert Lam. You know nothing about nothing, body or spirit. I'm going back to the *Rose*."

"You can't go without me!" I complain like a child. But she has gone, and I am left sitting on the uncomfortable beach all alone.

"Bitch!" I whisper. Then, "Bitch!" I shout as loudly as I can. The ugly word echoes round the hills, shaming me. The birds, the butterflies the comforting susurration of my surroundings, all quit. "Who is this man," says the quietness, "who carries such ugliness in him? Who is he?"

I have no answer to that, and so I say, instead, to myself, "Get hold of yourself, Robert Lam. Get hold."

I take the Chinese coin from my pocket. It shines dully. I lift it to throw it out into the water, for it has brought me no luck, but it slips between my fingers.

When I bend down to search for it, I find instead a glistening fist-sized object in the grass. It is a whale's eardrum. And so, naturally, I hold it to the side of my head to listen.

The gambling debt. The fine for drunkenness. The workingmen's association blacklist. Robert Haack was back where he had started some months earlier. At home in the Johnson Street ravine, with the companionship of his chastened dog, Charlie, and recently shamed in front of the woman he loved.

It was love he now thought about. For in that worst of all moments, when he'd been seen with his hand thrust up a dog's anus, he had known that he and India belonged together and never should part. There had been a shock, a physical jolt, as if love had progressed beyond their control in spite of his absence. It was chemistry run wild, irrational, unstoppable.

And he was certain that what he'd felt, she'd felt. And he did not want it to stop. He wanted to find her and ask her to marry him. He wanted a home, a family. He wanted to work and be happy. He wanted to take her with him to a new life in San Francisco. He wanted his life to turn out well, as his mother (the teacher) had told him it would. He wanted a happy ending.

So what was he to do about it?

Robert shook out the piece of canvas he had held over himself and Charlie to keep off the rain. He spread the canvas on the ground to dry. Charlie at once sank down upon it.

Robert Haack sighed. Somehow he had to straighten out his life. He had to show India he was the man she thought he was. Then he could go to her with something to offer. Not empty-handed like this, hungry like this, soaking wet and on the verge of a cold. With his clothes in rags and his hair unkempt. Not like a beggar.

He took off his hat and began to swat at the flies, which had risen from the dust the instant the rain had stopped. There were problems to be solved. There were difficulties to overcome. There was the matter of money, for instance.

Slowly, Haack let the thought that had been in his mind all along rise to the surface. The seed that Smiling Jimmy had planted had finally germinated. Time and distance had done it. Plus the need for money. And the need for love. There was a way, if he were willing to risk it. Smiling Jimmy had made an offer to go into business.

But no, no, no. It was impossible. There was his conscience to deal with. There were promises to his mother, and others. There was Charlie to consider.

Charlie rose unsteadily to her feet and slurped at Robert Haack's face. He had seen her grow weaker. He had no money with which to feed her. A man and his dog. The bond between them. He remembered Smiling Jimmy's face as he'd kicked at Charlie's belly. After Charlie had bitten him.

No. He could not do it. No.

And wouldn't the risk be too great? But if he didn't risk it? Were his dreams to end here, like this? Besides, India was sure to understand once he'd given his reasons. And it wasn't her opium factory anyway, it belonged to Sing Yuen.

And so Robert Haack left the Johnson Street ravine behind, and also left behind (for obvious reasons) his dog Charlie, and went to call on Smiling Jimmy. For it was clear to Haack that he needed a partner. For while he could gather intelligence, such as the timing of opium shipments, the speed of manufacture of the raw material, the details of the Tai June defenses, he knew nothing about the considerable undertaking of distributing and selling the drug. And there was loading to do, and transporting to a suitable beach, and finding a boat and crew—not to mention an ideal hiding place—and there was navigating the straits at night. These matters, Haack thought, could best be handled by Smiling Jimmy, a former skipper himself, who had run up and down the coast in all manner of ships. Whose idea it had been in the first place.

And so, suppressing the counter-arguments, most of them to do with his feelings, Robert set out for the Dallas Hotel where Jimmy lived.

Thus, as it had to, the enterprise advanced. A decision balked at on a mountaintop, but taken because of love, became timetables and schedules, movements of guards, availability of wagons, trustworthiness of stevedores. It acquired a shape and momentum, a force of its own.

Haack and Jimmy met in the Metropolitan, where Robert lived once again (thanks to a loan from his partner), and worked on their plans. Or they met at the Dallas Hotel, and drank at the bar, with not a word exchanged between them as to import-export. Or sat outside on the hotel's benches, while the sun, pale as a handkerchief, suffused the sky then shrank, and rain spattered down like paint on the bathing pavilion.

New brides gazed out at them from smart bay windows, and new husbands polished windowsills with brand-new shirtsleeves. And if Jimmy and Haack didn't become close friends, well, they grew used to each other, and even Charlie learned to let Jimmy pet her.

Spring. As it changed to summer. And the weather settled.

While Robert Haack watched the Tai June factory from morning till night, and saw India arrive each day at noon and depart at six. And wondered what she was thinking. And wondered if she were thinking of him. And daydreamed.

While Smiling Jimmy took care of his share of the work. He gathered up charts. He found a boat, and a crew who, if they had known where the job would take them, would have refused it. He arranged for sale and distribution of the drug in the States.

In short, all was done that had to be done, and the date for the robbery of the Tai June factory was selected and marked.

Calendar time. Pocket-watch time. While the sun went up and down like a martinet. And there was nothing to do but wait.

And talk.

And so Robert Haack, destined to speak when he shouldn't, and to remain silent when it was vital he speak, told Jimmy about his love for India. How they had met, where they had walked, what they had done. What his plans were for her. The whole kit and caboodle of the relationship.

"But what," asked Jimmy, not unintelligently, "does a woman like that see in you?"

Robert was taken aback. It hadn't occurred to him quite that way. "Why, Jimmy," he answered, "it's not the seeing that counts, it's the feeling. We're like two halves of a peach. I don't know why it's so, but we fit." "Oh," said Jimmy, "so it's like that!"

"No, no," said Robert. "I mean, she'd do whatever I wanted, but you don't ask a woman like that. Not without marrying her, anyway. Aw, it's personal, Jim. I can't say it, even to you." And Robert Haack blushed.

"She'd do anything, you say? You're sure she feels like that?"

"I'd stake my life on it," Robert Haack said.

Which was a mistake. For there are some words that, once said, can't be taken back. Not when men have to trust each other. Not when a man's word is his bond. Not when what is said is what you want to be true.

And who could blame Robert Haack? He had said no more than any man might.

"I've been thinking," said Jimmy a few days later, less than a week before the planned robbery, "if things are as you say they are with your young lady, and certainly I've no reason to doubt it, in fact if I had any doubts at all we'd not be partners, I've been thinking, I say, that we can simplify our project."

"What do you mean, Jim?" asked Haack uncertainly. "We've got it all worked out now, there isn't anything more to do." He was rather hoping to avoid the subject of India. He feared he had been indiscreet.

"You can always make improvements, my friend Robert," said Jimmy Carroll. "That's one thing you learn with experience. Experience, as they say, is the best teacher, and experience is telling me there's an important factor here we've missed.

"Let's say," he continued, ignoring Robert's glum appearance, "that we didn't have to break into the factory at all. That we could walk up plain as you like and unlock the door. Wouldn't that be safer? Wouldn't that be the sensible course to take, if we had the choice? Why be caught in a robbery when all we have to do is borrow some keys? See what I mean?"

"I'm not sure that I do, Jim," said Robert carefully. He was examining a sheaf of drawings—location of locks and bars on windows, schedule of guards—as if it were the first time he'd come upon them.

"You could," said Jimmy suggestively, "just take them."

"I'm sorry, Jim," said Robert, "I still don't see... "

"Don't be stupid, man," said Jimmy impatiently. "Go to see her, take her out to eat, take her to bed. Whatever is necessary. Just bring back the keys!"

"Oh, no!" said Robert in a thin, shocked voice. "I couldn't do that! It wouldn't be right! She trusts me! She thinks I'm her friend!"

"Friend be damned," said Jimmy, "you said it was more than that."

"Well, it is," said Robert.

"Then what's the problem, boy?" asked Jimmy, squeezing Haack by the shoulder. "You said she wouldn't let you down. She'd do anything you wanted, you said."

"That's not what I meant!" cried Robert Haack desperately.

Jimmy released his grip on Haack's shoulder. His eyes narrowed. His face looked more than ever like a well-sharpened hatchet. "You wouldn't have lied to me about this woman, would you, son? You know what I think of liars. I can't stomach them. I'd as soon see a man dead as have him lie to me."

"Oh, no, Jim," said Robert. "I told you the truth. I swear I did."

"Then that's all right," said Jimmy sweetly. "You just remember that I'm your friend. You've not got so many of them in this old town as you could afford to lose one. There are a lot of men who'd like to see you go down, if you catch my meaning."

Robert placed the sheaf of papers on the bed. "There's just one problem, Jimmy," he said turning to face him, although his hands were shaking. "If I took her keys she'd know it was me that had them. I'd get the blame for it. I'd go to jail. Who knows what I'd have to tell them if they made me? You know what they're like. You've said so yourself." Haack thought, with a sense of relief, that this was a clinching argument.

"That fine girl! That woman who loves you, who'd give you her life! Why, she wouldn't let the man she worships go to jail! Not for a minute. If there's one thing I know, my friend, that's women. She'd go to blazes herself before she'd turn you in."

Robert rubbed his hand on his forehead where the sweat had broken out.

"Don't worry so much," said Jimmy. "This'll make things easier. Besides, you'll enjoy it," he said with a wink, "and she won't feel a thing."

When a man like Jimmy Carroll, who had spent his life as a smuggler, who knew the ropes, who had been (for the most part) successful, appears to be simple, to believe, word for word, what his partner has told him, and when the subject his partner has talked of is love; and if this apparent credulity appears a few days in advance of a well-planned robbery and means a change of plans for that partner, and if the idea of burglary is abandoned in favour of keys, then it is time for that partner, Robert Haack, to look after himself. To harbour no illusions about his future. To think deeply about what he is involved in, and with whom. To wonder why a man like Jimmy Carroll needs him.

In other circumstances, with his mind free of worry, with affairs between himself and India settled, with no concerns as to how he was going to present himself, these self-preserving instincts might have made their appearance.

But as it was, once he grew used to Jimmy's suggestion, Robert Haack quite welcomed it. It meant he would have to see her at last and explain himself, reveal his hopes, and begin his real life.

And so, when he should have been figuring out what Jimmy was up to, instead he went shopping, buying new shoes, a suit and shirt, plus a hat. And getting his hair cut. And standing in front of the mirror in Mrs. Lush's roominghouse, trying out phrases. What he should say first to India. What she might say back. Where it would go from there.

Poor Robert Haack, so immersed in the mist of lies he had told himself that he was lost.

I must have fallen asleep, for when I awaken the tide has floated the dinghy. A fog, thick as snow, has rolled down from the mountains and piled up in the inlet. I can see the stones beneath my feet, the rope that leads to the floating dinghy, but very little else. My feet and hands are tingling but are no longer numb. I stand up.

"Fan!" I cry. "Where are you?"

"Out here, Robert Lam," she answers faintly. "On the *Rose*. You'd better get out here, the wind's coming up."

"It can't be, Fan," I tell her. "The fog's too thick, there's no wind at all."

"Maybe where you are," she shouts, "but not out here. The barometer is falling, and I think we're dragging anchor. I can't see you, either, the shore has vanished. Hurry up!"

I am shivering in my shirtsleeves. The wet folds of the fog surround my body. I clench my teeth to prevent them from chattering as I step into the sea in pursuit of the dinghy. I pull it in by the painter and climb into it. Now where? For already, only ten or fifteen feet from shore and carried by the tide, I have lost my bearings.

"Fan!" I cry. "Keep shouting. I don't know where you are."

"Here!" she cries. And "Here, here, here," the mountains echo.

"Again, Fan. Keep shouting."

"I'm here, I'm here."

Her voice seems to move in circles around me, and I feel the keel of the dinghy scrape a rock.

I swear and rummage in the bow of the boat for a life jacket. If I can find it I can blow the whistle attached, listen for echoes, and at least know where I am in the channel.

But there is no jacket. I must have taken it out. "Fan!" I call again. This time there is silence.

I row the dinghy and try to think. Cachalot is a narrow inlet, lying approximately east to west. I can feel the first breath of wind on the back of my neck. It has to be a southeaster, despite the fog, tunnelling down through the valleys. If the *Rose* is dragging anchor, as Lam Fan says, then the wind should move her north and towards the entrance. And the dinghy is being carried west on an ebbing tide.

But before I have it worked out, the squall hits, dumping the dinghy's nose in the water, wrenching the oars from my hands, and tearing the fog into shreds. I scramble for the oars and manage to rescue one. The dinghy is sinking fast, but ahead, just ten feet away, is the *Rose*, pulling on her anchor and riding the wind and waves like a thoroughbred.

"Help, Fan, help me!" I cry through mouthfuls of water. "Throw me a line! For pity's sake, help!"

I scrabble at the water with my oar, inching the dinghy onwards. "Help, Fan, please help me!"

"You'll have to help yourself, Robert Lam," she cries, "there is no one else."

And so I do. Calling on tired muscles for further effort, making use of the force of the wind and water to drive the half-sunken dinghy a few feet forward, until I can reach out for the anchor chain of the *Rose* and pull myself up. Refusing to give up hope.

And so, muscles spasming in pain and desperately afraid of falling, I finally flop over the stern and onto the deck. Where I lie for some minutes spitting out water and laughing. Each breath I take hurts my ribs. But I can't stop laughing.

"Start the engine, Robert Lam, we're far too close to the rocks!"

I do what I'm told.

We have run out of Cachalot Inlet, the *Rose*'s engine purring and humming, and down Kyuquot Channel about three and a half miles to Volcanic Cove. It is just big enough to take us and is sheltered from all winds but northerlies. The storm has blown itself out, and we are basking in the rays of a pale, weak sun.

I have a stern line out: the cove is so narrow that without it we'd swing into shore.

"How'd you find this place?" asks Fan.

"Genius," I answer, lying on the deck with my eyes shut. I open one eye to see her face screwing up to a question.

"I looked at the chart, Fan," I tell her. "It was marked as an anchorage. I don't think that's cheating."

"Oh!" she says, as if surprised.

"I'm not as dumb as you think," I say.

We rest while a deer stands still at the top of the cliff and watches us. "There is just one thing I want to know, Fan," I say. "Were you afraid like I was?"

"Me?" she says. "Of course not, Robert Lam, I have you to take care of me."

I smile to myself, then sleep.

And so my mother, waiting for Robert Haack to come to his senses, knowing he was embarrassed by the scene she had stumbled on, eager to help him but not wanting to interfere, asked herself questions.

Did she trust him? Would she want to live with him? Was she willing to have children? How much did she like her life as it was, and would she be willing to change it? Her dreams about him became vivid and frequent. So that she woke up thinking Robert Haack was dead, that he had killed himself or been murdered; or that they were making love. For she was a woman in her thirties, and if not quite experienced then no innocent, either: for she and Fan had seen life as it was in the streets of Hong Kong.

My mother, a woman like and unlike others of her generation. Who had had no mother to protect her. Who believed in reform as taught by her father. Who wasn't afraid to take a chance with appearances. Who had an inquiring mind, yet knew how to look to her heart for answers.

The pink skin showed above Robert Haack's ears, where he'd just had his haircut, as he stood with his derby in his hand in front of the door of the Fisgard Street house in which India lived. He was dressed in a blue worsted lounge coat and trousers. The trousers were pegged over black town boots, the jacket was single-breasted with rounded fronts, four buttons and five pockets, and around the small stand collar of the shirt, Robert had wrapped a sailor's tie. To say he had taken pains with his appearance would not be enough; in fact, he felt so unlike himself, as if the costume had defeated his personality, that he kept patting the cloth to reassure himself that he was inside it. Mrs. Lush hadn't helped: catching a glimpse of him as he'd come down the steps of the Metropolitan, she'd burst into laughter. He could hear that laughter still.

He raised his hand to the door and stopped. What in the world was he there for? To see India, of course, and to borrow the keys to the Tai June factory. But which came first? The woman or the robbery? It was a puzzle he had to sort out, for deep in his heart it remained unsolved.

Although it was obvious that when a man turned up on a lady's doorstep, after a long absence, washed, groomed, and dressed as never before in his life, that she was entitled to take for granted what he was there for: namely, for her. And, in this instance, to assume that he was sorry for all he had done and was ready to make it up. Although the fact was that he wouldn't be there at all, at least not at this moment, if he hadn't had a job to do in which she was involved.

Robert Haack sighed and screwed up his courage. He knocked. Rehearsed for the thousandth time how he would start, and began to shake. Inside the house footsteps approached the door. His eyes filled up in anticipation with grateful, reconciling tears.

The door opened a crack. "Is that you, India?" he asked, peering into the opening through which he could see a fragment of a familiar blue dress. "It is I, Robert."

She said nothing. Was she afraid of him? Or so surprised to see him there that she couldn't say anything? Or hadn't she made up her mind yet how to receive him?

He plunged on. "I know it's been a long time since I've been to call," he said. "It's not that I haven't wanted to, please understand that. It's just that I've been afraid of what you'd think, after all that's happened." He waited, but she maintained her silence. He tried to ease the door open a little further with his foot, but she resisted.

"Well," he said sadly, "I've sure missed you. I've been hoping that we might have a chance to talk things over. There's a lot to be said between us. I should have said it before. But the truth is, India, I love you.

"Please," he begged, as he squeezed his body through the narrow opening and into the hallway, "can you ever forgive me?"

There are moments in our lives when we see ourselves through the eyes of others, when the ego's self-deception is torn away and we know exactly how we appear. Such a moment was this for Robert Haack as he looked, stunned, into the bright, inquiring eyes not of India Thackery, his beloved, but of Gook Lang, the reformed child prostitute.

Whom he had helped to rescue some months earlier from the prison of a star house. Who had witnessed his fatal encounter with Henry McMullen, workingman. Who had gone (as he'd forgotten) to live with India, and who now stood before him with her hand covering her mouth in embarrassment, wearing a cut-down version of India's favourite blue dress.

What lurked behind that hand and in those eyes? Was it laughter, or just incomprehension?

"Where's India?" he demanded angrily, feeling he'd been fooled. "What are you doing wearing her clothes? What are you doing here?" He pushed past her and peered into the drawing room. It was empty.

"Answer me!" he cried, returning to the dim hallway. He grabbed hold of the girl's wrist and twisted it.

"She is not here," Gook Lang whispered painfully.

Robert twisted harder. "I can see that for myself, now where is she?" Gook Lang whimpered. The wrist that Robert held had been broken twice.

"She has gone out," said the girl, in tears. "She has gone to work."

Haack let Gook Lang's wrist drop and watched his reflection shrink to nothing in the child's frightened eyes.

"That can't be right," he said in a wondering voice. "She doesn't work on Sundays. The factory is closed. Why are you saying this?" He felt tired, he wanted to sit down and think, but he could not before he was sure he understood what the child had meant.

"I need the keys to the factory," he said. "You just get them for me, then I'll leave. I'm sure you know where they're kept. You won't need to tell your mistress." He did not know why he felt so weak and helpless, what it was that had turned his body, inside the blue suit, into a fixture of wood. He pushed Gook Lang away from him. "Hurry up," he said.

She turned to face him. "I cannot," she said.

A flash of his anger returned. "You'll do what I say or else!" he threatened.

"No," said Lang. "I already told you, she took the keys with her, she has gone to work."

Haack's wooden body turned icily cold. "No, she didn't," he said. "She doesn't work today."

"Yes," Gook Lang countered, rubbing her wrist and regarding him scornfully, "Sing Yuen sent a message for her to go there. There is a big shipment for Tai June coming in. Sing Yuen asked her to make the place ready."

Robert Haack slumped against the wall and put his hands over his face. Jimmy's visage, as it had appeared at their first meeting, shortly after he had kicked Haack's dog, Charlie, swam up in vivid detail before Haack's eyes. He saw the anger and heard Jimmy's voice as he snarled at Robert, who had threatened him, "We'll see, Mr. Haack. We'll see or I'll be hanged. I won't forget this." A warning if ever there was one. A promise of revenge, which he, Robert Haack, had, to his folly, ignored.

Numbness crept from the tips of his fingers into his entrails. He could scarcely breathe. He straightened himself, no longer aware of Gook Lang, who stood alertly nearby, and manoeuvred himself outside.

He was like a man who had awakened from a long sleep, or like a grief-stricken man forced to appear too soon in public. He staggered down the road into the June sunset as a golden sheen of light spread over the boardwalks, the windows, the faces of the passersby. His new clothes, his brushed hair, and shiny skin held a hint of gold. The glitter and shimmer of the street was like a dream, and he was caught fast in it.

Where was India, his pounding heart asked over and over. The drumbeat of his feet on the boardwalks repeated the question.

If India was there with Jimmy and his men.... If Jimmy had known she would come.... If she hadn't been able to get away.... Why hadn't she come back? He couldn't remember if he'd asked Gook Lang what time she'd left.

He took his inert body as fast as it could be moved towards the Tai June factory, towards the chasm of his own double-dealing.

The gold faded from the buildings, and as he arrived at the factory, followed by Charlie, who had chewed through the rope that had tied her to a post outside the Metropolitan, night fell like a sudden blow.

All was still. The Tai June flag was lowered. The chimneys were smokeless, as on any other Sunday. But at the side of the factory Haack found a broken window with the bars sawn through, and from inside he could hear the groans of the tied and gagged guards as they began to come to.

The lane gate was open. Robert swung it wider, and exposed to view the gaping doors of the empty warehouse in the courtyard. The place had been ransacked. The guards had been surprised on their rounds, knocked unconscious, and blindfolded. There would be no witnesses.

While the city had gone about its Sunday business, its citizens gathered in churches or at picnics; with its policemen sleeping or playing cards; and with Sing Yuen courting Lam Fan with tea at his restaurant, Jimmy had gone efficiently about his work. Passing cartons of tins out of factory doors and windows, manhandling crates and strapping them into carts; swatting the backsides of horses and sending them and their drivers and wagons into the streets. Where they clattered away into the distance.

The stillness was oppressive. Robert Haack stumbled over broken crates and shards of glass. He looked into the windows; he walked through every room of the factory, ignoring the trussed-up guards; he paced clear to the back of the empty warehouse, where he struck a match. Within the darkness created by this small patch of light, and where the odour of opium mocked its own absence, he saw on the earth floor a swatch of blackness no bigger than his hand, which was not black at all when he looked at it closely, but red. "India," he said. Charlie, who had followed him on his rounds began to whine. A torn piece of India's clothing lay nearby. Pinned to it was the brooch that Haack had given her. He sank to the floor, touched the dry, hard blood, and passed his hand across his eyes.

For the first time in days, his thinking cleared. Jimmy, who had taken over the scheduling when Haack became otherwise occupied, would have known that the opium was expected. He would have known that, as always, India would go in the day before to make sure that the factory was prepared for it; that the earlier shipment had been fully dealt with and was ready for export; that the incoming warehouse was empty; that the processing plant was cleaned up and ready for Monday. He had known, that is, that she wouldn't be home when Robert Haack called. For, after all, it was Jimmy who had selected this as the day for Robert to obtain the keys.

He understood, at last, that he had been deceived. Jimmy hadn't needed the keys at all. What he'd wanted, and what he'd accomplished, was to get Robert Haack out of the way for a few crucial hours, and to get India into his clutches. Robert: who had given Jimmy not only his drawings and plans, but all the information he had gathered about Tai June, and who didn't know, in turn, very much about the actual execution of the robbery, or what was to happen after it. He didn't know where the boat was kept. He didn't know the names of any of the crew. He didn't know where, or for how long, Jimmy would hide the drug, nor what his plans were for distributing it.

Pity Robert Haack. Pity the terrible combination of loss and responsibility that confronted him. Pity this man in his new suit of clothes, his freshly revealed ignorance, his dead-end thinking. He was afraid to move. He did not want what he was thinking to be true. And so he stayed where he was, with the factory cats watching him from the shelving, and his frightened dog howling, until the police finally arrived.

"But, Fan," I say, sitting up on the deck of the *Rose* in puzzlement, "what did happen to my mother? Obviously she came to the factory while Jimmy was there, and she tried to stop him, but what did he do with her? She can't have been killed, or else I'd not have been born. It doesn't make sense."

"Think, Robert Lam," instructs my stepmother. "Robert Haack had found no body, only a small stain of blood."

I think. "She wasn't killed, she was kidnapped," I say. "But why would Smiling Jimmy do that? Why not just kill her? We know that she was the only witness to the burglary—the guards who were knocked out and blindfolded could have identified no one." I go on, working it out. "And Jimmy would never have let her testify as to his guilt. We know that he feared jail and would do almost anything to keep out of it."

"Except reform," says Lam Fan dryly.

"On the other hand," I say, "he was a smuggler, not a murderer, he must have had his ethics." I shake my head, unable to go further.

Fan nervously taps her long red fingernails on the hatch combing. "You've forgotten one thing," she says.

"What's that?"

"Jimmy hated Robert Haack because he had insulted him. Jimmy never forgave a slight."

"Which was why he made a fool of Haack over the robbery," I say. "I know that."

"And?" she asks.

"India?" I say, the light dawning. "She was part of his revenge, as well?" Lam Fan nods.

"So tell me," I say, "what *did* Jimmy do with her?"

"He put her in a perfect place," she says. "A place that no one would think of.

"Just remember," she adds as she gets to her feet, "that Robert Haack believed, at first, that India was dead. He was so guilt-stricken over his part in the whole terrible affair that he assumed the worst. Once he realized there were other possibilities—that indeed she could have been kidnapped and hidden somewhere—he'd been taken away by the police. He did hear, though, while in jail, that Jimmy had returned to town and was looking for him. But before he had a chance to find out why, whether Jimmy wanted to torment him, or make sure he kept his mouth shut about Jimmy's role in the robbery, Jimmy was killed. It was in a brawl in Chinatown, and it was said to do with money."

"But Fan," I ask her, "why on earth would Jimmy come back? Wouldn't it have been better for him to stay out of the country? After all, he had to go to the States to get rid of the opium."

She shrugs her shoulders. "I don't see why," she says. "There was no one left who could connect him to anything illegal but Robert Haack."

I pause to think about this. There is something troubling me. Some thread or loose end, but I can't catch hold of it.

"Also," says she, "Robert Haack was the man on the spot in this instance—he'd been found at the scene of the crime and so was the logical suspect."

"And Haack never said anything about Jimmy's involvement?"

"Of course not," said Fan. "Not while he knew that Jimmy held the key to India's disappearance, and not while Jimmy had the power— which he did—to have Robert Haack silenced even where he was.

"He was trying to find a way to get a message to Jimmy, possibly to make an arrangement of some kind, when he heard of Jimmy's death. He was devastated, of course."

"Devastated?"

"With Jimmy dead the secret of India's fate was lost. The police tried to implicate Haack in Jimmy's murder—they had suspected all along a connection between the two men—but I think even they believed Robert when he wept and cried out, 'Why would I want dead the only person in the world who could tell me what happened to the woman I love?'"

"You seem to know a lot about it, Fan," I say.

"Everyone did," she says indifferently.

"You had a personal interest, too, I suppose," I continued. "Sing Yuen must have lost a lot of money."

"We weren't married then," she says. She blushes. "He had insurance, he said."

"You still haven't told me where India went, and I still don't understand," I say as Fan turns to walk away.

"Just a minute, I'll be right back," she calls as she leaves the deck.

How futile and sad it is, I think. My mother's future husband left in ignorance as to my mother's fate, yet knowing he was the cause of it.

Failure after failure piling up.

Fan returns shortly carrying a small blue book that I dimly recall having glimpsed in the depths of the lawyer's briefcase. "What's that, Fan?" I ask.

"It belonged to your mother," she says. "She gave it to me, and now it is yours."

I take the book from her hands. The numbness and tingling in my own hands returns. I fumble at the covers to open them. "Help me, Fan," I say. "For some reason I cannot do it myself."

She gives me a look that chills my spine. "Fan," I moan, letting the book drop, suddenly completely helpless, "I can't, I can't read it."

"Do I have to tell you again to face the truth, Robert Lam? Do I have to keep on begging you to do what's best for yourself?"

I scoop the book towards me with cupped palms. The wind flutters the pages open at the beginning.

CHAPTER EIGHT

"There are three channels leading from seaward into Esperanza Inlet and of these, Gillam Channel is the widest and best, and is the only one recommended. North Channel and the passage between the reefs westward of Catala Island and between that island and the mainland northward of it are sometimes used by small fishing craft with intimate local knowledge."

British Columbia Pilot, Volume I

"Well," says Fan, "I suppose we have our diagnosis."

"If you're referring to my malady," I answer bitterly, elbowing her aside as I move from the wheel to glance at the chart table as we leave our anchorage at Volcanic Cove, "then you're wrong. I should never have listened to you in the first place. I should never have let you come along."

"Let me!" she says. "You practically begged me! You needed my help! You didn't know what you were going to do! You said you were desperate."

"I did not."

"You did so."

"Don't be so childish, Fan."

There is a pause while we both grimly examine the passing scenery.

"I can leave any time you want me to," she says. "You are perfectly welcome to give up and run away and go back to your nest in the Pilot House. That's where you belong, anyway. See if I care." She looks impassively seaward, but I know from the tightness of her lips that she is upset. My symptoms, which have terrified me and have set me to imagining all sorts of possibilities, have not left her unmoved. Despite what she says.

"Is this what you wanted to happen, Fan? I've become an old man before my time. Listening to your stories has turned me into a hypochondriac. I hardly know myself anymore. I'm weak and feel helpless and I don't like it."

"My stories! So now it's my fault! I'm only telling you what you've asked about. Don't you ever take responsibility for yourself, Robert Lam? I didn't make you sick. You are what you are."

"I'm a marine pilot, Fan," I say stiffly. "Hundreds of crewmen and passengers, millions of dollars worth of ships and goods have passed through my hands safely. I believe I'm what is called conscientious, and I am extremely responsible, in fact. I wouldn't be licensed as a marine pilot if I weren't."

"Bah!" she says in disgust. "If they could only see you now!"

"Who?" I ask angrily, as the chart slips through my useless fingers to the floor. The *Rose* is rising and falling on the smooth ocean swells of Kyuquot Channel.

"Who?" Fan echoes, her voice rising in pitch. "Your colleagues, fellow pilots, stuffed-shirt adventurers who think they're better than everyone else! And your fellow man, Robert Lam. All those you've fooled!"

"Well, Fan," I say with great restraint, "you could have fooled me. I didn't know you felt like that. I thought you were proud of me and my job. You should have told me earlier. It would have saved a lot of argument."

"That's not what I meant," she says.

"Yes, it is."

"No, it isn't."

"Yes, it is."

We listen to the put-put of the *Rose*'s sturdy Crown engine and the thump of the bow as the *Rose* drops off the tops of the waves into the troughs. I feel myself tensing as we climb each high comb. The *Rose* is not a youthful boat, and I never intended her to voyage on this coast. Each jolt is a threat to her framework. I am afraid of more spread planks or worse, and on these shores there's no prospect of help. We are all too old for this.

We leave Kyuquot Channel and round Rugged Point. We pass the two-story-high black pinnacle of Grogan Rock at the entrance to Clear Passage. There are a score of islets around us foaming with petrels, pigeon guillemots, and tufted puffins. My intention is to reach the town of Zeballos off the northern arm of Esperanza Inlet. We need fuel and food, and I am desperate for human contact.

"If you didn't mean what I thought you meant, then what did you mean, Fan?" I finally ask her.

She sighs. Then she takes several measured breaths. "It's not your job I don't like," she says, "it's what it has done to you. All that emphasis on safety. Rules for this, rules for that."

"But I love my job!" I tell her. "It's all I have. What's more, I'm suited to it!"

"That's what I mean," she says. "You are too comfortable. You know it inside and out. You don't have to think. You go from home to Pilot House to ship and back again, and that's it. You know so little about the rest of the world or the people in it." She folds her hands and refers herself to her surroundings as if they would back her up. The white froth of water round the black jagged rocks, the occasional splash of grassy green on the islets, the white beaches where the fossilized shells, which record the history of these islands, have been ground to powder by the ocean.

From here we can see Tatchu Point, the ceremonial beach, known for its abundance of shellfish, of the Ehatisaht band of Indians. There is also a shoal, which extends far from shore. Tatchu Point is at the northwestern entrance of Esperanza Inlet.

"What I do is dangerous, Fan," I tell her. "You should know, you've seen it for yourself, and when you did you wanted me to quit. How could I be in a rut when, every time I go out, I'm in danger for my life?

"Only a short distance from here, a few years back, a pilot drowned while returning from a ship in a small local boat. We take chances all the time—with ourselves, that is, not with the ships. Maybe that's why we seem closed to outsiders: no one else seems to appreciate, let alone understand, what the job involves. It's quite a burden to carry. If I give the impression that we think we're better than everyone else, then I can only apologize. That's not what it feels like inside. It's a lonely job, Fan, but it is very worthwhile."

"Listen to you!" she says. "You'd think there was nothing else to life but work! You should get out, meet more people, enjoy yourself. Why is it, Robert Lam," she asks, "that you won't try anything new? What are you so afraid of? You won't have a family, you won't take a holiday—this trip certainly doesn't count. You behave like a criminal, keeping your head down, hoping you won't be noticed, burying your nose in books. Why not, for a change, take my advice?"

"Why not, Fan? Because you won't accept me as I am. You want me to be someone different. I don't know who you are thinking of, but I'll never measure up. I like my life as it is. I'm happy, Fan. And if that's enough for me, then it should do for you."

"Should it?" she says. "Why are you unwell, then? What's wrong with you? What's making you sick?"

"You won't let up, will you, Fan?" I ask resentfully. "You won't let me be."

"No, Robert Lam, I won't!" says she.

So it was that my mother's future husband, Robert Haack, was tried and convicted for his part in the robbery of the Tai June opium factory. For there was much circumstantial evidence against him, plus his confession, for why pretend in his innocence, he thought, when his reason for living was lost. For my mother, who had stumbled into the robbery, had been abducted by Smiling Jimmy. And no one knew where she was.

There were painful interviews with India's friends. With Sing Yuen and Lam Fan, who pleaded with Robert Haack for information, and with Lam Fan's uncle, the herbalist, Lum Kee, who could hardly believe that Haack was the same man who had searched with him one night through a network of snowy tenements for his missing niece. As if it had suddenly become unclear who had been looking for whom, and what had been lost.

But to all of them Haack had little to say. Jimmy was dead and Jimmy was the only one who had known what had happened to India. And the opium was gone. And he had failed Lum Kee and deceived Sing Yuen. And Lam Fan didn't like him. No, he had nothing to say to them. There was nothing left of the world that had been.

D'Arcy Island. Six miles out in Haro Strait from Cordova Bay on Vancouver Island, seventeen miles from the harbour at Victoria, with the islands Sidney, James, and San Juan (on the American side) nearby, and with Vancouver Island extending the length of the western horizon. D'Arcy Island. The leper's island. Where there was no traffic. No boats landing or casting off. No passengers, no observers or witnesses. No customs officers. Where at the south end only there was a settlement, and the rest was forested. And the island was inches (or so it appeared on the map) from the Canadian-American border. The perfect place to hide some cargo if a man had the courage to do it. If he could outface his fears.

It was here, after a nightmare journey in the dark in the bilge of a boat, her hands tied with ropes, with the odour of opium surrounding her and with laudanum befuddling her mind, for Jimmy had forced her to take a number of drops before they set out, that India woke up. Her head, cut from the blow that Jimmy had given her when she'd stumbled upon him at the Tai June factory, was aching. She did not know where she was. And in her memory was a series of confusing images: Smiling Jimmy and half a dozen other men, the jolting of a wagon, the neighing of horses, and, beneath her feet, the treacherous give-way of sand. Plus a glimpse of a group of small cabins, then a boat painted green. Lamplight. A ladder to climb. Then the cold, fetid blankness of a boat's hold.

She pulled herself up from the sand. Her hip and back were stiff from the damp. Her dress was torn. Her hair had come undone and lay tangled over her shoulders. She was cold.

She looked about her. The sun was low on the eastern horizon; to the west lay the long parabola of Vancouver Island. And she was standing on the northern end of a piece of land that was set among islands. As to what islands they were, or on which one she'd been landed, she had no idea. A tangle of forest and bush shut off all views to the south, but in the surrounding waters, most notably in the passage to the east of where she stood, there were ships. Most likely, she thought, if she could build a fire she could attract their attention. For it seemed to her, just by the sense of things, that the island on which she'd been cast was not inhabited, and that any activity thereon would be sure to be noted. Certainly, she thought, she was in an unpleasant predicament, and no doubt there were hardships to come, but it was clear by the logic of chance that soon she'd be out of it.

How could she not be? For there were settlements on most of the islands. There was Vancouver Island itself, only a few miles distant.

There were steamers and fishing boats and freighters nearby; she could see them. And there were her friends—Sing Yuen, Lum Kee, Lam Fan, and Robert Haack—who would move heaven and earth to find her.

India followed a trickle of fresh water, which gullied through the sand, up the beach to the edge of the forest. Here the stream deepened enough for her to cup her hands and drink from it.

She washed her face, then dabbed the blood from her temple with a handful of leaves. She combed through her hair with a dry stick of wood. She tried to think, in spite of her headache. She needed to reconnoitre, to gain a better idea of where she was, for one thing, of how big the island was and what it held by way of supplies—that is, food and water and shelter. For if she had to stay here after nightfall she would need (at the very least) a fire and something to eat. There might be—and she would never know except by looking—a farm, or a fisherman's or Indian's cabin further round the coastline. Since the men who had abducted her must have left her where she was for a reason: that being how much time they needed to get away. For certainly, if they had intended to kill her they could have done so easily. And since they had not, she was expected to survive. And so it was up to her to further that end and get on with it.

So my mother reasoned.

India rose from her knees by the stream and brushed the sand and earth from her dress. She tied the edges of the tear in her bodice together: the dress in which she had set out on Sunday, lightweight and summery, just right for the weather. She wished she had chosen something sturdier: but how could she have known what she was in for? And so she kilted up her skirts, loosened the buttons at her neck, bent down and removed several pebbles from her shoes, and set out in a clockwise direction, with the woods to her right, to survey her island.

There was uneven sand and gravel underfoot; there were stretches of jagged, broken red rock. There was mud and marsh, and slipways of boulders oiled smooth with seaweed. The waves washed gently in, softening the shoreline with a thin fringe of foam. And as the sun rose higher, and the sky deepened in colour, India began to feel much better, almost cheerful. In the forest there was predominantly Douglas fir, but there were also yellow cedar and lodgepole pine. Arbutus trees, sculpted by weather, smooth-skinned and peeling, clung to the cliffs overwatching the sea. In their branches the seabirds rested. Wild roses and broom grew close to the ground, and there were honeysuckle vines in flower. A raven flew up ahead of her, crying loudly, and an osprey circled over the water. India hummed. Bees buzzed over her head, and she moved her hands carefully while climbing the bluffs, to avoid the tufts of flowers and clover where they probed for nectar. At the top of one such cliff, she rested.

The sea stretched below her, silvery and dazzling with light. A gentle wind cooled my mother's face, and as she watched, two seals surfaced in the water and called to each other. They were curious, as seals are, and when she called back to them: "Here I am, I'm here, where are you?" they turned their heads to look for her. She sat, hugging her knees to her chest, ignoring her hunger, and thinking, "I'm free, at last I'm free." Although she did not know, herself, what she meant. Except that it was years since she'd had such a thought: not since, as a girl, she had first ventured alone into the streets of Hong Kong. Not since, briefly, at the moment of her father's death, before grief had set in, she had looked ahead to the rest of her life.

When she had rested enough, she again began to walk.

D'Arcy Island. Wave-lashed, verdant, and perfect. Seaweed lay in long, pale drifts on its shores, and there were cascades of broken shells where sea gulls had been at work. There were clam shells, mussels, abalone, chitons, barnacles, and small crabs: these were pink and white, whole and in fragments, some with mother-of-pearl undersides. And in the tide pools, spiky purple sea urchins and orange or ink-coloured starfish idled. The air was heavy with the scents of sun-warmed herbs and grasses. A raccoon washed its dinner, and two deer crossed the tidal flats ahead of her.

Was she happy? If happiness can be found in Nature, then she was. If happiness is believing that one is doing what one wants, and that the will is free....

After an hour more of walking, she reached the southeast tip of the island. From here she could see across the strait to Mount Douglas on Vancouver Island. Just behind it, not many miles distant, lay the city of Victoria, where her friends lived. Where her home and work were. "It won't be long," she thought, "until I go back." It was a pleasant thought, but mixed with a sense of regret at having to leave her newly found island. She wished that she could stay where she was, surrounded by beauty, and with no one to fill it with misery; no human failings and human needs; no robberies and opium addictions and love gone askew; but she also wanted the world she'd left behind; for she had important work to do, and there were many loose ends in her personal life (such as her relationship with Robert Haack), plus the fact that the city was what she knew. With its tangle of friendships and business. Its buildings of wood, brick, and stone. Its meetings, partings, reformings, and failings: its fast-spinning changes.

And so, realizing that it was time to act, and keeping an eye on a fish boat straying within signalling distance as it followed a shoal of fish through Haro Strait, my mother tore a strip from the hem of her petticoat and began to wave it. Back and forth her arm moved. She shouted and smiled. She waved and waved and waved. Surely they must see her, how could they not? But the fish boat steered away.

This was disappointing, but not entirely unexpected, for there was no guarantee of instant success. Still, she was a little puzzled. She'd have thought they'd have responded in some way even if they hadn't wanted to stop to pick her up right then. Surely they could see that she was female; surely they'd have guessed she was in distress. They might at least have sounded a whistle to indicate they were sending help. Why not give a sign that she'd been seen and heard? But perhaps the fishing was good, and they did not think she was serious. She shrugged and walked on round the point and onto D'Arcy Island's southernmost shore. She would keep on trying. There were many other boats in the region.

But twice more, as she waved with her petticoat, as she shouted and called at the top of her voice, vessels that had appeared to be on the point of sighting her suddenly veered away.

They had to have seen her, they must have! And of course (as we know) they had. But what they had seen was not my mother. Not a stranded woman calling for help. No, what they had seen was what they believed would be there in the first place: a Chinese leper. With long flowing hair, and wearing a long Chinese dress, unlikely as that seemed. But then anything was possible in such a place. Hallucinations, even a ghost.

For so it is that we resist the pull of facts and of our senses, and refuse to believe our eyes. And so it is that we deceive ourselves with what we know to be truth. And so it is that we turn our backs on knowledge, on our own valid experience.

*   *   *

The island is as it has always been. Time goes backwards and forwards around it, spinning from top to bottom as if it were never ending. Long, long ago, lava spewed up from the earth's core, and the sun was eclipsed with ash. When the dust had settled there were mountains; when time had passed there were oceans; and then there were fires and middens and burial sites. And then there were the lepers. And then there was my mother, India Thackery.

And now, as my mother, in the pages of her diaries and in Lam Fan's stories, prepared to look behind her, still puzzling over what had happened, as she sensed a strange new element in her surroundings amidst the buzzing of flies in the seaweed and the grating of pebbles in the undertow, as she caught sight, for the first time, of the lepers' dwelling, I turn to my stepmother for help.

"Was it so long ago, Fan," I ask, with the sound of my voice echoing off the drying rocks that silt up our seaway, "that we started out on this journey? That we spent a night, our first night away from the city, anchored at D'Arcy Island? It seems like aeons have passed. How could I not have known my mother had been there? How could you not have told me? I would have made better use of my time."

"What would you have done differently, Robert Lam?" she asks me.

"I would have paid more attention to my surroundings, for one thing. I would have thought about my mother, understood her better, perhaps. I don't know, but it would have helped, I'm sure about that." And then I remember what I can't believe I've been able to forget. "Fan, it was there, at D'Arcy Island, that you made your first appearance and frightened me half to death! I suppose that should have told me something."

She nods. "What else, Robert Lam?" she says. I try to think back to what I had done before meeting my ghost. It seems so far away, as if in another life.

"I went diving and I found something," I say to her. "I had forgotten about that, as well." I reach down from my post at the wheel and draw out from the debris on the bottom shelf of the compass table the fish-tackle box. Inside, where I had carelessly placed it that long-ago day, is a spoon with a large, looped handle. I look over at Lam Fan questioningly. She raises her eyebrows.

"Of course it belonged to the lepers?" I say.

"Presumably."

"It might have been used by someone my mother knew."

"It is possible."

I turn it over and pass my fingers along its corroded metal, then I fit my arm through the handle. "When I found it, it didn't mean anything," I say.

"And now it does?"

"Now it does." I lift the spoon to my mouth, then lower it. It is easier, with my numbed fingers, to manipulate than an ordinary spoon. I put the implement away, and looking ahead, checking my bearings so as to steer safely between High Rocks and Obstruction Reef, I attempt to remember what I'd seen of the island in the few hours I'd had.

There were, behind a ribbon of bush at the shoreline, fence posts that had once marked out a garden. There was a long-overgrown house foundation. There was a muddy cistern receiving a thread of water; and overleaning the beach, an arbutus tree with hatch marks carved along its ancient length. That was all. Evidence of human history. Of people who had gardened and lived and cooked. Who had stood by a tree above the beach and marked off... what? Years? Burials? Boats? What?

We are anchored at Rolling Roadstead, between Catala Island and the west coast of Vancouver Island. I am not feeling well, and although this is not a quiet anchorage—the swells roll in here from both directions—we are safe enough. Zeballos will have to wait. I can eat nothing, drink nothing. My stepmother sits at the table humming, turning over papers, as if nothing has happened.

"How are you feeling?" she asks, between bars of phrasing.

"How do you think, Fan?" I say. "I feel sick to my stomach. I am worried. I've lost feeling in my limbs and face.... How do you think?"

"Seasick?" she asks, stopping her humming. "After all this time? I'm surprised at you, Robert Lam." She is paying me scant attention. Something in the pile of papers she's handling has caught her eye.

"What is it, Fan?" I lift my head from my pillow and peer over at what's in her hand.

"It is a sketch," she says, holding a small square of rice paper close to her eyes to examine it, then passing it to me. "See for yourself."

I lie back down and hold the drawing to the light. It is neatly done, in pencil, and is labelled, "D'Arcy Island." It bears my mother's initials in the bottom right-hand corner.

She has drawn a long, low building against a backdrop of forest. The building is divided into rooms, each with a door at the front leading on to a common veranda. Three steps connect the porch to the ground. The exterior is planking, and the pitched roof is shingled. On the earth in front of this house she has drawn several broken crates, wooden boxes, and a small wicker basket. A pan inclines against the wall of a lean-to attached to the left side of the building.

"There are no people in it, Fan," I say. "It's empty. You'd think she'd have put some people in."

"Yes," says my stepmother, musingly, tapping her long fingernails on the panelling by the porthole and looking out at the shores of Catala Island. "But it's only a drawing, Robert Lam. It is not the real thing."

India turned and saw the building that she later represented in the drawing. But there, as well, in front of the house posts that spaced the long cedar railing, were half a dozen men. She shaded her eyes, as if that could help her understand what she was seeing. For these were not ordinary men. They stood as if frozen; and the features they presented to her, even at a distance of some thirty or so feet, were monstrous.

A dozen explanations as to who they were came to India's mind as she stood there, irresolute, wondering how long they had watched her. Were they fishermen, who, due to an accident, had banded together? Was she dreaming because of her hunger? Were they a nightmare version of the men who had abducted her? Whoever they were, if they were men at all, they must have observed her futile attempts to signal a ship, and hadn't thought to assist her: they might have helped her build a fire, for example.... Slowly, so slowly that afterwards she couldn't understand why it had taken her so much time, she began to connect these silent men, some dressed carefully in trousers, shirt, and waistcoat, plus jacket, others with shirttails hanging out, strings around their waists, and wearing crushed and rain-soiled hats... she began, as if assembling an image made of individual motes of dust picked out by sunlight, to connect these figures with others she'd seen before. On the road to the cemetery at Happy Valley in Hong Kong, begging for money from the passing processions of mourners. Collecting drowning victims from Hong Kong harbour, which they would advertise and sell to relatives for a certain sum of money. And here, in the New World, she'd heard mention of one of these men having been found sleeping beneath a sidewalk in Victoria. Although, as to what had happened to him afterwards, she hadn't thought to inquire. For these, she finally understood, were lepers. Outside the magic circle of business, of hungry miners and prostituted children, of reform and plans and progress, in which she and others she knew were interested. Outside the magic circle of humanity.

And so there it was: she had been landed on D'Arcy Island, the lepers' island, and these were the sufferers who were exiled there. It was the last place on earth she'd have wished to find herself.

For, like everyone else in Victoria and in the rest of the colony, India had given no thought to the men who had disappeared so quietly, leaving wives and children, parents and friends in China in astonished ignorance as to their whereabouts. Leaving those who had known them on the west coast of Canada with the sad task of removing their names from all remembrance. For once stricken with the disease, they were considered to be dead, or as good as. And once they were taken to the lepers' island, most usually under extreme protest, all their property was left behind to be absorbed by the government or by their relatives—money, land, books, letters, whatever they had gathered. And no record was kept, either of what was taken from them or of their names or origins. Not even by the Board of Health. For they were Chinese lepers, immigrants. Carriers of the most dreaded disease on earth.

And so my mother stood and looked at these men and was badly frightened. Not just of contagion, for certainly in Hong Kong, where she had come from, the lepers weren't isolated, and their presence at the edges of the community hadn't seemed too worrying, although she knew it was important not to touch them or to share their food or drink. What she was concerned about was what they might do to her. For these were men who saw no change ahead of them but the advance of their disease; these were men with nothing to lose.

She stepped forward, impelled both by her fear and the imperative need to conceal it, calling out, "Hello! I didn't see you there at first. I'm afraid I'm lost. Can you tell me where I am?" She smiled charmingly.

But not one of them answered, and—she could sense it—they were becoming increasingly hostile. They neither beckoned her nearer nor waved her away.

For what need had they to explain themselves? This was their island. Their world she'd invaded.

Still, men, even men like these, who in the opinion of the outside world no longer existed, were individuals. They had come from seashores and mountaintops, from farms and cities and villages; from families; from particular genes and environments. They, as individual men, with personal histories, with wives and children and parents and sisters, were unlikely to harm her.

"No, Robert Lam," interrupts my stepmother. "At this moment these men are dangerous. You forget that they have seen no one but each other for months. And now India, a woman alone, comes along. What is there to stop them from doing what they like? Why should they not be bitter against those who have removed them so far from their homes? Who is there to report whatever happens to her? And why should they care, Robert Lam, when they have nothing to look forward to but staying where they are, and to death, and when nobody cares about them?

"You have forgotten, it seems," she goes on, "what you saw during the war. Did not men who lived together, who fought together, act as one? Did they not do things of which, as themselves, they would have been ashamed? Isn't that how it was?"

I cannot answer, for, of course, I have not forgotten at all. I remember the enemy sailors we did not take on board when we came upon them after a sinking, and of how one of our men trained a gun on them and fired, although no order was given. And how we did nothing. I remember what happened one day in Freetown, when, convinced of my imminent blindness, I turned my fear and terror on someone else. What Fan says is true, and has long been on my conscience....

And so....

And so at the bottom of the steps leading up to the veranda, India stopped. She swallowed several times to subdue the nausea that had risen to her throat. She hadn't thought of what it would be like up close—the stench of open sores and of rotting flesh. The lepers she had seen in Hong Kong had been seen from a distance.

"I'm very sorry to bother you," she said, attempting to smile unconcernedly. "I have come to this island by accident and I only want to return to my home. I'm hoping that you can help me. Perhaps you saw my attempt to signal?"

The lepers continued to regard her in stony silence.

"The trouble is," she went on despite this, "I've been walking now since early morning, and I'm hungry and thirsty. I'd be grateful if you could give me something to eat and drink."

("Why does she say this, Fan? She knows she must not eat their food."

"She has very good manners, Robert Lam. She is appealing to their better natures. Besides, it is only food they've touched she must not eat. It does not occur to her that this could be a problem. She is like those ladies long ago in China, missionary ladies who went places that were very dangerous, and yet no one harmed them. It is the strength of innocence, Robert Lam. It does not exist today."

"Some of those missionary women were not harmed, Fan. But I know there were others. There were ten nuns, for example. I remember reading that they were raped and murdered. Their breasts were cut off."

"I know, I know," says Fan, "but this does not change my point.")

"There is no food for you here, lady," said one of the lepers, a man whose name she learned later was Sim Lee. "You go away now, please, we do not want you. Go away!" he repeated, gesturing violently. India took a step back, but then stood her ground. "I'm afraid you do not understand," she said. "I have no choice but to ask for your assistance. I need food and water and shelter. I have tried to signal a boat to take me away from here, but no one answers. I have only the clothes I am wearing, I have nothing else at all."

A second man, who was called Nap Sing, smiled a grim smile at her as he said, "What is that to us? We have only just returned from burying one of our friends in the bush. The earth from his grave still covers our boots. Any one of us would have preferred to be in his place. Why should it matter to us if you are hungry or thirsty?" He spat and turned his back on her.

The others, looking from one to the other, nodded their agreement. Except for one man, Chou You, who hadn't been listening. Chou You, who was simple-minded and nervous and who spent his waking hours splitting wood, had noticed what the others hadn't: that there was a wound on India's temple, and that she was pale with fatigue, and frightened. Perhaps he half-remembered his mother, or a sister, or a long-ago sweetheart. In any case, he edged down the steps towards my mother. In his arms he cradled the hatchet he took with him everywhere.

"No, stop!" shouted Sim Lee, when he realized where Chou You was headed. "Chou You, go stand over there," and he directed his friend to the woodpile.

Chou You hung his head and obeyed.

"You see," said Nap Sing, who had turned at Sim Lee's shout, "already you are causing us trouble. What do you think would happen to us if you were found here? We would be punished, that is for certain. Lady, please go away, please leave us alone."

My mother, beginning to see the situation from the lepers' perspective, looked at the ground, but stubbornly she said, "What would you have me do? I cannot swim away from your island. I do not want to be here. I was brought here against my will, but if I am to leave, you will have to tell me how." For, of course, by now India understood why no passing boat would come to her rescue, and why none ever would.

Nap Sing, who had had to leave his twelve-year-old child behind in Victoria after living there for four years, turned away to enter his room, but returned in a moment with a cup in his hand. "All right then, lady," he said, dipping the cup into the water bucket on the porch, "I will give you a drink." He held the cup out to her, regarding her expressionlessly.

Time stirred and settled. Slowly, India, as if hypnotized, lifted her hand to receive the proffered cup. What would she do with it? There were murmurings from the other lepers who watched—they knew what was risked. How could she take it—but how could she not? For it was, as well as a challenge to her, an invitation to trust.

But Ah Chee, the youngest of the lepers, who was in the poorest health, had dragged himself along the railing, his face wrung with anguish. "No, miss, please!" he cried out, trying to lower himself down the steps to stop her, "I will show you where to find a drink."

Ng Chung, who, like Kong Ching Sing, had not yet spoken, and who had a wife and child in China, reached out to stop Ah Chee. "No," he said to him, "you rest. I will take her myself. There is a cistern at the back," he said to my mother. "The water there is clean. You can use your hands to drink. Please follow me."

On the back of an undated, unstamped letter to the Victoria *British Colonist*, which I have found among the other papers belonging to my mother, and which I have read sitting up in bed with a cup of tea steaming on the ledge beside me—a cup I have filled only half full, for the *Rose* at anchor at Rolling Roadstead, an anchorage particularly well titled, continues to rock on the swells—my mother has noted down the names and several details about the men she met on D'Arcy Island.

Sim Lee keeps his hands always hidden in his pockets. The disease has disfigured his face. He has no eyebrows or eyelashes, his nose is broad, and he has long, thick earlobes. He is fifty-two years of age, with a wife and child in China.

Kong Ching Sing is partially paralyzed. He has only stumps for hands and feet.

Chou You is a simpleton. He is forty-three years of age. He has no sense of taste or smell.

Nap Sing used to live in Victoria. His face is badly affected by leprosy; he has no lips or nose. He is forty-one years old.

Ah Chee is covered in sores. He is losing his sight and cannot stand without support.

Ng Chung, who, like Sim Lee, has a family, is thirty-nine years old. The fingers on his hands are contracted and almost useless. When being put on board the *Alert*, the steamer that brought him here, he tried to cut his throat.

I turn the letter right side over and read again what my mother—I would guess within a short time of her arrival at the lepers' colony—had written but never sent to the public.

Editor, the *Colonist*:

I am appealing to you on behalf of the lepers of D'Arcy Island, who mercilessly and cruelly are placed there out of reach of assistance, cut off from all communication with the outer world. Suffering or dying, not one friend near to soften their distress. When in more or less anguish they are forced away to their destination for life, their ears are ringing with promises of the good time they will have, how well they will be cared for, what plentiness for all, etc., and they are told in case of need merely to hoist the flag and assistance will be rendered promptly. Recently the flag was hoisted as an appeal for help to a dying man. For six long weeks the appeal was made to weather wind and sky, while the miserable man hourly and anxiously expected the promised assistance and possible relief, which never came. Soon the poor man was dead and buried and no more in need of or dependent on any human or inhuman assistance. Great outcry is made when we occasionally hear of the behaviour of the Chinese to their fellow creatures in similar cases. But the treatment of these unfortunate beings beats every cruelty, because the whole arrangement made for them is a permanently and systematically adopted way of inflicting long sufferings, which should not be allowed in a nation of people calling themselves Christians. What moral right have those responsible for the welfare of the lepers to keep them on an island without proper attention being paid them? No judge dare condemn a man to death through caprice. Therefore should no administration dare to punish with worse than death people in no criminal guilt but stricken with disease. If justice and right were done they should have been taken to a hospital where competent doctors and nurses are in constant attendance.

Yours, etc.,
Miss India Thackery

I put the letter down on the blankets. I like the rocking of the *Rose*: it reminds me of my younger days, when, as an apprentice, then as an officer, I'd sailed on long voyages. Where the motion of the sea entered the body and soothed the blood, and brought into rhythmic harmony one's work and one's thoughts; when the ship was the limit of the world, and within it, you were—at least if an officer—very well looked after. I always regretted our time in port and avoided going ashore. It was like being born, emerging from a perfectly comfortable womb into a cold, hostile climate. Where you were on your own.

I sigh. There is no one here to take care of me except myself, and I do not actually want to spend the rest of my life below deck, even on this boat I love, the *Rose*; nor do I wish to finish my tour of the world at Rolling Roadstead.

I turn down the blankets and get up.

*　　　*　　　*

From Rolling Roadstead up Esperanza Inlet—the inlet of Hope—to Zeballos Inlet, and down the length of this rocky steepto waterway—too deep for anchorage—to Zeballos settlement. With its government wharf and sawmill and its seaplane anchorage. With its post office, hotel, and hospital. With its old prospectors—for the town was the centre of a west-coast gold rush, until about ten years ago, I think—resting, in the sunshine, between rain showers, on their laurels. And where I find I am not so desperate as I had thought for human contact. A few hours is enough.

I have a couple of beers at the hotel, and a game or two of billiards. The people are friendly enough, but they are not what I want. For the men know each other, and are wary of outsiders, and the women are loud and desperate and ask me what I do to make money. And when I answer that I am a pilot, they ask me to take them away with me. Anywhere. Just away from where they are.

Islanded. Stranded. Isolated. Exiled. I suppose that's how they think of it. Out of reach of television and movies. Trapped, with their children. But they are living in paradise, an Eden of wildlife: where deer and cougar and bear and wolves inhabit the forest; and where eagles, ravens, otters, and mink patrol the waterways. And the whales, of course. Always the whales.

"I married on a whale once," an Indian woman, who does not want me to take her anywhere, says. I had just bought her table a round of drinks. She winked at me. "My other husband didn't want to share his woman. So he followed me one night down to the beach, and when the whale came to get me he cut off its dick." Her friends laugh, and she gets up to play the jukebox. One of the women explains to me kindly, "Don't mind her, she's drunk. She doesn't know what she's saying. It's a story she's telling. Maybe she heard it from her Auntie."

"No, no," the storyteller says, coming back to the table for nickels. "I'm not lying. It was the best ride of my life." She smiles quietly, as if she harboured a secret, then she goes away again to dance.

Later that night, when I am untying the *Rose* and getting ready to go, for I do not want to spend any more time in this town than I have to, despite my illness, for I see I have other things to do, the woman appears beside me out of the darkness. "If you ever need a cook, mister," she says, "you let me know. I'm a good one. I'd bring you luck."

Then she helps me cast off, and waves for as long as I can keep her in sight.

It is four in the morning, and we're retracing our tracks down the inlet. And I don't want to sleep on land again. And I don't know what is making me sick, but I do know what won't help. Doctors. Hospitals. Diagnosis. It's not medicine I need, it's..."

"What?" asks Fan, with a yawn, stepping out on deck. "What now?"

The first man who had been sent to the island, the lepers told my mother ("See, Fan? I was right. I knew they wouldn't harm her." "You are right this time, Robert Lam, but maybe not forever."), was the only one who had ever escaped it. He'd been left on D'Arcy Island alone, without facilities—not a shelter, not even supplies or blankets—of any kind. When the health inspector returned three months later to check on what had happened to him, the leper could not be found. India suggested that he might have died of exposure and been devoured by animals; or that he might have swum out into the treacherous currents of the strait and been drowned. But the lepers insisted that his family had come in a boat to rescue him. It was a story they repeated to each other often.

Those who could, namely Sim Lee, Ng Chung, and Nap Sing, had helped India set up a shelter in the middle of a small clearing. The dwelling was made of saplings tied together to form a frame, and it was sheathed with leftover planking and the remains of packing cases. Sacking covered the windows, and with a pair of hinges that they had removed from a cupboard in the dead man's room, they had managed to hang a door. It had also been agreed that, at least for the interim, India would take over the dead man's other belongings—his clothing and blankets and dishes, and, of course, his rations. Normally these goods were split amongst the surviving men, but in the circumstances, and after long discussion, the lepers had decided to make an exception. And so after cleaning and boiling and scrubbing, airing and drying, India had made her camp as comfortable as she could. She knew approximately how much time she had to wait. It would be five or six weeks before the supply boat—either the *Alert* or the *Sadie* came every three months—would arrive and she could leave the island. And in the meantime, there was the sunlight in the daytime in which to bask, and moonlight at night by which to watch the deer as they came to graze in the meadow surrounding her house. And there were plans to make: how she would take up the cause of the lepers on her return to Victoria, and obtain better treatment for them from the authorities. How she would raise funds for them, and hire doctors and nurses. How she would work for the building of a proper hospital. And while she was waiting, so as not to lose track of this brief but important experience, she borrowed writing materials from the lepers and continued to keep her diaries.

But as she wrote and made her drawings, she began to feel that the major, her father, had come to peer over her shoulder to examine what she was doing. And she would find herself sketching improvements to the water system, or working out the position of new latrines; or wondering who would help the lepers change their dressings once Sim Lee, Ng Chung, and Nap Sing had lost the use of their hands. And instead of staying by herself in her cabin, as she had planned, she was more and more drawn to these men whose appearance still filled her with revulsion. For she began to perceive the face that each carried within him: a second face of hope and youthfulness and strength. Of possibilities; what-might-have-beens.

Then her mother came to her in a dream, and asked her forgiveness. She enfolded India in her arms and rocked her. She sang her a song that was like the wind or the pulse of the ocean. She sang away loneliness, and when she had finished she made India look down at her hands. At the flowers that bloomed from her fingers: the violets and lilies and anemones. And her mother helped India pick them, not without pain, and they placed them on a windowsill where the sunlight touched them and set them aflame.

She only knew that the supply boat had come when she heard the shouts of angry men. The other noises—the throb of the *Sadie*'s engine, the scraping of the keel on the sand—had been obscured by the sounds of the forest in which India dwelled. Sounds, through which the hum of the wind and the rhythm of the waves also played, and to which India had become accustomed. She was annoyed when she heard these strange voices, that no one had come to warn her, for she had expressly asked the lepers to give her notice of the supply boat's arrival: she had wanted to look her best. Now she hurried to divest herself of her borrowed shirt and trousers and to put on her dress. She knew that the first impression she made on the sailors who had brought the supplies would be extremely important.

Sim Lee had warned her that the unloading of supplies would not take long, and that the sailors were always very nervous and in a hurry to be gone. And so India brushed back her hair with her hands, smoothed down her skirt, buttoned her blouse, then ran.

She could hear the men more easily now as she pushed through the brush and neared the shoreline. There was cursing as well as more shouting. She could almost smell their sweat as they rushed to finish their tasks. Crates were thrown on top of each other; sacks were thumped on the sand; barrels were rolled, and they crashed and clanged where they landed on stones.

India slowed down. Sim Lee had also advised her to be cautious as to how she approached these men. It was very easy, he had said, to put them into a panic. Once, when, during the unloading, the lepers had approached too closely, the sailors had run back to their boat. Despite the lepers' pleas, they had refused to return, and had left for Victoria with half the foodstuffs still on board the steamer. Which had meant three months of hunger for the unlucky exiles.

"Do not surprise them," Sim Lee had told her. "Call out to them first. Tell them a little of your story before you show yourself. Let them know who you are. And do not allow them to think that you have been near us. We will not give you away. We will act as if you are a stranger. That way it is more likely they will agree to take you back to Victoria."

It was hard to believe that he was not overstating the case: surely no civilized man, she thought, would refuse her his help. It was unthinkable. It simply couldn't happen. Nevertheless, she paused as she came to the fringe of forest at the top of the beach. She adjusted her dress and hair once more, and looked cautiously from behind the boughs of a fir tree, at the scene below.

Rice, sugar, flour, potatoes, chests of tea and of dried fish, plus a case of opium had already been unloaded onto the sand near the waterline. In addition there were some small sacks of seeds and a few wooden tools that the lepers would use in their gardening. As well as the sailors, who held at a frantic pace to their work, there was another man standing somewhat away from them. He was tall and well-dressed, and, as India watched, he opened a bag that he had set down on the shore beside him. From it he took out several instruments and a rubber apron, which he

193

put on. This, surely, must be the doctor who, Sim Lee had said, also sometimes came.

"How many, John?" this man called out to the lepers who remained above him on the slope below their cabin.

Sim Lee, as spokesman, and familiar with the routine, stood up and answered loudly, "Seven." The lepers had agreed amongst themselves to hide the death of the seventh man. That way, they would continue to receive his share of the supplies. The doctor nodded and wrote something in a notebook. Although there were only six lepers, in fact, and just as Sim Lee had indicated would be the case, no one troubled to count.

The doctor called again, this time beckoning to Chou You, who had been sitting a little apart from the others, with his axe, slivering a piece of wood. You, pleased at being singled out, smiled and, looking shyly at the doctor, who impatiently motioned him forward, shuffled down the slope towards him. The doctor put on his gloves, and without saying anything further, when You was within his grasp, took his scalpel and sliced off a flap of skin from one of Chou You's ears. This he tucked away in a pouch while You stood in front of him grinning stupidly.

"Get away now," the doctor said to You. "Go on, get back to your place." He turned away, stripped off his gloves and apron, gathered up his belongings, and signalled to the crew that he was coming. And walked away.

Chou You wept.

Surely now was the moment for India to speak, to shout out her name and call the men back. Surely now she must step out from her shelter of trees and make her appearance. For the doctor was helping the men push the boat off the beach. In moments the engine would start, and all would be lost!

But my mother couldn't move her feet. Her hands flew to her face. She felt its roughness, from sunburn and scratches. She touched her tangle of hair, her torn dirty dress, and thought of how she must look. But most of all, angered and humiliated, she thought of what she'd just witnessed. Of the doctor's lack of interest, of Chou You's hurt; of the sailors' fear of all the lepers.

And she made her choice.

For the world she had known no longer existed. Or if it did, then she had changed and it wasn't her world at all. She did not want to go back to it, not with men like this, not leaving the lepers behind, not this way, not at this time.

And as for whether India had lost her nerve—fearing that the sailors would treat her likewise—or if this was an expression of courage, there is no one to say. For the truth lay in my mother's eyes and in her heart as the *Sadie* floated into deep water and the engine eased her away.

The visit of the *Sadie* had lasted no more than twenty minutes.

CHAPTER NINE

"The coast between Cape Cook and Estevan Point, seventy-two miles to the southeast, presents a bold and rugged appearance. The high and jagged skyline of the mountains in the interior, upon which are patches of snow in summer, is remarkable; the mountains bordering the coast are for the most part high, precipitous and generally densely wooded. Between the above-mentioned points the coast is broken by several sounds and inlets; the principal of these are Kyuquot Sound, Esperanza Inlet and Nootka Sound. The stranger, wishing to enter any of these, is well advised to procure the services of a pilot, as the entrances, though lighted and buoyed, are encumbered by numerous above-water rocks and sunken dangers."

British Columbia Pilot, Volume I

"Well," says Fan, peering over my shoulder at the pilot book, "at least we're following directions."

"What do you mean?"

"We have our own pilot, just as it advises," she says. "We couldn't have done better if we'd tried."

We are in Tahsis Inlet, making a run down its twelve-mile length. It is rocky and mountainous and too deep for anchorage. We are heading for Nootka Sound. "You know, Fan," I say, "this is a very historical area. At the head of this inlet, near where Gibson's Mills have their sawmill, Captains Vancouver and Quadra met to discuss the Nootka Convention. It was there, in 1792, that Vancouver Island received its name; although, in fact, it was originally called the island of Quadra and Vancouver. The two captains, you see, despite the fact that their countries were enemies, were friends. Sailors are like that," I tell her.

"Like what?"

"Friendly. They don't stand on ceremony. Politics mean nothing to them. What matters to them is character."

She grunts noncommittally, giving me to understand that she's heard this before.

"Let me read you what it says in Vancouver's journal, Fan," I continue, determined to keep her mind (and mine) for once on where we are, and not on events hundreds of miles away and long ago. For I need a rest from it all. There is too much to think about. And today, at least, I am free from illness.

"Listen, Fan," I say, opening the book to my favourite passage. "'Conceiving no spot so proper for this denomination as the place where we had first met, which was nearly in the centre of a tract of land that had first been circumnavigated by us, forming the southwestern sides of the gulf of Georgia, and the southern sides of Johnstone's straits and Queen Charlotte's sound, I named that country the island of Quadra and Vancouver; with which compliment he [Quadra] seemed highly pleased.'" I close the book.

"But nobody calls it that anymore," she says.

"Pardon, Fan?"

"So much for friendship. What's left of it now? Who cares what Vancouver thought of Quadra anyway?"

We pass the light on the western extremity of the gravel spit on the eastern side of Tsowwin Narrows. It is a bright, sunny day. Two miles on and we will enter Nootka Sound, taking Princesa Channel between Strange and Bodega islands.

"He thought he had found the Northwest Passage," says Fan.

"Who?"

"Captain Cook, of course," she says. "He thought he'd found a way to link the Pacific to the Atlantic Ocean. But he was wrong."

"How do *you* know, Fan? I thought you never read books."

"Books?" she says. "What has this to do with books? I thought we were talking about history."

After the supply boat had gone, and my mother had made her way back to her house in the forest, and the lepers had set about the work of storing, as best they could, the new supplies in the lean-to next to their dwelling, it began to rain. It was the end of July, and this was the first rain that India had seen since arriving on the island. She sat in her hut listening to the drops spattering down from the boughs above onto her tin roof. She lit a fire in the makeshift stove the lepers had given her. She heated water with which to wash out some clothes. She made flat bread. She wrote in her diary. She rested on her uncomfortable bed. Then she got up and went outdoors. An old hat protected her head, and the dead leper's jacket kept the rain off her shoulders.

Breaking out of the brush that bordered the beach, India walked slowly along the shoreline. Pools of water lay in depressions in the sand, and sandpipers, dipping and running and dipping again, drank from them. The silver-grey castings of lugworms drew a cursive script in the sand. Moon snails and sand clams lay broken and scattered, and through the haze of rain and mist they appeared like torn white messages the waves had washed in. Further on, where fine sand gave way to a muddier and coarser grain, there were other shells: horse clams, geoducks, and cockles. In the low-lying wet zones there were beds of eelgrass, matted, tangled, and covered with a furry brown coating that could be scraped off with the fingernail. Sim Lee would know, India thought, if the grass were edible. She toed her boot among the roots.

Littleneck clams, pale brown or pinkish—these, she knew, were good for eating—could be seen in abundance, and when she bent to scratch at the gravel with a stick, she unearthed more shellfish. In her immediate vicinity she found butter clams, and there were oysters and horse mussels growing on the rocks. As to why the lepers didn't collect these to supplement their diet, she had no idea. They existed principally on salt cod and rice.

Now all that would change. For she had a program of work on which she was anxious to start. Not only would a variety of food do the sick men good, but (although aware that there were limits, because of their health) it was India's belief that what the men needed was a change in habits. Healthy activity; plus cheerfulness and common sense and cleanliness. This was her prescription for better living.

And why, come to think of it, had they no fresh fish? The Indians caught salmon in abundance and dried them on racks. Why could the same thing not be done here? If not salmon, then some other fish.... And here were crabs and mud shrimps: everywhere she looked there were possibilities for food. And since there was barely enough to get them through the three-month stretches between supply-boat visits; and since she was now another mouth to feed....

Round the next rocky point, and nearing the region of the lepers' camp, she came upon Chou You kneeling on wet sand and pushing ahead of him a large piece of driftwood. It moved by inches, and she could see from the short trail it had left that he'd only managed to shift it a little distance. He was stuck now in a patch of sea lettuce, and his trousers and jacket and hands were stained green and slimed with it.

India moved the wood to where he appeared to want it, then went back to fetch the hatchet he had dropped. Then she sat, a little distance away, to watch him as he took out his penknife and whittled. She grew chilled as the fine rain dampened her jacket, and soon she was restless.

"Would you like to go fishing, Chou You?" she said. Chou You looked up. He smiled at her and nodded.

"Come then," she said, and got to her feet. She had in her pocket, having made it a few days earlier, not knowing then how long she might be on the island, a rough fishing kit. There was a sharpened and bent nail, and a flattened tin can threaded onto a string. She had made dozens like it as a child when the major had taken her and Fan fishing in Hong Kong harbour. He had always made her wear a hat.

They went slowly to accommodate Chou You, but eventually they stood at the top of a staircase of rocks that fell away into deep water. She held a stick, around which the line was wrapped, in her hand and jigged the line up and down in the sea. "There should be cod down here," she said to the leper who watched her. "Perhaps we'll bring one in for supper." There were several nibbles—a soft tugging at the line like an infant trying a nipple—before one bit. With a quick motion India lifted the fish up onto the rocks. It lay there, blunt-faced and thick, with its gills fluttering. "Here, you try," she said to Chou You.

Chou You took the stick from her, but his hands, they found, were too weak to hold it for long. India wrapped the line around his wrist, and Chou You bobbed his arm contentedly up and down as she'd shown him. Suddenly, the line went taut and You fell to his knees. Slowly, inexorably, he began to slide down the rocks toward the sea. Frantically, India grasped him around the waist, at the same time struggling to unwrap the line from his wrist. Blood flowed down Chou You's arm where the line sawed at it, and his terrified eyes pled with her as the weight of the heavy, thrashing fish proved too much for his light, fragile body. He was on the last lip of the outcrop when someone splashed into the water near them and cut through the line with a knife.

It took both of them, Ng Chung who had come to their rescue, and India, to manoeuvre Chou You out of the water. His wrist had been opened to the bone by the bite of the line.

When he could speak, for the effort had cost him much and his contracted hands were bleeding from the way he had had to hold the knife, Ng Chung said, "You should have known what would happen. We never fish for this very reason. When will you understand that we are not strong men? The things that others can do are dangerous for us. You have almost cost Chou You his life, and me mine. It is only by chance that I saw you both and came to see what you were doing. You should not have stayed here. You should have gone when the supply boat came.

"Now I shall have to take Chou You and dress his wound. We are short of bandages, we have no medicines, and Sim Lee and I are the only ones who can bandage the others. When we become too ill, there will be no one."

It was the longest speech she had ever heard him make.

"I will help you," she said to him, helping to carry Chou You across the sand. "I will do everything I can." But Ng Chung did not answer. In fact he did not speak to her again for three months.

Time on an island. Where there are no distractions from its basic message—that is, that time lasts forever; for there are no distinctions between one day and another; there is no way to measure.

And time itself: a powdery, wind-blown ash spreading along magnetic lines to the rim of the universe. It stands still, with the faintest shimmer on its surface like a sugary spill of stars; it resists the centrifugal thrust that tears at mountains, oceans, horizons. It slides away, disappears in a blink.

There was the ritual of making tea in the morning. There was her walk. There were meetings with the lepers, and talks. She helped them with their dressings when they let her; she assisted with the garden, digging when they couldn't, hoeing and weeding, washing the blood from the tools after Sim Lee and Ng Chung—the only ones still with the strength—had finished their work.

It should have been perfect, shouldn't it? For where else would a reformer find such a place to work? It was a model of things to be done: of vegetables to be harvested and stored against the winter; of wood to be cut and stacked; of lectures to be given on hygiene and sanitation— for India, if nothing else, was Major Thackery's daughter.

And it was true that the lepers were cleaner, more settled: for it was hard to resist this woman who promised them hope. Impossible, at least for a season, not to believe in her magic.

Although the truth was that Ah Chee was now helpless, and Kong Ching Sing could take only liquids; that Chou You's wrist had never healed, and that Nap Sing, who had remained in a depression, wrote for hours, forming the same few characters over and over again with his brush, and not showing his work to anyone.

Of the other two, Ng Chung and Sim Lee, only Sim Lee would communicate. And the truth was that between my mother and the lepers there was tremendous distance.

We have sailed out of Tahsis Inlet and into Nootka Sound, passing Marvinas Bay as we coast down the western shore. It was here that the weapons maker Jewitt was captured from the American ship *Boston* by Chief Maquinna, remaining as a slave in captivity for two years. His account, written originally in berry juice, was eventually published. Despite his sufferings and the murder of his companions, Jewitt and Maquinna eventually became friends.

"Friends!" says Fan, in astonishment. "But the chief treated him brutally! He was beaten and forced to work, wasn't he?"

"Well, yes," I say, "but in the end it was Maquinna who saved Jewitt's life."

"Oh, life," says Fan dismissively. "You make too much fuss about it. You want to hang on to it at any cost. More wicked people have gone on to justify their bad deeds because they have survived and have written books about it than you can count. The good die young, truly, as it is said."

"Really, Fan?"

"Yes," she answers. "It is an old Chinese proverb." And she smiles.

"Then why do you think you lived so long yourself?"

"To trouble you, Robert Lam," she says.

We chug on south past Nootka wharves, where the cannery and pilchard-reduction plant are, and at which are also a post office and tele-graph system. We are in Cook Channel.

"I'd like to stop at Friendly Cove, Fan," I say. "There is something I want to take a look at there."

"You don't need my permission for anything you do," she says primly. And then, after a minute, adds, curiously, "What is it?"

"You'll see," I tell her. And shut my lips.

My mother, on D'Arcy Island, as the summer passed and the weather worsened. As she saw the results of her labours come to nothing. For she could not do it all herself. Dig a new latrine, carry water, chop wood, mend the roof, sew clothes, cook, clean, act as nurse. She was only human, after all, and there was too much work. And the lepers, who had watched her closely and had seen her energy run out, learned a lesson that they had learned before and had only briefly forgotten. That you cannot change the way things are; you cannot redeem the past; that there was nothing left for them in life.

They were waiting. For the slow exchange of cells in their bodies to come to a halt. For decay to set in. For spirits to sink and minds to turn inwards upon themselves. For nothing to happen.

However you looked at it, there were limitations.

Poor India. Who was doing what she had been taught to do, which was to work. Work that nourished, that was a reformer's raison d'être and means to progress. And that wasn't enough.

And so the summer went. In the garden, cabbages that had been planted too late began to shrivel, and carrots turned wormy; and in the sky ducks grouped up in vees and started to practise for the coming long journey.

It was autumn, with its gathering storms and its rain clouds high and lowering. Alder and maple leaves skirled in the wind, and small animals began to prepare their burrows: it was time for change.

One morning, as a cold sun softened the early gloom, and after she'd built her fire and washed and dressed and set out on her walk along the shoreline, India spied a carcass washed in at the tideline. She thought, at first, that it was a deer, for these often drowned as they attempted to swim between islands. And she began to plan what she would do with it. For such a gift—meaning meat as well as a skin for tanning—was a welcome event on the island. And it would give her a chance to contribute something. She had learned enough, she thought, to skin it herself, and she could certainly butcher the meat. And it would give her an answer of a sort for Nap Sing, who had said to her the day before, "If it weren't for you I would have died this summer. Now I shall have to suffer all winter." For it was true that those who would have perished quickly of infection or malnutrition, now, because of her interference, would die more slowly from their illnesses. It was up to her to make the time they had left as pleasant as possible.

And although no one else had said anything, she had begun to wonder if perhaps it wouldn't have been better, and certainly easier for all concerned, if she'd never arrived on the island.

And so, plagued by doubts as to what she was doing, India drew near to the deer, which as she came up to it began to change its aspect. It was the size and shape of a man, and it was clothed in rags the colour of driftwood. It lay on its side with its feet pulled close in to its body. Its hands covered its face, and as she bent over it she could hear its shallow breathing.

It was only when Sim Lee and Ng Chung, who had been watching from the veranda of their dwelling, came down to tell her to leave him alone, that she fully understood that what lay on the sand in front of her was a living man.

"How long has he been here? Why aren't you doing anything?" she said to them as she struggled out of her jacket and tried to place it over him.

"Leave him alone," Sim Lee repeated, putting out his hands to stop her. "You can do him no good."

"But he needs help!" cried India. "Can't you see that he's dying?"

"We have already talked to him," said Ng Chung, breaking his long silence to her. "He was put ashore last night by a boat. He is a leper like us and wants to be left to die in peace. Please let him be."

India looked at the two men who, although she felt she had come to know them a little, she could not comprehend. "I have to help him," she said.

They regarded her coldly. "He has told us what he wished. He has begged us to let him drown when the tide comes in. It is his decision," said Ng Chung.

"No," she said firmly, "he is too ill to think for himself. We must do what we can to save him."

"Who owns his life?" said Sim Lee angrily, glaring at her. "Is it me, is it you? I think it is the one thing he has left for himself. I think he knows what is best."

But it is against all human instinct! she wanted to shout. It is as good as murder! But, in fact, she was not as sure of herself as she'd put out. Could doing nothing also be a form of love? Could helping someone actually be harmful if it went against that person's desire? What about freedom of choice? What about someone's right to direct his life for himself?

These questions, troubling in the extreme, beset her at this least opportune of moments. Work for progress, for evolution, for salvation: that's what she had been taught. No one had ever suggested anything different.

And yet she hesitated. Watching the subtle rise of water over the land as the sea responded to the pull of the moon. Noting the dignified stillness of the dying man, the shift of light that made him take on the colouration of the sand, and appear to become part of it.

Ng Chung walked away from her. After a moment, so did Sim Lee. On the porch, Nap Sing was writing. Kong Ching Sing hummed a song, Chou You, nursing his wrist, rocked with his hatchet, and Ah Chee sat watching the horizon.

Never had she felt so alone, so tired of keeping the machinery going. What's the point, she thought, if this is all there is to it, if doing nothing is the highlight.

The castaway, between dry, caked lips, murmured when she tried to give him a drink. "Go away. Please go away. In the name of heaven, please leave me alone."

And so the earth turned through its hours, and there was a slow cycling of temperature and weather as the lepers and India kept their vigil. As the sun traced its secret path behind the clouds, and the magnet of gravity worked on the waters, as the waves rolled gently in, turning the dying man's body round by quarters, lifting it, catching it, excluding it from the world of pain and suffering. And so, and so, he was drowned.

It was dusk. India sat alone in her cabin. The ducks had settled, the first owl cried. Although the embers of her fire still burned, India was cold. She shivered, but did not move to fetch her blanket.

She had let a man die when she could have intervened. That was the thought that tormented her. Although she was sure that, in the circumstances, what she'd done was right.... Although she could have held his hand (but he didn't want to be touched!); or she could have insisted that the other lepers help her to move him (but they wouldn't, they wouldn't, and what then anyway, except more time dying?). She could at least, have found out his name. Round and round her thoughts went, sickening her. She could not eat. She could not sleep. Why? she asked, over and over. And then, even less helpfully, why me?

For it wasn't fair that she should be on this island, wasting her talents where no one appreciated her; and it wasn't right that she had no home and no family, that no one cared about her; that she had no job, no husband to comfort her, no child, no future to look forward to. Even if it had been her own choice. It wasn't fair that she had to endure this grief.

For that's the truth of it. That's what had made her sick. Death. The waste of it.

("No, Fan," I say. "I think she just feels sorry for herself."

"And you," says Fan, "can you not find pity in your heart for her? You who have had so much? Who have never lost anyone you loved, let alone shed a tear for a stranger?"

"That's not true! How can you say that!" I cry angrily. "What do you know about it, anyway? You were never there when I needed you."

"You never let me be," she says.

"That's not so."

"Yes, it is."

"Please, Fan, let's not argue."

"Then what, Robert Lam? Do you think because the man was a leper he didn't deserve your mother's sorrow?"

"No!"

"Then what? Do you think that because she cannot get her way your mother has given up?"

"I'm not sure," I say.

"She is sad," says my stepmother. "But she is also angry. That's how it is. As well, she is frightened. She did not know what death was before. She had never seen it come like that: welcomed, but surrendered to with a terrible struggle. Now she has seen it and she does not like it. She will have to sleep and heal herself.")

Which is what she does: a long sleep from which she awakened empty and dreamless; and after which nothing had changed except that time had passed, and that within herself was a vast burden of indifference. And weariness.

India lay awake for a long time with her mind sheltered in blankness. Eventually, feeling a little better and motivated by hunger, and thinking that she had heard a noise nearby, she lit a candle and stepped outside. On the doorstep someone had left a bowl of rice, plus tea and warm water. She took the gifts inside. In picking up the rice bowl, she found, folded beneath it and wrapped in a piece of oiled paper, several notes. There were words—Chinese characters—formed with a brush. She recognized Nap Sing's ink.

She put the paper aside. Washed her hands and face, ate the rice, drank the tea, then went back to bed. Unable to sleep, once more she got up and lit the candle. Then she settled down—not out of curiosity, but out of a lingering sense of duty—to read what Nap Sing had written. It was a poem.

> I am in prison because I covet riches.
> Driven by poverty I sailed here over the choppy sea.
> Had I not had to labour for money,
> I would already have returned home to China.

India blinked her eyes in surprise. She reread the words, made up and strung together by a Chinese leper on an island at the edge of the Pacific— words that insisted that Nap Sing accepted his fate with reluctance, and that he wanted things to have meaning—with increasing pleasure.

Why, in this he was just like her! With his disappointment and looking backwards: but here there was also form and beauty.

India examined the next page, tears polishing her face as she read.

My Wife's Admonishment

You go abroad to seek wealth because we are poor.
In your sojourn, do not sow your wild oats.
Before you departed, I enjoined you to remember
That you have a wife and children at home.
Please work diligently and be frugal with money.
Two years hence, return home to sweep your ancestor's tomb.
Remember, our backs are bare;
Not half a cup of rice can be scooped from the pot;
All our houseware is worn and torn;
Our house is dilapidated.
Your gambling has driven us to poverty.
In tears, I beg you to repent.
You are fortunate to have an older brother to pay your head tax.
Always, remember your gratitude to him.

All the letters not sent, she thought. Conversations not had, love not experienced. Duty, admonition, pity. They were all here. It was a mystery: for the sadness of the poems brought her relief. They were a victory over time itself, since words repeated—forever—the patterns of existence. They were an answer—possibly the only one she would ever have—to the unsolvable problem of what had happened earlier.

Inadequate, perhaps. A clutching at straws. But it soothed my mother's feelings that night as she sorrowed over her helplessness, and the fate of herself and others, the fate of the world. In which a man, even a nameless leper, could be left on an island with not a thought given as to his welfare.

She wept for hours. For Nap Sing, who had written the poems, and who had not the protection of ignorance; for his family, who would never know how he felt. For all that was lost in the realm of failures and triumphs. For the fact that no one outside would know of the poems' existence.

They were grieving, healing tears. And they reminded her, at length, that there was nothing in all creation that couldn't be reinterpreted and made into beauty if that was what one wanted, if one had the art: and that creation was impartial with its own implacable purpose. That there was more to life than progress, there was life itself.

*   *   *

We have arrived at Friendly Cove, near the entrance to Nootka Sound. It is situated "close north of Yuquot Point and sheltered from the sea by the San Miguel Islands," as the pilot book says. It is not an especially good anchorage, being used by the Indians only during the summer (the name of their village, "Yuquot," means exposed to the winds).

There is, situated at the north end of the village, which itself is on a small space of clear, cultivated, flat land at the head of the cove, a church and connection to the general telegraph and telephone systems. More importantly, it was not far from this village that the Nootka Indians (as Captain Cook mistakenly called them—they were actually Moach-ahts, or, people of the deer) prepared for the whale hunt. It is this place I have come to see.

I have said nothing to Lam Fan of my intention. She has already told me that she knew the last of the native whalers—Chief Atlin and Chief John Moses. She would only try to interfere. Either by insisting on accompanying me and telling me her stories, or by preventing me from exploring on my own. And so, after dropping anchor, I signal for a boat to come and get me (we no longer have a dinghy since ours was sunk in the storm in Cachalot Inlet). The man who arrives, rowing a punt that is filling with water even as he steadies it to take my weight, wears a knitted cap and a vast number of hand-knit sweaters beneath his plaid wool jacket. He gives me a toothless grin. He has a scarred, sun-weathered face, and when I ask him he says that, yes, he is a fisherman, but that it is his father who owns the boat, and is right now out in it.

"Your father?" I say in surprise, reassessing my ferryman, who must be younger than he looks, and who has stopped rowing to bail.

"We live up there," he says, pointing to a shack at the end of a row of shacks at the western edge of the village. "There are six of us children. I'm the eldest." He smiles again. And in a few more minutes we have beached the punt and are walking to the house he pointed out. Just above and behind it is the spire of the Catholic church. He has invited me for tea.

Large juice cans, potted with geraniums, flank the steps. On the porch, a long-haired mongrel sleeps. My acquaintance toes him over to open the door.

"Ma!" he cries. "We've got a visitor." A woman, thin and dressed in workman's jeans and flannel shirt, and towing two little girls wearing pink party dresses, comes from the kitchen. The woman shakes my hand.

"I've made biscuits this morning, they're still hot," she says, "we can have some with our tea." Her son goes to the stove in the sitting room, stokes it up with wood, and puts the kettle on to boil. We sit down side by side on a slumping sofa. The woman smoothes her hands over her knees. The little girls look at me curiously.

"It's awfully kind of you to invite me in," I say to her. "I'm sure you're tired of sight-seers. The name, Friendly Cove, must attract a lot of people, and everyone knows that Captain Cook came here."

"We don't get that many visitors," she says quietly. "But we have to keep an eye on those who do come to make sure they don't do any damage. There are many sacred burial sites here, and we have to protect them. No one is allowed to wander off alone."

"Oh! Of course not," I say. Although this is the first time it has occurred to me that there are other interests than mine to be considered.

We sit in silence, listening to the boy chop wood outside, and to the little girls, tired of standing still and staring, rustling in their stiff, starched dresses as they try to wake the dog that sleeps, as if dead, on the porch. On the wall to my right, above a large floor radio with its knobs twisted off, there is a crucifix. A Bible is the only book in sight. But on the wall behind me, so near that the frayings of a cedar-bark rope tickle my neck, are the ancient weapons used in the whale hunt.

I have been trying not to look, afraid that my hostess will wonder at my interest, but I can't resist. I shift myself round on the couch. There is a large harpoon, running almost the entire length of the room. Attached to this is a skein of sinew rope. There are several lances and sealskin floats, and more cedarbark lines. The head of the harpoon is a pair of pointed barbs made of bone. The blades are made of mussel shells, and the whole is wrapped up tightly with cord and strips of cherry bark.

The woman is watching me. "Do these belong to your family?" I ask her.

She nods. I smile at her and sit up straight on the couch. The boy comes in and pours the boiling water into the teapot. He stirs the contents with a spoon, then tips it into cups.

"So," he says, handing me a cup of tea, which he has whitened and sweetened with spoonfuls of condensed tinned milk, "what is there here that I can show you?"

*   *   *

We have taken the trail that runs behind the village. My guide, Sam ("My father took our names from the Bible."), shows me the little white-painted church, which all the villagers had helped to build. There is no bell in the steeple, but it is often used as a lookout for the fishing fleet. I admire the polished bone handle of the door, and inside, in front of the altar, a cedar wood screen bearing the likenesses of the killer whale and the thunderbird. The other item to interest me is in a locked glass case a few feet from the statue of the virgin. The case contains an Indian headdress.

"What's this?" I ask Sam. He looks embarrassed.

"It really shouldn't be in here," he says. "There was a lot of argument about it in the village. My uncle wanted to sell it to the museum in Victoria, but my mother wouldn't let him. She said it was part of her religion, and if it wasn't good enough for the Catholic church, then the church wasn't good enough for her. The priest didn't seem to care one way or another, and so my uncle said the church could have it while he made up his mind. It's been here ever since."

I look at the eagle feathers, each nearly a foot in length, and at the tiny carved whales, which are tied to the headdress with cedar bark. "I thought the church made the Indians give up all that," I say.

"What do you mean?"

I shrug, indicating not only the headdress but the screen and a drum, also bearing the design of the killer whale, which sits close to it. "Indian religion," I say, "shamanism and so on, the potlatch. We were taught, in the school I went to, that the church repudiated all magic arts. Remember the story of Saul, who went to visit a witch? He came to a violent end because of it."

But my guide has walked away from me, scowling, leaving me to find my way out of the church by myself.

Sam is waiting outside next to the cemetery. Long grass blows between the tumbledown headstones, but there are fresh-cut wildflowers in glass jars on nearly every grave.

I go and stand beside him. He has taken off his wool cap. His thick black hair is straight, cut to chin length, and tucked behind his ears. He does not look at me.

"I'm sorry," I say. "I should have learned by now not to talk about things I know too little of. I've offended you, and I'm afraid it's out of ignorance."

"We have a story," he says after a minute of silence, "about what happens to strangers who do not understand our ways. They are lured by dwarves into dancing around a drum. Once they start, they can't stop, and each step they take causes the earth to shake. They can't go back to their ordinary lives ever again."

Across the meadowland, on the other side of this curve of land from the cove, is the open ocean. The beach is long and pebbled, and from here we can listen to the sound of waves landing and withdrawing.

"The only reason I came here," I say to Sam finally, "is to learn something about the whales. I know that this is the village where the whalers made ready to hunt. I want you to take me to the place they prepared. Where they performed their rituals."

A small smile plays about my young guide's lips. How old is he, I wonder again? In his teens? Twenties? The smile turns into a grin. "You sure about it?" he asks.

"Yes."

At the edge of a lake, deep in the woods, inland from the village, I dance. Sam, who has seated himself on the ground, is beating a log with a stick. And singing.

Me. A middle-aged pilot, on the verge of being elderly, in the midst of a story concerning his mother, is dancing round and round, stamping his feet. Three times already I have dipped my body into the lake.

Round and round. While the sun does its turnabout.

And I do not care if the boy is laughing at me. I do not care what he thinks of my antics, nor do I need to know why he's agreed to help me. Whatever I am doing, I am doing it for me, Robert Lam. For myself.

Round and round and round. Drunk with it. Until the singing sits inside me. Clasps itself tight and will not be moved. And so does strength. No more weakness in my limbs, no more numbness in my fingers or face.

And on and on until I hear my stepmother calling, and find myself returned to the *Rose*, face down on the deck.

"How did I get here?" I ask her, sitting up.

"A boy brought you," she answers. "He left you this."

She holds the harpoon head of a whaling lance. I take it with both hands, cradling it. "You spoke to him?" I ask her.

"Of course not!"

I get to my feet, filled with sudden energy, and go forward to start the anchor winch. "Let's get going," I say to Fan. "We haven't got much time left."

"For what?" she questions.

I do not answer, but the hunting song still courses through my veins.

Time on D'Arcy Island. Where the only measure of progress is in the advance of winter storms blowing in from the Pacific and across the land, and in the deterioration of the lepers' condition. And in the gradual evolution of relations between the exiles and my mother. For more and more they must depend on her assistance, and more and more she must depend on theirs.

Keeping fires going, cooking communal food, sharing warm clothes, doing laundry, dressing sores. And, as well, writing poems, polishing stones (in a bag looped round a rock and left in the sea), identifying plants and insects. Keeping a diary. The actions of civilized beings.

Civilization. Without the wood, brick, and stone of buildings and cities. With conversation and memory and invention, and curiosity.

And suffering. And laughter.

Friendship.

But in the pass leading from the mainland and between the Gulf Islands, and heading for D'Arcy Island, there was a boat. And in this boat there were several officials: men who would be glad to finish the job they were doing and return to their homes in Vancouver. For without the knowledge of the authorities in Victoria, whose responsibility the leper colony was, these men—a doctor, two members of the Vancouver Board of Health, and two policemen—were secretly delivering a brand new inmate to the D'Arcy Island colony.

His name was Oung Moi Toy, and he had come from New York to Vancouver equipped with a travelling certificate of health and a train ticket. He had been an inhabitant of the lepers' island near New York City, but had been discharged from there with a changed diagnosis of syphilis. Because, it was rumoured, the New York colony could not cope with his conduct.

Having arrived in Vancouver, he had been held by immigration and diagnosed again as a sufferer of leprosy. Which diagnosis he would not accept. Nor would the Americans take him back. He wanted only to continue to Hong Kong by ship. But not a captain on the coast would agree to transport him.

He was a huge man, almost seven feet tall, with a shaved head, and covered with tattoos. His hands were in chains, because he had several times tried to assault his captors and escape. It was said that in his life-time so far, he had killed more than a dozen men, and numbers of women. This in San Francisco, and in New York City, before being confined to the east coast lepers' colony.

And because it had not been a pleasant journey, and because the men in the boat were anxious to be rid of their charge and return to the more normal run of their jobs, they left Oung Moi Toy on the landing shore at D'Arcy Island without supplies—no food, not even any blankets—and only removed the chains from his wrists at the very last moment.

And so he stood on the shore in ill humour, suffering from seasickness, rubbing his wrists where the chains had chaffed and cut, and swinging his head back and forth like a wounded animal.

For there was something in the air that alerted his senses: not just the lepers' dwelling nor the lepers themselves, who stood watching him, solemn as attendants, round a beach fire on which a kettle (into which they had placed dozens of shellfish, plus an onion and a carrot from their garden storehouse) was steaming, but some other element. Almost a scent. And unexpected.

For Toy was a man of instinct. And whatever was there that shouldn't have been troubled him and irritated him and set up a current.

The lepers trembled as they watched him. What they realized, and remembered now that they had forgotten, was the sheer impact of phys-ical size and strength. With its lack of perspective, and its imminence. Its potential for evil.

Their skins prickled, their scalps tightened, and it was with an effort that they stopped themselves from running. This was no innocent, no piece of human refuse (like themselves) on whom to take pity. This was no brother, this was a threat.

Moreover, they were aware, as Oung Moi Toy could not be, what it was that he searched for and sniffed at in the air.

It was the scent of a woman. Who was my mother, India, who had come to see who had landed by boat, but had remained in hiding at the edge of the forest.

A pall of smoke rose from the burning driftwood; the soup in the kettle boiled, and the lepers stood in silence as the sky appeared to wheel and blur with darkness: for they knew that with Oung Moi Toy's arrival on the island, their lives had changed for the worse.

Oung Moi Toy now turned to look at them directly, and as he did so he pulled out of his legging a knife.

Ng Chung spoke first. "Welcome to our island," he said politely. "We did not know you were coming and so have not prepared to receive you. But you are welcome to share our food until you are able to arrange for your own." Ng Chung indicated the boiling soup in the kettle. "What we have is the result of the labour of all of us. If you are willing to help, you will not find that the life here is too unpleasant."

Which was not, exactly, the kind of speech that Oung Moi Toy might have expected. He was used to having an effect on people. He was used to them being afraid of him. He advanced on the lepers, still looking about him uneasily, but concentrating more and more on the scene in front of him. When he had reached the fire, on the opposite side of which the lepers were grouped, he kicked out with his foot and spilled the kettle of soup. The hot embers steamed and hissed, and some of the boiling liquid splashed onto Kong Ching Sing's foot and burnt it. Although Kong Ching Sing felt nothing.

Unperturbed, Ng Chung continued. "As you see," he said, pointing to the building on the slope above them, "we have a house. Unfortunately it is small, and all the rooms are full. You may sleep outside on the porch, or underneath it if you like. We will be happy to share our blankets with you." Ng Chung smiled, as if to soften the bluntness of his words. But it did him no good. For Toy, knife in hand, simply walked round him and climbed the steps. He opened the doors of the cabins one by one and peered inside them.

"You!" he called after a minute, indicating Ng Chung. "You are going to sleep outside. I am staying here." He went inside one of the cubicles and shut the door.

The lepers looked at each other in consternation. Sim Lee, with an urgent gesture in the direction of where India was hidden, signalled that she should quickly move inland. Then Sim Lee climbed the steps while the others watched him, knocked at the closed door, and said, "You do not understand. Someone is already living here. There is a better place for you. Come, and I will show you."

The closed door opened and Toy stood, bending his head to clear the doorway and gazing out belligerently. He seemed to consider Sim Lee's offer. "Where is this better place?" he asked him.

"Over here," Sim Lee said, pointing to the storehouse attached to the building. "Down there is where we keep our supplies. It is warm and dry there. It is nice, you will see, there is more room." Toy followed Sim Lee along the porch as far as the steps. He was curious, and the mention of supplies had certainly piqued his interest. But to follow any further he would have had to pass Chou You, who had climbed the stairs in Sim Lee's wake.

Chou You: who had no sense of undercurrents, of what lay behind what had been said; and who was far too inexperienced to be afraid.

Chou You, who in a gesture of greeting to this new companion, held out his hatchet. A gesture which, of course, was bound to be misinterpreted. Moreover, none of the lepers realized that Oung Moi Toy, for all his size and strength, was terrified of being touched by them. Because he still believed, despite the evidence, that what had made him ill was syphilis, not leprosy. And he had no intention of contracting the other, more dreaded, disease.

Toy feinted at Chou You with his knife to warn him to step back and to lower the hatchet. But You, instead of acting as might be expected, took a step forward and in friendly response mimicked Moi Toy's action. And so Toy, with inevitable logic, for he had observed not the simplicity of You's ravaged face, nor the swollen hands with their weak grip, but only the all too familiar style of the movement, slashed his knife across Chou You's cheek.

"What makes a man bad, Fan?" I ask my stepmother as we head across the mouth of Nootka Sound in the direction of Estevan Point. We have to steer a fair distance west since there are sunken and drying rocks within one and a half miles of the point itself. The whole area is dangerous, with a propensity for sudden squalls, even in summer; and, with an ebb tide from Nootka Sound meeting the underwater ledge off Hesquiat Peninsula, the seas become confused and choppy. It is not my favourite point of passage.

"A man is bad when he acts without thought of the consequences," says my stepmother briskly.

"But no one is bad to begin with," I counter. "I'm asking you what makes him that way."

She gives the matter some thought as I scan the horizon for spouts. There should be whales near here. There must be.

"A bad man is only a selfish child grown up," she says. "He thinks only of himself and no one else. How bad he becomes will depend on circumstance."

"You mean it's up to chance?"

"In a certain way," she answers. "There are degrees of badness. Most of us have no chance to find out how bad we can be. What matters, if we do, is what comes after it. If a man can learn from his mistakes, then he is not wicked. He can change. If the man learns nothing, he will get worse. Like Oung Moi Toy, who I am telling you of."

"So what we have here, in your opinion, is a case of arrested development?" I ask sceptically. For I think she reasons too simply.

"More or less, Robert Lam," she answers. "It is men who do not grow up who do all the damage. Look at Hitler. He was too fond of dress up and parades and magic. Everyone said, 'Where's the harm in that?' But look what happened."

"For heaven's sake, Fan, be serious. What Hitler did was not bad, it was evil. There is a difference."

"Is there?" she says. "Perhaps you are right, but it has the same source. A man thinks of himself, like a baby does, and when he does not get what he wants, he is angry. When he is big he likes to give orders.... But why do you ask?"

"Why? I don't know," I say. But I am wondering if we are born like that—bad or even evil—and it is only by chance that we do good. For that's what it feels like.

There is a cool touch on my hand on the wheel. "You are too hard on yourself," says Lam Fan. "If you are unhappy it is because you forget you have a choice," she says. "You always have a choice, no matter what." Then she slides the pilothouse window open and puts her hand out to the spray blown back from the bow.

It was cold on the island, and it rained and it rained. The lepers grew thin from the scarcity of food. For once he had found the storehouse, Oung Moi Toy had all the supplies moved into his room.

And there he lay with provisions stacked around him; with spoiled fish on the table and rotting chicken drying in a pan, and with a pile of well-thumbed novels by his bedside.

Oung Moi Toy: within the foursquare boundaries of his room; and city-bred, who would no more think of venturing beyond the immediate clearing and the view of the beach than he would of letting the lepers forget to cook his food for him.

There were no more efforts at food gathering. For the lepers were not allowed out of Moi Toy's sight, and they had managed, so far, to keep India's presence on the island a secret.

Chou You's face wound did not get better. Ah Chee coughed and stayed on his pallet, where Ng Chung nursed him when he had a few moments to spare from his work. Kong Ching Sing, who could only sip fluids, looked like a cadaver, and Nap Sing, the poet, wrote only one new line.

"I had always yearned to go to the land of Gold Mountain," he had written, "But instead it is hell, full of hardships."

Sim Lee was also fully occupied attending to Moi Toy's needs, but from time to time he managed, with help from the others, to leave a bit of cooked food at the back of the clearing for India. Although the lepers themselves were near to starving.

Nevertheless, in spite of all this, they had not given up hope. There were conversations at night while Moi Toy slept, and whispered messages in passing as they went about their business in daylight. For months they observed their tormentor, alert to any hint of weakness. And as autumn progressed into winter and the rain gave way to days in which the sun appeared in pale, cold crispness, they began to perceive a change.

Oung Moi Toy was becoming restless. He began to wake early and to pace the beach. He could not sleep at night. For what was he to do now that he had his kingdom running smoothly, now that he had finished the liquor and smoked the opium and read all the novels? It was only now, with a surfeit of leisure, that he really felt imprisoned.

He practised meannesses: hiding the grindstone so that Ng Chung had to struggle with a dull axe to cut the wood; demanding more and better food and taking from the lepers the little they had; breaking dishes and commanding the others to repair them when they had no means of doing so; throwing their shoes and clothes into the ocean; taking Nap Sing's pen; and so on.

For this was what it meant to be a man like Toy: he was full of desires that could not be met; and he had tremendous appetites for all the ways in which men with weak intellects prove to themselves that they can and do remain alive.

Certainly, he was not a man at peace with himself.

And what the lepers had noted, and what made them think that it was nearly time to act, was the fact that Toy's restlessness, his feeling that the world had left him out, had made him vulnerable. He was lonely and unhappy, and there was nothing he wouldn't risk to be satisfied.

On a bright, cold morning, with the sun settled in the sky like a pale silver disk, Sim Lee and Ng Chung sat, wrapped in blankets, on the porch. From one of his pockets, where he had kept it hidden for months, Sim Lee brought out a pair of dice; he warmed them in his palms and breathed a prayer to his ancestors, then he winked at Ng Chung. For the dice were to be the weapon of choice in their assault on Oung Moi Toy.

Sim Lee shook the dice in a bowl, then emptied them onto the planking. He had thrown a six and a three. It was now Ng Chung's turn. He threw two fives, and, having the highest number, he then threw the dice ten times in a row, first predicting his final total.

So it went. They kept score with sticks, laughing and joking as they questioned each other's rough mathematics.

The click-clack of dice; the smell of cigarettes, for Ng Chung had saved, for just this occasion, a small store of tobacco; laughter; mild quarrelling; then the sounds of the other lepers joining in. Gathering round the scene of merriment.

Toy came out of his room to watch, his eyes heavy with sleeplessness. Sim Lee smiled at him, but took no further notice. Ng Chung shared his cigarettes and moved aside so that Nap Sing could take his place. Sim Lee, it seemed, had had a sudden run of luck. But as the others joked, and as the smoke spilled up to the height of the rooftop, Oung Moi Toy hung back. They knew, for he had told them over and over, that he was a lover of all games of chance. He had broken all the banks in all the gaming houses in San Francisco, he had said. But it is a funny thing about gambling: you cannot just step into a game, you have to be asked, for what is gambling but companionship and equality—for each player has the same chance.

Toy cleared his throat. He shuffled his feet (in slippers made from Ching Sing's socks) back and forth. He sighed. But the one thing he could not bring himself to do was swallow his pride and ask.

Although he wanted, he wanted to very much....

"Well," said Sim Lee, suddenly looking up, "we have played this game too long. Does no one know another one?" There was silence. "Perhaps you, Oung Moi Toy," Lee said, after looking around him, and letting his eyes rest at last on the giant man as if surprised to find him there, "could show us something. Surely there is much that you could teach us if you wanted. We would be happy to learn."

Shyly, almost as if he feared the invitation might be withdrawn, Oung Moi Toy stepped forward.

"Yes," he said simply, "gambling was my favourite pastime. I know many games." He sat next to Lee, close by, but not touching, and began to instruct them.

But now the rules changed. Since it was Oung Moi Toy, a real gambler, with whom they played, they had agreed to raise the stakes. They bet their clothing, their blankets and washbasins, even their dishes. And by the end of the day, even the coins that each man kept to be placed on his eyelids at death. No matter what the game, no matter how he threw, Toy could not help but win. Fortune, it appeared, had decided to favour him.

Then Nap Sing, who over the past few hours had said almost nothing, got to his feet. He dusted his hands and looked down at the others. His face gleamed in the late, but still silvery, light.

"Tell me, Oung Moi Toy," he said accusingly, "why is it that you never lose?"

Toy glanced up, puzzled. Then he looked away, embarrassed. In the pause that followed, Kong Ching Sing coughed, and there were the sounds of Chou You's laboured breathing from the open door of his room.

"Let us go on with our game," said Ng Chung, with whom Toy was currently playing. And he touched Toy on the elbow. Toy jerked away, but Ng Chung apologized, and so Toy shook the dice to continue the game. But before he could cast them down, Nap Sing again interrupted.

"Do you win because you are so smart?" he asked him. "Or is it because you are so strong and everyone is afraid of beating you?"

Toy, flushed with fellow feeling, hesitated to answer. He did not want to be bothered; he wanted Nap Sing to go away so they could get on with the game. At last he shrugged and said, "I am a lucky man, I suppose."

But Nap Sing would not be put off. "Oh," he said, "is it luck that makes you win? Thank you for explaining. For I was beginning to think that you were cheating."

This time Toy could not let the insult pass. He was on his feet in an instant, his bulk looming over his accuser.

"You take that back," Toy demanded.

"No," said Nap Sing. "You are not an honest man, you win by cheating. You dishonour all my friends."

Slowly, still not wanting to fight, still cherishing the earlier mood, Oung Moi Toy drew his knife. He held it in front of him like a piece of thoughtful evidence.

Sim Lee also rose to his feet. "I am sorry," he said apologetically, "I am sure that Nap Sing doesn't mean it. He is unwell." But as he spoke he laid his hand ever so gently on Moi Toy's wrist. Toy jumped away and stumbled against the veranda railing, then into Ah Chee. As he scrambled away from Ah Chee, tripping over his feet and losing a slipper, Nap Sing began to laugh, and the others, even Sim Lee, still crying apologies, also looked amused.

"Please come back and play with us," cried out Nap Sing. "You must not be afraid. You are one of us, too."

Oung Moi Toy recovered himself, and although shaken—since only moments before he had felt himself among friends—he brandished his knife with seriousness.

"I will kill anyone who tries to touch me again," he said, meaning it.

But behind Toy, where he had quietly placed himself, stood Ng Chung. In his hand he carried the axe. He raised it, his cramped fingers gripping the handle, ready as soon as he could get within striking distance to use it on Oung Moi Toy.

"Why are you afraid of us?" said Sim Lee calmly, hoping to keep Toy's attention on himself. "We are weak men, sick men, we cannot harm you." Almost, the moment was right. But at this juncture, pivotal as it was, Kong Ching Sing, who could not walk and who sat in Chou You's doorway, began to scream. For Chou You had suddenly stopped breathing.

"You have killed him!" Ching Sing cried to Oung Moi Toy, "you have killed my friend. Chou You is dead! It is all your fault! You struck him, when you came, with your knife! Murderer!" he cried, crazed with anguish, "murderer, murderer!" And he began to crawl across the porch towards the giant.

Toy halted, looked around him, and felt his strength deserting him. He was imprisoned by the building, by the sea that flowed inwards from the outside world. Overhead there were ravens, calling and beating their wings. The grotesque, misshapen, leprous men were beginning to encircle him.

What was he to do, this invincible man with the knife in his hand? For he could not kill them all before they reached him, and he knew that he could not stand it if once more they touched him.

Then, like a stir of mist in the mountains, he thought he saw a form emerge from Chou You's cabin. If it was a ghost, it wasn't that of the newly dead man—for that simpleton's shade could not have moved him. It was himself he saw. Vague, shrunken, disfigured. Leprous. And it smiled at him in welcome.

He broke before that phantom, pushed through the ring of lepers, and vaulted over the railing, scattering men behind him. And, dropping his knife as he stumbled across the garden, he ran like an animal diving for cover, inland.

"There she blows!" Several plumes of spray are spouting in the distance. "Quick, Fan," I shout, "make ready the gear!"

I push her out of the pilothouse, grab the glasses, and, with one hand on the wheel, scan the spot where I saw the whales blow. The sun is flaring from the ridges of the swells, and I have to blink several times before I can see the next columns of vapour.

"Fish on the port bow!" I cry and push the throttle wide open. As we close with the whales, I shout, "I think they're sulphurs, Fan. When we're within a few hundred yards I'll throttle down and you take over the wheel. Hand me the lance."

I turn to take it from her, but she is empty-handed.

"Hurry up, Fan! You're wasting time. I told you to get the gear!"

"Leave them alone, Robert Lam," she says quietly. "There's a mother and calf there, can't you see that's why she's lying on her back? The young one is feeding."

"I can still kill a male, Fan. Now do what I told you, get me the gear!"

The whales have stayed on the surface, perhaps because of the calf. I throttle back to almost nothing. The *Rose* tosses uneasily. Holding the harpoon head in my hand, I leave the wheelhouse and creep forward onto the fo'c'sle deck. We are within thirty yards of the glistening, rounded creatures. They lie quietly, as if waiting for us.

"Dive!" I scream at them. "For Christ's sake, dive! I dare you!" I raise my hands, feeling not just the weight of the harpoon head but the whole length of the lance. Mussel shells to cut through the skin, flukes made of antlers, which will open up as barbs and hold the lance in the body.... The whales swim gently away from us.

"Easy, Fan," I cry, "easy after them."

The mother and calf are in the centre, shepherded by four adults. One on each beam, one ahead and another astern. Like a convoy. Like the *Silverbell* that long ago day of the war, when we were picked out from the middle of our escort and struck with torpedoes.

When all the men who were below, or whose quarters did not give access onto the deck like mine did, were lost. Unlike me, Robert Louis Lam, who was rescued. Despite what I had done. With my eyes on the mend, and my hands stained with blood. Lifted from the middle of that wreckage and burning oil, with the submarine poking up its periscope nearby, and the Free French ship bearing down to save us. Not leaving us behind. Not thinking of herself.

When we are within a range of twenty feet, I throw. Eighteen feet of yew, with the cherry-bark rope coiling off the deck. The harpoon strikes, then all the other spears of all my comrades strike as well, although mine was first. And the sealskin bags keep the beast from going under, and as the blood pours into the sea, and the desolate calf swims dizzily, the men jump onto the whale's back, and are still holding on when she stands up straight on her tail, then topples over, lashing the sea into a frenzy of foam. And I jump from the deck of the *Rose* to join them all in the water. With a knife in my hand. And strike and strike and strike, even as I go down....

As Oung Moi Toy ran into the forest, afraid for his life. Ran and clawed his way through the brush, his clothes torn by brambles, stumbled and fell over roots and windfalls, and got up to keep on running, until even he, in his terror, had to stop to catch his breath.

At the edge of a clearing.

With his chest heaving and his ribs aching, and the feel of each place the lepers had touched him burning.

He sobbed with his bleeding hands clasped over his face. His heart thudded, and the veins in his temples throbbed. When he dropped his hands from his eyes, his vision was clouded with a thin red mist. He was under a sentence of death. For he knew what he had never admitted before: that he was a leper himself.

Suddenly Toy dropped to his knees and vomited. He spewed, over and over, into the leaves, filled with self-loathing, and the decay of his body, the sharp sourness of the pain in his belly. His weakness.

But slowly, for instinct was Toy's great gift, in the midst of his wretchedness and the revulsion that shook him, body, soul and spirit, he sensed that he was not alone. He wiped his face with clean leaves, and slowly, as if fearing to startle a nervous animal, he raised his head.

At the far side of the clearing there was a cabin almost hidden beneath a fir tree. Branches embraced it closely, but its tin roof caught the last of the light that fell from a dull pewter sky. Standing in the doorway of that place, alertly watching him, and dressed in men's clothing, was the unmistakable figure of a woman.

Toy stared at her, at first fearful of finding himself with another apparition. But the woman was real. The light touched her hair and flamed it. Clothes had been hung to dry on nearby bushes. There was the smell of smoke, and smoke issuing from a chimney. A neat pile of wood. Drying seaweed.

The fine hairs along the length of his spine lifted. He rubbed the tips of his fingers together, he loosened the cord that bound his queue, stretched it between his hands, stood up, and advanced.

As on that evening in Freetown, on the verge of blindness and sick to death of myself and the loss of my future—for what would become of me once I could not see, and had nothing to offer in the midst of a war—I came upon a girl standing quietly beside her bicycle outside her door.

And even as she smiled at me and offered to read the future in my palm, I knew what I would do: oh, Lord, Fan, she had her hair tied with a scarf, and wore gold earrings, and those platform shoes that the women wore and in which they couldn't run.

I was drunk, Fan, but I did know what I was doing when I pushed her inside that room. She crouched in the corner, with her pee running down between her legs because she was so frightened. I talked to her, urging her, trying to reassure her, although nothing she could have said would have stopped me.

I didn't care, Fan. Her eyes were red with fear, her ebony skin glistened with sweat: I thought she was the last woman on earth. I remember every detail. The way her nostrils fluttered like butterfly wings with her breathing, the stiffness of the buttons on her new cotton dress. The blood that spilled in a little gush when I was through.

She was the husk of herself by then, Fan, not real at all. Pale, insubstantial, despite the stink that filled that room as she emptied her bowels. Still, I thought it would be all right. That I could fix it up. For I promise you, Fan, I did not plan to leave her like that. I would have stayed, explained, helped her dress and clean up, told her about myself, what had happened to my eyes, why I had done what I'd done.... I was a grown man, Fan, I wouldn't have left her alone....

"You know what happened to your mother, Robert Lam?"

The voice, deep under the water where I am falling, darkened by the shadow of the body of the whale above me, reaches me clearly. "Yes," I whisper.

"Tell me," says Fan.

"No, I cannot."

"Then look, Robert Lam, as the cord is stretched across her neck and he falls on top of her. She had nowhere to hide, Robert Lam. She had no chance. She could not even scream as the muscles of her struggling arms and legs gave way. As he spread his weight upon her, not out of lust, Robert Lam, but just like you, out of fear of death.

"Do you think that she could be comforted, reasoned with, *explained* to? What did you say, Robert Lam, a husk? Yes, that's it. There was nothing left."

"No, no, Fan," I cry, fighting to get away from her, for she is holding me under, in the bloody swirling icy ocean. With the surface blacked out and the bottom a hundred and fifty metres below.

"Oh, no, Fan," I say, "but you still don't understand what happened. There is more, I have to tell you!"

"What," she says, "more than the death of the spirit? For the spirit is what gives us choice, and without it we are nothing. Nothing at all."

"I know, I know. But, please, Fan, please don't lecture, let me go before I die. I am begging you."

"No, Robert Lam, not yet. You have to see what she saw, feel what she felt, suffer her annihilation. And the pain, Robert Lam, we must not forget the pain."

Or Oung Moi Toy as he knelt on the dirt floor of my mother's crude house with her woman's body splayed out beneath him. As behind him there were steps, and two frail men joined hands on the knife that Oung Moi Toy had dropped as he fled, as they plunged it—Ng Chung and Sim Lee did—through the muscles and ribs of Moi Toy's back.

And the giant released his hold at last.

Or how, when I had finished with that girl, and was smiling at her, imagining presents, a bolt of cloth to brighten up that dusty room furnished with beer crates; or maybe a set of combs to nest in her thick black hair; and money, of course, some money... a thin old woman entered that room.

She looked at us. The girl rigid and bleeding on the floor, and me with my pants hanging down around my boots.

She did not say a word, Fan. She went to the girl and kissed her while I grinned foolishly. Then she pulled a curtain aside from the closet. And all in one motion—I swear I couldn't have stopped it—she brought out a gun, an old service revolver, I can't think where she'd have got it, and shot the girl and then herself.

And so there are some acts beyond forgiveness, that play themselves over as long as forever. There are some that can't be faced without losing the world as we know it; all that's worth it.

My mother lying under the dead weight of Oung Moi Toy's body. Myself, moving too late to stop the grandmother. Too late. For you cannot push time back even a step, Fan. It cannot end, and there is nothing I can do to amend it.

She is holding on to my hand. "Time to swim for it, Robert Lam, you still can do it. You just might make it. But don't breathe yet, look up, look up!"

Yet, even now, holding on to my stepmother's hand as she drags me to the surface of a blood-filled ocean, I hear the echo of an earlier judgement.

And I want to die a thousand times for the shame of it. But can't.

CHAPTER TEN

"A light is exhibited at an elevation of seventy feet from a red lantern on a white pole set in a square concrete base, situated on the southeastern side of an island at the western side of the entrance of Refuge Cove.

There is a wharf in a small bay situated on the eastern side of the cove, about a mile northward of Sharp Point, where there is a post office, known as Hot Springs Cove, and which is connected to the general telegraph and telephone systems. Diesel oil and gasoline are procurable. The local steamer calls regularly. There is an Indian Village on the western side of Refuge Cove, about half a cable north-northwestward of the light.

Anchorage.—Good anchorage, well sheltered and secure from all winds, may be had in the position indicated on the chart, at from three-quarters to one mile within the entrance."

British Columbia Pilot, Volume I

"Did he give you anything to eat?" Lam Fan asks me as she helps me along the trail.

"Who, Fan? I don't know what you're talking about," I say, grimacing with pain at the cramps in my stomach. I walk hunched over, with scarcely the strength to lift my feet over the edges of the rough boards, laid end to end, that form a path through the mud. The odour of skunk cabbage is pervasive. Giant ferns, devil's club, and salal are tangled to head height, forming impenetrable walls on both sides of us. There is light somewhere high above, but it falls in fragments through the thick roof of rain forest.

"The boy," she says impatiently. "The one who brought you back to the *Rose* at Friendly Cove."

"I don't know," I say, wishing she would stop bothering me. Then faintness and pain bring me down to my knees, and I spend a miserable ten minutes vomiting over and over into a mess of fir needles, pine cones, and fallen branches that have wedged between tree rounds placed as stepping stones in a small, dribbling stream.

When I feel better and can get to my feet, I try to answer her question. "I don't see how it could have been him, Fan. We all ate the same food in the house, tea and biscuits. It tasted fine to me."

"Think, Robert Lam. Are you sure he gave you nothing else to eat or drink at all?"

"Nothing else?" I try to concentrate, ignoring the nausea that promises to surface if I admit its existence. I lean my back against an ancient cedar and lift my face to the faint patches of light that mottle the shade. "After tea we visited the church," I tell her, reciting our itinerary, "walked past the cemetery and beach, then arrived at the lake. The next thing I remember is that I was dancing.

"You're right, Fan," I continue. "He could have given me something: I can't remember anything after I first saw the lake until I heard him drumming. But why would he have given me poison?"

"Not poison, Robert Lam," she says, "but the drug the Indians took when they prepared to go whaling. Only they'd be used to it, or at least know how to deal with its effects. It might have been mushrooms, there are several kinds that produce the kind of visions you experienced." She looks amused. "You must have said something to annoy him."

"I believe we reached an understanding, Fan," I say frostily. "It's not the sort of thing on which you'd be an expert."

She says nothing, but continues to smile like she knows what happened better than I do.

We stumble ahead, splashing through mud and water when the trail breaks down, tripping over knots of roots and negotiating roadblocks set by fallen trees. They are enormous, some of them, and seem to be sleeping under a primitive spell like giants in a fairy tale; they put us in our places by their scale.

"Keep walking," Fan encourages me when I want to stop. "It's not much further. We're almost there."

I groan, crumple at the knees again, vomit for another interminable length of time, then, as she badgers me to move, once more stagger to my feet.

This time I ask the question that has been on my mind for hours. "What did I actually do, Fan?" I say. "It couldn't have been what I thought I was doing. You said yourself they were hallucinations, visions. But something must have happened."

"You mean on the *Rose*? Last night?"

"Of course," I say. "What else would I be talking about?"

"You don't remember?" she says, surprised.

"It's like I said. I remember, all right, but it doesn't make sense. I don't understand it." I am about to say more when, like a wall of water rushing down a dry river bed, I find I am overwhelmed with feeling. My voice is choked with tears; and I stand there in the midst of the forest—with the faint sound of the sea thrumming in the air—and begin to weep. "I'm sorry, Fan," I say, wondering why it is that my heart has broken open now, "I'm sorry, oh, so sorry." And although I'm ashamed of my blubbering, of the animal wailing that bounces back and forth between the walls of bush and forest, there is nothing I can do to stop it. I am hugging myself as if I thought my bones might fly apart, and I am rocking. "Maa...." I sob. "No...." For I am a prisoner of two pictures vivid in my mind: two women, both innocent, both violated and bloodstained. One with the body of Oung Moi Toy stretched out on top of her, and the other with a dazed man looming nearby; a man who has shut his eyes to what he's done, and so looks puzzled at all the blood and death he's caused. Me. Robert Lam. Myself.

Fan touches her long, cool fingers to my cheek. I feel the glass-smooth polish of her nails. "Come on, Robert Lam," she says, softly, "come on. It is too late for crying."

And so I unlock my arms from around myself, wipe my eyes, and follow after her, until the path dries out and the walls of bush and forest diminish in height and depth, and the thrum of the sea divides itself into the regular stroke of waves flooding ashore. Until Fan, gingerly pushing aside a spike of blackberry canes, announces, "Here we are."

The ground falls away at our feet to a ragged, grassy edge of beach. To our left, a slight greasy stream disgorges into a scummed rock basin. Fumes, sulphurous and thick, roil above the surface of the greenish water.

"Come on," says Fan again, "you can't really see it from here." She steps across the basin to a rocky ledge. Once through the curtain of steam we look out at clear blue water and to the deep green islands of Clayoquot Sound. The serrated silhouette of their forests is laid like paint over the washed-out blue of the sky. The little stream runs clear, showering down into a deep ravine that, at the bottom of three pools, is open to the sea.

"Clothes off," says Fan.

"What's that?" I say.

"Your clothes," she repeats. "Take them off and get into the water." Obediently, although reluctantly, I begin to strip.

"Are you coming in?" I ask her. But she does not answer, keeping her head turned away out of decency.

"One thing I want to know, Fan," I say as I am lowering my pants and exposing my hairless legs and voyaged-in underwear to the critical view of Nature, "were there actually whales in that ocean? There must have been some level of reality to the visions, mustn't there? I couldn't have made them up out of air."

"Yes," she says briefly.

"Yes, what? They were real or I made them up?"

"There were whales in the ocean, many of them. Now it's time to get into the pool."

"But even if the whales were there," I persist, "I couldn't have killed one, could I?"

"No," she says, urging me, shivering, forward to the lip of the rock, and over. There is a pause, just long enough for me to commit myself to the descent, before she adds, "That is, not exactly."

I stop, one foot gripping a fractional ledge, the other waving unsupported in air. "Either I did or I didn't, which is it?"

"Why must everything be spelled out for you," Lam Fan complains wearily as she has before. "That's the trouble with you pilots. You think that facts are all that matter. You never know what's really going on." She sighs.

"You raped a girl, and her grandmother killed that girl and herself out of grief," she says without regard for my freshly wakened feelings, pressing on my arms to force me down the face of that cliff. "The girl didn't matter to you at all, except as something you had done to hurt yourself," she says. "*She* was real enough—but what about you? Were you? Are you? That's the question I ask myself. What kind of man can do a thing like that and cover it up?"

She says this academically. As I slip and slide and scrape my chest down that rock. "An ignorant man; a foolish one," I answer. "One who is ashamed of himself." I say it as if she has the key to the heart of the matter. She tries these on in her mind.

"Perhaps," she admits. "Your mother was a sensitive woman, and your father was...."

"My father?"

She smiles at me shyly and shuts up.

"Well," she says, after a moment's thought, "we won't go through all that again. What counts is what happens next. And shame is the strongest emotion."

"Stronger than love?"

She looks sad and nods.

"But what about the whales, Fan?" I ask again, inching my way into the pool under her spurring. "You haven't answered my questions."

"Did you believe in them?" she asks.

"More than anything before in my life," I say fervently, thinking of the great, dark forms that had filled me with terror as I fought for my life in the blood-coloured ocean.

"And the girl? Do you see what you must have been to her? You'd have made as much sense to her as a nightmare. Less, in fact."

I think about this as I gather my courage to sink my buttocks in the steaming-hot water. "Yes," I say finally, "I wish I had gone to her funeral, or knew where she was buried. I wish I'd had the courage to face up to it. I'd still like to do something. Although I don't know quite what it could be, after all this time," I finish lamely. I stare at my feet, the toes bobbing up and down in the jet from the spill of hot water.

"You should have gone to jail, you know," says Fan. "Instead you carried your prison inside you. But from now on, every time you think of one—the whales or the girl or her grandmother—you will think of the other. You will see the blood on your hands for what it is. You will know that it is you, Robert Lam, who throws the harpoon head at the whales and puts the gun in the old woman's hand.

"Can you live with that?" she asks me.

Can I? I wonder. I have avoided it for over fifteen years. I can never forget it now, Lam Fan has made sure of that. But to *live* with it? I cannot take the heat of the topmost pool for very long, and so I slide down into the relative coolness of the next basin. Where, as the water loses its relativity, I'm still not comfortable. Self-consciously, apologetically, I ease my way to the coolest of pools. As Lam Fan laughs.

I lie back with the hot mineral water soothing my spine and neck, and the cool ocean currents washing against my legs. Lift and drop, hot and cold. As the hot water floods to the ocean and the ocean surges in. And all the knots of pain and sickness flow out of my body as if they could never return. And I think of absolutely nothing.

"Ready?" says Fan quietly.

"Hm?" I murmur. "For what?"

"I've a story to tell you," she says.

"Oh, no, Fan," I cry at once, my eyes flying open in alarm and my muscles tightening up. I feel the sobs, deep in my belly, beginning to gather again. "Not now, please, I couldn't take it. Please, not yet!" I look around wildly as if for an exit.

She grins, stretching the parchment skin tight across her cheekbones. "It has nothing to do with you, Robert Lam," she says. "It is an old, old story, it is just to relax you."

"What's it about, then?" I say mistrustfully, fluttering my toes up and down nervously.

"You have heard the first part before, many years ago, when you first came home from the war. I told it to you then, though I'm not sure you were listening. It is the story of Lo Bing, the Chinese warrior. But it is the end of the story, after he gets to be an old fellow like you, that I want to tell you now. He feels the same inside him as when he was a young man. Only his body has changed, nothing else about him."

"I'm still not sure, Fan," I say with a hint of whining. "I'm doing just fine. It's nice to be quiet for once." My voice is quavering. Fan, afraid of nothing, finds my fearfulness amusing.

"Please don't tell me anything that will upset me," I plead. "Let me enjoy this place in peace. Later, perhaps, when I feel more ready."

"Hush," says Fan. "Don't be such a weakling. I am not going to frighten you, I promise. Haven't I always been your friend?"

And so she begins.

Although I lose the first part of the story because I am thinking. A friend. Which is certainly what I need. A friend who will not probe or question. Who neither accuses nor is overly sympathetic. A friend who will help me find my way myself. For I will have to find a path around the name calling and recriminations, the punishment I've been giving myself, to recover the world of alternative possibilities I have long done without; to uncover truth and expose lies, to float my mind on a sea of ideas and find a home in them; to know that I have been on the wrong side of evil, and that life is not a fairy tale with a happy ending round the corner, but still to make a contribution, to be forgiven, to forgive myself and put it in the past.

For it does no good to think about it. To weigh up costs and consequences time after time—for these take their toll regardless; or to make resolutions and determine to endure—for what else is there?

And I see, as I lie in that hot and cold water, watching the thin wisps of cloud melt from the sky, and with a ghost at my elbow droning on and on, that all the time I have ignored what happened, have refused to consider it or let it touch my life, I have been thinking of nothing else. That everything I have done since the day I saw that woman, and since the *Silverbell* went down, has been done because of that single event, the mistake of my life.

Ashamed of who I am. Of my name. Of what I am capable of doing. Of getting to know another human being. Of giving up secrets. Of telling the truth.

And so it is time, past time, to make plans and be cured of this self-indulgence. Not to pretend it didn't happen, no, just the reverse. To change. So Lo Bing will do for a start.

"What's that, Fan, what is it you're saying?" I interrupt her.

Patiently, more patiently than I recall her ever having been with me before, she begins the story over. And I say goodbye to that youthful self who has stood so long in my way, and that young man cries, as he's leaving, knowing he can never come back, "There's no telling what might come up, now you've left yourself open, now you've lost your protection."

Old man. For that's what I am. With my skinny arms and legs, and a belly like a stone trapped under my skin....

puffing out around her like wings in the freshening wind, turns and says, "It is what happens to you if you refuse to change."

"Yes," I say. "You grow old and die."

"Yes," she agrees.

"And what if you do change, Fan? What happens then?"

She shrugs, but I can tell from the tilt of her head in the dark that she is smiling as she says, "You grow old, Robert Lam...."

"And die," I finish for her. "Do you think that's all?"

"I don't know," she says thoughtfully. "Let me think about it."

We stand together. The two of us. Lam Fan, a ghost, and Robert Lam, washed clean by a west coast hot spring. While the wind plays music on our shivering bones, and the sun sinks into the ocean. The fire on the shore only fifty yards distant suddenly goes out.

"How are you feeling?" asks my stepmother.

"Exhausted. Empty. But I'm not in pain."

"Back to the *Rose*, then?"

"Back to the *Rose*," I say. Wondering how we'll find our way in the dark, but not much caring.

My mother woke up at night in Oung Moi Toy's old bed in the lepers' house on D'Arcy Island. (For there was nowhere else to put her.) She had been washed and dressed in an old pair of long johns. Her hair had been brushed and braided. A fire burned in the stove, and the bed was heaped with blankets. She moved, and felt the pain begin, but she didn't know why, for she wasn't fully awake yet, still sorting through the puzzle of those last conscious moments.

Before she could solve it and give intelligible shape to the frightening sensations that ran through her body, before the full horror of what had been done took form in her mind, a friend stepped into the lamplight.

A friend who had been watching over her, who, ignoring his own wounds and bloodstains had come to look after her. Who brought her hot soup and tea he'd prepared himself. Who made her sit up and open her mouth. So that before she could think what to say, or begin to ask questions or weep, she was swallowing, spoonful by spoonful, the nourishment she needed to recover.

This friend was Ng Chung, who along with Sim Lee had saved her life. And he, surprising himself by the sureness with which he made decisions

Lam Fan taps me gently on the knee. "Are you listening, Robert Lam?"

"Long, long ago, in ancient China," she says, checking to see that at last she has my ear, "there was an illustrious gentleman, known not only for his superhuman qualities—for he had fought for his emperor and had won many battles—but also for his virtues. This man, Lo Bing, had made a humble but satisfying marriage in his village, and had built his small house there: this despite the wars he had won for his mandarin, and despite his many rewards and honours. He could have lived anywhere in China, in any style he wished, but he had chosen to remain loyal to the place and station of his birth.

"But when we meet him, the height of his glory has passed and Lo Bing has grown older. Having reached this point in his life, he has wearied of all his accomplishments. Even the loving kindness of his peasant wife and of his children no longer means much to him. He walks by himself along the seashore, watching the birds. He sits by himself on a rock and thinks, 'Is this all there is? Is it enough to have done so much, and then to have stopped? What do I want out of life?' As he questions himself, he feels the soft wind that blows from sea to land brush his skin like a shiver of panic.

"One evening, although it is growing dark, he cannot bring himself to go home. He knows exactly what he would find if he did: his wife waiting with his dinner of rice and fish; his children, hungry but not touching their food without him; the earth floor of his simple house swept clean; a straw mattress to lie down on, and his wife, thin and brown from years of hard work, lying stiff as a dried-out branch beside him.

"'I am as I always have been,' he tells himself. 'It is the others who have changed. I have given them everything yet they treat me with indifference. I owe them nothing.'

"He stares hard into the distance, while crows return to their rookery on a nearby island, and the moon rises like the tip of a young girl's fingernail in the sky above him.

"'Maybe it's not too late,' he thinks at last. 'They are wrong if they think I am finished. Maybe it is up to Lo Bing to help himself.' So thinking, he falls into even deeper contemplation: it is clear that things cannot go on as they are. The story of his life must go back to its beginning: for he doesn't like at all what he senses coming.

"For the next two months Lo Bing spends every waking moment building a boat. He works outdoors in all weathers until it is finished. No one helps him, in fact they laugh behind his back to see the old man building a boat for nothing. But at length he slides it into the water, hoists the sails, and, trusting to the tides and all the gods he knows, he sets a course for the horizon.

"Already he feels much better, having left his old life behind him. The wind and sunshine cheer him, rain doesn't bother him. 'One thing I know,' he cries out loud, 'I am now a new man!'

"Oh, it was long, long ago," says Fan. "There were no lighthouses to warn him of rocky coastlines, no radio beacons or channel markers, no engines to power him in dangerous storms. There were times, certainly, when he feared he would lose his life to his wish to adventure, and when his hands grew numb on the fragile rudder.

"But fortune was on his side, and at last, and against all odds, he sailed smoothly into a foreign harbour. There was a crescent of beach on which to land his boat; there were grasses and wildflowers perfuming the headlands; flocks of sheep and goats stopped feeding to watch him. As did a phalanx of men carrying weapons.

"Lo Bing stepped onto the shore with his robes gathered over his arm. He sat down to wait for the armoured men. He faced the ocean and said his prayers.

"'Welcome!' cried the men, who had marched right up to him. 'We have been watching for your arrival. Our priests said you would come.' They placed a garland of flowers around his neck and made him their leader.

"Truly it happened that way. The world did not end for Lo Bing, not as he'd feared. In fact he began to make a name for himself in this new land exactly as he had done before. Once more he led men into battle and was victorious. Once more he was given titles and riches and the rights to a kingdom. Although this time, instead of refusing, he accepted them as his due. He married again, a woman related to the king of that country, and they had several children.

"But gradually, as time passed, he tasted the same old poison. 'They are whispering about me,' he said to himself. 'My wife doesn't think I am worthy of her. My children show me little respect. They think I am old, finished.' Disconsolately, feeling unappreciated, he began to haunt the

shoreline, looking out at the watery regions from whence he had come. Day after day he sat there until the twilight shadows lengthened.

"But now something happens. A sail is sighted, and a ship tacks in through the harbour entrance: a ship Lo Bing doesn't recognize. He gets to his feet and lifts his hand to his eyes. He thinks, 'This must be what I'm waiting for. A ship that will bring me a message. Once more I shall be saved from those who do not value me enough.'

"At first it seems that this indeed will happen. For in the ship are Lo Bing's grown-up children and his long forgotten wife. But while he had had his new beginning, his wars and victories and second family, his second chance, they had been suffering. Without Lo Bing they had had to make their way alone. Thrown out of their village, angry, having suffered years of cold and hunger on account of his desertion, the children had sworn to find Lo Bing and to kill him.

"'My children, my dears, how I've missed you!' Lo Bing greeted them, holding out his arms once they'd told him who they were. But even as he moved to embrace them, the knives were out. In short order Lo Bing's cast-off wife stood with her foot on his neck as he lay on the sand, and as one by one his children stabbed him.

"They burned his bones on the beach and thanked the gods for their intervention. For it was only by chance that they had been able to find him."

"And so," concludes Lam Fan as twilight spreads from island to island in Clayoquot Sound, "it is a story with a happy ending."

I moisten my lips to speak. My voice comes out in a croak. "But not for Lo Bing," I say to my stepmother.

"No," she replies thoughtfully, "not a happy ending for him."

Someone is camping on the little island near us. A fire has sprung up on the shoreline. Perhaps it is the Indian boy I had seen an hour or so earlier manoeuvring a herring skiff against the current. Having engine trouble.

My face feels cold. My skin is rubbery and coated with a fine white powder as I climb out of the pool. My feet are dead weights at the end of my legs, and I have to use my arms to pull myself up the face of the ravine.

"That was a terrible story, Fan," I say once I've put on my clothes and have had a few minutes to rest.

My stepmother, standing like a sentinel at the top of the cliff, silks

and knew what to do, as he fed her began to speak. Not about what they'd just been through—for that was all too evident, and would not bear discussion, at least not yet—particularly as when he and Sim Lee had returned to bury Moi Toy's body they hadn't been able to find it—but about himself. He wanted to tell her a story to add to the one she was telling herself. So that as she remembered Oung Moi Toy and the rape, she'd not be alone with it. So that if there was suffering, it was not only she who had suffered, but those in the story as well; it was all mankind. For there is comfort in that. And so he told her his story, the only one he knew by heart, the story of his life.

Cooking smells, mud smells, excrement; the River Pei-ho curving north-west towards Peking; a stone bridge arched over the river, and houses built across it; people gazing down from their wooden balconies at a bamboo raft drifting by with waterfowl strung up on its decks, the birds upside down, like arrows. These were some of Ng Chung's earliest memories of the city in which he was born, a city of a hundred thousand people, Tientsin.

Ng Chung, aged six, in the year following that in which a Hong Kong baker, Lam Fan's father, had attempted to change the course of history with arsenic, paddled his feet in the waters of the Pei-ho, waters in which people were washing their clothes and bathing, and in which foreign ships, British and French, were floating. For they had come to negotiate a treaty with the Chinese, and had destroyed the Taku forts at the river's mouth. And they had spread their armies over the plains outside the city, and camped on the city's defensive walls, and put up white tents, and pastured their horses, mules and gun carriages.

In a temple by the river, a temple called Supreme Felicity, near where Ng Chung was wading, British officers propped shaving mirrors against the gods on the altars. Soon, although the child could not know this, they would be bringing more gunboats, and legalized opium, and missionaries and traders, "cutting ruthlessly and recklessly through that glancing and startled river, which until the last few weeks, no stranger keel had ever furrowed," as one observer would put it.

But in the meantime, a small boy watched the foreigners from the corners of his eyes, and trailed a bamboo stick through the Pei-ho River, stirring up reflections of the red-roofed temple and its arches, and the dark-green foliage of its terraced gardens.

Then, drying his bare feet in the air, he continued on his way, foraging for fuel to take to his mother. He gathered tufts of grasses, dry cotton stalks, whatever he could find in that flat, arid countryside.

That morning, or another very like it, it was difficult after all these years to remember exactly when it was, he had come across a man pushing a wheelbarrow to which a pig was tied. The pig squealed and cried, but its limbs weakened by the home-brewed drink it had been fed, would not co-operate, and it lay in the barrow, helpless. The boy followed these two for more than an hour, in lanes and out, past mud and straw houses, through the market, until the man, sweating and wishing to rest, stopped at the outer rim of a circle of spectators. The boy watched the man for a minute or two as he emptied the bottle of liquor he carried into the pig and himself, then the child pushed his way in from the outside of the circle to its centre.

There, in the middle of a ring, was a kneeling prisoner, and even as the boy poked his head round the stomach of the man in front of him, the executioner raised his axe, the axe flew down, and the prisoner's head was cut from his body.

This sequence—the river, the invasion of the foreigners, and the rhythmic spurt of blood blotting the dust of the public market—had all run together in Ng Chung's memory. So that as soon as he thought the word "river," he knew he would come to it: the jerking limbs and the staring head yards apart. This was his childhood, and some of what he wanted to tell my mother. That all parts of the sequence had equal value: the feeling of the cool water against his boyish legs; the smooth white skin and vivid uniforms of the foreign soldiers; the pig's intimation of its fate, and its pathetic cries for help; plus the shock of the blow that severed a criminal's neck. He wanted to tell her that the end of any memory, even such a memory as his, was not an end at all.

For even as he had watched and begun to cry, the relatives of the executed man rushed forward with needles and thread: it was their job to join the head and body of the dead man back together, for his spirit needed help if it was to be whole in the afterworld.

This was the way of the world, he said to her. So that when she remembered her sadness—whatever it might be—she must also remember the shade of trees, the fall of light on a wall, the poems of Nap Sing.

They sat together in silence. And then he drew for her a further picture of his city, with its crowded streets and scenes of poverty; its sedan chairs carrying nobles and carts transporting vegetables; its street scribes and barbers and village chiropodists; its rows of caged criminals and men being strangled on tall wooden crosses.

It was a brutal world, but not so different from the one she'd been born to that she couldn't see the truth of it. And be glad it was not hers.

("Being thankful for small blessings, Fan?" I ask.

"No," she answers, stretching her muscles and settling down for the night as we ride at anchor in Refuge Cove, "for big ones. She does not carry the burden of sorrow that Ng Chung does.")

Ng Chung's family were cotton weavers. His mother and two sisters worked day and night at the loom and spinning wheel. The mother turned the spinning wheel with a pointed stick that she rolled with her foot, and walked, when she walked, with a limp, because the muscles in the leg that rolled the stick were overdeveloped. There was not much demand for the coarse cotton cloth they produced, and eventually, when their mother could no longer feed all of them, the youngest sister was sent to the missionaries' orphanage. The older sister got work in a rattan factory where there were no windows, and where she sat on cold stone flags gathering up palm fronds and slowly going blind. The father had died years before in an accident, drowned when he had fallen from a freight barge into the Pei-ho.

For Ng Chung there was hunger and cold in winter and never-ending hard work. In summer instead of cold there was thirst. He carried mud from canals to the cotton farmers; he helped with ploughing and planting and tending; and once the cotton flowers had ripened, he picked them and cleaned them of their seeds and husks. When he was older, he laboured on the barges of the Pei-ho as his father had.

Time passed, as it does. Treaties were signed with foreign governments. More missionaries came, and more of the traders grew rich. The empire was crumbling, and the emperor departed on a permanent hunting trip north. Even the empress dowager had no answers. And so, as the people grew poorer and the foreigners made money, the people began to ask, each time more loudly, "Whose fault is it? What can be done? How shall we stop it?"

Then some children, including Ng Chung's younger sister, died in the Christian orphanage. The nuns of St. Vincent and St. Paul continued to walk through the city in their long black habits as if nothing had happened, and the priests kept on burning the Chinese gods of their converts. Pamphlets were printed: the Christians ate dead babies, the pamphlets said; the children who had died had been tortured, and the nuns earned their livelihoods as prostitutes.

All this the people believed. Because they could not blame the emperor or empress for the pillage of their country. Because there had to be a way to end their sufferings. There had to be a pattern to their lives.

"What shall we do when even our children are taken from us?" the pamphlets said. "Without children there is no future. Why should we let this new god, this Christ, destroy our civilization, when he has only made his appearance since the second year of the Emperor Ai Ti of the Han dynasty? Why should we?"

What happened next was all too easy to forecast. Under a hard blue summer sky the Tientsin mob gathered. They banged on gongs and waved the swords and sticks they'd kept hidden for years in the rafters of their houses. When the priests came out of the church, they were murdered. When the nuns were found in the orphanage they were raped, their eyes gouged out, their breasts cut off, and their bodies fed to the flames that soon consumed the orphanage buildings.

Then the crowd fell silent, and all of them, including Ng Chung, who had waved a stick and sword with the others and had cheered the deaths of the missionaries, went home to wait for things to get better.

But what happened next? Children went on dying in the epidemic. Foreign gunboats returned to the river. The workers remained as hungry as ever. In fact all that the uprising managed to accomplish was the execution in the marketplace of eighteen Chinese citizens to satisfy the anger of the European governments.

Heads severed from bodies, then stitched back together.

Now the season changed. And Ng Chung, piling wood in the stove, glancing now and then at my mother's pale face, evoked a different scene. The many faces of the crowd became the single face of a girl riding towards his house in a red-papered chair. Along Tientsin streets, skirting the Pei-ho, crossing Tientsin squares. Past open windows and curtained doors, watched by onlookers and bystanders and waving children, followed by dogs. It did not matter that he had never seen her before, that the marriage had been arranged by relatives, for from the moment he lifted the crimson veil from her face he had loved her.

It was a tender, unquestioning love. A pupa emerging from its sleep in the chrysalis. A meeting of minds, of bodies and spirits, as sometimes happens to the very fortunate. They prayed to their ancestors. They sat down together, each on a scrap of the other's clothing so that neither would dominate. They talked, and ate, and made long, passionate love. It made up for a lot, this marriage....

But here Ng Chung grew embarrassed, and his face turned red. He had loved. He had wanted my mother to know that: for love can surprise and make one forget. And nothing else matters. But love is private and makes its own net. And it was long, long ago....

And Fate had other lessons in its syllabus, and the world is a wheel that seldom stays upright. Knowing this, that for every up there is a down, for every love there is a loss (he glances at my mother as he says this: since the corollary is obvious, that for every loss there is love to come); he was not surprised at what happened next.

The weather changed. As to why—because of sunspots or gases or volcanic dust—was anyone's guess: but instead of seasons with a succession of sun and rain, there was only dust. The cotton plants and wheat, peas, and beans shrivelled up. The people went to sleep thirsty and awakened thirsty. Dust whirled, blew, and gathered in heaps. And Ng Chung's wife, who had given birth to their first child a few months earlier, lost her milk.

Their days were dry seas into which their lives emptied drop by drop. Their skins cracked, their lips were parched. The grass hummed as it dried under protest, as the fertile land was transformed into desert.

Villagers began to arrive in the city from the surrounding countryside. They camped on the banks of the dropping Pei-ho. They slaughtered their animals and sold their implements; they ate next year's seed.

"We were told that grain would be sent on big ships from the south," Ng Chung explained. "We watched for these ships day and night, but they did not come. All we could see was the clouds gather and dissolve without bringing rain."

When skeletons had piled up in the streets, and carrion birds, wild dogs, and wolves roamed close to the houses, Ng Chung's child died. They buried him in secret, for the city, it was rumoured, was full of cannibals.

"How long can this go on?" the people asked. "Is there no limit to our tragedy? What's to become of us?"

The answer, if they had wanted one, was not long in coming. One night, as a plague of typhus swept through the shantytown along the river banks, there were six hundred deaths.

In the morning the butcher's stalls in the marketplace opened. There was fresh meat where before there had been none. The flush-faced merchants went about their business as if in a dream; and in the air was the odour of overripeness. And the truth was that those children who had not died of disease were drowned by their mothers out of pity. And many of the carcasses in the butchers' shops were pink and neat and clean.

The truth was that nothing went to waste; not even death. That those who were left were determined to stay alive. But by the time the grain arrived, from most of the hovels crumbling next to the Pei-ho there came a telling silence. During the famine, in the country at large, over five million people had died.

"I'm against suffering, Fan," I say as I listen to Ng Chung's story. "It shouldn't be allowed."

"Everyone's against it," she says. "Especially for themselves." And she thumps her heels, as she sits on the capping with her legs hanging over, against the side of the *Rose*.

Night in Refuge Cove at the north of Clayoquot Sound. I can hear the tide grappling with the anchor chain. And the sound of fish feeding nearby. In my nostrils is still the sweet, bitter odour of the hot springs. The stars are like sprays of blossoms in the slightly misted sky. I identify the ones I know. The others stray—to my eye, formlessly—round these pivot points.

"I wonder, Fan," I say after a minute, "if Ng Chung's approach is the right one. I understand what he is doing, you've explained all that, but is it always best to see one's life in context? Doesn't that, in this case, rob my mother of the anger and pain that are rightfully hers?

"Or put it another way," I say. "Do we have to lose all innocence? Do we need to know about every evil there is in the world?"

"What evils would you leave out?" asks Fan as her feet keep going thump, thump, thump. The noise seems to make no difference to the tree frogs, or to the owl I can hear hooting on the shore. Perhaps they're used to drumming from the Indian village on the other side of the cove. I find it annoying.

"This boat has got to see us home, Fan," I say irascibly. "For that, if for no other reason, I wish you'd stop."

"Which evils?" Fan repeats. "Which would you leave out?" Catching my eye on her, she stills her feet. "Natural disasters? But they're not anyone's fault, and evil, of course, is a human event. How about the nuclear bomb, then? Or the deaths of all those millions of people in the concentration camps?"

"Don't be silly, Fan. That's not what I meant."

"Isn't it? Well," she says dismissively, "I don't think you know what you meant. I thought you'd learned your lesson about avoidance. Burying your head in the sand has brought you nothing but trouble."

"Yes," I say sadly. "I suppose you're right. But isn't it a little hard for India to take? All that on top of... all that," I finish weakly. Fan gives me a withering look. Her face, I note with surprise, reflects the sheen of the stars. Not like a mirror, but like scratched, polished, opaque glass.

"The doctor at Coal Harbour, the one who sat on the dock staring out at Japan, was right, I suppose," I say. "We've run out of time in the world. We should stop having children. We should all just quit."

"I wouldn't say that."

"No?"

"No, Robert Lam. But you must know what evil looks like and how to avoid it. You must make yourself step outside its trap."

"But how, Fan, how!"

"You should think about consequences," she says. "I say 'think,' and not 'give up.'"

Silence. While contending tides and currents push and tug at my boat.

"Did you know," says Fan, as the owl hoots again, and the night wind walks a delicate shiver up and down my arms, "that here in Clayoquot Sound, and in Nootka Sound to the north, the Indians fought for their land? These are the only places on the coast where this went on for any length of time."

"I've heard something about it," I say. "Everyone who sails in here knows a little because of the many ships that went down. Some of them are still hazards and are marked so on the charts. They sank some of the trading ships, didn't they?"

"There was the schooner *Kingfisher*, for one," she says. "Indian villages were shelled in reprisal, and many people killed. The *Tonquin* was another vessel the Indians burned. At Nootka there was the killing of the crew of the *Boston*, of course, and in Clayoquot, at the time your mother and I were girls, some traders were killed. The settlers who came here did so at the risk of their lives."

"All right, Fan, I get the drift. The Indians fought to keep their land, so what about it?"

"They knew that the merchants and settlers meant the end of things for them. They knew they were fighting for their very right to existence."

"I don't see what good it did them. They lost it all in the end."

"Yes," she says, nodding vigorously. "But they kept their self-respect. They did not forget, as so many Indians did, who they were and where they had come from."

"What do you mean?"

"What you do from this point on is up to you, Robert Lam. There is nothing holding you back."

A plate of light is showing above the mountains on the shoreline. Fan stifles a yawn. "Ng Chung had lost his mother and his remaining sister and also a child," she says, going back to her story. "Yet he considered himself to be lucky. There was still himself and his wife left alive.

"You should do what he did, Robert Lam," she says, blinking as the rim of light grows wider. "You should count them up."

"What, Fan?" I ask, feeling as I often do, that her logic is beyond me.

"Your blessings, Robert Lam. Count them one by one."

A call had gone out from the New World to the Old. Labourers were needed to build the cities, the roads and railroads, to work in the mines and to set up businesses. Ng Chung, having found no way to improve his prospects in the city he was born in, Tientsin, answered that summons.

The old ways were done with. It was a relief to put them behind him. Only, when he travelled to North America to build his future, his wife could not accompany him. For the labourers were not permitted to take their families with them: they had to go alone. For this was contract labour and there was no thought, indeed no intention, that the workers would stay in the New World and become New World citizens.

Moreover, in Ng Chung's case, and this was cause for rejoicing, his wife was pregnant again.

A child! An emblem of hope! And what a miracle it is: sperm and egg uniting, implanting in the womb, and then the long climb towards birth. And the future. What the world has going for it....

("I didn't know you cared about children, Robert Lam," says my step-mother as I start the *Rose*'s engine. "Of course I do. Just because I haven't any of my own doesn't mean I'm ignorant about them," I say as I ease the *Rose*'s nose towards the mouth of Refuge Cove. "There are many things I haven't experienced about which I know something. God, for example. Or technocracy. Or cold baths in the morning."

"I thought you were an atheist," says Lam Fan shortly.

"Then you thought wrong, although I have to say it's not my fault. That school you sent me to, the Chinese Christian School for Boys, did its job. I was taught to think as if I believed in Him, whether I did or not. It was in everything we read or talked about. I can't get rid of it now," I say. "It's far too late for that.")

Put-putting across the pastel waters in the early morning and heading down the western shores of Flores Island. With its rugged and broken coastline, and the brilliant green of its mountains rising steeply in the interior. A white-foam outline of an island, cut out and stuck against the transparent glass of the atmosphere....

Ng Chung, with one thing left to do before he went: to hold a proper funeral for the child they had buried in secret. His wife sewed a small red bag, and they filled it with tea and salt and candy, plus a piece of silver from his wife's wedding earrings, so that the poor starved infant could buy its way past the spirit dogs that lived and hunted on the route to the afterlife.

Ng Chung, wearing loose trousers and sandals, a padded vest and cotton jacket, with a round blue cap on his head. His oval face like smooth tanned leather, his back and legs well-muscled, young still and for the most part unmarked. Although it was not easy to let go of a wife and a dead first child, nor to leave a child as yet unborn.

But still he went, travelling first to the south to the immigrant ship, which then set sail for San Francisco. Eighty days in the hold, with not enough to eat or drink.

*   *   *

And my mother listening to all this. While rain fell on the roof of her room like water from an upturned bucket. While time ran fast on its clock, and her thoughts went out beyond the hut in the forest to the rim of the island and beyond. To Vancouver Island, to the ache and the wish that had come together in her heart as a woman, as Ng Chung told the story of his life.

For he has had the family she never had. Not as a child or as an adult. The major didn't seem to count. And there was no mother, not to speak of; and surely that was the glue that made it all work?

Motherless children. India, Lam Fan, and myself. And childless. Although for India, of course, only up to a point....

But it was a new beginning, and clearly worth it. Ng Chung found work first as a dishwasher, then as a cook. Although sand blew along Market Street, and the buildings went up overnight, there were Chinese restaurants and Chinese laundries everywhere you looked. Even a Chinese newspaper, with its office on Grant Avenue. And there were saloons and gambling houses, the usual city labyrinths.

He liked to climb up Telegraph Hill where the streets, paved with grass, were too steep for horses to walk, and look down at the ocean. At the fishing boats criss-crossing the harbour, at the currents twisting and turning and returning—surely some of them would be—across the Pacific Ocean to the shores of his home.

It was a connection of sorts, more concrete than the simple letters his wife paid a scribe to write. It was here he went to think about the birth of his second child in his absence.

Another son. Whom he wanted to have an education, a better chance at a fulfilling life. And whom, as well as his wife, he desperately wanted to visit.

Which meant more work, and more money, although he was saving almost everything he made as it was. And so he went back down to his communal room in the Chinese hostel and packed his belongings, and, pushing a cart, made his way far away from that city of thousands to the emptier north.

It was a huge continent. Men moved up and down it on a conveyor belt of rumour: gold in California, gold in the Yukon, abandoned claims not worked out in the Cariboo. Men needed to carry supplies, to run grocery stores, to labour on roads and bridges and railways. Men paid to lay track and blast tunnels and dig.

And so he walked, mile after mile, week after week, over the snow-bound mountain passes and into the rain forest: a six-week walk north to British Columbia.

The men lived in tents or in sod-roofed huts along the Fraser River. There were no hospitals, although there were dozens of accidents. There was never enough rice, and no meat or vegetables, and there were scores of deaths from black-leg scurvy.

Once the main lines were finished the men were laid off: some three thousand of them turned out of the tents and houses, and hiding like animals in caves by the river. Where they ate dead salmon and rotted abandoned stores. Men without work. Who starved and fell ill, and who were put in jail where their queues were cut off.

Men who were worthless.

But Ng Chung was lucky. He was hired on as one of a crew of twenty-five workers clearing land on the outskirts of Vancouver. It was densely forested land, thick with brush and full of promise. Land that now is bounded by Burrard Street and Stanley Park, from Coal Harbour to English Bay. It was land that made a profit of twenty-one thousand dollars for the contractor who knew the market and who knew what he could get the Chinese workers to take for their sweat.

They cut down trees and hauled stumps and burned scrub. At night, when the green mountains were muted in mist, and heavy, wet snow froze to the cedar trees, Ng Chung sat in the bunkhouse shanty. Where he lifted the edge of his damp straw mattress and counted his money. Soon there would be enough to buy a house for his wife and the baby, and to send the boy to school. Soon, very soon, in only another month or so he would have enough to go home.

But then, just as it always did—yes, he should have seen it coming—the wheel of his life gave another quick turn.

It was a long, hard winter. There was ice on top of the mud, and in the growing settlement of Vancouver, a few miles distant, there was much unemployment. Citizens, with no jobs and loud voices, painted crosses on the wall in front of Chinese businesses, and organized boycotts. And those who employed the Chinese immigrants were also singled out for punishment. With so little money to go around, few could take the chance of losing everything. And so the Chinese lost their jobs and many Chinese businesses closed. It was a sad time in the life of the city. When sad men, most of them failed miners and farmers and storekeepers, with their dreams of riches spoiled, sought revenge where they could. Men who had grudges. Men with one outlook.

Someone said that a headless white child had been found in the Chinese dump, and the rumour went round and round until it was not one child, but dozens. Sacrifices, it was said, to the heathen rituals of worship. And if there are parallels that might be drawn, if Ng Chung thought of the death of the orphanage children and the pamphlets that led to the murder of missionaries in his home town, Tientsin, then he must have guessed what could happen.

In the last week of February 1887, speeches were made, mass meetings were held, and the rumours attained the status of truth through public utterance. Thus, when someone shouted from the back of the crowd, "We should burn them out!" the response was a roar from three hundred throats.

They burst forth from that meetinghouse like a stampede of cattle. They ran down the trail through the tarry wet night the full two miles to the Chinese camp. Leaping over chasms, careless of injury, they rushed up hills and skirted ravines until they came to the shacks where the labourers lived.

And pulled them down and set them alight. Food, bedding, clothing—it didn't matter what it was, it was destroyed. While the Chinese workers hid in the snowbanks, or, like Ng Chung, stood up to their necks in the icy water of the inlet all that long night. Shivering, numb to the bone.

No one was killed—which was something. But some wellspring, some inner source that had kept Ng Chung going had come to its end. The money he had saved was burned, and with it all hope of returning to his wife. A trap had sprung shut. There were no new beginnings, no more fresh starts.

With the first cracking of dawn in that cold, soaked sky on that shameful morning, while the last of the mob were still rioting in town, breaking windows and burning houses; while hundreds of men were still solving their problems, Ng Chung and the others came out of hiding. They gathered round the embers of their burned-out property, and they tried to get warm. At first he didn't understand what had happened to him. There were numb patches on his skin, which remained numb no matter how hard he rubbed them. And there were white blotches and scaliness. There must be some mistake, he thought. It can't have happened overnight. But there it was. He knew what he was up against; he had seen too many lepers in the streets of Tientsin not to know the disease for what it was when he met it.

He took the steamer *Princess Louise* from Vancouver to Victoria with the other refugee workers. He slept in a tenement. He half-starved, and floated on the crosscurrents of men without families for three more years. Adrift, fed on mussels and vegetable peelings and the garbage from restaurants. That is, he existed. Waiting, until his life should take a turn for better or worse.

Until, in the year and month that India and Lam Fan arrived on board *Thermopylae*, he was caught in a roundup and taken into custody.

At the harbour, where the lepers waited for the steamer *Alert* to take them to D'Arcy Island and permanent exile, he had grabbed a knife, and as India had been told when she first met the lepers, he had attempted to cut his throat.

But unlucky in all he tried, and by now growing weak, he lost his hold. A policeman, Sergeant Walker, seized his arm and saved his life.

"But think!" my mother said as much with her eyes as with her voice, "if you had succeeded in your attempt at suicide, think what would have happened to me! A man saves your life against your will, and you, in turn, along with Sim Lee, are alive to rescue me!"

Her eyes shone with the thought of it: how fate is a chain of cause and effect and we can't see where it starts; how luck depends on timing as much as on anything else.

Ng Chung stirred the dying fire with a stick. Perhaps he was asking, "Was it worth it?" Not saving her life, for he had shown no hesitancy at all when it came to that, but life itself.

At what cost are we on this planet? How does it all add up?

"I'm sorry," my mother said. "I can't undo the bad or do much good, but I want you to know I'm sorry."

Ng Chung resettled her. He tucked the blankets in beneath her chin. He blew on the fire and added more kindling.

Then he told my mother to sleep, and he put out the light, and stepped outside to wait for the rain to stop and for the sky to show first light.

It was the one thing he could count on.

CHAPTER ELEVEN

"Tofino Village is situated at the northern end of Esowista Peninsula. In the village are stores and a post office, which is connected to the general telegraph system. There is a government wharf, one hundred and twenty feet in length and with a depth of nineteen feet along its L-shaped head. Diesel oil, gasoline and water may be procured from the oil wharves at the village. A local streamer calls regularly. There is a hospital.
"A motor life-boat is stationed at Tofino."

British Columbia Pilot, Volume I

Dust and ashes,
dust and ashes,
was my fortune
and my fame,

dust and ashes
was my fortune,
when shifting sands
revealed her name.

*   *   *   **

I am singing—to the tune of "Found a Peanut," a melody that once heard is never forgotten, even on one's deathbed, I should think—in rhythm with the *Rose's* engine as it runs a little roughly through its cylinders. Lam Fan has covered her ears with her hands. She cries out, from time to time, against the monotony of the tune and lyrics. It is a strange kind of song, I suppose, for a fine summer's morning, when shoals of fish are surface feeding, and a stray blue jay (resting between islands?) is clinging to a mainstay and giving me its greeting: a morning when every breath taken should be a hymn of praise to creation. Silvery waters, prisms of sunlight, burgeoning life, and so on.

But dust and ashes are what remain to me of Ng Chung's story, and I cannot get it out of my mind: for it seems a useless waste of a life to me, even though, as Fan has said, if nothing else, he and Sim Lee saved my mother from certain death.

And shifting sands are set out right in front of me: for we are approaching the eastern half of Clayoquot Sound, where shoals and shallow bars make navigation a nightmare. Even for a sailor like myself, with years of experience on the coast.

Nearby, for instance, off the southwest corner of Flores Island, called Raphael Point, a score of ships has gone down. The *Lord Weston* (although her final resting place is still a mystery), the *Transport*, and the *Mololo*, which was wrecked the same day that my pay went up to seventy-five dollars a year, which is why I particularly remember it. A red-letter day for young Robert Lam, who felt he'd balanced too long on the bottom rung as mess boy, deckhand, and coal passer, and who planned to work his way up from ordinary seaman to able seaman and then through the hierarchy of officers to captain. Although it could have been the end of the climb even then, and should have been, in fact, considering the small detail of which I was then ignorant, that no Chinese before me had made it onto the upper decks.... But I looked European enough, I guess, and although the navy would only take me on as a steward and wouldn't count my sea time, the SilverLine thought more of my prospects and was willing to take a chance on a half-caste. For make no mistake about it, however I spelled my name later on, they knew as certainly as I did where I had come from; where I had lived and with whom; and all about my schooling. It was the school, indeed, I was eventually told, that had helped to shift the balance in favour of signing me. "No trace remains in Robert Louis Lam," the principal had written, "of his Chinese father's heathen origins."

But it was a long ladder to climb, and a slow rise if ever there was one.

Breakers, rocks, and reefs. We are giving the southern shore of Flores Island a wide-swinging berth. There are shoals offshore for a mile, stirring up steep, breaking seas. We proceed slowly, steering for Bartlett Island through water that is only forty feet deep: wooded Bartlett Island, one of the Whaler Islets, with its pale yellow sands; and all the islets are havens for seabirds—auklets, petrels, and guillemots—that pay us no attention, so secure are they on their nesting grounds.

And so on south to the low and undulating western shores of Vargas Island, where, at Ahous Bay, the migrating grey whales are known to gather.

"I thought you said they'd be here, Fan."

"I said they might be, I said they often were; I didn't promise," she responds testily.

We are both standing on the deck of the *Rose* gazing at the surface of the bay. No plumes of spray, no glistening, mottled bodies or echoes of resounding tail slaps, just the steel-blue, unmarked waters. The whales like to come here, to rub themselves on the sand of the bottom, and to browse amongst the kelp. But not today, apparently. The surf falls steadily along the beach. The tides make their predictable advance. Below the surface prey and predator work through their daily contests. Each diatom has its place, and the absence of the whales should make no difference. But it is sad, somehow, not to see them. It feels like I've lost some friends.

"Come on, Fan," I say to my mother's adopted sister, "let's go back the way we came. I think we took a wrong turning."

Retracing our course by voyaging round the northwest shore of Vargas Island, then into Calmus Passage. With the high peaks of the Catface Range to the north; going as slowly as we can, for the currents flood in and out around the islands in various directions, and the sandbanks keep changing position, and so I must watch for the bottom. But I yawn, and my eyes keep straying to the perfect volcanic shape of Lone Cone on Meares Island ahead of us, as if it is a beacon. Although I should be watching for beacons and buoys in the path of the *Rose* instead....

"Wake up, Robert Lam! Pay attention!" cries Fan.

"I am awake. Stop shouting. I just closed my eyes for a second," I answer.

"Well, you can't!" she says. "Snap out of it!"

Open enough to make the south turn into Maurus Channel and around Elbow Bank where the north- and south-going tidal streams meet. But closed, I'm afraid, as we putter along the western coast of Meares Island and into Father Charles Channel.

Seven years on D'Arcy Island. During which Ah Chee, Kong Ching Sing, and the poet, Nap Sing, died. Fathers, husbands, and sons they had been as well as India's friends. And which included a visit from the missionary steamer, *Glad Tidings*, with the Reverends Crosby and Winchester attending. "A most interesting service was held," they reported upon their return. Years which, as well, saw four new arrivals.

One, Alexander Sundy, a white man, had been one of the earliest settlers in Victoria, living latterly in Alert Bay. He was dead by June 1895, and the only reason he is remembered is that the other lepers refused to bury his body, and were only made to do so by the withholding of their supplies.

There was also Ah Sam, and two other Chinese, unnamed.

Ah Sam had been living near Kamloops in the interior of the province when he was discovered. He had been cutting wood, winter and summer, and getting along well enough with the aid of his companions. After someone reported him, he went away by himself to a place called Notch Hill, where he spent the spring of the year planting a garden. Still they came after him—men on horseback, and carrying weapons.

He was put into a boxcar and shipped by rail to Vancouver, a journey that lasted more than twelve hours, during which he was given no food or water.

Constable McKenna, who picked him up at the station, transferred him to a large wooden box with a hole cut in the top of it and placed the box on a cart, then drove to the dock of the Victoria steamer.

On board that ship, sometime during the lonely journey across the strait to Vancouver Island, Ah Sam put his mouth to the breathing hole and cried out loudly, "Me very hungry!" How many times he called before he was heard, no one knows. But it was late in the day before he was finally fed and watered.

McKenna, struggling with his fears, worried that he would contract the disease of leprosy himself—despite what had been learned in the rest of the world of its minimal degree of infectiousness—towed Ah Sam to D'Arcy Island from Victoria Harbour in a small boat tied behind the police launch.

Ah Sam: with his hands roped behind his back and his stomach sick, who arrived on D'Arcy Island without any food or clothing, and who was nearly dead—not from his disease, but from the coarseness of his treatment. And whom India, Ng Chung, and Sim Lee nursed back to a semblance of health.

And Constable McKenna. Pursued by nightmares, travelling the whole way back to the city alone; and who sank the boat that had carried Ah Sam, then incinerated his clothing and washed his hair in alcohol; and who had seven long years ahead of him in which to dread the appearance of leprosy in himself. A policeman following instructions. Who could not be blamed. For it wasn't his fault, it was the whole system.

("That's an easy out if I ever heard one," says Fan.

"Don't be so critical," I say to her as I doze in the sunshine. "Everyone's not perfect like you."

"What do you mean, Robert Lam?" she says, her feelings hurt. "I am only telling you that McKenna should have thought for himself. It wasn't right to treat Ah Sam so cruelly."

I suppose she is right, I think to myself, considering what our leaders said at Nuremburg after the war... but I haven't the energy to admit it.)

The two other men, who, along with Ah Sam, Ng Chung, and Sim Lee made up the lepers' party, had been taken off a CPR ship while attempting to return to China. They were arrested and locked up in the Vancouver rail yard. Vancouver City Council, the Dominion government, the province, and the CPR all refused jurisdiction over them, so that the men stayed in the shack, with no heat and only salt pork and water to eat and drink, all winter. Lawyers argued, telegrams were sent, meetings were held. One man offered, if paid three hundred dollars, to dispose of the lepers, "no questions asked." Another man, arriving at the shack with food and blankets, was driven off by the guard. And so the two lepers lived, in semidarkness, without exercise, and unable to let their families and friends know where they were. For, as always happened, any letters the men managed to write were taken away and burned.

The question of whose responsibility it was, and who should pay, revolved through the courts. The city of Vancouver "refused to become a dumping ground"; the province said it was a Dominion quarantine matter, and the Dominion that it wasn't. At last, the City of Victoria, under pressure from all of them, agreed to place the unwanted prisoners on D'Arcy Island.

Only one letter was written on behalf of the suffering outcasts. A Mrs. Kerr, of Norwegian extraction, stated that, in her country, lepers were not isolated and were treated in hospitals and were set at liberty. Why could not the same be done in British Columbia? Not a single case of infection had resulted from these practises, she claimed, except for that of a laundress who had washed the lepers' linen with an open wound on her hand. "The lepers sell knitting and weaving and woodcarving; the citizens of Norway buy these goods with no evil effects. Why not, at least," she suggested, "send the Chinese lepers to the lazaretto at Tracadie in New Brunswick where lepers are cared for in humane conditions?"

The answer was printed in the *Victoria British Colonist.* To do such a thing "would pollute the gentle Acadians whose hospitable forefathers caught the disease by rescuing shipwrecked sailors from the Levant who were cast upon the wild shores of the Bay Chaleur, and whose thoughts dwell day and night on the glories that will be theirs in the Other Land." Et cetera.

("Wake up, Robert Lam, wake up! " cries Lam Fan, pinching my arms and my thighs. "Better boats than this have spent the day on the sands."

"Leave me alone, Fan, I'm having a little rest," I murmur as the *Rose* steers herself at low speed south. "I'll get up in a minute, I'm just tired, that's all.")

My mother, losing and gaining friends and companions on D'Arcy Island. Working, day after day, for the good of the community as a whole. Trying not to put the interests of one man ahead of the others, so that personal feelings would not intrude on the larger social picture; so that the job would get done. Yet feeling the pull of her friendships. The closeness that had developed between her and Ng Chung as they shared the stories of their lives, and worked together, the affection she felt for Sim Lee, who was like a father to her.... Attempting to find a place for herself in this context through intelligence and practical reasoning and the needs that they met; through thought-out action. Through conversation and musical evenings. My mother, who had done all that she could by the book, and yet had come to the end of her rope. For there were limits to what she could accomplish. She could not cure her friends of leprosy, for example, and this failure was breaking her heart. Moreover, who could she unburden herself to, with whom could she share her fears as well as her hopes?

My mother, growing older, and believing that it was time to look after herself; for what hadn't she given up? And what was there to show for it?

And so she sat on the beach as the sun went down, and watched the dimming of the shore of Vancouver Island. "Restaurants," she thought. "Churches, post offices, horses, and people." It was an unused vocabulary, and she rolled it around, like foreign food, on her tongue.

Sim Lee, who had been scuffing up and down the sands with his hands in his pockets, hiding his fingers, his worst disfigurement, stopped in front of her. She looked up at him: his face, bare of eyebrows and lashes, was almost expressionless, but she knew that there was no way he would let her drop the subject. The Japanese fishermen, who had anchored their boats offshore for the third day in a row, and who had sent ashore a dinghy full of fresh-caught fish for the lepers, and who had offered to take away letters and messages and—more to the point—had made India realize that she could leave the island if she wanted, for she had seen that they were upset by her predicament and would happily assist her, being more familiar with and less afraid of contagion than their European counterparts—were stringing up the lanterns with which they marked their position.

"You say," said Sim Lee in a voice made rough by the progress of his malady, "that we may have been better off if you had not come here at all; but tell me, how could that have been? We suffer because of our lack of physical strength. What we have been able to do together could not have been done by ourselves. Surely, after all this time, I shouldn't have to tell you that! It is a question we settled years ago: and, as I recall, you were on the opposite side of it!"

"It was different then," said India. "You don't understand." Sim Lee shook his head in bafflement.

"Don't bother to reason with her," said Ng Chung, who was seated nearby, and whose hand rubbed back and forth nervously at the scar on his throat as if he still regretted that the knife had missed its target. "She doesn't want to hear what we have to say, her mind is made up."

"It's just common sense," said my mother in exasperation, then stopped. For how to tell them the truth that she had lost heart? That something was missing from her life, and that she had no more to give until she found it. "You would have been more independent," she said at last weakly. "You would have tried to do for yourselves the things I have helped you with." Ng Chung looked at her in amazement.

"We were independent when you met us," he said. He searched India's face with his eyes. "What is it," he asked softly, "what is it that is troubling you so badly? Please tell us."

Sim Lee kicked the embers of the beach fire, around which they were gathered, to life. The fire had slowly died down during the afternoon hours, and none of them had bothered to tend to it. The last rays of sunlight lit the undersides of the clouds above Mount Douglas. Then quickly faded.

"I'll find some kindling," said India, getting to her feet. She walked a short distance away to gather up driftwood.

"What do you think is the matter?" said Ng Chung worriedly to his older friend. "She has not been like this before. She seems sad. I can't put my finger on it."

Sim Lee indicated the Japanese fishing boats riding calmly at anchor. Their lines clinked gently against their masts. "She wants to leave us, and she doesn't know how to say it," he said. "She feels badly about it. She doesn't understand it herself."

Ng Chung regarded the boats as if he had failed earlier to read their meaning and now saw what they threatened. "Do you really think so?" he asked. "Has she said anything about it to you privately?"

Sim Lee shook his head. "No, but I am sure that I am right," he said. "Ever since she saw the boats she has been restless. It is finished for her. And now that she wishes to go, we must help her. We don't have to know why," he said simply, "for she is our friend."

"But I can't understand it," Ng Chung persisted. "Haven't we suffered together and given each other strength? Haven't we, as much as can be, been happy, all of us?" He looked down at his hands, which were clenched in his lap. "It's been almost like being a family," he said.

"Your family is in China," said Sim Lee sharply. "Even if you have forgotten them, she hasn't." He looked away from his friend as if he had said too much.

Ng Chung, willing the muscles of his fingers to open a fraction, picked up his hat, which lay in the sand beside him, and kneaded its brim. He said nothing.

"Happiness is not an animal to be trapped and killed," said Sim Lee quietly to him as India returned with the wood. "You cannot keep it in chains beside you while you decide what to do with it."

India placed the kindling on the embers, then blew until the flames caught. Carefully she laid on larger pieces of wood. She sat down stiffly between the two men. She blew on her hands to warm them.

As to what had made the hole she felt in her heart—an emptiness that kept her from sleep at night—and as to what could fill it, whether poetry or love or art—or nothing at all on this earth—she was frightened to think. Sim Lee put his arm around her shoulder.

"The cultivation of feelings," he said thoughtfully, "is the greatest of human arts. It is of this you are speaking, I think. You have worked very hard for seven years. Hard work alone is not enough to nourish a life. I am sorry you have not found what else you need with us. Nap Sing, our poet friend, would have understood at once."

"Perhaps," suggested Ng Chung, who had been listening attentively, "it is because you are a woman and have no children...." He seemed not to know how to continue this thought. He put his hat on the ground. He picked it up again and turned it by the brim, round and round.

India, who had lifted her head at these words and had waited for more, said at last into the prolonged tense silence, "I feel tired. I think I will go to bed now." And she walked away, with lowered eyes, into the darkness.

The silver oblongs of the fishing boat lanterns along the water danced and dazzled. Sim Lee sighed. "Tomorrow," he said to Ng Chung, with his eyes upon the lights, "we will talk to the fishermen. I think they will do what we want. They are kind men at heart."

"She will never come back," said Ng Chung, gazing at the cold expanse of water he could never cross. "If she leaves she will forget all about us. We have forgotten the truth. We have forgotten the only thing that matters," he said despairingly. "We are lepers and she is not."

*   *   *

"Wake up, Robert Lam, wake up, I say!" My stepmother, Lam Fan, is shouting in my ear.

"I can hear you, Fan, please speak more gently," I say with a shudder. Suddenly, ice-cold water splashes into my face, and, like it or not, I am wide awake.

"You didn't have to be so brutal, Fan," I sputter. But then my mouth flops open, and no more words come out. We are a hair's breadth away from a sandspit. The *Rose* is running in circles, drawing ever closer to the shallows. We are just inside a light buoy, painted black, on which a green light should be flashing and isn't, and which is moored, I see when I run to the chart, on the southern side of the eastern end of Heynen Channel. The sandspit forms the northeastern tip of Stubb's Island.

"That was close, Fan," I say, wiping the sweat from my brow once we are safe. My heart is pounding and I am experiencing, from the stress, some moments of double vision.

Fan, sallow-faced, refrains from comment until I bring the *Rose* round again right up to the buoy.

"What's wrong with you, Robert Lam! What are you doing now?"

"Don't worry, Fan, I'm about to perform a public service. Someone else will get in trouble if that light isn't fixed. Whoever should be looking after it has fallen down on the job. You stay here, and I'll just have a look."

"The light had nothing to do with it!" she shouts as I jump from the deck of the *Rose*, which is idling in neutral, onto the buoy. "You fell asleep! For heaven's sake, what's wrong with you! How will you get back on?"

"Don't worry, Fan," I say. "I know what I'm doing." I flourish the rope, tied to the *Rose*, that I'm holding. "When I need to get back on board, I'll pull her in." I knot the rope to a crossbrace and begin to examine the fixture. A wire has come loose. It should take me a short time to fix it.

When the light is flashing satisfactorily, I turn around. The rope, still tied securely at this end, has fallen slack. The *Rose*, drifting into the channel with the current, is about a hundred feet away. "Fan, come back!" I shout. "You can't go without me!" She waves, a small, bleak figure in the bow, a solemn farewell.

Cursing, angrier than I can remember being in years at whatever carelessness has let that rope work loose, I dive into the frigid waters. It is summer, or I wouldn't take the chance of swimming at all. In winter the cold water can kill you in less than ten minutes. As it is, with the current carrying me in the direction I want, I should be able to catch up to the *Rose*.

Stoke, stroke, stoke, stroke, puff. I can almost hear the nasal voice—from years of infected sinuses—of my swimming instructor in my ears. "Rhythm, Lam. If you can sing to yourself, sing. It will help your endurance." Swimming relay laps in the Crystal Gardens in Victoria during my childhood. While overhead the gymnasts swung out on trapezes and somersaulted through the air, catching each other by the tips of their fingers. Or missing and plummeting into the water on top of us. Swimming in the oil-slick waters of the Atlantic Ocean after the *Silverbell* went down. And swimming in my dreams, half drowning as I tried to hunt a whale.

"Endurance, Lam! Don't be a sissy!"

Summer or not, the ocean cold is tugging at my heart. I glance up to see how much further the *Rose* has drifted, and view a scene my brain can scarcely credit.

While I have been considering my swimming history, and counting out beats, a speedboat, with an outboard engine, has popped out from the Indian village of Opitsat, just south of Mission Point, and has placed a tow on the *Rose*. Just as I shout at him—a bellow of rage that couldn't fail to reach him—the salvager guns his engine and shanghais my boat, departing in the direction of Tofino. I am so sick at heart that I almost panic. But getting a hold on myself, I tread water instead, tipping my head back to look at the sky, which is a benign, pacific blue. I watch the sky until a wave from the wake of the pirate boat splashes into my mouth, then I turn around and swim the long, cold way back to the buoy.

It is not a very big purchase for a man of any size. Moreover I am wet, and not in the best of shape. My fingers and feet grow numb as I wait for someone to see me. Luckily, when they modernized the buoy they kept the original wooden float. Otherwise I'd be embracing this light from the water instead of balancing on it as if on a soap box.

Clouds, which obscure the sun and increase my shivering to tremors, arrive in numbers. Sounds, which I think at first are powerboat engines, but which must be chain saws from the shoreline logging, wail in chorus. Vague grey shapes underwater circle the buoy to which I am clinging. They say that the Japanese current used to come into the sound. They say that, not thirty years ago, there used to be sharks.

Hours pass. The sun is on its afternoon descent when I hear the gruff alarm of the lifeboat engine. My clothes are dry, but now I am shaking from sunburn. The underside of my lips sticks to my teeth, and I taste blood when I open my mouth to cry, "Help! Please help me!"

Strong hands lift me from the platform and into the boat. The hands wrap a blanket around me and give me water to drink. They put a wet cloth over my eyelids, which are swollen and caked with salt.

"I thought it might be you, Lamb," says a man as he tips a little more water into my mouth. "I heard you'd bought an old sea bucket and were somewhere around the coast. When I phoned in the registration the salvager brought in and they gave me your name, I couldn't believe it. I thought you were going up north. Well, I said to myself, old Lamb must be out there swimming. So I called out the troops."

"Brian?" I say, lifting the cloth from my eyes. "Brian Chapman?"

"None other," he answers proudly. He gives me a slap on the back, which shakes my ribs. "Ha, ha ha," he guffaws, "that Indian bought himself nothing but trouble when he found your boat drifting. Ha, ha ha. What the hell were you doing out there, anyway?"

"The light," I say, "it was broken and I stopped to fix it."

"Nobody bothers with that damned old thing. It always goes out. They say it's haunted. Years ago a light attendant died out here from exposure. His boat drifted off while he was repairing it." Chapman eyes me oddly. "Say," he says suddenly, "the sun's taken off your eyebrows, did you know that?"

"Has it?" I say as fingers of fear count the bones of my spine. "But what about you? The last I heard of you, you were chief engineer for Imperial Oil. It must be some drop in pay, working the lifeboat."

Chapman's large, florid face suddenly looks grim as if a particular but well-known horror has appeared in front of him. "You know my boy," he said, "the one who wanted to go to sea, just like me?"

"I remember him," I say. "We took him out once or twice in the pilot boat."

"He got on in the galley of the *Petrel*. They never should have taken him on, he was far too young. He didn't tell me about it. He knew I'd object. I didn't know he was on that ship until the police were at my door."

Chapman spits over the side of the lifeboat, now running through Deadman Passage on the way to Tofino. "Bloody steel hulls," he says.

The *Petrel* had gone down with all hands in a storm off Cape Mudge.

"Well," says Brian, as if he could put the tragedy behind him, "it was another time and place. The wife wanted a change after that, and so we came up north. It's not a bad life when you get right down to it."

We are close to the village now. I can see the public floats ahead.

"Your lady's anchored at the fish dock about a quarter mile from here," says Chapman. "We're not taking you there just yet." The steersman is drawing up to the smaller of the public floats near the village.

"Why not?" I ask. "Unless you're volunteering to buy me a drink."

"I might," says Chapman, grinning, "although I'd say it's you that owes me one. First, though, we have to get you checked out."

"For Christ's sake, you can see that I'm all right."

"I know, I know," says Chapman, holding up his hand to silence me, then stepping onto the dock to secure the line. "Rules and regulations, Lamb. You know how it is. I gotta follow them. Once the doc at the hospital signs the sheet, we can do what we want."

Seven years is a very long time. Not just for a woman on an island, but for a man in jail. For Robert Haack, to be exact, who had languished there since 1891 and who was about to be let out. Robert Haack: a man who had made a mistake and paid for it; who was sorry for what he had done; who was determined to recover what there remained of his life and to live it as a wiser, more reflective, less selfish kind of person. A man who could learn from experience, and yet who was full of contradictions: guilty and yet innocent, naive and also cynical. A man who had determined what was important. A man who would never forget the woman he loved.

Haack blinked in the dim light of the Victoria city jail cell—to which he'd been transferred from the red house on the hill—as he read over the papers that would shortly let him go. All seemed in order as far as he could tell. What was more crucial, he told himself, was to remember the sequence of events that had brought about his downfall: the betrayal of the Workingmen's Protective Association by his involvement with Chinese; the ensuing blacklist proclaimed by Noah Shakespeare; his gambling debt, still unsettled with Yong Sam; his partnership with Jimmy Carroll; Jimmy's subsequent treason over the Tai June robbery; and, most important of all, the disappearance of India Thackery. Not a day had gone by of the long years in jail but that he had thought of her.

"I must not do it again," he told himself, folding up the release papers. "I'm a better man than I was." But even he could sense the uncertainty in his thoughts. But what could one expect when he'd been so long by himself? For he had refused, as much as possible, to mix with the other inmates of the provincial jail—murderers and scoundrels that they were. Except for Starkey, a fellow American, who had been his friend until he escaped, climbing up onto the roof in his stocking feet, jumping to a lower roof, and leaping the twenty feet to the ground. Starkey, last seen by Haack as he dashed into the woods, and last seen by anyone as he had passed through Cloverdale Farm. Although it was said that he had turned up in Portland and committed a robbery.

Starkey, who had known Smiling Jimmy, and who had sworn that Jimmy had told him about a woman, a woman he had kidnapped and who he'd certainly not killed—"I've never murdered a woman yet!" Jimmy had cried, offended at the very idea of it. "He had something to tell you," Starkey told Haack. "He was going to send you a message in jail. He said it would make you suffer terribly, and that you deserved it." Starkey, a small, well-built man who liked to dress neatly, blew his nose discreetly into his handkerchief. "He was a wicked one that Jimmy," he said, shaking his head over the memory of Jimmy. That was all. There were no further hints, that Starkey could recall, as to where the woman might be, but the message meant—Robert knew it in his heart—that India, at least up until the time Jimmy had died, had been alive.

Once Starkey had vanished, Haack had asked to be put on the chain gang that worked the streets of Victoria so he could at least keep acquaintance with the city to which he planned to return. He had seen too many men over the years no sooner out of jail than right back in because the world they reentered had left them behind. It would not happen to him. He would be prepared for whatever was out there. He would meet it on his terms.

It was an early morning in the summer of 1898. Through the open, barred window Robert could hear the noise of shops unlatching their shutters. For close to the square in which the police station resided there were cigar stores, trunk shops, and gentlemen's clothiers. And not far away was the customs house; from the field next to that there came the cacophony of barking dogs—hundreds of them, as he had seen during his work on the road gang, chained up or running loose or being trained by the men who had gathered to wait for the issuing of mining licences.

Dogs to carry packs, dogs as companions; plus the forlorn wailing of pack mules braying. The outfitter's goods had overflowed onto the boardwalks. B. Williams, Simon Leiser, Lenz and Leiser sold snowshoes and fur-lined parkas; and Pither and Leiser were the wholesale liquor dealers.

Men—even at this time of day, who had stumbled from tents pitched hastily by the harbour—crowded the streets. They piled onto the paddle wheelers and side-wheelers that were tied up at the Wharf Street docks; they wore high leather boots despite the heat, for they had invested all they had in the feverish enterprise that had racked the city ever since the news was first received of the Klondike gold strikes.

Gold fever. That took sons away from parents, husbands from wives and children. That turned good men, churchgoing men, into gamblers and drinkers and frequenters of brothels. From his position of enforced abstinence in the city jail (even though soon to be released), Haack shook his head over these evildoers. First steps, as he had had the leisure to perceive in the last few years, were all-important. As soon as he got out, he would look for a job; and as soon as he had made some money he would search for India. Since the foundation of stability was work with regular hours, and the family was the fundamental element in making society bearable. He wanted to be part of these worlds. He wanted to be on the inside, not on the outside of all-important matters, as before, and always odd man out.

Robert Haack, turning away from the window, took a fresh, if somewhat vague grip on his newfound principles. He touched the oft-read poem in his pocket, presented to him by Robert Louis Stevenson, an author who had become more famous with each of his books: *Treasure Island, Dr. Jekyll and Mr. Hyde, Kidnapped, The Master of Ballantrae*, and so on; a very model of a man who had died, unfortunately, far too young, yet who had grown, year by year, in Robert Haack's mind, to take the place of the friend and adviser he had never had. "If only we hadn't lost touch," Robert Haack often thought. As if more wise words from a poet would have changed his life.

He was fatter, and his muscles had grown a little slack. His hair was not quite so bushy. But, as the jailer turned the key in the lock and ushered him out, Robert Haack's broad, pale face was suffused with hope.

He left the square and walked south down Government Street staring straight ahead, not allowing himself even a glance at the Garrick's Head or the Grotto or the Central, where drinks were two for a quarter and there was no such thing as a measure. Drunks rolled out of one bar and into another, Haack stepped over and around them without taking thought. But as he continued, and grew gradually accustomed to the idea of freedom, he felt his neck muscles loosen. Soon his head was swivelling from side to side, taking in the life around him, the gentlemen out for a stroll or on their way to their offices; the women walking their children. He tipped his head back and gazed up at the opaque white sky of the hot summer's morning. He emptied his lungs; he breathed air in. He did this again and again until he felt his blood to be purified of the prison atmosphere he had too long lived in.

Although he could still do with a bath; he could do with a change of clothing.

Haack kept on going. He came to the wooden bridge at the foot of the harbour. Here the tide had receded, revealing mud flats and foam from the soap works. Old bottles, tin cans, stoves, and other materials less clearly distinguished decorated the sludge like fruit in a pudding. The flats, as always, smelled very bad. Haack plugged his nostrils and began to cross over.

Below him a few canoes were pulled up on shore. In these, whole families lived. In the shallows on the sea side of the bridge, a man with rings in his ears and a long black beard poled back and forth, gathering garbage.

Between the cracks of the planks Robert could see more garbage, miscellaneous sea wrack, mussel-covered rocks. It was all as he had remembered it, and thus reassuring.

He needed his courage, and any reminder that the world he was entering was full of familiar things was welcome: for by crossing the bridge he was taking a risk. For on the far side were the prosperous suburbs, where tree-lined streets hid doctors and lawyers. It was here, and in the newly constructed quarters of the Legislative Assembly, that decisions were made and careers prospered. It was here that Robert Haack wanted to live. To be taken at face value for what he did, not for what he had done long before. It was, he believed, his only real chance. Not just a change in environment, but a revolution in outlook. It would alter how he thought of himself. And that, as he well knew, counted for much.

But first, now that he had crossed that bridge and taken that step, he wanted to view the city from his new vantage point. And so he climbed up on top of the heap of rubble, the granite, andesite, and slate, that had been discarded from the Belleville Street building site of the new Parliament.

Northward, on the shore from which he viewed, were the rowing club and boat house, the yacht and canoe clubs, and the boat-building premises of David Jones. In a few years, Haack thought, he would be on intimate terms with all these dwellings. In the harbour itself, commercial boats bobbed at their stern lines. On the far shore were the livery stable, holding two hundred horses, all of them hired out by prospectors, St. Andrew's church, and the post office. The customs house stood alone next to the field of stirring dogs.

Beyond these—landmarks, all of them, and noble and solid in demeanor—there was a border: not indicated by barriers, but by shanties and tenements and balcony urinals. By opium factories, boot works, and smoking laundries. This was the world on which Haack intended to turn his back.

To the west a bridge crossed an arm of the harbour to the Indian camp. Further to the north were the market gardens, where long ago he had lived. And way beyond these were the two little mountains he'd so often examined: Mount Tolmie and Mount Douglas, on which he and Charlie had built their cabin.

Robert Haack sighed. It was all laid out in front of him: a map of his choices.

He put his hand in his pocket. In it was the poem he'd been given by Stevenson. In it as well was an envelope that held the money he'd earned in jail. It was enough to rent a room and to get him started. It was enough to tide him over.

But tide him over to what? And for what? And is it money that counts?

Robert climbed down from the jumble of rock and set his face to his task: to the three-storey houses, to white-painted fences and gazebos and sun parlours; to vegetable and flower gardens neatly attended; to old families with servants.

Down Menzies Street, up Simcoe, along Oswego, down Niagara, through to Carr, then to Birdcages Walk and Belleville Street he walked. There were a number of signs in windows saying "Boarder Wanted," but when he applied, it turned out that the rooms were rented.

Perhaps it was his clothing, a jigsaw assembly if ever there was one; or perhaps it was his prison pallor, or it could have been his telling lack of luggage. Whatever the reason, he wasn't wanted. He spent all day trudging those streets backwards and forwards, and when the sun went down he was no further ahead than when he had started.

Except that he'd lost confidence.

And so, was it any wonder that, as he passed back over the wooden bridge at the onset of darkness, he was discouraged and was tempted to answer the call of an old fellow hawking bad whiskey from a half-sunken boat? Was it any surprise that Robert Haack, just out of jail, wanted to return to it?

There was a chill in the air as mist blew in from the ocean, and there were long, dark hours ahead to fill. But suddenly, drawing on an inner strength he had somehow accumulated, Robert Haack turned away from the bottle and again crossed the bridge to the prosperous suburb. Past gaslit houses and through the quiet streets all the way to the beachfront. Where, behind him, the Dallas Hotel, where Jimmy Carroll had stayed, was lit up like Christmas.

The world, Robert Haack's world, was empty. There was only the dimming landscape of the American shore opposite. He scraped a hollow in the sand and pebbles; he rolled up his jacket, and he lay down on top of it. And he began to shiver as the moon climbed through its last quarter.

Bitten by sand fleas, pierced by sharp rocks and sticks, chilled and feverish, Robert Haack, on his first night at liberty, slept.

He was a boy again in Monterey, California, having just left his home. His life was all ahead of him. As yet he had made no mistakes and had nothing to regret.

"You can't let yourself drift, man," said the poet, Robert Stevenson, whom the boy had just met. "A life needs a purpose, you have to give it shape."

"Yes, sir," said young Robert. The boy turned to Fanny, who was seated beside him. "You remind me of my mother," he said.

Fanny nodded and gave him a book. "Read this," she said.

He opened it up. On the first page, in delicate handwriting, there was a dedication: *To India Thackery*, it said.

"But where's the rest?" the boy protested as he leafed through the blank white pages. The poet handed Robert Haack a pen.

"Write it yourself," he said. Hesitantly, the boy dipped the nib in black ink. He wrote carefully on the first page, *Treasure Island*. He looked up at Stevenson, but the poet shook his head. Robert Haack thought. He turned to a fresh page, dipped the nib again and this time wrote, more certain of what he was doing, *Kidnapped*. Both Fanny and Stevenson smiled at him, and nodded.

Kidnapped! Robert Haack woke up with a start, as if he were being taken by force. Instead, he found that the tide had advanced to the top of his boots. He took them off and poured out the water, shivering all the while. Fortunately, there was no other damage. He removed his bed and belongings to a more sensible position.

He took out papers and tobacco and rolled a cigarette. He smoked it. Perhaps he had started off wrongly, he thought. It could be that that was the message sent by the poet. It wasn't money that mattered, or how he got it, or where he lived; it was finding India that counted. It was *Kidnapped* not *Treasure Island* that was meant to be first on his list.

He tamped the cigarette out in the cool, damp sand. He regarded the sinking moon. But still, he thought, the stumbling block remained. He had to have money, there was no way around it. Rightly or wrongly—as the dream had suggested—he had made his plans and would follow them.

"Mr. Lam! Mr. Lam!" a female voice says in my ear. "Can you hear me? The doctor will see you now."

I open my eyes slowly. Spirit, if spirit you are, stay with me now. She has short blond hair beneath her white nurse's cap, deep grey eyes, and a fine-boned hand, decorated with a large diamond engagement ring, that is shaking my shoulder. "Mr. Lam, are you all right?"

I sit up straight. "I'm fine, just fine. What is it you want?"

"The doctor," she says with a hint of exasperation that makes me wonder how long she's been trying to arouse me, "the doctor is ready to see you now."

I smile at her. Although I deeply resent having had to wait in this dark cave of an office while half the village went in ahead of me, and with nothing to eat or drink.

I haul myself out of the sprung-seated armchair and stumble against the chrome-and-glass coffee table that bears the marks of the village hands, feet, cigarette ash, and jam sandwiches. At least some of the doctor's patients knew enough to bring provisions.

"Mr. Lam!" exclaims the young woman, who I wish didn't look at me as if I were her grandfather, as I stumble.

"It's all right," I say, "my legs are a little stiff from sitting, that's all." Clutching the nurse's arm, I make my way into the inner medical sanctum. The grey-eyed nurse lowers me into a chair. "She'll be with you in a moment," she says.

Not grey eyes this time. Not eyes at all, but painted stones. The doctor is a woman in her middle thirties. Her blond hair (unlike the nurse's) looks scarcely human. It has been bleached and dried to the texture of grass. I have to resist the temptation, when I look at it, to blow—as I did as a child near the Christmas Hill house—to tell the time on a dandelion clock. I feel even more like a child—that is, puzzled, humiliated, and near to tears—after she's had her hands in my every possible orifice. She strips off her gloves, washes her hands, then begins to manipulate an impressive series of swabs, small scalpels, needles, lights, and hammers.

"Dizziness?"

"Yes."

"Numbness in the limbs?"

"Yes."

"Hallucinations?"

"Does it matter?"

She pulls a pair of spectacles out of her lab coat pocket, puts them on, and scribbles a page of notes.

She has looked, listened, assessed, examined, and told me absolutely nothing. She turns away, telling me to get dressed, and once more carefully washes her hands.

"I don't know what all *that* was about," I say resentfully, having recovered my courage along with my shirt and trousers. "A couple of hours on a light buoy hardly makes me a candidate for major surgery."

She turns around. The flinty eyes are unlit. "Exposure is no trivial matter, Mr. Lam. You, of all people, in a job like yours should know that."

"What do you know about my job?" I say with annoyance. "I don't recall telling you a goddamned thing about it." Immediately the words are out, I am embarrassed. I don't know what it is about her that makes me lose my temper. Perhaps it is because I feel she is looking at me from such a distance: miles of space or hundreds of feet of dimmest ocean water.

Doctor Annette—as she tells me she is called, as if to compel her patients to think of her as a friend—unexpectedly smiles. The effect is star-tling. She looks like Einstein. Formidably intelligent, slightly mad, and not unkind at all. I have an impulse to ask her what she's doing in a place like this, but I cannot quite so quickly forgive the nipping of her fingers at my privates or the repeated jolt of her hammer blows on my bones.

"When the lifeboat makes a rescue we have to write it up," she explains. "We write down who you are, where you're from, and so on. You'd be surprised what the government wants to know."

She smiles again. And I remember that it was Einstein who helped to make the atom bomb. "Brian Chapman told me all the answers so I wouldn't have to quiz you. He said you were a private kind of man."

"Tell him thanks," I say bitterly, having pulled on my socks. "Tell him I'd prefer to be asked to my face and not have my affairs made public behind my back."

She looks at me as if my further bad temper is no more than she might expect. Brian Chapman, insists the reproachful downturn of her mouth, just saved your life, you ingrate.

It takes me several long minutes to tie the laces of my shoes. My fingers fail again and again to form the loops. Doctor Annette simply watches. She must know that I am afraid of her and her knowledge.

"I'll tell you what," she says, when at length I've finished. "You put up with one more set of tests from me, then I'll let you go."

"More," I ask her. "What can there be left?" She turns away and begins pulling out forms from a shelf by the sink. "I want X-rays," she says. "I think we need to have a look inside."

"At what?" I say. "I hardly think exposure has jumbled my organs."

"Not exposure," she says carefully, not looking up. "You're fine as far as all that goes, except for a touch of arthritis. I'm interested in some of the other symptoms I've noted."

"And if I refuse?" I say, putting on my coat.

"Well," says she, putting pen, spectacles, and stethoscope into her pockets, tidying up for whoever is next, "I cannot make you, of course, but I can say that you're not fit to pilot a boat."

Ten minutes' walk through the streets of the village, with the general store and the post office being the principal buildings, brings me to the fishing docks; and a quick survey of the floats finds me my boat.

She is undamaged. They have even remembered to put her bumpers out. She rocks gently, emptily, when I jump on board. "Fan?" I call softly. But no one answers. I give the *Rose* a quick look over, but all seems shipshape. I check the level of the fuel tanks and am pleased to find them filled to the top. The salvager must have had a conscience. Maybe next time, before he goes to take a boat from its owner, he'll look in the water for swimmers. Or it could be Brian Chapman, knowing how I'd feel after going to the hospital and seeing Doctor Annette, who was the good Samaritan.

Doctor Annette. Who did not answer when I asked where she was from. Who had a hint of an accent. German? French? Belgian? Who would have been in her teens when the war began. It could only have been the war, I thought, that could turn out a woman as competent and uncompromising as she was. I shiver as I think of the X-rays she took of my head in an iron clamp: "Don't move! Don't breathe!" she commanded. I refused to wait for results and gave her the name of my regular doctor at home.

Heading down Templar Channel past Wickaninnish Island where the *Tonquin* went down. And by the Lennard Island lighthouse; keeping to the east of it and hitting, at long last, the great, rolling swells of the open blue Pacific. Staying about three miles offshore as we pass the foaming line of Wickaninnish Bay, and so on down the coast, carried along at speed by the wind and waves. While Lam Fan, who reappeared once we were at sea and looked pleased to see me, has made herself at home on deck. She calls out above the noise of the wind and the engine, "I thought you'd never come back, Robert Lam! I thought you were done for! You should never have taken such a chance for the sake of a light."

"It was to help save lives, Fan. Mariners depend on those markers."

"But that one never works," she says.

"Who told you that?"

"Oh," says she, "it's common knowledge." It wasn't to me, I think, but don't say so out loud. "So, Fan," I say instead, hoping to take her by surprise, "what can you tell me about the rope?"

"What rope?" asks my stepmother innocently. She looks around, as if casting about for what I might mean. "There are many ropes, Robert Lam, you will have to be more specific."

"The one I knotted before I stepped off the *Rose* onto the buoy. The one that couldn't possibly have worked its way loose by itself. Is that specific enough for you?"

"There you go again, blaming someone else for your troubles," she says. She closes her eyes and leans back to take the sun.

"Fan," I say. "I want an answer. I want the truth and I want it now. You don't know what you put me through. I could have died out there from exposure."

"It is summer," she says, "and the weather is good."

"Fan!" I exclaim, shocked to hear her so easily admit what I only suspected was true. "It was you! It wasn't an accident at all!" I leave the wheel of the *Rose* (my craft is nicely throttled down and running steady) to confront her. She regards me complacently.

"Don't throw stones from behind a glass window," she says.

"Oh, for Christ's sake, Fan! I could have slipped off and drowned. As it was, I was lucky not to have a cramp while swimming. What would you have done then? Waved bye-bye as I went down the third time?"

"I didn't know someone would take your boat away," she says defensively. "Don't make such a fuss about it."

I am left almost speechless. But not quite. "I had no idea you could be so heartless," I say to her. "I simply don't understand it. Despite all our differences I always thought you were on my side."

She has the grace to hang her head. "I meant it as a joke," she says into the the bosom of her silk shift. "I didn't mean you harm by it."

"A joke? A practical joke? You, Fan, were playing tricks? I don't believe it." I stop, in doubt as to other choices. She nods, shamefaced. I think about this. What was she really up to back there? Whatever else Fan is, she is no great kidder. Yet I can't believe that she meant to hurt me, and when I consider the circumstances, that we were near enough to land— we almost ran aground on that sand spit—and surrounded by settlements filled with seafaring men; that someone was bound to take note of us in good enough time, the fact is that I was uncomfortable for several hours but in no real danger of losing my life.

"Fan," I say, believing I am nearing enlightenment, "are you worried about me? Did you want to get me to land to see a doctor again? Was that it? You mustn't worry about me. I'm going to be all right. I don't need any doctor's help, I just need to get this job done, finish what we've started. I'm much stronger than I look. I have you to give me courage.

You were wrong to think you could put me off so easily. I won't quit now, Fan, whatever happens, please believe me." I watch her carefully, to see if I've hit the mark, and as I do I see a struggle take place on her face. Moisture springs to her eyes, and she blinks it away. Her mouth quivers, and a distinct sniffle flutters her nostrils. There are new lines drawn on her flesh amongst the others: deep lines of worry, and beneath her bright black eyes are grey circles. She scrambles to her feet with the wind folding her clothes tightly around her stick-thin body. Her sharp, thin shape is outlined like a knife blade; and she embraces me.

We stand, the two of us, as my arms go around her in turn, like mother and son. Like the mother and son we never were. I can feel the trembly beating of her heart in the region of my stomach. For the second time in several days I begin to weep. These sobs, however, don't tear me apart like the others. They bring me joy, and relief.

It is not easy, when a man has been cut off from his fellows for seven years, and when he finds that even when he gets out of jail he is still not wanted by them, and that old scores remain to be settled, and that the blacklist stands, for him to make a new life. So it was for Robert Haack.

It is even more difficult if, with a little money to tide him over burning a hole in his pocket, he cannot find a home in the respectable suburbs, and must camp where he is when the sun goes down while he thinks of a way to alter his circumstances: afraid to ruin his chances by a single misstep. For so much depends on what he does. Including my mother's future life.

It is difficult, nay, nigh well impossible, under these conditions with no one to help him, for him to pass by saloons, night after night, and not go in. To hear laughter emanating from doorways and to have no part in it; to have no one to talk to—for even the stray dogs have been taken away from the city by the hordes of prospectors.

Robert Haack, on one of these lonely nights, footsore from his tramping up and down the streets, and weary and discouraged in spirit, paused outside the Commercial Hotel. He was hungry and cold, but most of all he was lonely. He listened to the tinkling of glasses as if it were music; he heard chairs scraped back as more rounds were ordered; he heard actual music as a piano began to play a tune that he knew. Men's voices and women's laughter. The sound of humanity. He peeped—surely no harm would come if he only looked—inside.

The room was golden with lamplight. Mirrors reflected happy smiles. The colours of the women's dresses ranged through the rainbow. Just inside the doorway, on the edge of the cigar smoke with which the room was encircled, there was an empty table. Robert Haack crossed the threshold and sat down at it.

He remained there quietly sipping his beer. There was no one in the hotel that he knew. He gazed about him with an expression of longing. A man, one of a party of five at a nearby table, catching his eye, called out to him and suggested he join them at cards.

There were more drinks, a bucket of steamed clams to eat, a singsong around the piano as the evening wore on. These were all innocent pleasures, and all the more to be savoured for being so long denied.

But would he never learn: was it a thirst or a demon that ruled his throat? For the end of all this apparent innocence was a new appearance in court.

Robert Haack to the court: After leaving the Commercial we went to the Bee Hive and then walking on Cormorant Street, and hearing the sound of gambling found ourselves opening the door of number eighty.

Prosecutor: Did it not occur to you that this was no gambling house, but a private dwelling? Had you no conception that you were not welcome?

Robert Haack: If you'll pardon my saying so, the trouble was one of drink. And then there were so many Chinamen throwing stones I couldn't tell what was happening. [Laughter in the court]

Prosecutor: Well, why did you run from the police?

Robert Haack: It seemed to me that it is very seldom that the police arrive without arresting someone. [Laughter]

Prosecutor: Indeed, and that would be a matter, I am assured, with which you have had some experience.

Robert Haack: I cannot deny it. But anyone passing would've done what we did. We heard the sound of dominoes and went in. The door was open.

Prosecutor: Let the court take note that not only has this man an extensive police record, and that he has not been long out of jail, but that this so-called "gambling house" is directly across from the police station itself!

It is a sad story, not any less moving for being so public. Robert Haack, with his future all mapped out, with the best of intentions, had made a mistake and found himself again in prison. But for two weeks only this time, and that because he could not pay the fine and damages of one hundred dollars that the judge had assigned.

Poor Robert Haack: who took one step forward and two more back. Yet this seeming hardship had one desirable effect. It brought him, through the columns of the *British Colonist*, which reported the case, to the notice of his former friends, Sing Yuen and Lam Fan. It gave him another run at his desired fresh start.

A man with a goal in mind; more than a goal, a sense of mission, which is, not only for his own sake, but in homage to the memory of his meeting with the now-dead author, R.L. Stevenson, who had favoured him with a vision, to retrieve my mother from wherever she had been hidden. And once she was found, and as he'd intended from the very beginning, to make her his wife, and to go with her to live in San Francisco, his previous home.

That is, if he could get together the necessaries, the funds, the needed contacts, and so forth. That is, if he had some luck and knew where to look.

For as for money and luck, there is never enough of them. And as for contacts, whether he has any left, he intends to find out. And as for who they are and what their sentiments might be regarding him, the first indication arrives at once in an envelope presented to him as he is let out of jail at the end of two weeks.

He opened the envelope. He took out the paper inside it and read it. Tears sprang to his eyes, and he wiped them away with the tips of his fingers. He folded the paper up. For the paper was nothing that he'd expected. It was an invitation from Lam Fan and Sing Yuen, who had been alerted to Robert Haack's whereabouts through the newspaper account of his trial, to the funeral of Lam Fan's uncle, the herbalist, Lum Kee.

It was a shock (although death comes to us all). It was an icy hand travelling his spine, a midnight blizzard through which the figures— himself, India, and Lum Kee wended their way searching for a missing person, Lam Fan. It was rooftops caked in snow and icicles depended from gutters. It was an opium den and the workingman, Henry McMullen, found inside it. It was years and years ago; and it made him think about what we can't afford to lose and yet abandon anyway, and how we hurt others and hurt ourselves and wait too long to ask forgiveness. For Lum Kee had been a good man, a kind and helpful friend, who had continued to send Haack letters and medicines while he'd been in jail; and who had begged, time after time, for anything he could tell him about the whereabouts of India: for Lum Kee, alone of all India's friends, had refused to believe that she was dead.

This herbalist, this student of medicine, had been convinced that all would turn out well in the end: not only for India, but for all of them. He had believed and worked and never given up on anything as long as he lived. He was that kind of man. Honourable, faithful, and kind.

"Is that you, Robert Lam, who I hear, if I'm not mistaken, praising optimism?" says my stepmother, who stands beside me as we speed, from roller to roller, south. Past Florencia Bay where the brig *Florencia* sank and towards the light—a red lantern on a white concrete building erected to the north of the end of Amphitrite Point. "Can it really be you, who have looked at the worst of things as long as I've known you, espousing these sentiments, these noble characteristics?"

"It's only what you've always preached yourself, Fan," I say to her. "It must be rubbing off at last."

She glances at me suspiciously. "Lum Kee has become your model?"

"I'm perfectly sincere, Fan," I tell her. "You've been right all these years. It is important to stick to what you believe in, to be truthful with yourself no matter what anyone else thinks."

"I know you've changed, Robert Lam," says my stepmother. "Believe me, I'd be the last to deny it. Still, I'm surprised." She peers at me concernedly. "You should ease into it, if you're going to be a saint," she says. "Too much change all at once can throw you off. You run the risk of going too far, becoming someone you aren't."

"What, Fan!" I cry in mock astonishment. "Now that I'm the man you want, taking your advice, an optimist, as you say yourself, you say I've gone too far. Make up your mind. Which is it you want? Robert Lam as he is, or Robert Lam as he was?"

Disconcertingly, she appears to give the matter some thought. "All in all," she says, "there's no going back. But not everything you've always done is wrong. Don't throw out the baby with the bath. You can't be more than human, Robert Lam. No one can. Not you, not me, not anyone. We have all made mistakes and will continue to make them...."

"Not anymore, Fan. I'm a new Robert Lam." To my chagrin she takes what I say at face value.

"Still thinking only of yourself," she says disappointedly. I feel a flush stain my cheeks.

"That's unfair, Fan. I was only pulling your leg. You don't have to remind me that I can fail. I'm used to it. But I am trying to do my best. Surely that's what counts."

"I meant only," she says calmly, "to remind you that there are others in this world. Many men and women—and I include myself—carry heavy burdens of guilt and suffer from them."

"You, Fan? What have you ever done but smoke a little opium?" My words sound crude to my ears even as I utter them. The face that she turns to me now lacks all expression. It is the impenetrable face of a stranger. Closed by my clumsiness. What's more, she is right. I am selfish, and I am undone by my pride. And the assumptions I've made. That my guilt and my remorse are more important than the burdens of anyone else. All people must have their secrets, their private hurts and injustices. Why can't I allow Fan hers?

"I apologize, Fan," I say. "Please forgive me if what I said was offensive. I am still the fool I always was."

"At least some things never change," she says dryly, dropping the mask of blankness, which has frightened me. "I shall be thankful for that."

I take two deep breaths. One for gratitude that I have her back, and one for luck. A solid black fist of clouds has suddenly blotted the horizon. "We're almost past Amphitrite Point," I say. "Why don't I make us both a cup of coffee?" I don't like the look of the weather coming in. If we want something hot in our stomachs we had better get it now before I empty out the kettle. The last thing we need is boiling water on the stove in a storm. "Take that old jacket of mine and put it on. It'll be cold once it starts to rain and blow." Already our gentle roller-coaster ride has assumed a new motion. The waves are breaking up. Moving as quickly as I can, I stow loose items. One test failed, a new one coming up.

Fan sits close to the exhaust shroud and shivers. I drape the jacket over her shoulders. She is smoking a cigarette. She puffs, coughs, and puffs again. "Don't sink the *Rose* before you get us home, Robert Lam," she says.

Robert Haack buffed his shoes and stuffed newspapers into the soles, which he had worn through by walking the streets of Victoria looking for lodging and employment. He brushed his threadbare coat clean of dust and dandruff. He put on his ancient brown hat and proceeded to that Fisgard Street address where he had last stood, seven years before, so full of hope. A man about to commit a robbery; a man longing to see his future wife.

He raised his hand to knock, trembling slightly with anxiety—for it was just so he had been placed when his life had fallen apart—as the door cracked open a notch and the fabric of a woman's dress was painted brightly in a strip of sunlight. The maid—for that's who it was, a girl Haack didn't know—showed him into the parlour, where there were tables laden with food and drink. The food—roast duck and sweet-meats—was, so far as Haack could see, untouched. The other guests stood quietly, or talked among themselves, sipping ceremonial liqueur from tiny china cups. They spoke softly of Lum Kee's goodness and his skill at treating ailments. They recounted stories of the many people he had helped: new immigrants, students, and crib girls who had run away from their owners. He had been a man, it was agreed, who had lived a life of effortless virtue.

Robert Haack could not settle. There was no one in the room that he knew well enough to speak to, although present were many leading busi-nessmen and dignitaries. He gathered, from what he overheard, that Lam Fan would inherit Lum Kee's property and carry on the business. She was, apparently, so deeply distressed by her uncle's death that she could not attend the funeral. Sing Yuen was in the room next door with Lum Kee's coffin, and the arrival of the hearse was momentarily expected.

Haack examined the heavy velvet curtains, which were tightly drawn against the afternoon light. He lifted up and put back several books and ornaments that lay on several tables. He dusted off a horsehair chair and sat down upon it. He stood up. He started to light a cigarette, then thought better of it. There was the sound of horses' hooves as the hearse arrived at the portal. Then Sing Yuen, in a black business suit, came in and shook hands with all who had gathered.

"Would you mind staying on when the others have left?" he whispered to Haack as he took Robert's hand. "My wife wishes to speak to you."

Lam Fan? But why on earth would she want to see him privately at a time like this? He waited nervously as the funeral procession lined up. He watched them, through a parting in the curtains, as they started off down the street. He stood in that darkened room and twisted his hands fretfully as the clip-clopping of the horses' hooves grew ever more distant.

A servant came into the room to remove the comestibles, and Robert was smiling at her when Lam Fan entered. He rearranged his expression more suitably.

Only half-awake because of the quantities of opium she had smoked to steady herself, and stricken with conscience because she had promised Sing Yuen she would not resort to it, Lam Fan, with her hair twisted into a knot on top of her head, and with her nails freshly painted, and in full formal dress, seemed to Robert not to have aged at all. Although there were lines of strain crisscrossing her forehead.

He coughed discreetly, for he could not tell if she had seen him.

"I know perfectly well where you are, Mr. Haack," said Lam Fan to my mother's future husband. "You need not lurk in the shadows. Come forward, please."

Haack did as he was bidden and Fan motioned him into one of the chairs that he had so recently quitted. He shifted his weight back and forth uncomfortably while Fan settled herself nearby. There was silence for several minutes.

The servant returned with tea and poured a cup for each of them. Haack blew on his and drank it. Lam Fan did nothing.

"You wanted to see me?" said Robert Haack finally. For he feared that Fan was drifting away permanently inside herself.

She sat up straight, and for the first time looked him full in the face. Haack said, "I'm sorry about your uncle. I didn't know he was sick or I would have come to see him. He was a very fine man."

"Yes," said Fan. "He was." Then she sighed. "It is not your fault you were out of touch with Lum Kee, Mr. Haack. He often talked of you. He would have liked to see you again before he died but we did not know where to find you. It was only because of the newspaper report of your recent misfortune that we were able to reach you. Although by then it was too late."

Haack turned his teacup over and examined its markings, embarrassed.

What is it she wants? he wondered. He was just as glad, when it came to it, that they hadn't found him in time to have that last interview. He did not see how he could have stood it. He felt bad enough to have failed Lum Kee as it was. Lam Fan's head drooped to her chest. "Ah," said Robert, feeling desperate, worried that Fan wouldn't come to the point, that he'd never know exactly why he'd been summoned, "there were one or two items concerning your sister that we discussed when we last met.

Of course I told your uncle all I could at the time. But I heard something while I was in jail, that I think we should start to investigate...."

Lam Fan's head came up with a snap. "Investigate, Mr. Haack? Would you turn up all that grief again for nothing? We tried every means we had to trace my sister. You assured us that you knew nothing, absolutely nothing, that could help us. You're not about to tell me, when my uncle died sorrowing that he hadn't done enough to find her, that you weren't telling the truth!"

Haack, taken aback, cried, "Oh, no! Of course not! It's just that I have reason now to think that she might be alive. Starkey said that Smiling Jimmy had said...."

"My sister is dead," interrupted Fan, her face hardening. "My uncle is dead. We cannot bring them back."

"No, I agree, of course not," said Robert Haack, retreating, who had planned, in the case of India, if it were at all possible, to do just that.

"It was a long time ago," said Fan. "No, Mr. Haack, I did not ask you here to talk about my sister." There was another pause, during which Robert felt more than ever puzzled. Not about India? What other connection could he possibly have to this woman?

"There is something else that concerns me," said Lam Fan. "It does not matter to me whether you understand it. It is a matter of conscience and of importance to me alone.

"Before I tell you what it is," she continued, "let me remind you of certain facts. And let me first assure you that I bear no grudge over the past. I accept that whatever happened was an accident. I know that you cared for my sister and would never have knowingly hurt her."

Robert nodded vigorously.

"On the other hand," said Fan, "there is still the matter of the robbery of my husband's factory. For that you owe him very much money. As well there is your indebtedness to Yong Sam. He has come to see us already to remind us he has first claim on your income. Do not think he will ever forget it." Fan stopped to let this news sink in. Haack slumped dejectedly, although it was, in truth, no more than he'd expected.

"Furthermore," Fan went on, her need to unburden herself surmounting the effects of the opium, "no one, not a European or Chinese will give you a job in this town. You need to make money, Mr. Haack, but there is no way you can do it."

Robert felt his hands trembling. He put his cup down on the tea tray with a rattle. "I know all this, Mrs. Sing," he said. "What you say doesn't help. I can only do my best. I give you my word that I am trying. I don't need any more criticism. Lum Kee would have understood. He, at least, was my friend."

"Lum Kee was everyone's friend," said Lam Fan abruptly. Robert looked at his knees.

"I will give you a chance to prove yourself," said my stepmother. "You will work for me, and I will pay you well. You see," she said, her face softening, "you are not the only person ever to make a mistake. I, too, feel sorry for something I've done."

Robert looked up at her in amazement. Fan nodded. "Yes," she said, "it is true. Do you remember," she continued, "a little girl that India and I looked after? We brought her here from a star house in the city. She was all by herself in the world. Her name was Gook Lang."

Slowly Haack retrieved his teacup. His throat had constricted, and he needed desperately to drink. He could scarcely breathe. Not remember a child chained to a table leg at their first meeting in a tenement; not remember the advent of Henry McMullen, workingman, coming up behind them; not remember the heroics of that movement? And more than that... not remember the thin face above the thin body in a borrowed dress in this very house, and the adolescent laugh that had shattered his heart at the moment he was declaring his love for India? He only wished he could somehow forget.

"I think I remember her," said Robert Haack cautiously. "Wasn't she a little, you know, funny in the head?" he said, twirling his finger round at his temple.

"Oh, no," said Fan. "That was not her. She was a bright girl, very smart. But the day that India vanished she ran away and did not come back. I think she believed my sister's disappearance was all her fault. You know how children are," said Fan, "they always blame themselves.

"I should have searched for her then, but I was too upset," said Fan. "I thought she would come back home in a day or two. I didn't think she was gone for good." Fan made a helpless gesture, which made both of them consider how opium makes time appear no more than a moment. "I know I should have tried to find her before," said Fan.

She slid her long red nails round the edge of her saucer, back and forth. "You will bring her home, and I will pay your expenses plus a good deal extra. Out of this you can start to pay your debts. Two-thirds to Yong Sam, and one-third to us."

"But it will take forever that way!" objected Robert.

Fan regarded him coldly. "What else are you going to do?" she said. "Do you have another benefactor?"

Robert didn't answer. He thought of the gentleness of Lam Fan's uncle, Lum Kee, now dead. He thought of Sing Yuen's fairness in business. And he thought of my mother, India, and longed, more than ever, to find her. But he shrugged his shoulders and said to my stepmother, "I suppose you're right. I have no choice. I will do what you want."

Fan stood slowly and held out a package, which she had kept concealed in her sleeve. "Here is money to begin with. I don't mind how long it takes or what it costs. You will, of course, give me a full accounting and provide me with receipts."

"Of course," said Robert Haack, also rising. He felt he had never been so overburdened. That he was stuck on a track and he couldn't get off it. That each time he tried to free himself the past entangled him.

"Come and see me every week," said Fan.

"Yes, Mrs. Sing."

"Don't worry, Robert Haack," said my stepmother, "everything will be all right in the end, I can feel it." She led him towards the door. For the grief-dimming effects of her pipe were wearing off, and she wanted to go upstairs to smoke before Sing Yuen returned.

"You're not going to the cemetery yourself?" asked Robert Haack as he parted from her at the steps.

"No," said Lam Fan. "My responsibilities lie in the house. I must return to them at once."

CHAPTER TWELVE

"The Broken Group is composed of a number of islands, islets, and rocks through which are several passages, and amongst which are a few anchorages. With the exception of those hereinafter described, none of the passages should be attempted without local knowledge."

British Columbia Pilot, Volume I

"Sechart Salad—3 cups cold roast whale, chopped coarsely; 2/3 to 1 cup cooked green beans, cut in pieces; 1/2 cup cooked green peas; 4 radishes, sliced. Moisten with salad dressing, mix lightly with a silver fork, serve on a crisp lettuce leaf, and garnish with slices of hard-boiled egg or tomatoes."

Whale Meat as Food,
Twenty Delicious Whale Meat Recipes; Tried and True

We race ahead of the storm, crossing Loudon Channel into Peacock Channel among the Broken Islands of Barkley Sound. As we reach the lee of Dodd Island and some protection from the wind and waves, a grey veil of fog begins to slip quickly between the islands, filling in sea, rock, and reefs, and then covering the land with a smothering hand. Here, as nowhere else I can think of, wind and fog make an insidious partnership.

The chart, open in front of me, is suddenly useless. I slow the *Rose* to a virtual halt. We are at the mercy of Fate.

"North," says Fan, appearing at my elbow. "That's the route we want. I'll go forward to keep a lookout." I have no time to doubt her. I turn the wheel at once. Seconds later she appears at the stem.

Wind that flattens the waters; cold fog that ices the waves with a deceptive calm, and which obscures everything outside this cabin. Even Fan, only a few yards away, is hazy in outline.

We are surrounded by islands, a maze of flooded mountains, and I might as well be blind. Yet the passage from Peacock Channel, up towards the Pinkertons and to the anchorage at Sechart, where we are headed, is wide and deep enough. And there are few dangers other than running aground. As if that weren't enough....

Fan waves her arms, and I adjust my course accordingly. I can almost feel, as I watch her, the humps of land that she indicates. I am steering by instinct: that is, by the instincts of my fellow traveller. And trusting her as I would trust no one else. Not because I have no choice, but because I know her; that she wouldn't let me down. Although I sound my whistle and study my charts intently as well.

The minutes fly by, then the hours. The wind has dropped to nothing in this sheltered network. The fog lies still and stiff as a shroud. We are in the Broken Islands, Inner Group. With Hand Island to the west as we bear northeast. On our way to the last old whaling station on the coast, at Sechart. That is, if the compass is correct; and the tide tables are accurate; and the heartbeat of the *Rose*, her elderly engine, keeps up. If we can thread our way through this pattern of islands on the right circuit. I can sense the storm massed all around us, like an arrangement of magnets with us at its centre, a circle of power, yet letting us pass.

Essential patterning. That guides us outside the dim grey outlines of the Pinkertons. That sweeps us along without thinking. That makes the hull of the *Rose* cleave a white split in the fog that closes up behind us.

Through it my stepmother helps me find my way. And through it my mother grows restless at her home on D'Arcy Island, as Robert Haack, fresh out of jail for the second time, takes steps to find her. Through it we find what we have to find.

And so we glide, Fan and I, on board the *Rose*, through the milky shallows and onto the landing beach. A gentle slope in a gentle curve of a pristine bay, where once hundreds of whales were hauled out and processed. We stand on the deck of the *Rose* and peer like explorers into the close-knit muffler of white that surrounds us; as the *Rose* gives a minor shudder, shifts, then settles, as Lam Fan takes my hand and says, "Come with me, Robert Lam. I have something to show you."

She leads me to the side of my sturdy old boat, and I clamber down after her. Clattering over the side with one hand on a rope, then a leap of faith onto sand and gravel. Then hauled along behind her by the hand like a child to stumble past a blur of shore phantoms: logs that shift and breathe like slumbering saurians, and birds that call from every side at once; plus the ragged figure of a she-bear with cubs that resolves, as we near, into the round and broken fragments of a tower. We continue beyond this sole remnant of the station buildings through a perimeter of bush and into a region of uneven hills: small cupolas, irregularly sprinkled with the broken spars of driftwood. At the base of one of these Lam Fan bids me to sit. "We'll wait here for the sun, Robert Lam," she says as my eyes try and fail to probe a few yards further down the path we've followed. "The *Rose* is safe for the moment. We'll know if the wind comes up, and there's a better anchorage to the east that we can reach in twenty minutes."

"How did you know how to find this place?" I ask her. "You could have got us here blindfolded. The fog made little difference. I watched you. You had your eyes closed. It was as if you had a direction finder."

She raises a hand to hush me. "Speak more quietly, Robert Lam. You should show some respect. You'll see soon enough for yourself."

"Don't *do* that, Fan," I say peevishly, but lowering my voice as she asks. "You know how annoying it is to be put off like that. I asked you a question I have a right to have answered. It was my boat we risked."

"Yes, of course," she says quietly, brushing off my protest. "Now tell me what you know of this place."

I sigh, but decide to answer. There is little else I can do, trapped as we are by this fog and with nowhere to go. "We're at the old whaling station at Sechart. It is the last station there is to visit on this coast. The Tseshaht Indians used to camp here in the summers. The station itself was built in 1905, I think, although I've forgotten the names of the men who started it. My friend Captain Larson, whose father was a whaler, told me a little about it. They did well here at first and took hundreds of whales from these waters. One ship could capture several hundred by itself in a season. They only shut the station down when the herds were so depleted it wasn't worth it to send out ships."

"Ah," said Fan. "Yes, that's it." She nods reflectively.

"And so?" I prompt her.

"Hm?" she says absently.

"What does where we are have to do with how we got here? I wanted to know how you were able to find your way so easily through the fog."

"Did I say it was easy?" she says. A crow drops down from the ceiling of white above us to sit and peck at the grass on the hillside. Its caw, caw grates on my nerves.

"For Pete's sake, just tell me, Fan!" I say.

"I followed the path the whalers took," she answers.

"You did what?"

"Think about it, Robert Lam," she says. "You'll see it makes sense." Doubtfully, but out of respect born of experience, I take her at her word. I think about it. As a light stirring of wind begins to tatter the fog.

Like the man on the lookout that he was, Robert Haack took note, as he scoured the city for word of Gook Lang, of changes in the city grid. There were more merchants, more tailors and shoemakers and pawnbrokers. There was a new jeweller, a tinware dealer, one more manufacturer of ladies' silk underwear. There were eighty or more businesses on Cormorant Street alone, and seventeen new ones on Fisgard Street—five groceries, one butcher, one tin shop, and ten general stores. All in all it made for a prosperous picture.

Even at the windows of the upper storeys, where faces arrived and departed as if on schedule, there had been additions. Not just in new brickwork, or painted scrollwork, but in the faces themselves. For some of the women were white. Tired women, most of them, washed up in the wake of the Klondike gold rush. Who were out of money or time or looks, or who had simply travelled far enough west or north.

Haack called up to these windows—"Do you know a girl named Gook Lang?" But the faces were quickly withdrawn.

Haack kicked along the cobblestones of Fan Tan Alley. Through vegetable peelings and coffee grounds, past men squatting over games of dice, and others eating their breakfast. Through the noise, like a massing of insects behind the walls of the tenements, of gambling chips and dominoes. There were twenty-five fan-tan houses in this alley alone, plus numerous opium dens, smoking cupboards, and star houses.

But Robert Haack's mind was not only on his quest for the missing girl, whom he doubted he would find. He was also thinking about his prospects: for there was no point in dwelling on the past, he had better look ahead and make his plans, and assume, as Lum Kee would have, that all would turn out well in the end.

This boom, he was thinking, this wealth he had observed in the city, how long could it last? There were notices for men to work in canneries and in the coal mines, and for brick makers and lime burners: but what did it mean? Was it going to last? Could he start a business for himself and be assured of making a profit? Or was it the same old routine he'd seen time and again: gold miners coming first, and leading dancing girls and merchants in a long, thin line, and all of them after the same few nuggets. And the working man at the bottom, and the Chinese, with no work at all, at the bottom of that.

It made a man cautious. It made him look more than once at the provision sleighs that sat unsold on the sidewalks, and caused him to notice that there were fewer boats in the harbour than he might have expected.

Was it a beginning? Or was the boom at an end? Or was this simply a lull in between?

Economics. Investment. Multiplication factors. There was over half a million dollars in capital investment in Chinatown alone, Sing Yuen had told him; over a million dollars in business turnovers, and revenues to the city government of some fifteen thousand dollars annually in water and sewer rents, property and road taxes, and licences. There was enough, surely, for everyone. But how to get at it? This was the problem. For every penny that went into his pocket was already marked for Sing Yuen or Yong Sam.

No, Haack thought to himself. Even if he shared a room with three other men, ate little, and had no unforeseen expenses, he wouldn't live long enough to pay his creditors back. And what if he should get sick? And what if he should find India and marry her, what about the family they might have? Was it fair to them to begin with such a burden of debt?

No, no, he said to himself. Even if he should start a business, let's say a tailor's shop, employing five men from 9:00 A.M. to 8:00 P.M., seven days a week, he couldn't do it. There were wages, plus the building rent and taxes, plus his merchandise. And if he did make a profit, even more than he might have expected, would he get to keep any of it? Would Sing Yuen allow it? Would Yong Sam accept it? Hardly likely. Yong Sam, in particular, would send the Tong to collect it at once.

It was a thoughtful, sombre-faced Robert Haack who turned his steps in the direction of his day's appointment. Even if he worked as a business agent, hiring men out to the lumber camps and fisheries at ten percent, making sure that they were soon laid off so that he could hire them out again, destiny had him by the scruff of the neck. There was no escaping it. All he could do was to oppose mathematics with good intentions and hope that the ledger would somehow balance.

For that's what it came down to: trust that the signs of the season— wasps in the garbage heaps, a wedge of ducks honking and squawking as they gathered in vees to fly south—that these pointed to a conclusion worth having, not just another winter of pointless suffering.

Faith. Hope. Dreams. Intuition. The words of a poem and a poet in a vision; debts paid to society, the desire to change: these were his assets. And whether he found Gook Lang, or whether India was well and ready to marry him, he had these to count on.

For what is hope, after all, but the sense that the world we move through must be just.

And so Robert Haack, feeling a little more cheerful as he put the logic of economics behind him, mounted the steps of the Oriental Mission and Rescue Home on Cormorant Street.

It was a modern brick building, raised entirely by subscription and unencumbered by debt, which housed not only a women's day school and home, but a night school for boys and a kindergarten plus a mission band. And it had grown out of India's small beginnings in the Fisgard Street house: a dream that had had its origins in Hong Kong with schooling by the major in reform, had been carried across the ocean, and had blossomed, after India's disappearance—for there were those who did not want the work she had started to come to nothing—into sewing classes and learning English; into a substantial refuge for slave girls and crib girl runaways.

For once a dream is born it seeks out avenues, supporters, ways and means, budgets, an agenda, and a program. It turns into business.

Robert Haack followed the girl who had opened the door into the black pool of the mission's parlour and shook hands with the directress, Miss Powell. He looked curiously around him in the heavily curtained gloom. The girls, children most of them, were ranged round on chairs, staring at him.

Miss Powell, reading Haack's expression of concern, said, "You may speak freely in front of them. None of them know English well enough to understand you, but they are used to men."

She led Robert to an armchair in the centre of the room and continued. "Please try to feel comfortable. These racial boundaries, Mr. Haack, they are nothing in God's scheme; it is we who make too much of them." She smiled at him, got him seated, and poured his tea. He balanced his cup on his lap and tried to speak. But he found the presence of the children too unnerving.

"We've taken in far too many immigrants in my opinion," said Miss Powell, waiting for Robert to find his voice, "but this is home to them now, and it is up to us to assist them, in the light of the Gospel, however we can. Wouldn't you agree?"

Robert nodded, and she laid a hand on his arm. "We are all God's children, Mr. Haack, and we mustn't forget this. Although I myself am a Methodist, we welcome anyone, anyone at all who cares to help us, even the Catholics. Why, the early missionaries to Tibet saw Buddhist priests using censers and the crosier and mitre, and beads for saying their prayers, and thought that Tibetans were instinctive Catholics! Instinctive Christians, possibly, although I wouldn't go so far as to say so myself. But whatever your persuasion is, Mr. Haack, you are welcome in our house." She gave him the friendliest of smiles.

Robert cleared his throat. "Actually, Miss Powell," he said, overcoming his hesitancy, "I'm not a religious man at all, although my mother was a teacher and used to read to me from the Bible. It is a private matter I've come to see you about. I'm searching for someone, and I hoped that you might help. It... she," he corrected, "is a child I knew some years back. I'm asking for a friend who wants to find her."

"Oh, I see," said Miss Powell coolly. Haack felt the temperature in the room drop by several degrees. "Whatever you have to tell me will, of course, be kept in strictest confidence, although we do have to take some measures to protect ourselves." She regarded him severely. "Many men come to us to make restitution for the past. Some feel better if they make a small donation to our running costs."

"No, oh, no," protested Haack, appalled. "It is nothing like that. Why, I never in my life...." He stopped, for he saw he could only make things worse. He started over, hoping that this time she would believe what he said.

"Please, Miss Powell, I truly have come at the request of another person, a woman. The case is nothing to do with me at all, except that I had met the girl when we removed her from a star house. I was assisting Miss Thackery at the time." Haack took out his handkerchief and wiped his face.

Miss Powell put her cup down. "Miss Thackery I have heard of, naturally, in this work, but of you I know nothing." She clapped her hands to gain the girls' attention, then, raising her voice, called, "Toy Kee? Would you come here a moment please?" Obediently, a girl stood up and, feeling her way with her hands—for she was blind—came to stand in front of the directress.

"Go ahead, Kee," said Miss Powell turning her towards their visitor, "no one can harm you here."

The girl stepped forward and placed her hands on Robert's face. She drew her fingers slowly down from his hairline to his chin until she had thoroughly mapped his features. "No," she said at last with a sigh of relief, "it is not him. I do not know this man at all."

Robert let his breath out.

"You must forgive us our caution," said Miss Powell, now smiling again. "But, as I'm sure you'll understand, Mr. Haack, there have been some terrible incidents."

Robert swallowed and tried not to imagine what the incidents had been. Toy Kee felt her way back to her seat. "This girl," said Robert returning to his purpose but with shaken confidence, "we just want to see if she's all right. She vanished seven years ago without a trace. Seven years is a long time, Miss Powell. I myself doubt that you'll have heard of her."

"You say 'we', Mr. Haack," the directress observed, "who is this other party?"

"My employer, Mrs. Sing. She thinks she owes Gook Lang an apology."

"Lang, you say?" said Miss Powell. "Gook Lang?"

"That's right," said Robert. "She'd be grown up by now. Or dead, maybe. Long gone, anyhow, I'd think."

Miss Powell appeared tired. She placed her cup and Robert's side by side on the tea table. She patted her lips with a handkerchief. Then, briefly, she covered her eyes. Haack thought she might be praying.

"The Almighty works in mysterious ways, Mr. Haack," she said, looking up. "There's no telling who can be His instrument." The girls, at Miss Powell's signal, stood and filed out.

Miss Powell took down a short jacket from a wall hook and began buttoning it over her blouse. "If you would be so good as to come with me, Mr. Haack," she said. "I'd rather not go alone."

It nagged at him, as he held Miss Powell's elbow and steered her, at her direction, through the streets he'd already walked that morning. From Cormorant Street along Government Street to Fisgard Street; past Sing Yuen's restaurant, the Place of Ten Thousand Occasions, and down the alley next to it. What was it about the situation that bothered him? It was like swimming upstream, a feeling of moving against the current, of overruling his better judgement. Yet he allowed himself to be carried along.

What was it about this place, these creaking wooden steps that they climbed, this broken door opening inwards into a dimly lit hallway? Whatever it was, it evaded him, though he saw the shadows of pigeons scuttering across the skylight, and a door cracked open on the left as Miss Powell knocked at another on the right.

She was saying, "We are so lucky in this country, Mr. Haack. We have an abundance of natural resources, our mines, our forests, our unsurpassed scenery. But what about people, Mr. Haack? Can we let them take second place while we build sawmills and fisheries? Jesus said, suffer the little ones to come unto Him. He meant all mankind, Mr. Haack, no matter in what condition."

She waited a moment, then opened the door herself. It was not until they were actually in the room, not until he was peering at the figure seated by a table at the window, that his mind released its hold on his memory and he realized where he had come, and to whom.

"Lang!" cried Robert Haack in wonder. "Lang," he repeated in astonishment as the familiar profile turned slowly towards him. "I never thought... I never dreamed... How have you been?"

For despite the conditions of their last meeting, he was genuinely happy to have found her. It would please Lam Fan and Sing Yuen. And perhaps he could make amends, explain to Gook Lang what had happened: for he did not like the thought that she had known him at his worst.

He moved towards her, but Miss Powell gripped his elbow and pulled him back. "It is so sad," she was saying. "There is nothing to be done. It is a loathsome infection." Her words meant nothing to him. But something in Gook Lang's attitude did. He knew, even before he was near enough to see her clearly: for it was a kind of nemesis—justice with hindsight, justice retributive—that the young woman who regarded him bore the unmistakable hallmarks of leprosy.

Gook Lang, whom he had mistaken through a partly closed door for India at a crucial moment in his life. Gook Lang, the living image of Haack's self-blame.

The magnitude of the cruelty overwhelmed him. Not just to Lang, but to him. How was it that everything he did went so terribly wrong? How was it he could find no way out? How was it that he was caught in a loop that had started with a falling coal bucket; and that had led to a woman named India on board a sailing ship, and from there to a profitless robbery and worse? A loop that had passed, on its way, a child named Gook Lang. A child who had once been rescued, and who had now come to this.

"What should we do with her?" Miss Powell asked him, as if he were the one who knew. "We can't leave her like this," said the mission directress, "we have got to take her somewhere: but where? She can't go to D'Arcy Island; only men live there. And it would be a terrible shame to introduce her among the other girls in the rescue home."

Haack was afraid to move. He blinked his eyes, half hoping that the vision of Gook Lang would disappear: but although she slipped in and out of focus, her ruined head floating like a pale white disk above her body, there was no denying her presence. A sudden shift in a heap of rags on the floor then caught his eye. The bundle rose and turned into a human. It advanced towards them, opening its mouth and crying, "She is a good girl. She works very hard! You no take her away!"

It was all Robert Haack could do not to faint. "Tai Ho?" he cried in horror, recognizing the old woman from whom he and India had taken Gook Lang so long ago. "Not you here also!"

Miss Powell tugged at his sleeve. "This is a difficult woman to deal with, we had better leave," she said.

"I'm sorry, Lang," said Robert weakly. "I didn't know. I'll try to do something. I'll tell them. It will be all right." But he was backing out, his legs trembling under him as if they would break like sticks.

Outside, Haack, having managed to say goodbye to Miss Powell, who had another call to make, and having given her Lam Fan's address so that the two of them could consult as to Gook Lang's fate, stood, shocked, on the boardwalk. He could not stop shaking. Each breath he took made him choke. But as he wheezed and gasped, the blur of impressions that swirled through his brain began to achieve a focus. It then moved to his heart. More than regret, it was grief that he felt.

Wasted time, he thought. And cost. Even now it could be as late for himself and India as it was for Gook Lang. He had no way of knowing.

Cost, thought Robert Haack as he stumbled along the boardwalk. You build for years, then it all goes up. Gambling debts, Smiling Jimmies, jail sentences, lost opportunities. And Gook Lang's visage. That's what it cost to live a life.

He saw himself as a small boy in his California valley home. He heard his mother's voice. He met the poet R.L. Stevenson once again and was given a poem. He walked through summer nights with India Thackery. He found the life he wanted, then he lost it.

In the beginning there was a man of mixed character who had come to many turning points in his life; who had taken every avenue he could think of, and yet had found that whatever he did he achieved the same result. A man who, as the sun set brilliantly in a smoke-coloured sky, was once more face-to-face with himself. A man who had seen the truth at last, and with no illusions left. A man who would do what he had to because he knew nothing else. A man who could no longer delay.

And so he made his way through a familiar labyrinth, but with no more mathematics and no more weighing up chances. No further attempt at balance. There was no more time to consider right and wrong. No time to hedge on the future. It had to be now, and it had to be first things first. He would do what he must to get money in order to find India.

We are sitting, Lam Fan and I, among the low hills of Sechart as a sea breeze begins to whisper and to shift the mist. The track we have followed is slowly revealing itself. I think about what Lam Fan has said about how we came here—by following the whaling ships. As if their well-worn routes from the open sea through the islands were like a path through the woods: trodden down and flattened, worn to bedrock. So that all who chanced this way could read the history of the whaling ships ever after. It is possible? Have both sea and land a record to keep? Do ship lanes and whale migrations and the blood trails left by the sea ravages of men—just like roadways and railways—tie strings of traffic round Mother Earth herself? And can these be observed by those with the eyes to see them? Like the light sent out by stars, which light-years after its origin is made manifest to earth?

It makes a sort of sense, I suppose, at least to a ghost. Who need not concern herself with what is now and what is past. It is all one line she treads.

It makes sense, of course, in the light of death.

The death of lepers on a tiny island. The death of a girl and her grandmother because of my actions. The deaths of fellow crewmen when the *Silverbell* went down near the Canary Islands; and the multitudinous deaths of whales and other fellow creatures, up and down this coast, for the sake of commerce. Sing Yuen dead in the frightful trenches of France; my mother dead not long after my birth. Even Robert Haack, who seems to me to be as alive as any man I know because of the pain he causes himself. And my father, of course, whoever he was, is long dead as well. It is only I, Robert Lam, who lives.

And who watches in anguished suspense as the lifting drapery of fog reveals a figure on the path. And then there is not just one, but several, and I know them all. Not the dead as one might expect in this desolate place, but those who have recently helped me: Joe Alexander from Granite Bay, who had walked from Siberia, so he said, and who gave me a coin for luck, good or bad; and the doctor at Coal Harbour, riddled with guilt for the Japanese destroyed by the atom bomb; and the Indian woman at Zeballos who had taken a whale for a lover; and the boy who made me pay for my vision at Friendly Cove by taking a drug, and who had sent me out to do battle with whales with the weapons of his fathers; and Brian Chapman, who had lost a son and now spent his time saving other men's children; and Doctor Annette, a refugee from Europe, who breathes a brief puff of life back into herself by trying to heal others. People with stories more important than mine, who had given me something; who I would always take with me, like it or not; who had traced, for a way, with me, my path.

They pass by me quietly, not looking around, and in a minute or two they are gone. "I think I see now, Fan," I say softly as I watch them go. "If I could observe myself, I'd be in line with them, too."

She nods. Then she touches me on the elbow. "Look, Robert Lam," she says. I turn my eyes reluctantly from the place where my visitors had vanished. The fog has risen foot by foot, and now it has revealed the hills, and the trees that body out the forest behind them. But the hills, the hills are not what I'd thought at all. They are made, every one of them, of the broken bones and skeletons of whales. We are in a dumping ground, a rubbish heap, graveyard, if you like, of beings that once lived and swam and breathed and birthed in the oceans. And sang. For so I believe I have heard them, time and again.

Thousands and thousands. Tens of thousands. Mute, and yet vibrant still with the life that once flowed through them. I reach out a hand and trace the rough filaments of one of these relics of bone. Fishermen won't have whalebone on board their vessels. It causes wrecks, brings bad dreams, ruins the catch. But sailors take the bone and polish it, then carve upon it the memories they want to keep: desert islands, Caribbean docks, beautiful women; plus sailing ships, storms, sharks, even their fights with the whales themselves. We sailors are made orphans of the world by our need to roam it. And we are not at home on land and are restless at sea, and are half human only. For our souls cry out to join with something better than we find in our own species. Or if not to join it, then to kill it.

Leviathan. Sea monster. A seascape of dreams we cannot see beneath.

I sigh and put the whalebone back where I found it. "Well?" says Fan with an anxious look.

"I guess that's it, Fan," I say, "we should say goodbye to the whales here. It's time we were heading for home."

"Jimmy Carroll did it," said Robert Haack to the customs officer with whom he had made the appointment. For he had realized that the only thing he had to sell was information—even if he had to make some of it up. "He planned the whole thing. I knew about the robbery and did nothing to stop it, but that was the extent of my crime."

The police officer, who had been asked by customs to sit in on the interview, rolled his eyes. He could not keep quiet.

"Jimmy Carroll is dead," he said. "We thought of him from the first, but before we could question him he was killed. You could accuse Carroll of whatever you wanted; there's no one to say any different."

"Yet you spent seven years in jail, Mr. Haack," added the customs officer, "without telling us any of this. Why have you changed your story now?"

Robert Haack looked wistfully out the window of the room in the St. Nicholas Hotel, in which the three men had gathered, to the street below. Along it men and women sauntered at leisure. The customs officer was waiting with pen poised above paper. "Conscience," said Robert Haack at last. "I wanted to make a new start. I didn't want this business left on my mind. Besides, Sing Yuen, the factory owner, is a friend."

"I see," said the customs man. The policeman unbuttoned his collar and tugged at his jowls.

"You said on the telephone," said the officer—for Haack had called him up from the Trounce Alley office of the telephone company—"that you might be able to tell us what had happened to the opium. A great deal, a very great deal, as I'm sure you know, was stolen. Naturally we would like to get it back and return it to its owner, Mr. Sing. Or, at the very least, have duty paid on it when it is sold. But there has been no trace of it in all this time. That is unusual, Mr. Haack, wouldn't you think?"

"Quite so," said Robert, who was surprised to hear that none at all had turned up. Usually some of it trickled through, one way or another, into the customs net. This was better than he'd hoped, and he adjusted his story accordingly. "But there are many ways it could have been hidden, it happens all the time."

"Yes," said the customs man, "I'm sure it does."

"Sometimes," Robert Haack went on, warming to the topic, "the opium goes from Victoria to Vancouver, where it is shipped on the Canadian Pacific Railroad to Fort Hope. From there it goes to the Similkameen Mines near the American border. From the mines there is a trail leading into the United States. A great deal is smuggled into the country by this route."

The police officer closed his eyes and gave a small groan. The customs officer gave him a sharp look and said, "We know all that, Mr. Haack. We have checked that route, and none of the Tai June opium is there to be found."

"Other times," said Robert Haack, soldiering on, "the opium goes from here to Golden, then to the Kootenay Mines, and, once it is considered safe, from there to Bonner's Ferry in Idaho. From there it is taken to the Northern Pacific Railroad and thence to a number of destinations."

"Indeed, Mr. Haack," said the customs man with infinite patience. "But this is hardly news to us."

Robert looked somewhat taken aback. "Do you know then," he asked sceptically, "that opium is shipped as Chinese wines or merchandise? And it is often billed to Winnipeg, then taken across the border there into Montana and Dakota? Or sometimes on to St. Paul and Minneapolis? Or it is carried by railroad to Port Windsor and ferried across to Detroit?"

''Yes, yes," said the customs officer, nodding calmly, but taking notes furiously, "we know all that." The policeman was fully alert. "But what has this to do with the Tai June opium in particular?"

Robert Haack leaned back in his chair, sure that he had established his credentials. "I know for a fact where the Tai June opium was stored," he said. "It is of no use to me. I do not hold with that sort of business in the first place, and in any case I have not the means to do anything with it.

"The point is," he continued, "that I am quite prepared to tell you where it is. But we must agree on a price first."

"Money!" the policeman cried. "I thought you said you were hardly involved at all! If you know where the opium went, you were right in the thick of it! You don't deserve a penny, not a penny. If I had my way you'd be hanged for it!"

"Please," said the customs officer, raising his palms to silence his associate, "we are not interested in blame at this late date. If Mr. Haack is a reasonable man I'm sure something can be agreed between us. What had you in mind, Mr. Haack?" he asked. He smiled pleasantly, but Robert saw that he had drawn a gallows on his paper.

Haack returned the smile expansively. He had it all worked out. "You'll find I'm a fair man," he said. "I want only one third now, when I give you the location, one third when you find the opium, and the final third when I bring you Smiling Jimmy's accomplices and you put them in jail."

"The whole crew?" said the policeman with a snort. "Don't tell us that you know where they are, as well?"

"I have my thoughts on the matter, but the less said now the better," Robert advised. "There are others who would like this secret, too. This much opium is of interest to anyone."

The two officials looked at each other, then, as if of one mind, stood up. "We shall return in a matter of minutes, Mr. Haack," said the customs officer. "I shall tell you then whether we can agree to what you want. Any monies involved must be approved, however, by my superiors, although that can be arranged quite quickly, if necessary, by telephone." They shut the door behind them, leaving Robert by himself.

He strolled up and down the thin red carpet. He believed he had them hooked. Once they gave him the first third of the money he asked, he would be all set. It was enough to take himself and India, once he had found her, out of the country, yet little enough in itself. After that they'd look after themselves. And once out of the country he'd be free (so to speak) of debt. For even Yong Sam wouldn't know where he'd gone; they'd take care to tell no one. He gazed out the window. He sat down on a settee and picked up the morning paper, which the policeman had left there. He turned its pages, scarcely aware of what he read until he came to this:

D'Arcy Island Lepers: Unfounded Report of Japanese Fishermen Carrying Vegetables From the Island to their Marketing Operations on the Mainland and Vancouver Island.

It has been stated most circumstantially that vegetables grown on D'Arcy Island are being sent across twice a week to Vancouver and Victoria in Japanese fishing boats, which had been seen working in the vicinity of the island. The object of the lepers in raising and selling these vegetables, it was alleged, was to procure opium, money being of no use to them. A thorough inspection has shown that the gardening operation, which, by the way, is very limited, is not more than sufficient to supply their own wants at the very outside. Further, there is no evidence of Japanese fishing boats being involved, and absolutely no evidence of any person visiting the island, except for those who are called upon in the official capacity of supplying the wants of these poor unfortunates.

A good deal of indignation is expressed that such a statement, calculated to do a very great deal of injury to the cities in question, should find such wide currency. It is evident that the person who had supplied the information in question had drawn altogether upon a fertile imagination.

Robert Haack let the paper fall into his lap. He sat wrapped in thought. Here might be an answer to another problem—what to do with Gook Lang. For he had not been able to get the young woman off his mind. Lam Fan was willing to pay for keep if they could just find somewhere to put her. To leave her where she was, with Tai Ho, was unthinkable.

What if, Haack thought, the Japanese fishermen, who did not seem to be afraid of leprosy, could be persuaded to look after her? Despite her appearance, she was still in reasonable health and would be able to help with their cooking and laundry. It was worth a try, he thought. The fishermen lived on the shore near Mount Douglas, not far from the cabin he had built and had shared with Charlie. It was all falling into place like magic. Each loose thread of his life was beginning to tie up. Now if only customs would give him some money, he could begin his search for India. Then his luck, he could say, would have changed character utterly.

The door opened. The policeman entered first, looking sour. The customs officer followed more cheerfully. "Well," he said most heartily, "Mr. Haack, I think we're in business."

Business. A shady business indeed, said Robert. For Jimmy Carroll had been up to his old tricks. Just like he had a dozen years previously, when he had smuggled opium on board the *Idaho* and he had hidden the drug at his 'cannery' in Alaska.

Only this time the opium from the Tai June warehouse had gone up the coast, just north of Nanaimo, to the abandoned whale fishery at Deep Bay. There, in an old whaling ship that lay rotting at anchor, Carroll had sealed up the opium. He'd been in no rush. He'd planned to wait until he was sure that customs had lost all interest before he distributed it. For this time he had wanted nothing to go wrong: he was frightened of jail, and he was not a young man. That is why he'd come back to the city so soon: to throw customs completely off track. And then, of course, he had died before he'd had a chance to put the rest of the scheme into practise.

And where, exactly, Robert was asked, was the opium to be found?

In the carpenter's room, between decks, and some in the bilge, said Robert Haack instantly.

"Would you come with us?" They queried him.

"If you think it wise," said Robert agreeably, "if you don't think it might alert other interests before you're ready for it."

The officers considered this. "No," said the senior man finally. "I think it's better if you stay here while we do the search. That way we have you in reserve if we should need your further assistance."

The men shook hands. And Robert Haack, with a certain advance sum of money in his pocket—meant to encourage his public spirit; money for which he didn't have to account to Yong Sam or Sing Yuen—for how would they know he had got it?—walked into the street a free man.

He turned on his heel, and, in the early autumn of the year of 1898, headed for Hillside Avenue, then took the turn north at the Jewish cemetery onto Cedar Hill Road; past the church at the crossroads and the farmhouses nestling under blankets of smoke, with cordwood stacked neatly and rain sizzling on chimneys, past the schoolhouse and grazing cows and fallow fields, all the way across the Cedar Hill plain to the foot of Mount Douglas. And further.

Down a trail that wound through great stands of timber, with the smell of the sea growing stronger, to the sudden give-way of sand underfoot as the green-black shadows of the primeval forest separated. To show the white narrow crescent of Cordova Bay beach.

The light was grey and silvered with rain. There was a gun-metal sheen on the waves. There was a clutch of fishing shacks, one sending up smoke, nearby. Nets were laid out to dry, and there were a few upturned boats.

Robert looked out into the mist of the strait and watched a fishing boat navigate between Little Zero and Zero rocks, its mast ticking back and forth. It drew nearer: it had white-painted planks and a small green cabin from which the head of its skipper poked out. Robert turned to greet a small brown-skinned man who had come out to meet him. The man was barefoot, and he wore a tight woollen cap on his head. He bowed in greeting. The two men stood companionably side by side while Robert wondered how he could broach the subject. How to bring up leprosy, and a young woman named Gook Lang, and, "I'd like you to take care of her." For he had to do it right. He took deep breaths as he watched the fish boat set its anchor and the crew move busily on deck and a blanketed figure stand up and be helped down a ladder into a rowboat. The Japanese beside him took his pipe from his pocket. He poked at the bowl with a knife. Then he indicated the dinghy that was bobbing in and out of sight.

"Did you come for the lady?" he asked.

We are huddling in the rain round our camp fire on the shore at Sechart. There is almost no wind. The *Rose* is still up on the beach, and we are waiting for the tide to lift her off. "Hush," says Lam Fan when I go to speak. And she points out to sea.

There is a whaler in the bay with a killed whale floating near it. And the shadows of men moving back and forth, busy at their work. It is not flesh I see, of course, but a memory. Time released from Fan and me and making a bridge between us. An alignment of place and date and ship and current. Like the aurora borealis, with its own music, the sound of coloured glass.

To the east, on a leper's island no larger than a thumbprint on the map of the Pacific, my mother, India Thackery, took a step. To the west of her, there was Robert Haack. And where they met, just as here, at Sechart, where Fan and I sit, there were the crosshairs of a magnet: time rising from the storehouse of experience, more real than remembering, immediate and complete. Time past. Time present. Time in coincidence. Time boundless.

Like clouds seeded with silver nitrate; or codes and signals, gathered in gasses, which rain down on earth from the planets and asteroids. With a beginning but no end; with its true habitation in the brain.

I reach for Fan's hand. "Goodbye, goodbye," I hear my mother, India, call to her leper friends. Ah Sam takes out his handkerchief and blows his nose. Then he says, "Don't forget to say that we need sugar. If we have sugar we will be all right." And Sim Lee says, with his face turned seawards, watching the fisherman as he sets up the oars, "Send us a little dog, a small black one to bring back sea gulls if I shoot them." And Ng Chung, with his hat brim funnelling rain down the inside of his jacket, says, "Here, I have something for you. Please take it." And he holds out his hand to my mother, who is even now beginning a future without him. In his palm is a Chinese coin. It is one of two he has saved to be placed on his eyelids at death. Slowly my mother opens her hand to receive it.

And then they wave until the dinghy reaches the fishing boat and the fishing boat vanishes from sight. Until Robert Haack arrives at Cordova

Bay beach. Until Lam Fan and I light our fire on the coast at Sechart, and watch the shades of long-dead men bustle about at their work.

The whale carcass, big as a zeppelin, the tunnel shape of an atom bomb, the shadow that blots out cities, the cloud without end... drifts and bobbles until the whalers draw it in, and the *Rose* takes heart and struggles upright on her keel, and floats free.

CHAPTER THIRTEEN

"Approaches to Juan de Fuca Strait—Navigation is simple in clear weather; but, owing to the irregularity of the currents and tidal streams, every precaution must be taken in thick weather. The strait is liable to all those sudden vicissitudes of weather common to these latitudes, and in few parts of the world is the caution and vigilance of the navigator more called into action than when entering it from the Pacific Ocean."

British Columbia Pilot, Volume I

We leave Barkley Sound by Imperial Eagle Channel, then pass through Folger Passage between Folger Island and Hornby Rock. Off Cape Beale there is a sharp and choppy sea, but once around the cape we are carried along swiftly by the swells. Although the roller-coaster ride is exhilarating, and the strong northwest wind merely helps us on our way, I am far from forgetting that this is one of the most dangerous stretches of coastline that there is.

We sight Seabird Rocks, on which many a vessel has come to grief at the entrance to Pachena Bay, with foul ground lying both southwest and southeast; then Pachena Point light. A distance-finding signal emanates from there, but we have no equipment to pick it up. If I ever sail this coast again, I will be better equipped.

I glance at Lam Fan, who sits pensively on a stool beside the exhaust shroud in the wheelhouse. She has been quiet for several hours, and in some inexplicable way seems to be absent. She looks windblown, sun-bleached, salt-stained, not the elegant Fan I've always known. And weary.

"Happy to be going home, Fan?" I ask her, for I am looking forward to our arrival. We could make port at Victoria, if all goes well, by the next midday. Or earlier, with favourable wind, tide, and currents. I am anxious, now that I can glimpse the end, to finish this journey, and to give myself and the *Rose* a well-deserved rest. We could both do with a tune-up.

Klanawa River and Tsusiat River—we can see the latter's waterfall even at this distance; then we fly past Nitinat and Clooose. I keep a look-out for the local steamer, which calls there regularly.

Stretches of white beach and an unending framework of trees line the coast of Vancouver Island; and pockets of haze burn off as the sun climbs the rungs of its ladder. To the west is the Swiftsure Bank, where the fishing boats gather, and where the lightship flashes out its warnings and forecasts. To the northeast is Carmanah Point light.

"Landmarks, Fan!" I cry out happily as I mark these off on the chart. "Every one we pass brings us one step nearer home."

Fan stirs at her post near the warmth of the shroud. Her subdued face, her travel-faded garments paint a hangdog picture. She decides, at last, to break her silence. "It's all right for you, Robert Lam," she says with a whine in her voice. "You've got a future to look forward to. But what about me? For me it's all over." She subsides again. Her head lolls weakly on her shoulders. Her spine—usually straight as a lodge pole—is curved.

"Why, Fan!" I say in an effort to raise her spirits. "It's because of you that the future looks bright at this late date in my life. My conscience is clear at last, and I'm freed of the past. Can't you see what that means? Anything is possible, anything at all!" I do a little dance to illustrate, although I stumble a bit as the feeling in my legs gives out. I sit down and rub and pinch them until the nerves respond.

"See, Fan," I say to her, with my feet again under me, "I'm a new man. Reborn. I've got my family, my history, my sense of identity. Yes, it's all due to you."

She stirs again, self-pity gaining ground on apathy. "But what about me?" she says again. "What will happen to me once you return, have you thought about that?"

I push my cap to the back of my head. It is stained, sweat-caked, and beginning to smell, but I'm proud of it. I've earned this captain's head-gear as I've earned no other. "Of course I've thought of it, Fan. You'll rest in peace, presumably."

She glares at me, her sharp black eyes sparking to life angrily. "Over and done with, is that it? Now it's back on the garbage heap? I wouldn't have thought it even of you, Robert Lam," she says disgustedly.

"But Fan," I say, "why is it up to me at all? It was your choice to come on board the *Rose* at D'Arcy Island. I'd already buried you. I'd said good-bye. You came to help me of your own free will. When I said 'rest in peace,' I meant it. For that's what you deserve, at the very least."

She looks sad. "I made you a promise and I kept it," she says. There is a pause during which I try to guess what's coming next, for it's clear she's not finished. "It wasn't much of a funeral," she says regretfully.

I look at her in surprise. "I did my best, you know. You never told me what you wanted."

"It's not what I wanted that matters," she says, "it's what I got that counts." She wipes a tear from her eye.

"I don't understand you, Fan," I say. "We've been in this thing together all along. I can't see why you're unhappy all of a sudden. If there's anything I can do to help, please let me know." I am beginning to worry, for it's not like Fan to be like this. I'd counted on her all these miles, and she hadn't failed me yet.

We are now in Juan de Fuca Strait, on the homestretch. I can feel the pull of my life on land: the pilot station and the men I work with; the little house at Christmas Hill that I don't think I'll sell after all, at least not for awhile; there are the boundless possibilities of travel after retire-ment, of other journeys in other company. Of friendship and compan-ionship. Of knowing where I fit. For I've almost got the whole of it. There can't be much more left.

Fan squirms and looks supremely uncomfortable. She twines her legs round the rungs of the stool. She leans forward, then tips back. She knocks down my wet socks, which were hung on the shroud, gently steaming.

"Come on, Fan, out with it," I say a little impatiently as I look for the flashing light on the buoy by Port San Juan. "I'm here for as long as you need me, but I want to get on with it."

She gives me a bleak look. She drops her eyes. "There is something I haven't told you yet, Robert Lam," she says quietly. "I'm afraid it is very important. You see, we can't go home just yet."

To Robert Haack's thinking India had changed very little since he'd last set eyes on her. Certainly she was badly dressed, in a man's shirt, trousers, boots, coat, and hat; and there was a streak of grey in the brown hair under the derby; and the blue eyes were pale in her sun-browned face; but he would have known her anywhere. With a great sigh of relief he threw his arms around her.

"I can't believe I've found you, I can't believe it," he cried over and over. Tears of release from all the years of worry streamed down his face as he sobbed against her shoulder. As for how he'd come to be there, and what had occurred to bring about the chance of their meeting, he did not think to tell her. It was enough, for the moment, that they were together.

India stood with her arms around him, comforting him as she would a troubled child. She could sense that he'd suffered—was it all because of her? Had he known she'd been on D'Arcy Island? And if not, what must he be thinking now? For the Japanese had told him at once where they'd come from. There were questions she had to ask, things she had to say to him; but she also needed time to think. For it was a shock to find Robert Haack back in her life. Not that she'd never given him a thought: for of course, she had, she had loved him once: but he was part of the world she had left behind on the day of the robbery, so long ago. But what now? What was to come?

Robert wiped his eyes and composed himself. "We've got to hurry," he said suddenly, taking charge. "We must get up to the cabin before it's dark. I've had no chance to fix it up. We can think what to do with you once we've got you safe."

His sense of urgency was infectious. Still in a daze, still bewildered by this unexpected turn of events, unsure of herself, India let him lead her away from the circle of onlookers. He strapped her few belongings onto the saddle of a horse he had borrowed from the fishermen and helped her climb up. Then he took the reins and mounted the horse behind her.

It had happened so quickly: as when the moon eclipses a star, the star touching the edge of the moon, then winking out: the star is there, then it isn't. So it was that India exchanged one way of life for another. And all calculations, considerations, and second thoughts were blacked out. They left the past behind them as they rode away from the beachfront.

The sun began its magnificent descent behind Mount Douglas. The horse whinnied and twisted its neck for a last long sniff at the fishermen's dinners, then horse and riders were encompassed by forest.

Fallen leaves slushed underfoot as the horse retraced its step as far as the path that wound up Mount Douglas. Here they started to climb, with Haack clucking the animal round the turns and guiding it up gullies, through streams, across deer trails, up and up, to the top of the mountain where a half-ruined cabin slumped.

Lights, miniature as fireflies, flashed on in the plain below them, indicating dinners and card games and family recitals in a dozen farmhouses. India could only stare at them in wonder.

How had it happened? Where had she been? Her life on D'Arcy Island was like a dream. It was as if it had never been.

Robert helped her down and began to unpack their belongings and prepare the cabin. India stumbled over to a rock and sat upon it. She watched her old friend as he hurried to fix things up. He looked happy, full of hope. He kept turning to her and smiling as if he could hardly believe his good luck.

She turned to look over the edge of the mountain. Beyond the little lights of the Cedar Hill plain the city was haloed in gaslight. Shopping districts and government offices, ships riding at wharfside, telegraph and post offices: they were all spread out before her, indistinguishable from this distance, but evident, nonetheless, in the general outline of memory. Her sister, Lam Fan, was there, and her other friends. There was the work she had left behind. Her whole other life. All suddenly attainable, but impossible, yet, to realize.

"We'll only stay here a few days," said Robert Haack, coming up behind her and looking over her shoulder at the sprawling vista. He turned her towards him. "We'll put this whole damned place behind us. I've got it all worked out.

"After we get married, of course," he added, noting the flicker of doubt in her eyes. "I love you, India," he said, tracing the bones of her face with his fingers. "I've thought of nothing but you for all these years.

We'll get married, I'll buy the steamer tickets, then we'll go to San Francisco." He wrapped his arms around her and held her tightly.

She looked beyond him, blankly, feeling the warmth of his body seep into hers, not knowing quite what to say, suddenly full of longing for all she had missed: love and a home and family. Someone to look after her, for a change. She sighed, and Robert bent his head to kiss her.

"It doesn't matter," he whispered, a moment later. "Whatever has happened, wherever we've been, whatever we've done, it's all over now. It's at an end."

Then it was all returning, as her memory, dormant from years of hard work, began to awaken: the long walks they had taken together; the talks about books; the rescue work; the sense of unhampered vision. They seemed, in retrospect, to have been so young. And now she felt young again.

The horse, left free to graze, whinnied as its nostrils picked up a dozen scents. In the circle of light from the lantern that Robert Haack lit, India watched their shadows dance and melt. Then she turned her face eastwards, searching in all the blackness for D'Arcy Island. As she watched, a light sprang up on the island's southern tip.

"I'll put some water on to boil if you want to wash," said Robert, who had noted at what she looked. "Then I'll cook us some dinner. The fishermen gave me a few fish."

"I'd like that," she said, turning to him with a smile. Once more he took her hands. "I thought I'd never see you again," he said. "I thought I had lost you. Can you ever forgive me? If only I had known what Jimmy had done to you."

She looked at him, puzzled. "Forgive you? But what for, Robert?" she asked. "It wasn't anyone's fault. It was an accident. There was a robbery at the factory, and I stumbled into it." She shrugged her shoulders. "You mustn't blame yourself for what wasn't your fault."

Robert dropped his eyes, weighed down by his burden of guilt. "I'll explain it all later," he said. He had forgotten how little she knew, how great the gaps would be, how much he would have to reveal. What should he tell, what leave out? Was there any point in risking their happiness when they had only just found it?

He boiled the water on the fire as he had promised, then left India alone in the cabin to tidy herself. He sat outside and took deep breaths. He examined the stars. A simple life with simple pleasures was all he wanted.

And it seemed to be possible, here and now, at the top of the universe. Why bother about what had been? Why let the past destroy them?

He returned to the cabin and lay down beside her. He blew the lantern out. Once more he took her in his arms and kissed her. Once more they remembered what both of them had missed.

As for what followed, as for jackets and shirts and torn Chinese vests, as for the aurora borealis displayed on closed eyelids....

"As for sex," says Lam Fan bluntly.

"As for that, Fan," I say with annoyance, "it is none of my business, as you've often told me."

She looks sheepish. "But the point is, Robert Lam," she begins in her own defense....

"The point is," I tell her, "that it is the autumn of 1898, almost a year before my birth. Whatever happened that night between Haack and my mother, it had nothing to do with me."

She sighs as if life has passed her by and is sorely regretted. "You have so much, and I have so little," she says resentfully.

"For God's sake, Fan," I say, "you lived to be a hundred years old!"

"It's not the same," she says.

"The same as what?" I ask her.

"What's gone is gone," she says, "it doesn't make up for anything."

I look at Fan again. My stepmother with emotions and feelings? As a woman? My stepmother with a private life?

Bliss. To be released from the claims of creditors, on the one hand, and from isolation on a lepers' island, on the other. And free, for the moment, of convention, of civilized mores, of the judgements of others. Of responsibilities and the hard facts of illness. Why shouldn't my mother and Robert Haack have been lovers, even if he wasn't my father? Why should I begrudge my mother her pleasure after all she's been through?

Because she *is* my mother, and to condemn her for what I'd do myself is only traditional. Yet my heart isn't in it. Rather, I envy them their respite, of whatever it consisted. I envy them their innocence.

And so Robert Haack lay awake for hours with India's head on his arm. He considered the future; he did his best to forget the past. He watched the face that he had loved so long in its absence. She lay serenely beside him as if that's where she truly belonged, calm as a child, never doubting. She slept until the sun crept into the cabin.

It was not much of a wedding in the normal scale of these things: there were no banns posted, there was no wedding dress for my mother, no high neck and long train or lace veil to cover emotions; no jewelled hairpins or orange blossoms, no choir to sing "Praise Ye the Lord all Ye Heathen," and no organ playing Mendelssohn. No bridesmaids or weeping spectators; no groom in frock coat faced with silk, and wearing cashmere trousers and boots and patent leather.... There was only my mother and Robert Haack, plus the minister, and his wife for witness.

They were married outdoors beside the Cedar Hill church. Leaves fell from the oak trees as the wind blew in gusts; and crows scattered from branches as the minister read the text. The minister joined their hands, closed his Bible, then had them sign a paper. And their two separate lives were joined together forever.

Robert walked a little distance with India on the way back to the cabin, where she was to wait for him. He was going to the city to purchase their tickets: for they had no time to waste, since the past that he'd outdistanced for a couple of days could quickly catch up with him. There were Yong Sam's men, for example, and Sing Yuen's friends, plus the customs officers, who would be on their way home from Deep Bay empty-handed and eager to find him.

He had told her as little about his problems as he could. But it was obvious, in any case, that it would be best if their movements were kept quiet. Moreover, India was still in a daze, stunned by her sudden change from one life to another; and they would have to find a way to account for her long disappearance. That she had ever set foot on D'Arcy Island was a secret they would have to keep hidden.

And so they stood for a moment and talked as the sun steamed moisture from the wet wood of the forest. And they forgot, in the obliterating joy of their marriage, about loneliness and unhappiness and plans gone wrong; they lost the very knowledge that these things could happen as they indulged in the language of hand-touch and lip-touch, in the everyday intimacies of love. They were at a fulcrum, a point of balance, suspended in time between city and cabin. There was one final kiss— with teeth clinks and inner lips, surfaces tickled and underpinnings undone, with tongue on top of tongue in advance and retreat.... It was like hunger and thirst.

That is, they kissed for the last time, time and again, then they parted.

My mother on top of a granite monolith, flea-sized in proportion to its mass and surface, as the sun sets into the saucer of the ocean and the stars blink open their cold all-seeing eyes; and the black bowl of the sky turns until she is dizzy with it. My mother, with her arms clasped around herself, alone on a mountain on her wedding night.

With the city to the west and the island to the east like perfect opposites. Waiting, while time, like time in space, elongates.

Time elastic. As when a spaceship (as scientists speculate) approaches a star at the speed of light, and time, relative to earth time, slows down. So that when the ship reaches its destination, thousands of light-years from home, the crew is no older than when it started out....

And then the return, where they land on earth and wander like ghosts in the future they've arrived in, in exile, *out of time* in the world that produced them.

My mother, India, on the brink of reentering the world she'd been torn from. Can it really be done? And what about the names she must never mention? What about those men who had been her friends, Sim Lee, Ah Sam, and Ng Chung, plus the others now gone?

And where does love fit in? And was it love that she felt? And how can she put the halves of her life together inside a marriage to Robert Haack?

"But *why* can't we go home, Fan?" I ask my stepmother, having turned her pronouncement over in my mind. "I can't think of anything we haven't done that we should have, and we can be there in a matter of hours."

"You can do what you want," she says as we coast by the Sheringham Point light on as gentle a passage as I've ever had in these waters—it seems as if we are blessed: all obstacles melt before us—"but I'll have to go on by myself."

"But why, Fan?" I ask her again, exasperated. "You know we're in this together, and I won't leave you alone with whatever it is; but I do think I deserve an explanation."

Fan looks unhappy but stubborn. "I can't tell you before we get there," she says. "You know I wouldn't ask if it wasn't important." I sigh.

Banks of cloud, low and enveloping, have softened the sky. Yet the sharp edges of the sea are aglitter with light. A troller passes us on its way to the harbour at Sooke, filled to the gunwales with fish.

"It's important to whom, Fan?" I ask her. "To you or to both of us?"

"I can't say any more," she answers evasively. "It will become clear to you once we get there."

"Where is there, Fan? I do have my limits. I'm not travelling around this island again, whatever you say. Let us have done with it."

"Oh, no, Robert Lam," says Fan instantly, "I wasn't thinking of that. I just want you to take me back to where we started. To where I came on board," she amends.

"To D'Arcy Island?" I ask in surprise. "Why go back there? We've just got my mother off it. Why should we want to return?"

She continues implacably. "That's how it has to be."

"It's not good enough, Fan. You've got to give me a reason. I'm not a child to be ordered about at your whim."

The mask of defiance drops, and I see on my stepmother's face tight lines of fear. "Please, Robert Lam," she whispers. "I beg of you. I shall never be at peace until we both go there and do what must be done." She wrings her hands pathetically.

The cliffs of Beechy Head come into view, and I prepare to run Race Passage. For here, and in the vicinity of Race Rocks, the tidal streams can reach six knots. We must keep Bentinck Island shore aboard, that is, at a distance of about a quarter of a mile, or just outside the kelp, for the outermost danger on the southern side of the channel is covered at high water, and the strongest eddies are found near it.

Tide rips that have sucked men down within twenty feet of land. And with Bentinck Island on the port hand. Bentinck Island. Where the leper colony was moved from D'Arcy Island in the 1920s, and where one man, a Chinese who has been there from the age of seventeen, still lives. I have seen him myself as he stood on shore to watch the pilot boat go by on its way to meet ships. There is a doctor who visits him regularly, and a nurse who lives on the island. I wonder, suddenly, if he has ever heard of my mother.

It is only a second of inattention, but in that instant the wheel of the *Rose* slips through my hands and spins wildly. We are caught by a surge of the tide. The engine coughs as I push the throttle forward and try to power her through the whirlpool.

"Can't you read the tides!" shouts Lam Fan sharply, her voice choked with fear. "I thought you knew your job!" I do not bother to answer. The *Rose* shudders and skids sideways as the engine misses. "No, Robert Lam!" cries my stepmother in despair as we draw nearer and nearer to the rocks. "Now it will never be finished!"

There is panic in her voice and in my heart as I fight to keep us afloat. We hold our ground, the Crown engine performing nobly, and then, just as I feel the *Rose* giving up this fight that is far too hard on her aging timbers, her boards shuddering and groaning as if they will split apart any moment, the tide slackens. I feel it in my bones half a second before the engine responds, then, as if it were nothing, the *Rose* leaps free of the eddy.

Fan's face is ashen. The rocks that were so nearly our downfall have dropped far behind. "How could you be so careless, Robert Lam?" she asks as if she can hardly credit it. "We were almost shipwrecked." She shakes her head in wonderment.

"I don't know, Fan," I say to her, badly shaken. "The tides in the passage are very irregular, but you can usually hit them right by reference to those at Turn Point. This has never happened to me before."

We pass the quarantine station at William Head, the fixed red light at the end of the breakwater in Quarantine Cove, Mary Hill, Constance Bank, and Albert Head before I've regained my confidence enough to leave the wheel for a moment. I tick the points of our passage off on the chart.

Then I bear north-northeast for Baynes Channel, and the inside coast of Vancouver Island, once again.

Robert Haack had made record time on the walk from the scene of his wedding on the Cedar Hill plain into the city of Victoria. Anvil-shaped thunderclouds, unusual for the season, hung over the city with dark foreboding. The air pressed down on him, and his joints ached. Yet his buoyed-up heart was full of hope, and he touched now and again, for reassurance, the money in his pocket. He turned from Hillside Avenue south of Government Street, and the pace of his heartbeat picked up. For now all was up to chance. If he could avoid meeting Lam Fan or Sing Yuen or any of Yong Sam's men—for they would all be wondering what had become of him—he'd achieve what he'd sworn to accomplish. Even if they came upon him, he thought he could parry their questions, at least for a time. All he needed was an hour of freedom in which to buy the steamer tickets and get out of the city. Then, under cover of darkness, he and his new wife, India, would return to the docks and, as soon as the steamer came in, board it and be on their way to a happier life.

All he needed was a little luck.

But a man with an unquiet conscience, who doesn't want to be noticed, is at a disadvantage. A man who owes a great deal of money, who had been blacklisted by the Workingmen's Protective Association, who had taken part in a failed robbery and spent time in jail; a man who had deceived the customs officers of his adopted country and who had taken their money; a man who had just been married, labours under a heavy burden of guilt. And such a man, in his attempt to mimic unconcern, could only succeed in conveying the reverse. His hands twisted in his pockets, and his attempt at a casual smile resulted in a grimace. There was, in fact, a general unease in his movements, which broadcast itself in a ripple effect throughout the streets until, not surprisingly (for he had garnered the attention of the most incurious), he was noticed by someone who mattered.

Robert Haack, who had stopped in front of a store window to pull down his hat—as if that would help!—and who lifted the lapels of his jacket to hide his neck, and who brushed the last of the dust of the country off his jacket, was watched with interest by one of Yong Sam's entourage.

Haack peered about him—the thunderclouds were dissolving like smoke, and the sun had come out—then strolled down Johnson Street (with a quick backwards glance) past grocers and outfitters (with their snowshoes and blankets), past clothiers and hatters, all the way to Wharf Street.

Here he jogged south to the Canadian Pacific Navigation Company wharves, sidled down the ramp to the ticket office, and went inside. Where—as seen through the window by Yong Sam's observer—he paid for two tickets to San Francisco from a large wad of cash, which he took from his pocket.

Tendrils of steam rose from the decks of the docked paddlewheelers as the sun dried the wood; schooners and steamers unloaded their goods, the stevedores rolling barrels and carrying pallets into a warehouse; and a rainbow struck the cupola on top of the post office. Haack surveyed the scene with pleasure, for his job was half done.

It was a world of light, of optimism that unrolled before him. Men at work, and ships from all nations, and the promise of the rainbow, that sign that God gave Noah at the end of his suffering. He was gazing upwards at this phenomenon, in an unwatchful moment of self-satisfaction, when the two men came up behind him: for Yong Sam's observer had found a friend. One held Robert's arms while the other turned out his pockets. And found a shopping list, a pencil, a damp handkerchief, a marriage certificate, a poem on an old piece of paper, the two steamer tickets with receipt, and, of course, all Haack's money.

Ah, pity Robert Haack, my mother's new husband, as he stood amazed at the trick Fate had played on him; pity him as all his planning and his sacrifice—his sale of himself for the customs' best price—came to nothing. And as he thought of the wife who was waiting on Mount Douglas, who was counting on him for her future; pity him as Yong Sam's men took the money and tore up the steamer tickets in front of him.

He stood there, a man with the noose of accident tight on his neck, until the two men had finished. He watched them walk away, laughing. Then he tried to think. He had to, he absolutely had to find a way. The steamer left in the morning: if only he and India could still be on it. He was sure Sam's men wouldn't bother to check the passenger list—they thought they had done for him. But how could he get the money it would take?

It was not a new question for poor Robert Haack. It was one he'd asked himself, in a thousand ways, almost all his life; and it was one, alas, that so recently he'd thought he'd finished with.

Perhaps it was the press of the moment, or perhaps because the visit to the docks had revived old memories of his work on a coal barge in these same waters, or perhaps it was the thought of former kindnesses, that brought his former employer, Mr. Redford, to his mind. Mr. Redford. A man who had tried to help him, who had visited him in hospital after his injury and had given him the job that had led him to India. And who had invited him to his house several times for dinner.

A house whose whereabouts, and floor plan, Haack well remembered. There was its artwork and fine furniture and silverware, not to mention the jewellery and wardrobes of its owners. There was bound to be money. It was an inspiration and temptation together; it was an answer to his need. But could he do it? Was it any way to repay a benefactor, to treat a friend?

But, on the other hand, looking at the circumstances in which he found himself, did he have any choice? Haack turned the thought over, then he made up his mind. He couldn't waste any more time.

*   *   *

"Why, Robert!" exclaimed Mr. Redford as he met Robert Haack outside the door to his house, "it's been a long time, hasn't it? How have you been? Were you coming to see me?"

Strangely to Mr. Redford, who liked Robert Haack, Robert did not appear pleased to see him. He lowered his head and tried to brush past him. But Redford, concerned, caught at his arm. "Is anything wrong? Are you in trouble? Can I help?" Robert tried to pull away, and Mr. Redford took a firmer grip on his elbow. For his hands had encountered familiar material. Still keeping hold, he took a step back.

"Why, isn't that my overcoat you're wearing?" he said in surprise. Then he caught sight of an object clutched in Robert's hand. He pried Haack's fingers apart. "My watch chain!" he cried in horror, as Haack hung his head.

"My pocketbook," said Mr. Redford unhappily inside the police station. "Yes, that's my money and my case, my Sons of Hermann badge, my trousers, and my jacket." The rest of Robert's pockets for the second time that day were emptied, and Redford continued the catalogue in mounting sadness: "My wife's jewellery, her watch, her pocketbook. And yes, her undergarments, too."

"What have you to say for yourself?" asked the policeman disgustedly. But what was there to say? And what did it matter at this late date? Robert, stripped of Redford's belongings, stood, naked but for his shoes and socks and underwear, and said nothing. Slowly, as if his neck bore a terrible weight, he raised his eyes to meet Redford's. His eyes begged forgiveness and understanding, another chance. But they met disheartened puzzlement.

Ice formed on the inside corners of the glass (behind bars) in Robert Haack's jail cell. He cleared the window of condensation with his fingers and tried to peer out. The city was in darkness; but from life on the outside, in whatever state, Robert Haack was forevermore shut out.

Robert Haack: a man who had a wife, and who once had money with which to make a future with her, but who now had lost it; a man who had no future at all, at least in this country. For despite the fact that Mr. Redford had dropped the charges, Robert Haack was to be deported.

"Men like you we can do without," said the magistrate. The policeman had nodded, the customs officer had agreed, even Mr. Redford, still bewildered and hurt, had acquiesced. "It's the best thing for you, Robert," he'd said. The papers had been signed. The United States escort was on its way. Haack would sail away on the steamer in the morning.

Going home at last. But not as he'd planned. With no means of ever coming back; no way to send for India. For at least he had that—he had not betrayed her. For what would these men, and the rest of the city, think if they knew where she'd been? Among lepers? The marriage certificate was safely in his socks.

As for the Tong, with the deportation order made public, they would never give up. Yong Sam had come to tell him so himself. Robert Haack would be deported along with his debts.

He sighed. The snipped-off threads of his life dangled. It felt as though his heart had abandoned his chest. There was more ice on the window: no question but that it was cold outside. How would India manage? What would she eat, how would she survive? How long would she wait before going for help? And what must she think of him, her new husband, Robert Haack?

A static charge crackled his hair as he ran his fingers through it. There was the nip of shock as he touched the iron bars over the window. He was gathering his courage. He bent down and took out the two pieces of paper he had inserted into his socks at Redford's house. He read through his marriage certificate, folded it and replaced it in its hiding place. Then he stood on tiptoe and squeezed as much of his hand as he could between the bars of the window. And pushed, and pushed, until his fingers, behind which he had focused his entire weight and will, broke through the glass. It was not much of a hole in size, and it made his hand bleed badly. But it was just large enough.

Ignoring the tears that watered his face, Robert tore up the poem that Robert Louis Stevenson had given him so long ago—"Praise and Prayer." He pushed the pieces through the break in the window, then watched the wind take them. Fragments of the past. Prospects of hope. Pieces of light that lifted, then dropped and drifted in the darkness. They glittered like snow; they stirred in a dance of atoms and caught a current. Then were gone.

Through a switchboard of streets and into the country. Over farmyards and cattle pens, through forest, then climbing high on the wind to the top of a mountain—Mount Douglas. Swirling, dancing, eddying. And reaching my mother.

Or so Haack intended. And so it seemed to him.

India watched and waited on top of the mountain. She kept the fire going. She heated water and made tea. She forgot to drink it. She folded blankets and talked to the horse that Haack had left behind with her. She watched the gaslights flare in the city, and the flicker of lanterns on D'Arcy Island as they sparked on and then, one by one, as the hours passed, went out.

The moon rose, and under its gaze the rippling dark skin of the strait came alive. All was as it should be. Except that Robert had not returned.

Another light appeared on D'Arcy Island, and even as, in his jail cell, Robert Haack tore up his poem and sent the bloodstained words on a whirl of wind towards her, my mother watched the tiny flame on D'Arcy Island grow larger.

From pinprick to glowworm it expanded, from glowworm to many-armed monster, sending out tributaries, streams, ribbons, and oceans of fire all over the island. All night India watched as the fire extended itself then slowly, ever so slowly, burned itself off.

> There has been a brush fire [reported the medical office] on the last day of November, 1898, on D'Arcy Island. I did not learn of it for three days. The building and some of the surrounding bushland burned. What was lost—food, etc.— has been supplied again. The survivors have not suffered undue hardships. One man was badly burned on the face and hands. Only one patient, Sim Lee, one of the original inhabitants, was burned to death.

So many factors, Fan, had gone into it. My mother between her choices, sitting up on a mountain, wondering why she'd scarcely thought of Robert Haack when she lived on D'Arcy Island; wondering why he hadn't come back. And Robert Haack, in the city, finally out of luck. So many signals going out. As a hand, misshapen and helpless with leprosy, failed to retrieve a live coal that had fallen from a stove front onto the wooden floor of a cabin. As a fire flared up and ravaged the surface of

D'Arcy Island. And as my mother watched and trembled for the lives of her friends, and saw she could not bear to be without them. As she wrote her farewell in a note to her brand-new husband.

And in the morning, that morning of the first of December, in the year before my birth, a Japanese left his shack to check his boat at the Cordova Bay landing. And he found, near the boat, a woman.

"Oh, Miss," he said, his voice tinged with sadness, to my mother, India Thackery, who now knew where her life and her heart belonged, "you've come back so soon!"

CHAPTER FOURTEEN

"A light is exhibited, at an elevation of twenty-three feet from a red lantern on a white pole set in a concrete base, erected on the western side of D'Arcy Island.
A black can buoy is moored close eastward of the eastern-most of the D'Arcy Shoals."

British Columbia Pilot, Volume I

There is no fog, this time, to mar our passage, and no killer whales, either, to guide us. And this time we know where we're going: not to the southern shore of D'Arcy Island, where the lepers had their colony, but—at Lam Fan's direction—up the west coast of the island, inside the D'Arcy Shoals, and to a beach at the northern end.

"Isn't this where Smiling Jimmy left my mother after the robbery?" I ask my stepmother as we carefully guide the keel of the *Rose* onto the sand.

"Yes, I suppose it is," she says nervously, looking around. Her hand returns to her mouth: she has been biting her nails for hours. Two fingers are bleeding at the quick, and the other nails—once long and polished red—are in ruins.

I jump over the side into knee-deep water. "Come on, Fan," I say, "I'll give you a hand." I wait for her: she moves ever so slowly, sits on the bulwarks, and tentatively puts her legs over the side. Now that we're here she's lost her compulsion to hurry. I hold out my arms.

"Come on, Fan, jump."

"Don't rush me, Robert Lam," she says, tucking her toes out the scuppers. "I'm not young like I was." I stand patiently, with seawater filling my boots and with the lines in my hands unsecured. It is a hot, clear afternoon. I can smell seaweed crisping and drying on the beach. Sand fleas leap in the air, and the trees are filling with birds too dazed by the heat to move.

The snap of pods exploding; the buzz in the grasses above the tide line; the head of a seal, further out in the water, bobbing up for a peek at us: we could be the first to have set foot on this island. And I, suddenly in love with the peace of this place, don't care if I ever leave it.

"Well," calls out Lam Fan crossly, disturbing my reverie, now that my attention has strayed from her, "I'm waiting."

I lift her down and carry her, like a parcel of dry sticks and swansdown, to the beach. I leave her sitting on a log with a shy raccoon for company, and return to make fast the lines. "There," I say, going back to her, "that should hold us for a couple of hours until the tide turns. Now tell me what's so urgent about us coming here."

She bows her head, she starts to bite her nails but thinks better of it. She sighs as if the woes of the world are weighing upon her. "I don't know what to say," she says. "I'm so ashamed of myself. I know there's no excuse."

I sit down beside her. This Fan—defeated, embarrassed, and anxious— is a new facet to my stepmother. I put my arm around her shoulders and draw her closer. "Never mind, Fan," I say, "whatever it is, I love you."

She looks up at me, astonished. I smile. I can't help myself. Then I pick up stones and skid them across the water. One, two, three, four skips. A thin, cold hand covers mine.

"I should have told you before, Robert Lam," she says quietly.

"Take your time, Fan," I say to her. I throw another stone. Three skips only. But it startles a heron who had just come in for a landing. He flaps his great wings, and his reedlike legs pencil two lines in the water before he lifts off. I feel a tug on my fingers.

"It's not so much what I have to *say*," Lam Fan says to me, pulling me up to follow her, "as what I have to show you."

"Come on, Robert Lam," she cries over her shoulder, as if, whatever it is, she's decided to get it over with. "It's now or never." And she crosses the beach at speed and heads into the depths of the forest.

So it was that on the first day of December 1898, my mother returned to D'Arcy Island with the Japanese fishermen, and found that Sim Lee had burned to death in the fire, and that several of the other lepers, including Ng Chung, had been badly injured.

There was no particular joy or surprise at her reappearance: there was far too much to do for that, although it was clear that the surviving lepers were relieved to see her. There were burns to clean and bandage, there was food to prepare from the meagre stores that remained, there was a shelter to make to protect the sick men from the worst of the weather. At night she stayed awake to feed the bonfire, for it was hard to keep the injured men warm in the damp of the winter. In the daytime she combed the wreckage for salvage: every scrap of clothing or blankets, every tool or implement she could find, was of vital importance.

When there was time, and when Ng Chung had recovered enough to help her, she buried Sim Lee in the little graveyard unmarked by headstones, whose occupants only she and Ng Chung could now name. There were no files in government offices, no notes anywhere as to who had lived and who had died on that island, except in their memories.

It was nearly a week before the supply boat came with a work crew and the doctor. The doctor changed the injured men's dressings and noted Sim Lee's gravesite. The work crew erected a cabin in one afternoon: six rooms beneath a single roof, plus a shed for a storeroom, on the old plan.

Then the supply boat hurried away.

The British Colonist, *December 14, 1898*

They wanted spoons: The distress flag at the D'Arcy Island lazaretto displayed on Saturday and Sunday last gave the impression to a number of passing mariners that something serious was amiss at the home of the exiles. It appears, however, that they merely wanted a few teaspoons, everything else required for their comfort having been taken out the previous Friday when Dr. Fraser and his associate workers learned details of the fatal fire of November thirtieth. The new buildings were then erected, a great improvement on the old, and each leper provided with an ample store of provisions; two complete shifts of clothing, "from the skin out," and even coffins for use should death release any of the colony. The teaspoons were taken out from Sidney on Monday.

And so life went on, with little change except for the day-to-day recovery of the lepers from their burns, and except for the new measure of grief they had stored up in their hearts.

And except for the miracle in which I am concerned.

For my mother, who had left the island thinking she wasn't needed, and who had acquired a husband and left him behind, and who had returned to D'Arcy Island after the fire, knowing it was her true home, found that something new and wonderful was happening right under her eyes. Ng Chung, her old friend, with whom she had shared more than seven years of her life; who, along with Sim Lee, had rescued her from the rapist, Moi Toy; who had saved her sanity with his stories; Ng Chung, who had lived tide time, sun and moon time, death and life time on the island with her, and who was the last of the original lepers of D'Arcy Island left alive, was not only healing from his burns, but was healing with no signs of leprosy.

The new skin was smooth and clean. And although he could hardly believe it himself, day by day, the evidence of the miracle remained.

Consider, Fan: a man who had left his family in China to make his way in the New World; who had done his best but who'd been struck down in his prime by an illness; a man who had lived for years within the limits this illness set, now found himself free of it.

And with the return of the strength of his body came renewal of spirit. And with that, the restraint he had laid upon himself regarding my mother fell away. That is, he spoke to her of his feelings for her as a woman. Of the fact that they knew each other as well as any two people could; that they'd worked together, sorrowed, laughed, shared all there was to share in this world except for....

Love, Fan. It was of love that he spoke. Of how it grows in stages, and has nowhere to go but up; how it can be harmed by fear and loneliness or take wings to rise above it. Of possibilities. Of the future. Of happiness.

And my mother, Fan. Who had watched the fire on D'Arcy Island spread, from her helpless position on a mountaintop. Who had wondered why she'd married that day when all she loved in the world was in danger of being lost. Who had known even then what had happened. That Fate had bound her to a place and a man. Who had known that she had to see that love, in whatever form it could take, through to the end.

Consider this, too, Fan. When two people who love each other, and who have not dared to talk about it; when these two people believe their reason for caution has vanished. Consider how it must be when they sit together on a grassy cliff above the sea, and survey the ocean vista, holding hands, feeling the pulse of life between them. What vows they make and looks they give and take. What sweetness it is not to have to explain, but to whisper, "I know, I know." To weep together. To laugh at their clumsiness as they begin to explore and touch. To feel the difference that the union of bodies makes. Especially for my mother, who had so recently been the lover of Robert Haack.

For this was not love out of lack and bewilderment. But love out of time-tempered wisdom; love out of thoughtless hope.

And so it was that Ng Chung and my mother took the step that gave me my life.

We emerge from the tangle of underbrush into a meadow. Lam Fan, her silks torn by the clawing branches, looks around carefully. She takes her bearing on a solitary rock that sits like a sentinel in the middle.

"You've been here before," I say to her.

"Many times," she answers shortly, then adds, "but it's been awhile, and the trees have grown up considerably." She makes a foray in one direction then turns about and returns to the rock. She examines its surface carefully, finds a mark on it she likes, and paces straight westward towards the forest. And, of course, I follow her.

A new year had begun. The year 1899. The year in which I would be born. It was a period in which to look ahead, to believe in the advance of mankind. To catch a glimpse of a future that would encompass aeroplanes, and the automobile, the talking pictures, and television. Not a time to consider wars. Not a time to imagine a weapon like the atomic bomb. Not a time to think of the truth.

It was also the last time that people could live on an island and not consider the world around them. And when the world outside would be content to forget about them. When a leper could be healed of his wounds; when prayers could be answered; when a woman who had been brought up to believe in consequences could let the barriers of discipline down. And so it was that India and Ng Chung thought of nothing but themselves.

Ng Chung and India. Full of amazement that they had found each other at last, that Fate had brought them together on an island for a purpose; that the scourge of disease that had kept them apart had apparently vanished. That the life that had been so difficult had suddenly transformed into paradise. For so it seemed to them as they went about the work that had once been so tedious: looking after the others, changing their bandages, helping them to wash and dress; doing household tasks, cooking, gathering firewood. They talked late into the night, going over and over the chance that had brought them together. Rejoicing in the odds they had overcome. Rehearsing the parts they had played, as if it were not themselves who had suffered. Hardly daring to believe it could last. Yet believing as well. For surely they, in their innocence, deserved it.

Ng Chung and India. Rising above the world of nature to the world of spirit. Blinded by love. For it was clear to all but the lovers that the colony was in some trouble. A stranger had come to the island. Someone was watching their movements. Rice, dishes, and blankets had disappeared. And several of the colonists had glimpsed the intruder's face between a parting of the bushes. Yet nothing was said. Even when his footprints—larger than any of the lepers'—were found in the mud by the spring. For what could be done about it? What resistance could be made to whatever chose to menace them?

So the newer colonists—those who had not lived through the lessons that the earlier lepers had—so they, in their weakness, thought. And so out of kindness, or apathy, or indifference, they let my mother and her lover, the former leper, Ng Chung, remain in ignorance of the threat.

And so it was that India went by herself one afternoon to work in the garden. There was weeding and mulching to do for the few winter greens, and compost to spread to rot before spring. Ng Chung had gone far down the beach to gather driftwood for burning, and the other lepers were ill in their rooms or were sleeping.

He appeared out of nowhere, standing still a few yards away from her as if he had grown there along with the trees. She raised her hand to her eyes so as to refute the vision, but this didn't change anything. It was Oung Moi Toy, the man-mountain from years ago, who had raped her and had been killed by her rescuers, Sim Lee and Ng Chung. He was dead, she was sure of it, and yet he was here, too, as large as life and certainly living.

India tried to speak, but no sound would come forth from her lips. "Toy," my mother finally whispered, "Oung Moi Toy!" At these words, pleased that she knew him and even more pleased at her fear, the man-mountain advanced. Closer and closer he came, while the hoe, with which she might have driven him off, slipped from her hands. For logic told her that she was wrong, that the man she saw crossing the short space between the woods and the garden couldn't be him. But her senses—the bristling at the nape of her neck, the weakness of her limbs—told otherwise. She knew that weight and shape. She knew the sick taste of despair as it welled up from her stomach. And his smell: that stench of lust and anger was all too familiar.

Oh, it had been long ago that it had happened, but she had not forgotten any of it. He reached out to touch her, as if this was a moment he had imagined and practised over and over. She saw the rope looped round his hand, and knew it was almost too late: that logic had made her delay when she should have tried to escape. But she ducked under his arm anyway and grabbed the hoe where it lay on the ground, swung it round without looking, and struck him a strong blow with the blade beneath the curve of his jawbone. Blood spurted onto the ground, but he was only stunned for an instant, then he was after her.

"Ng Chung!" my mother screamed as she ran towards the beach. Toy caught her by the legs and brought her down just as she reached the sand. He thrust his arm across her throat, choking her, and with the loop of rope bound up her hands. He lay on top of her and began to tear at her clothing, while my mother struggled and fought for her life. But then he went slack, as if he were suddenly tired. He yawned and tried to sit up as the blood poured from the wound in his neck. He rubbed at his eyes like a puzzled child, then his head dropped, and this time, truly, he was dead.

My mother, with Toy's blood soaking her breast and hair, rolled away from him and all the way down the beach.

Which was where Ng Chung found her.

Fan's face is scratched by brambles, her hands are dirty, and the remnants of her nails are torn and bleeding. She has been, for the last few minutes, unwilling to speak to me; scrabbling through a heap of stones, while I sit nearby and weep. I weep for my mother, for the horror that came upon her at the happiest point in her life. For the resurrection, which I still don't understand, of Oung Moi Toy. And I cry for myself, for the man I once was, and for the girl and the old woman who died because of it. And for the good in the world, which is so often destroyed by the bad. Fan takes a deep breath and lets it out.

"Well, Robert Lam?" she says, sitting back on her heels on the floor of the forest. "There is always one more surprise, isn't there."

"That's one way of putting it, I guess," I say wiping my eyes. "But I suppose that's the end of it."

"There are a few loose threads," she says. She changes position and begins to poke her hands into the pile of stones again. She shifts some of them over.

"But where did he come from, Fan?" I ask her. "I thought Ng Chung and Sim Lee had killed Moi Toy at the time of the rape of my mother."

"They thought they had," she says as she moves some pieces of wood, "but you may recall that when they went back to bury him, his body had vanished."

"But even if Toy was alive when they left him, he couldn't have survived on the island without anyone noticing. And he couldn't have escaped by himself—it's not possible, because of the tides and the currents and so forth. We've been all through that."

The colour rises in my stepmother's face, then quickly recedes, leaving her as pale as I've ever seen her. "I took him off the island," she says, looking at the ground. "He must have gone back on his own, years after, for reasons of revenge. I knew nothing about it."

"You, Fan?" I say, stunned. "But how, why? What could you have had to do with Oung Moi Toy on D'Arcy Island?"

She holds out an object she has retrieved from amongst the wood and stones. What she holds is unspeakable, and instantly recognizable. It is the forearm and hand of a human. A few scraps of blue cloth are attached to the bones, and the fingers are spread in entreaty. "Whose is it, Fan?" I ask her, scarcely breathing, watching the finger bones curl as my stepmother moves them.

"Don't you know?" she asks, surprised. "I thought you'd have guessed it all by now, Robert Lam."

All winter long, through the spring and the hot days of summer my mother went about her work like a sleepwalker. For to be with child at this time in her life was taking its toll. She felt well, for the most part, although occasionally her dreams were bad, but she was always tired. Ng Chung took special care of her, he searched out herbs and cooked her favourite dishes. Most of all, he stayed with her, not leaving her alone for a minute unless she asked him to. Talking to her about the child—their child. Who the child would be, what it would mean for their lives. Once or twice they spoke about Oung Moi Toy, then did their best to forget him.

And the other lepers—once the pregnancy was evident—began to behave like uncles.

Giving advice, counselling walks or rest, arguing over names and sex of the child, watching, waiting, sewing scraps of shirts and trousers into baby's clothing.

And once the child began to kick in the womb, to make its opinions felt, all were eager to listen and to touch.

For a child speaks in the womb, Fan. It cries out to the world that awaits it. It protests and asks questions, it requires answers and brings messages. It gathers its courage and grows impatient; or becomes reluctant.

And can be miscarried or stillborn; or develop too slowly ever to function. Or, quickly birthed, arrive too weak for the shock of the world that it meets. And some children, Fan, never emerge at all. They sink back on their cushion of fluids; too discouraged or too pleased with themselves to take any risk, they gradually turn to stone in their mother's abdomen. The *lithopedions*, Fan, the stone children, too wise or too stubborn to ask to be born.

But not I, Fan. I listened and heard and took note... and despite all of it, I swam out from my mother as all children should, and howled.

A birth on an island. Not a simple matter for a woman as old as my mother, but not too difficult, either. For there were the medicines that Ng Chung had prepared, plus a little opium to mute the pain.

And after it all, after the great surge of energy that had carried her through the event, she slept. While Ng Chung cleaned me up and wrapped me in the warm clothes that were ready. And held me in his arms.

I was placed in a coal scuttle lined with a blanket, and kept warm in front of the stove. I was given red string and ginger and fern to protect me from all sorts of harm, and I was hefted, tickled, and generally inspected and approved by my uncles, the lepers, while my father prepared tea and vinegar to aid my mother's recovery.

It was a happy time, by all accounts—that is, according to my mother's diary and to what she later told her sister—with the child, me, safely launched, and Ng Chung a man in full strength and vigour.

Time on an island. Where a group of exiles became a family; where a dread disease faded into a memory. And even the ghosts of violence, of friends loved and lost, were finally laid to rest. It was time with a happy ending.

Except that time kept on running. And soon, within a few scant months of my birth, Ng Chung and India had to face facts.

For the fact was that Ng Chung was no longer getting better: the clean new skin was showing signs of the return of leprosy, and he was weakening daily. And the fact was that my mother could no longer act as anyone's nurse—far from it, she needed looking after herself while she rebuilt her strength. And one final fact, which they'd pushed to the backs of their minds for these first few months: they had to get me off the island. For a newborn is safe from leprosy as long as it has its mother's milk. But not after that, Fan; it's not safe at all. And both my father and mother had seen, in China, the tragic results.

Joy and anguish, Fan. And the facts were bitter every which way they looked.

In the meantime, a thousand miles to the south....

My mother's husband, Robert Haack, surfacing for a moment from the swamp of crime in which he had established himself at the New Swanston boardinghouse on the San Francisco waterfront, wrote two letters. One was to a Victoria lawyer, and to accompany it there was another, addressed to India in care of Lam Fan.

For Robert, in ignorance of the fire that had devastated D'Arcy Island and of my mother's return to the lepers and of all that took place thereafter, including my birth, had assumed that India, when he had not come back for her, would have gone to find Lam Fan—for who else had she to turn to? Moreover, being in fear for his life because of the company he kept, and worried that all he would leave to India, in the case of his death, would be enormous debts, he had determined to give my mother a divorce at once.

Robert Haack: overweight, sallow-faced, drinking too much, but capable of one last decent act, struggled with pen and paper. In the lawyer's envelope he placed his marriage certificate and a statement concerning his desertion and adultery. To my mother he wrote:

> My dearest, my dear dear wife,
>
> I know you'll forgive me for not coming back that night. You'll have seen the notice, or Lam Fan will have told you that I was deported and could do nothing to reach you. I have waited this time to write to you, in hopes that we'd find each other again. But I fear, my darling, that all hope of that is gone. I can't change what has happened to us. It is best if you try to forget. You could find a new husband—no one need ever know that you were married to Robert Haack, except for the lawyer, and I have told no one at all about the years you lived with the lepers on D'Arcy Island. So there is nothing to stand in the way of your chances of happiness.
>
> I did love you, and I love you still, more than I can say, but God has kept us apart. Please do what the lawyer says: I know it is for the best. I can pay for whatever it costs. Tell Lam Fan and Sing Yuen I am sorry, and make sure that they care for Gook Lang. Tell them to speak to the Japanese fishermen.
>
> Don't forget the mountaintop and our short time together. I keep you in my heart forever. Goodbye for now, and no regrets from the man who only wished to be
>
> > Your husband,
> > Robert Haack

As for tear stains on the paper; as for a pen held so tightly between thumb and forefinger that the letters quavered; as for broken hearts and broken promises, and untold sorrows. As for truth and consequences....

Lam Fan read the two letters over in the lawyer's office. Sing Yuen, sitting beside her, saw her blanch. "Now," said the lawyer, who had observed her reaction, "do you believe that the papers are genuine?" Lam Fan nodded. "Then you'll undertake to deliver them as the writer requests?" She nodded again. And the lawyer showed Lam Fan and her husband out into the early winter light of mid-December of the last year of the nineteenth century.

Drawing her scarf more closely around her as the wind whirled the falling snow into her face, and as her husband drove the sleigh along the flat, winding road of the Cedar Hill plain, Lam Fan thought how time reverses; how one is abandoned then is rescued, or acquires a family only to lose it; how husbands arrive and sisters vanish then reappear on islands in letters; how tides alternate and the wheel of fortune turns; how one swims in the river of change, or drowns.

The horse's nostrils blew steam into the atmosphere, forming a torn white ribbon of moisture. Sing Yuen, next to Fan, snapped the reins as they emerged from the woods below Mount Douglas and sighted the Japanese fishermen's cabins.

It was too late for the laying of blame. Fan knew what had done the damage; what had numbed a corner of her heart and impaired her thinking. It was the haunting suspicion that her sister had left her behind on purpose. Not that it made any sense or followed any logic but that of an orphan's experience.

This was the root of it. And of this, as much as anything else, Lam Fan was deeply ashamed.

"And so," I say to Fan, as we crouch in the middle of the forest on D'Arcy Island, "I think we are getting close to the truth at last. Although I see you've been careful to leave some things out. You've still not told me what you had to do with Oung Moi Toy, for one."

Fan, still holding the gruesome relic of bone, says nothing.

"What happened next, then, Fan?" I ask her, trying to be patient and determined to get to the end of the tortuous path down which I'd been led. "I imagine that you and Sing Yuen arrived on the island and found—what? This?" I indicate the bone she holds, and the mound that must contain the rest of the skeleton. "You'll have to explain it, Fan. I still don't know whose grave this is."

She shakes her head, but at least breaks her silence. "I had found these bones long before, Robert Lam. Sing Yuen never saw them. In any case it doesn't matter. It's not a grave exactly, you see," she says, almost shyly, "but a hiding place.

"It was in midwinter, about six months after the Tai June robbery, that I came here for the first time by myself. Your mother had disappeared, and my life...." She pauses as if searching for a suitable word, sighs again, and starts over. "My life, for various reasons, as you shall see, had become quite difficult. Sing Yuen had grown preoccupied with his business, and he blamed himself for sending India to the factory on that terrible Sunday. I paid a man to bring me here, and he dropped me off not far from the spot where you and I left the *Rose*.

"It was there," she goes on, "that I saw Oung Moi Toy for the first and only time. He had terrible wounds on his body that were healing badly. And so, when he asked me to help him leave the island, I said yes."

"But Fan!" I exclaim. "How could you!"

"I knew nothing of what he had done!" my stepmother protests. "I did not know until your mother told me herself, long after!"

"He was a leper! You must have known that! Surely you had some responsibility there. You knew he should be in quarantine."

"He did not look like a leper," she says defensively. "He told me he was there by accident and that the lepers had attacked him out of jealousy."

"And you felt sorry for him and, out of the goodness of your heart, decided to help him. Come on, Fan, I don't buy it. You'd better tell me the rest."

She looks around uncomfortably. "All right Robert Lam, I have already said that I would, but let me tell it my way. Don't rush me."

And so another journey, eight years after the one she has just told me about, in which she helped Moi Toy escape from D'Arcy Island. This time my stepmother travelled in a Japanese fishing boat with her husband, Sing Yuen; and with Robert Haack's letter burning a hole in the pocket of her overcoat. It was bitter winter weather in the first year of my life. And the Japanese fishing boat in which they travelled tilted and rocked and shipped water as they moved through the thick swirling snow and approached the rocky coast of D'Arcy Island.

"We cannot land you at the colony," said the skipper to them, "the wind is too strong. I will drop you off at a more sheltered spot and return in the morning to pick you up." And so it was that my stepmother and

Sing Yuen landed where Smiling Jimmy had dumped my mother after the Tai June robbery, and where Lam Fan had come ashore alone to find a giant of a man encamped in the forest; and at the same place, too, where I had secured the *Rose* and stepped ashore with my stepmother.

"We were not sure which way to go, Sing Yuen and I, when we went to the island in response to Robert Haack's letter," Lam Fan says quietly. "Although I had been there before, many times, as I have said, I had never seen any sign of the colony. All we knew was that it was to the south, for so the skipper had told us: I suggested that we try to make our way across the interior of the island so as to be out of the way of the wind and the blizzard."

And so they came to a meadow, one that Fan knew well, and ploughed their way through the drifts; they sheltered in the lee of the rock that dominated that clearing to catch their breath, and then Lam Fan told Sing Yuen that she had to go into the woods to relieve herself.

He waited while she pushed her way through the trees and found the path that she was looking for. And when she stopped, it was not to gather her skirts up, not to stoop near the stump of a fallen tree to empty herself, it was to push aside the snow-dusted broken branches that lay atop a rock heap; branches with swatches of cloth attached; branches that were not branches at all but the weathered bones of men.

"But why, Fan?" I interrupt, appalled that now we are talking not about one, but about the bones of a number of men. "What could make you do such a thing? Why not go back even then and tell Sing Yuen what you'd found?"

My stepmother draws the dignity of her years around her like armour. The look she gives me is a challenge. "You must take me as you find me, Robert Lam," she says. Then she pushes the rock and earth and remaining bones aside to reveal what the mound contains.

Wind and weather and falling leaves and branches, the growth of new trees, the decay of old, the vegetable turning and regeneration of the earth have altered the scene from what it was. But then, even with a sprinkling of snow filtering down through the trees, the glint of metal beneath the bones and shreds of flesh of the long-dead men was obvious. A heap of tins, stacks and cases of them, some split open, some gaps where Fan had already removed a quantity. But all stamped "Tai June" and displaying the rooster emblem. It was the opium, cached on the island after the robbery and never retrieved by Smiling Jimmy.

"And the dead men, Fan," I say, tears again blinding me as I watch the casual way in which she shunts their remains aside. "Who were they?"

She shrugs. "Smiling Jimmy's crew, I think. He killed them here after the opium was stored. He wanted it all for himself. As well," she goes on, "he had been betrayed once before by a crewman. Jimmy never forgot a lesson once learned."

"And you, Fan, what did you want and what did you learn?"

She is silent.

"Tell me then, Fan," I say, having wept myself dry, "how did you come to know of it? Please tell me now, although I am almost afraid to ask." I put out a hand to touch the bones of these poor wicked murdered men. They lie as if there had never been a scrap of humanity in them; with their brave, wind-lifted flags of cloth their only testament; and a stash of unopened tins of opium, perhaps a hundred or so, that's all, as their witnesses.

Fan closes her eyes, then opens them. "It was an accident, Robert Lam, I swear it. I had nothing to do with the robbery. I knew nothing at all until the day Smiling Jimmy died. He had been badly injured in a fight in Chinatown in a saloon a few doors down from the shop of my uncle, Lum Kee. They brought Smiling Jimmy in for Lum Kee to treat him, and while my uncle was preparing some medicines I was alone with him.

"Smiling Jimmy opened his eyes and said to me, 'I know you, Lam Fan.' I did not know what to say. I had never met him before, but I knew his reputation. He was as vile a man as ever lived in the city.

"'I know you, Lam Fan,' he said again, and a shiver of fear went through me. He smiled at me, Robert Lam, then he closed his eyes.

"A few hours later, when it was clear to all of us that he was dying, I was left once more for a minute on my own with him. I was holding his hand out of pity for his suffering. 'Come closer,' he whispered to me. 'I have something important to tell you.'

"I bent near him, Robert Lam, I did it out of feeling for his plight as a human being. I could never have guessed what he would say, or made a worse mistake in my life. 'I know you, Lam Fan,' he said very softly. 'I know everything about you. I even know what you will do.' And then he laughed. Not loudly, of course, he was far too weak for that, but as if this were the world's greatest joke. 'You will deceive your friends,' he said to me. 'You will betray everyone you love.' Then he started to cough. I thought he was out of his mind. But then Jimmy recovered himself and went on. 'You will do all these things, Lam Fan,' he said, 'because of the opium I have left on D'Arcy Island for you to find.'"

"And then what, Fan?" I say to her, saddened.

"And then," she answers me softly, "he told me exactly where it was, and then he died." Her face is a mask. She touches it carefully with her fingers as if to test if it is frozen. Then her hands drop to her lap.

"You didn't tell Lum Kee?" I ask her, numb with the magnitude of her sins and with compassion for the hell of remorse she has lived.

She shakes her head.

"It never occurred to you to tell Sing Yuen, your husband, whose opium it was?"

Tears, scant as drops squeezed out of an onion form in the corners of her eyes. "I tried not to think about it," she whispers. "I tried and tried, but I couldn't get it out of my mind. And I didn't know for sure that the opium was his. I didn't really believe it until I saw it for myself."

"And what about Toy, Fan? Tell me the rest of that."

Oung Moi Toy. Who had raped my mother and been left for dead. Who had hidden himself away until my stepmother—an orphan addicted to opium, who thought that opium was her one true friend, and who could not forget the evil words that Smiling Jimmy, out of the blackness of his heart, had spoken on his deathbed—had come to rescue him.

"I didn't know," Lam Fan says, shaking her head stiffly like an automaton. "I swear I didn't know. I only helped him to leave because he was camped so near to the place where the opium was hidden."

Lam Fan. With enough opium for a lifetime put away where no one but she could find it. On how many occasions had she returned here by herself? How many lies had she told to Sing Yuen, and to me, later on, her stepson, to get away with it?

I take both Fan's hands in mine. I rub them, towards the heart, the way blood should run, as I used to long ago, to warm them. "And my mother, Lam Fan, did you know she was on D'Arcy Island as well?"

"Oung Moi Toy told me," she says in her almost voiceless whisper. "I guessed at once when he mentioned a woman."

"But because of the opium...?"

"They would have thought I'd been in on the robbery. Even Sing Yuen. No one would have believed I was innocent."

I sigh a sigh that travels through the wasteland of my being. I pull

Lam Fan to her feet. "We've got a lot to do in the next few hours," I say to her, "and I'll need your help."

We bury Smiling Jimmy's crew as they should have been buried sixty-six years earlier. Then I gather up the tins of opium, and laboriously, taking several trips, carry them to the shore. And there, with Lam Fan's help, I place them on board the *Rose*.

We are sitting in front of a beach fire. We have cooked some fish and some mussels. We are drinking tea.

And so it was that Lam Fan returned to her husband, Sing Yuen, explaining how she had lost herself and walked in circles, then they both made their way down the coast to the lepers' colony. They gazed up at the cedar planking of the cabin, and at the snow-speckled roofing and the smoke issuing from chimneys, and at snow melt running from gutters. At a front door opening, and at the man who came to stare at them. He held one hand crooked close to his chest to carry his axe, and he wore a broad-brimmed hat. He stopped where he was, forgetting to close the door behind him.

While, from out of the room he'd just left, out of the dark of the cabin, came the sound of a baby's crying. For it was my father, Ng Chung, who had stepped out for a load of firewood, and found, instead, my mother's sister and her husband.

Does it matter that my mother wept, or that my father held me in his arms for one last time while Lam Fan and Sing Yuen turned their backs and examined the frosty horizon? Does it add to the scene to know that my mother promised to visit Ng Chung, and to give him frequent news of his son? Does it signify at all that I stopped crying and smiled my way through my parents' parting, or that Lam Fan carried me all the way to the Japanese fishing boat, which had returned to the cove to wait for them, while Sing Yuen supported my mother as she stumbled over rocks and kept half turning back in the direction from which she'd just come?

Nothing was said about the missing years, about robberies or vanished husbands, about babies born on islands, until the two sisters were safely at home upstairs in Lam Fan's bedroom in the Fisgard Street home. There Fan made certain promises, which she afterwards kept: to preserve my mother's secrets, and to have the child—me, Robert Lam, grow up in blessed ignorance.

*   *   *

Thus we have come full circle. To the first reading of my mother's papers, found in her diary, on board the *Rose* at the start of our journey as we anchored off D'Arcy Island. There was the divorce decree, signed and passed by Parliament; the account of Robert Haack's tragic death by shooting in Los Angeles; and the newspaper account of my mother's death by drowning.

"There's still an unanswered question, Fan," I say to my stepmother as she warms her hands on her tea mug, and as we watch the sun go down. "Did my mother drown by accident or not? It seems strange to me that she—used to climbing on rocks all over an island—would slip to her death. Moreover, it was stupidity, was it not, to put the rescuer's rope around her neck instead of beneath her arms? There is also the note in her diary, about kissing me goodbye and giving me to you to look after. It bothers me, Fan. But on the other hand, why would my mother, after all her grief and trouble to take me to safety, suddenly abandon me? I didn't get the impression, from what you told me, that she was the type to give up easily. I just can't imagine her committing suicide for no reason at all."

It did bother me. In fact, the fear—rational or not—that I'd been responsible in some way for my mother's death had plagued me from the very first reading of the account.

"You see, Fan," I continue, voicing my concern out loud, "she would have stayed with my father if it hadn't been for me. I could never have taken his place, of course...."

I glance at Fan, looking for reassurance. I want her to say that I'm wrong, that my mother didn't kill herself; that it was an accident; that nothing on earth could have made her leave me behind on purpose.

But Fan, watching the *Rose*, which is lifting on the incoming tide, says instead, "It was no accident, Robert Lam. She did what she intended to do. I am only sorry that those men came along to trouble her. At least she was able to make them believe that they had done their best to help her. She wouldn't, for all the world, have wanted to hurt their feelings."

A feeling of utter desolation washes over me. To be unloved, or not loved enough at the outset to give my mother a reason to stay alive. To have been, instead of a lifeline, an unbearable burden.

"No," Fan goes on, running her bitten nails round the rim of her teacup and looking into a past that excludes me, "she only wanted to do what was best for your future.

"You see," she adds gently, as if by her voice to avoid giving hurt, "we found on your mother's skin, shortly after her return, the first signs of leprosy."

"But why, Fan," I ask when I find my voice, relief and dismay contending equally within me, "why didn't she just go back to D'Arcy Island? At least she could have been with my father; and I could still have stayed with you. That seems to me the simplest answer."

Fan shakes her head. "No, Robert Lam. You didn't know Ng Chung. He would have blamed himself for the rest of his life for India's illness. Far from a consolation, their being together, in those circumstances, would have been constant bitterness. In her sickness he would only see his failure. Your mother told me that's how it would be, and I believed her."

I move my feet back and forth in the sand, turning up a baby crab, some wood lice, and a score of shells. And try to fathom these parents I never knew. The wind blows smoke from the bonfire into my eyes, and my eyes sting with tears.

"Your mother didn't want him to know about it, Robert Lam," says my stepmother. "Please try to understand. I went to visit him several times while I was on my other errand, and I never told him."

"You mean your trips to the cache of opium," I say to Fan, my anger rising. She nods agreement sorrowfully.

"Yes, that is so," she says. "I killed two birds with one stone."

"It must have made the perfect story to tell Sing Yuen," I say sarcastically. Hoping that she'll start to argue, that I'll have someone to blame. But even as I recognize the thought, I see that it's all at an end. My need to hear the story and Lam Fan's to tell it. Slowly, solemnly, she nods again.

"I told Ng Chung that India had returned to Hong Kong with you. That she had work in her father's old firm of Jardine Matheson. That she was happy, although she missed him, and that you were thriving. I told him that she would write when she could."

My father: alone on the island despite the company of the other exiles, waiting for Lam Fan to bring him a letter that would never arrive. My father, abandoned.

For somewhere, inside—it would be better this way—he must have known that my mother was no longer alive.

I sigh, get up, and throw wet sand on the fire, then help Lam Fan to her feet.

"Well?" I say to her. "Are you ready?"

She smiles at me her smile of infinite sweetness. "Is there wine, Robert Lam? Are there chickens and cakes to give me a send-off?"

I shake my head. "Not at your first funeral, Fan, nor at this one either. But I think what we've got is better."

"All the opium?" she says as I lift her in my arms and wade out to the *Rose*. "Every single tin? You're sure they're all on board?"

"Positive, Fan," I say as I lift her feather weight on to the deck and pull myself up by a rope. "I checked more than once."

There is nothing more to say, and so she gives me a final embrace, then seats herself on the hatch cover and begins to prepare her pipe.

I make a pile of all the paper in the wheelhouse—charts, documents, photographs, all of it, except for one last scrap, which I put in my pocket—and set the whole bundle alight. I throw the stool on top and add frayed rope, oily rags, all the flotsam and jetsam we've gathered over these weeks. I stay for a moment to coax the flames. The *Rose* is old, dry, and brittle. She won't take long to burn.

My stepmother waving to me, as I stand on the shore of D'Arcy Island, as the *Rose*, caught by the current, bobs out into Hughes Passage. As tendrils of fog drift in to mix with the fire. As the clouds lower their blanket and cover her; as the fire reaches the gas tanks and a great wall of flame splashes to heaven a heartbeat before I hear the explosion.

There is a crown of black smoke in the shape of the cloud of the atom bomb. And then there is nothing.

Ng Chung had taken his blankets from his cot and rolled his belongings up in them. He waited with all he owned on the beach as the supply boat landed. Fresh bread, boxes of oranges, bags of wheat, pork and chicken, as well as new boots for all the men, were unloaded. But Ng Chung paid these improved provisions no attention.

He listened impassively as the doctor offered to amputate Ah Sam's useless hand. He heard Ah Sam say, "It is getting better now. Please don't cut it. If you cut it off, I cannot cook."

He heard the Presbyterian Chinese missionary read the Gospel story, in St. Mark, of Christ healing the lepers, while one of the other exiles kept up a flow of questions: Had they remembered to bring the chicken wheat? Could they bring more chickens the next time? Was the sugar they'd brought the Chinese kind, or was it granulated?

A younger man, one of the recent arrivals, the new strong man on the island, rushed back and forth with boxes and cases and bags of supplies. When the missionary told him to sit down and listen, he cried, "I have no time to listen!" And then he cursed the uncle who had brought him out from China to Victoria, knowing he had leprosy. Had he remained in China, he said, he would never have been imprisoned on an island.

Ng Chung, my father, crouched at the water's edge with his arms around his bundle. "See," he said when the doctor came near to treat him, "the only knife I have is the knife of a dead man. I cannot get any other. Can a man use the knife of a dead man and expect to have luck?"

"He told of how he wanted to go to some other island," says the report in the *British Colonist*, the one item I have saved from the papers on the *Rose*. "He would do anything, he said if he could only be taken away to some small island and left there all alone. He would live in a cabin as small as the chicken house fronting his cabin, in anything, if he could only go to some other island.

"But, of course, his request was turned down."

I follow the eastern shore of D'Arcy Island. I watch the ships and ferries sail through the strait. I wave at them, but they appear to take no notice.

I'm not sure what I'll do when I reach the part of the island where my mother and father once lived. I suppose I'll rest for awhile. My legs are shaking with tiredness, and the numbness in my face has returned.

Someone is bound to find me. I can always light a fire that will draw attention. There is nothing to fear on this island any longer, and mariners are curious persons. And I am a pilot; and if anyone does, I know the right signals to bring them.

ABOUT THE AUTHOR

Marilyn Bowering was born in Winnipeg and grew up in Victoria, British Columbia. Her books of poetry include *The Killing Room* (1977), *Sleeping with Lambs* (1980), *Giving Back Diamonds* (1982), *The Sunday Before Winter* (1984), *Anyone Can See I Love You* (1987), *Grandfather Was A Soldier* (1987), *Calling All the World* (1989), *Love As It Is* (1993), and *Autobiography* (1996). She has lived and worked in various parts of Canada, the United States, Greece, Scotland and Spain.